Lat

These passion
Mediterranean sun…

Three passionate novels!

In December 2006 Mills & Boon bring back two of their classic collections, each featuring three favourite romances by our bestselling authors...

LATIN AFFAIRS

The Sicilian's Passion
by Sharon Kendrick
In the Spaniard's Bed
by Helen Bianchin
The Italian Marriage by Kathryn Ross

CHRISTMAS, KIDS & KISSES

The Christmas Baby's Gift
by Kate Walker
The Christmas Child
by Diana Hamilton
Gift-Wrapped Baby by Renee Roszel

Latin Affairs

THE SICILIAN'S PASSION
by
Sharon Kendrick

IN THE SPANIARD'S BED
by
Helen Bianchin

THE ITALIAN MARRIAGE
by
Kathryn Ross

MILLS & BOON®

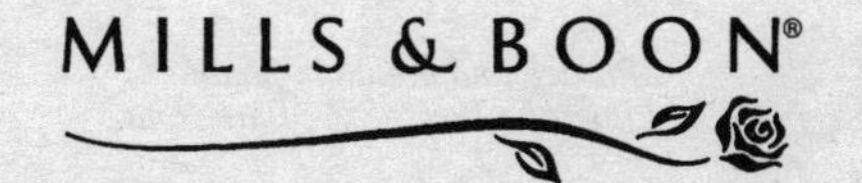

Harlequin Mills & Boon Limited,
Eton House, 18-24 Paradise Road, Richmond, Surrey, TW9 1SR

The Sicilian's Passion, In the Spaniard's Bed and The Italian Marriage were first published in Great Britain by Harlequin Mills & Boon Limited in separate, single volumes.

ISBN 10: 0 263 84975 9
ISBN 13: 978 0 263 84975 2

05-1206

Printed and bound in Spain
by Litografia Rosés S.A., Barcelona

THE SICILIAN'S PASSION

by

Sharon Kendrick

Sharon Kendrick started story-telling at the age of eleven and has never really stopped. She likes to write fast-paced, feel-good romances with heroes who are so sexy they'll make your toes curl!

Born in west London, she now lives in the beautiful city of Winchester – where she can see the cathedral from her window (but only if she stands on tip-toe). She has two children, Celia and Patrick, and her passions include music, books, cooking and eating – and drifting off into wonderful daydreams while she works out new plots!

Don't miss Sharon Kendrick's exciting new novel *The Sheikh's English Bride* out in March 2007 from Mills & Boon Modern Romance™

With special thanks to Mary D'Angelo of the
Italian Cultural Institute and Sarah Locke
(of Winchester!) and Victoria and Alexandra
and, of course, dear old Goethe.

CHAPTER ONE

IT WAS probably the sexiest car Kate had ever seen. Black and sleek and gleaming, it positively *screamed* testosterone! And it looked all wrong on the forecourt of such an imposing mansion.

Kate smiled. In her experience, only dull little men drove around in cars like that—as if compensating for their own inadequacies with an excess of horsepower!

She squinted at it curiously. Lady St John, her client, was a very wealthy woman, yes—but in a restrained rather than an over-the-top way. Since when had she taken to entertaining people who owned such outrageously powerful cars?

Unless she had taken to driving one herself, thought Kate, her mouth quirking in amusement. It wouldn't surprise her.

She studied the car again. Maybe not. Lady St John had an abundance of energy—but you would need to be pretty agile to gain access to *that* long, low and mean machine!

She took one last glance in the driving mirror before she presented herself and looped back a stray strand of fiery hair. Considering that she had been up since six that morning she didn't look *too* bad! And appearances, as she knew, were everything. Particularly in her business.

Kate Connors; interior designer to the rich and—sometimes—famous. And, as jobs went, it was... Well, as she often reminded herself, it was pretty cool. It paid well, it had variety, and what was more—it enabled her to meet all kinds of interesting people.

Like Lady St John—an intrepid aristocrat who had travelled to all corners of the globe and then produced exciting—if somewhat under-read—books all about her journeys.

The St John house was as rugged as the magnificent sweep of coastline which lay to the front of it, and as Kate jangled the old-fashioned doorbell, she could hear the thunder of the sea as it crashed and foamed against the craggy grey rocks.

Such an elemental place, she thought, wishing that her job was not almost at an end, as the door was opened by the housekeeper.

'Hello, Mrs Herley,' smiled Kate. 'Lady St John is expecting me, I believe?'

The woman gave a brief smile as she pulled the door open to usher Kate inside. 'I think that your appointment may have slipped her mind,' she confided. 'Lady St John is a little…er…distracted today.'

Kate knew better than to ask why. It hadn't taken her long in the job to discover that domestic employees never gave away information about their employer—and particularly not one as naturally autocratic as the rather formidable Elisabeth St John, who was nearly eighty, and yet Kate had never met a woman of such advanced years who could exude such beauty and such grace. Who could still wear clothes with the style of the fashion model she had once briefly been. If *I* look like that at her age, she had thought at their very first meeting, then I would be a very happy bunny indeed!

Mrs Herley shut the door again. 'If you would like to wait in the Blue Drawing Room, Miss Connors, then I will tell Lady St John that you are here.'

'Thanks,' murmured Kate rather wryly.

Her early appeal to Mrs Herley that she 'call me Kate' had fallen on polite but deaf ears—and she had remained Miss Connors ever since! Some people's worlds were built on different structures from her own. But such formality suited this beautiful old house, she decided dreamily, making her way to the enormous room which she was almost through with decorating.

Kate let out a sigh as she looked around. She would be

sad to let it go—but then, that happened with nearly all her jobs. They were her babies, in a way, and the final parting always proved more of a wrench than she expected, even after nearly nine years in the business.

The floor-to-ceiling windows were filled with the image of sea and sky—a breathtaking view and one with which the room had needed to compete so that it didn't fade into complete insignificance.

Kate had chosen the colours carefully, and now the walls were bright with an unusual shade of blue. A deep and stunning and startling blue, and one which made the most of the Gothic mouldings which adorned the cornices.

And if she said so herself—it did look pretty good!

'Kate?'

She turned around to find Lady St John walking into the room, in a cashmere cardigan and matching ankle-skimming skirt.

'Hello, Lady St John! Almost my last visit to you, sadly! And I…I…' Kate's words faltered and then died completely, stuck in her throat like an insult one had thought better of saying.

For Lady St John was not alone, and insult was the very last word you would associate with the man who had quietly entered the room behind her. For who could possibly criticise pure perfection on two such long, muscular legs? This must be the owner of the car, she realised, and her heart began to race. Had she thought that only dull little men drove cars like that? Because she had been totally and foolishly wrong.

Lady St John performed a seamless introduction, waving her hand in the direction of the man who stood like a dark, silent statue behind her. 'Kate—this is my godson.'

'Your *godson*?' echoed Kate, in breathless bemusement.

Lady St John smiled. 'Mmm! I met his mother on my youthful travels to Europe and she became one of my closest friends. I'd like you to meet Giovanni Calverri.' She turned to the man at her side. 'Giovanni, this is Kate Connors, who has just been turning her rather spectacular talents to this room.'

As he glanced around the room, Kate couldn't take her eyes off him. His name implied Latin blood, as did the jet-dark hair, though the eyes were—rather disconcertingly—a bright, dazzling blue. But the term Latin implied warmth and passion, and wasn't there something awfully *cold* and aloof about this tall, striking man who was eyeing her with a face that was closed and shuttered?

She matched his look with one of her own. Men in suits that looked as if they had only just left the designer's show-room the previous day were simply not her type.

'Hello,' she said coolly.

Giovanni froze. He had never seen a woman quite so tall or so slim, nor with hair of such a bright, beaten fire—and her very unexpectedness beat a deep, inevitable path into his consciousness. He felt the muscles of his thighs clench, as if his body was instinctively telling him that he wanted to…wanted to… His mouth hardened as he acknowledged the rampant flurry of his thoughts.

He forced himself to make his introduction as bland as possible, although the moist gleam of her mouth filled him with an overwhelming urge to crush its soft pinkness beneath his.

'Giovanni?' prompted his godmother, looking at the forbidding set of his shoulders in mild perplexity.

He pulled himself together. 'I am delighted to meet you,' he said, in the most beautiful accent Kate had ever heard—rich and dark and overlaid with the slightest and sexiest trans-atlantic drawl.

Say that again like you meant it, thought Kate indignantly. But she didn't stop staring, because, even though he was not her type, he was still remarkable, and men who looked like this one were few and far between. Even in the rarefied circles in which she mixed.

Olive skin, an aquiline nose and a hard, sensual mouth. Combine those attributes with a body which was tall and lithe and didn't possess even the tiniest bit of excess flesh, and you had a man who was most women's fantasy come true in living, breathing form.

'Delighted to meet you, too,' she murmured, tempted to echo his own lack of enthusiasm, but good manners brought her up short and she gave him a polite smile. 'You're Italian, are you?'

'Italian?' His mouth twisted with a derision which made it look very sexy indeed, and Kate felt her heart race again. What on earth had she said to make him glare at her so?

'*Diu Mio*!' he uttered softly, a warning glitter lighting up the depths of his blue eyes, as if she had inflicted some silent blow on him. 'I am a Sicilian, not an Italian!'

He made the claim as if he owned the world itself! 'You mean there's a difference?' she questioned lightly and batted her eyelashes playfully at him.

'Oh, dear,' murmured Lady St John.

Giovanni felt his muscles tense once more as he met the flirtatious challenge which had suddenly made her eyes look very green indeed. Eyes which were almost on a level with his own. It was a new and unsettling sensation not to be looking down on a woman—from a purely physical point of view. Disturbingly, he found himself wondering how their bodies would feel if they were touching head to toe, horizontal. *Naked.* He swallowed the thought down and sublimated his desire, preferring instead to dwell on her ignorance.

'You mean you don't know the difference between Sicily and Italy?' he demanded.

'I wouldn't have to ask if I *knew*, would I?' she returned, though his rudeness was doing nothing to dampen down the heat in her blood.

Giovanni bit back his irritation, for why should this pale and unknown Englishwoman know anything about the deep, secret place which was his home? The place in love with its own silence, which shaped the impenetrable character of all Sicilians.

'The difference is almost incalculable,' he told her coldly. 'And would take far more time to explain than I have at my disposal.'

'I see,' said Kate faintly, thinking how well he spoke English—whilst at the same time acknowledging that she could not ever remember anyone being *quite* so rude to her!

'Giovanni!' said Lady St John, with a mild air of reproval. 'Much more of that severity and you'll have Kate leaving!'

He turned then, and a sudden brief flash of warmth transformed the chilly face as he looked down at his godmother. 'Forgive me,' he murmured, 'but it has been a very long week. You must make allowances for me if I am not up to giving a history of Sicily this close to lunch!'

Kate was furious. Was he going out of his way to make her feel as though she was something he had found squashed beneath the sole of his delicious, handmade shoe?

'Oh, don't worry about *me*, Lady St John,' she declared airily. 'It would take a lot more than *that* to make me cut and run!'

Giovanni observed the fire which was spitting from eyes as perfectly shaped as bay leaves. For a brief moment he wondered what it would be like to see those same eyes sleepy and satiated in the aftermath of passion, and then hardened his heart against their emerald appeal, astonished to find his body stubbornly attempting to disobey his will.

And yet he had had a lifetime's practice of seeing beautiful, intelligent women looking at him with open invitation in their eyes. It happened with such monotonous regularity that he was nothing more than bored by it. Usually.

He told himself that she was a predator—that she must put

out for every man she wanted, in just this way—and thankfully the fire began to leave his loins.

Confused, Kate turned away from that beautiful, condemning face and tried to pretend that he wasn't there. 'I have the curtains in the van, Lady St John,' she said, gleaming a small smile of pleasure at her client. 'And I'd like to begin hanging them, if I may.'

'I can't wait to see them!' enthused Lady St John. 'Shall we ask Giovanni to help you carry them in? They must be very heavy indeed.'

Ask for help from the cold-faced man who had been so rude to her? Like hell! Kate shook her head, and the red hair shimmered like a windblown wheat-field all the way down her back. 'That won't be necessary!' She gave him a defiant smile. 'I'm used to managing on my own!'

'How admirably independent!' His blue eyes mocked her as did the smile which hovered around his lips. 'But I am afraid that consideration for the weaker sex is inborn in all Sicilian men. I insist on helping you.'

Had he deliberately said that just to inflame her? The weaker sex indeed! And how could he insist against her wishes? Kate opened her mouth to snap back some suitable retort, until she realised that it wouldn't make very good business sense to be rude to her client's godson. Even if he did need a few lessons in manners! And the curtains really *were* very heavy.

'How terribly *sweet* of you,' she emphasised deliberately.

Giovanni silently registered the affront, with another stab of heat to his belly. Sweet was not a description which most red-blooded men strove for. Was she hoping to goad him into some kind of reaction, perhaps? His smile grew even colder. Women were notoriously predictable and he was in grave danger of giving her back just the response she wanted. 'Why, you are much too kind!' he murmured back.

Kate felt more than a little out of her depth as she led the way out of the house towards her van. Not a feeling she was used to—and certainly not one with which she was comfortable.

She was sunny and enthusiastic—qualities which were normally contagious. When you worked closely alongside people in their own homes, you had to get along with them. And normally she didn't have a problem getting along with anyone.

So what was the problem here? Or was Giovanni the problem?

It's not his home, she reminded herself as she pointed to her van. It belongs to his godmother. He's obviously just into all that macho stuff—maybe he thinks it turns women on. Well, she should let him know loud and clear that it didn't! 'All the stuff's in there!' she said, pointing rather frustratedly at the van.

'Yes,' he said, narrowing his eyes to look at her as she unlocked the back of a van only a little more flamboyant than she was, and began to climb inside.

She wore a pair of slim-fitting trousers in a soft green as vibrant as the newest buds of spring—stretched closely over a bottom which was high and taut. She half turned, and Giovanni swallowed as his eyes flickered over a tangerine Lycra T-shirt which clung to the lush swell of her breasts.

Most redheads would never have worn a shirt that orange, he decided. But, then, hair that thick and bright was rare indeed. It hung almost to her waist, clipped back from her pale, freckled face with two clips of glittering pink plastic which matched the bangles that jangled around her narrow wrists.

Giovanni had been brought up to believe that a woman should only ever wear gold. Or diamonds. That their bodies should only ever be clothed in silk or cashmere, or the lightest of cottons. Pure, natural fabrics to enhance feminine beauty—not these clinging, man-made clothes. He wondered if her underwear was just as garish and his mouth hardened. What in *Diu*'s name had made him think of something like *that*?

'Here we are!' said Kate breathlessly, hauling out a huge, plastic-sheathed package from the depths of the van. And then she looked up to find those cold blue eyes studying her with an intensity which was almost…almost… Her own eyes narrowed in response as she realised that the overriding expression on his face was one of censure!

What made this arrogant stranger think he had the right to look down on *her*?

She curved her lips into a smile. Be pleasant, she urged herself. Or, at least, be outwardly pleasant. Don't react. Reacting will look like a challenge and this man looked too ruthless an adversary to risk challenging.

'Think you can manage it OK?' she asked kindly.

The insincere smile was almost as insulting as her question. She was employed by his godmother, for heaven's sake—and here she was looking down that freckled snub of a nose as though he was some kind of odd-job man! Giovanni fought the desire to retaliate, even though she was just asking to be put in her place.

'Give it to me,' he instructed softly, his voice dipping in Latin caress.

And to her horror Kate found herself responding to that silky order as if he had been talking about something entirely different. She felt her senses spring into some kind of magical life—inspired by nothing more than a throwaway comment. Since when had her self-esteem been so low that she found something as derogatory as that a *turn-on*?

'Here.' She would have dumped the precious package in his arms if it hadn't been worth a small fortune. As it was she laid it there as tenderly as if it were a newborn infant, and just for a moment their hands brushed and she felt the unwelcome sizzle of longing. 'I'll bring the rest of the stuff inside,' she said, hoping that he hadn't noticed.

He had, of course. It had happened too often in his past for him not to. Desire could strike inappropriately and randomly; he accepted that. And sometimes, though not often, he was tempted as any man would be tempted—but he had never yet succumbed to the lures of fleeting desire. His sense of honour was too deeply ingrained in him to ever do that.

But Giovanni could never recall a temptation as potent as the one he was experiencing now. He turned his back on her and without another word began to walk back towards the house.

Lady St John was still in the Blue Drawing Room and she turned around with a smile as Giovanni brought the heavy package into the room and placed it on a table.

'Would you like us to leave you alone now, Kate?' she asked. 'I know you prefer to work undisturbed.'

'Oh, yes, please!' answered Kate gratefully, trying to imagine hanging heavy brocade under the scrutiny of that critical blue gaze. Why, she would probably break the habit of a lifetime and drop the curtains all over the floor!

'And afterwards you'll join us for lunch, I hope?'

Usually, of course, she did. But today? With this moody-looking godson? Thanks, but no, thanks! 'Well, it's very sweet of you, but I think I might run over time, and I'd hate to delay you—'

'No trouble at all,' said Lady St John immediately. 'Giovanni has expressed a wish to see the gardens—and I can't wait to show him how many exotic plants we have acquired in the conservatory!'

'But perhaps Miss Connors has lost her…appetite?' he murmured, and his eyes darkened in predatory challenge.

She most certainly had—and he knew it, too! Kate met a mocking blue gaze and knew that this was something she could not refuse—and when she thought about it, why ever *should* she? Why let this contemptuous individual put her off, when during every other visit she had enjoyed a congenial and delicious meal with Lady St John before setting off back to London? Surely she was accomplished enough in the ways of the world to be able to act indifferently when she wanted to?

'I haven't eaten since six this morning,' she said truthfully. 'I'd love lunch!'

Giovanni looked at her, and wondered if she was one of those women who could eat with genuine appetite and remain as slim as a blade of grass. Or would a hearty lunch mean that she would exist on nothing but water and fresh air for the next three days?

'Good! Come on, Giovanni,' said Lady St John resolutely. 'Let me show you colours that could rival your Sicilian flora!'

He gave a benign but disbelieving laugh. 'I do not think so!'

Once they had gone, Kate took out the heavy brocade curtains, and set about pinning them up, running her fingertips down their shiny pleats. When she worked she was focused, seeing nothing more than colour and texture taking shape before her eyes, and she put the dark-haired Sicilian out of her mind.

She had just finished when she heard a soft footfall behind her, and she turned on her stepladder to find Giovanni standing there, his gaze arrested by the brilliant glimmer of deep blue and gold.

And then the gaze was lifted almost reluctantly to her face, and Kate felt herself imprisoned—impaled, almost—by a shaft of blinding sapphire light.

'You look surprised,' she observed in a low voice.

He was. He had expected…what? That she was too modern, too up-to-the-minute, and that the fabric she chose would look shockingly out of place in this beautiful old house.

'A little,' he conceded, with a very Sicilian shrug of his shoulders.

'You thought I would have poor taste?'

He looked at her. She had perception, he noted. And such green eyes. And hair like fire. He felt some unknown and unwanted sensation washing over his skin. 'You should not ask questions to which you do not wish to hear the answers.'

How ridiculously old-fashioned he sounded! 'I'm a big girl, Mr Calverri—'

'*Signor* Calverri,' he corrected softly.

How could he possibly make his own name sound so beguiling? 'And?' she challenged in a husky voice she didn't quite recognise as her own. 'On the question of taste?'

He saw the quickening of her breath, and felt it fire a rapid response in his heart. 'Your taste is quite exquisite,' he said quietly.

Kate let her eyelids flutter down before he read the unwelcome hunger in her eyes. She didn't *like* him! So why did she want to keep running his compliment round and round in her head like an old-fashioned record?

'Thank you,' she said breathlessly, feeling as uncoordinated as a giraffe as she slowly stepped down off the ladder, unspeakably relieved to see his godmother appear, her face one of delight as she surveyed the finished effect.

'Oh, Kate! It's perfect!'

'You're sure?'

'Better than I could have hoped for in my wildest dreams!'

Kate found herself having some pretty wild dreams of her own—and most of them seemed to involve the unsmiling face of Giovanni Calverri, trying to imagine what it would be like to be undressed by him or to be kissed by those hard, sensuous lips.

'Why, Kate,' said Lady St John, with a little frown of concern, 'you'd better come and have some lunch—you've gone quite pale!'

'H-have I?' She touched her fingertips to her cheeks, and prayed for co-ordination to return.

The three of them walked to the light-filled room which overlooked the garden and Giovanni found his eyes being drawn to the graceful curve of her neck, feeling his senses spring into life as he told himself that she was resistible. Easily resistible. But the sunlight that flooded through the windows had made her hair look even brighter—as though someone had put a flame to it, and the waves were made of dancing fire.

He was unsmiling as he waited for the two women to sit down, and Kate thought that she had never seen a face quite so devoid of emotion. Or so compelling. And she became aware of the sudden soft rush of colour to her cheeks.

Giovanni saw her blush, and interpreted the unmistakable reason behind it, feeling his heart begin to hammer in his chest as he realised how much she wanted him.

'Have a glass of wine, Kate,' smiled Lady St John.

Kate shook her head as she tried to avoid the clash of that blue stare, the small but knowing smile which was playing at the corners of a mouth which looked almost *cruel*. Wine was the very last thing she needed. 'Just water for me, thanks—I'm driving. And I have to get back to London straight after lunch.'

What a pity, Giovanni found himself thinking and then, with a huge effort of will, pushed her green-eyed temptation to the very recesses of his mind.

It was an endurance test of a meal which Kate forced herself to eat. Because if she pushed her food round and round her plate, wouldn't he be able to tell how debilitated she felt in his presence? How aware she was of those long, olive fingers as they casually broke bread and then sensuously placed a fragment in his mouth? Why, she was in danger of acting like an overgrown schoolgirl, with a schoolgirl's crush! At twenty-seven, for heaven's sake!

She cleared her throat and forced herself to look directly at him, unprepared for another sudden, sharp tug of longing. He isn't your type, she told herself again. He isn't!

'So are you just over here for business or for…for—' she got the next word out with some difficulty '—pleasure?' she finished on a gulp.

He noted the faltering quality of her voice without surprise, the tremble of her mouth which made him long to taste its sweetness, and was appalled at his own weakness. 'Business brings me to England,' he said, his accent deepening. 'But it is always a pleasure to see my godmother.'

Kate persevered, forcing herself to continue as if he were just anyone and she was networking. 'And what is your business, exactly?'

'This!' Lady St John waved an elegant hand at the solid silver candelabra which adorned the centre of the table and at the exquisitely fashioned knives and forks they were using. 'The Calverri family exports silver all over the world,' she said proudly.

And suddenly Kate made the connection—if she hadn't been quite so reluctantly dazzled by the man she might have made it a whole lot sooner. 'Calverri silver?' she asked him faintly. 'You mean, *the* Calverri silver?'

'There *is* only one,' he told her arrogantly.

Which explained the outrageously expensive car and the outrageously expensive suit—his air of only being used to the very best. Because Calverri silver—recreating classic, antique pieces, or creating timeless new ones—was a must-have for anyone with taste and plenty of money.

'Your company is doing very well,' Kate offered.

'But of course! Under Giovanni's guiding hand, it has become truly international,' said Lady St John, with another proud smile at her godson.

He shrugged. 'We have an exemplary workforce,

Elisabeth,' he murmured. 'I am simply a small cog in a very well-oiled machine.'

Kate thought that modesty did not become him, and something in the look of challenge which he glittered across the table at her told her that he probably had a good idea *exactly* what she was thinking. She broke the stare and looked down with determination at her salmon instead. Was she going completely mad? Since when had anyone ever been able to read her mind?

'This is delicious,' she said politely.

Liar, thought Giovanni as she chewed without enthusiasm. You have barely touched a thing, *angela mia*.

The plates had just been cleared away, when her mobile phone began shrilling from her bag, and Kate stared down at it in consternation as she heard Giovanni's unmistakable click of annoyance. What had she been thinking of? She *always* switched her phone off when she was eating!

'I'm sorry,' she said, reaching down for her bag.

'The curse of technology,' came his low, mocking response.

'You'd better answer it, hadn't you?' asked Lady St John mildly.

'If you don't mind.' Kate grabbed the bag and rose to her feet. 'I'll take it outside.'

But she was happy to escape from that unsettling stare and equally unsettling presence, and even happier to discover that it was Lucy who was calling. Lucy, her beloved older sister, who worked for Kate and ran her life like clockwork.

Kate clicked on the 'talk' button. 'Lucy, hi! No, no, no, of course I understand—it can't be helped! An emergency is an emergency!'

'Kate, what on earth are you talking about?' Lucy sounded confused. '*What* emergency?'

'No, of course I can come back immediately,' babbled

Kate loudly. 'I've just finished here, and I'm sure that I can be excused pudding and coffee!'

'No doubt you'll give me some kind of explanation later,' came Lucy's dry response.

'Oh, definitely! Definitely!' breathed Kate. Though how on earth would she put into words that she had fallen for a man with a cold, contemptuous face? The most beautiful man she had ever seen? And she wanted him, this blue-eyed stranger.

She shivered as she acknowledged the awful truth.

She *wanted* Giovanni Calverri!

CHAPTER TWO

'KATE, what on earth is the *matter* with you?'

Kate looked at her sister with an unaccustomed blankness in her eyes.

She had spent the whole drive back from Lady St John's house in Sussex veering between disbelief and self-disgust. In fact, the whole journey had been negotiated on some kind of auto-pilot. She had gone straight upstairs to Lucy's flat, and it wasn't until she was inside its elegant interior that she began shaking uncontrollably—like a person who had just come down with a fever.

'It's stupid. It's nothing.' She shook her head distractedly. 'It would sound too far-fetched to explain—'

Lucy's forehead creased with perplexity. 'But Kate, you *never* leave your phone switched on during lunch. It's one of your "unbreakable rules", remember?'

Oh, yes, she remembered all right. And another of those rules was that she didn't fall victim to grand and irrational passions. That she was ruled by her head, and not her heart. That she liked and respected herself, so that falling for a man who played the 'treat them mean and keep them keen' ticket was simply *not* on her agenda.

'I just met a man,' she said slowly, and ridiculously it sounded like the first line to a love song.

The frown disappeared, and Lucy relaxed. 'Oh! And about time, too,' she smiled, with the approval of someone who was happily established in a long-term relationship. 'I've been waiting for you to fall in love for years and years!'

Kate nodded. So had she. But love was not an appropriate word, not in this case. If she was being brutally honest—and she always tried for honesty—then wouldn't falling in *lust* be a more fitting description of what had happened to her some time over lunch?

She compressed her mouth into a determined line. 'It isn't like that,' she insisted. 'I don't love him. How can I when I barely know him?'

'But Cupid's arrow has hit you with unfailing accuracy?'

'A thunderbolt,' admitted Kate in a dazed kind of voice. 'The kind of thing you read about but think will never happen to you.'

'Yes, I know.' Lucy gave a wistful smile. 'The French call it a *coup de foudre*.'

Kate shook her head. 'That would imply that it was mutual.'

'And wasn't it?'

Kate thought about it. There had been an undeniable fizzle between them, yes, but...but... 'He looked at me as though he didn't really like what he saw.'

'Or what he *felt* perhaps,' said Lucy perceptively.

Kate looked at her sister. Two years older and the most beautiful woman she had ever seen, with her dark copper hair and thick-fringed green eyes.

Lucy had been born with looks to burn and a certain irresistibility to the opposite sex. But in the end she had fallen for her boss, unwilling and unable to stop the relationship even when the powers-that-be had threatened her with the sack if she did not.

Lucy had duly lost her job, and although Jack had not he had left anyway, using the opportunity to work for himself at long last. But at least they had stayed together, thought Kate, even if Jack now spent the majority of his life abroad. And Kate had been able to offer her sister a job as her assistant at just the right time. That was the pay-off for being neighbours as well as workmates, she realised. As sisters, she and Lucy looked out for one another.

She looked around Lucy's flat, which, with Jack helping to pay for it, was much larger and more opulent than her own.

'How's things?' she asked absently, still unable to get Giovanni out of her head.

Lucy stared at her. 'Tell me about him,' she said suddenly. 'This man who's making you tremble like that.'

Kate looked down with surprise at her unsteady hands. What could she say? That he had the coldest, proudest and most beautiful face she had ever seen? And eyes so startlingly blue that the summer sky would have paled in comparison? She shrugged, but her shoulders felt unusually heavy. 'There's nothing to tell. Like I said, I don't know him. I've barely exchanged half a dozen words with him. He's Lady St John's godson—'

'Mmm. So, he's well-connected, then?' murmured Lucy.

'Oh, yes. And he's Italian—or, rather, he's Sicilian.'

'There's a difference?'

'That's exactly what I said! And apparently there is. A huge difference.' Kate thought of his quietly furious response to her innocent question. 'His family owns the Calverri silver factory. You must have heard of them.'

Lucy's eyes widened. 'You *are* kidding?'

'No, I'm not. He's rich. He's handsome.' Kate shut her eyes and forced herself to see facts rather than fantasy. He is curiously unsmiling and there is an impenetrable barrier between him and the rest of the world, she thought with an instinct which seemed to come from nowhere.

'He sounds perfect.'

'I'm sure he is,' said Kate lightly. 'For someone who doesn't mind a man who looks arrogantly down his beautifully patrician nose at you!'

'Hmm! So you've got it bad!'

'Not really. A passing fancy,' answered Kate tightly. 'And anyway—I'll never see him again. Why should I?'

Never. It sounded so brutally final. Oh, what *magic* had he woven during that tense, short meeting? she wondered despairingly.

She had gathered up all her belongings and left the house in an unseemly rush, driven by some self-protective instinct which was quite alien to her. She had just known that if she didn't get out of the St John mansion quickly she risked making a very great fool of herself.

Because for one brief, mad moment as he and his godmother had accompanied her into the hall she had actually thought about *asking him out*!

Oh, not in the kind of 'would you like to go out with me?' way which was perfectly acceptable nowadays. Some of her more liberated girlfriends wouldn't have hesitated.

No, Kate would have been more subtle than that.

She could have said that she would be interested to see the latest Calverri silver catalogue on behalf of one of her clients. And that wouldn't have been a lie—she could think of at least half a dozen people who would doubtless love to choose something lavish and expensive from the latest glossy Calverri brochure.

But she had recognised in him a steely intelligence—and an innate ability to see what might lie behind a request such as that. He wasn't stupid. Women must react to him like that all the time—hence the contempt for her, which he had barely bothered trying to conceal.

So she had shaken his hand and given him a cool smile, and hoped that her body language hadn't betrayed the shimmering thrill of pleasure she felt to have his fingers closing around her hand.

She frowned as Lucy went to make some coffee, walking over to the window where the Thames glittered by in tantalisingly close proximity.

Flats like this didn't come cheap. Her own had been bought with the proceeds of her work after her salary had started surpassing even her wildest dreams. And everyone knew that you should put money into property.

She had the perfect job. The perfect home. And the perfect life.

So stay *away* from him, she told herself fiercely, and then she remembered that their paths were never going to cross again.

Thank God. Because she wasn't sure just how strong her will to resist him would be if they were to meet again.

Crazy.

Crazy to think that a man could arouse that amount of passion in a woman who was normally so self-controlled.

She turned to smile as Lucy carried in the tray of coffee and put him out of her mind with an effort.

Giovanni's mouth tightened imperceptibly as he put his foot down hard on the accelerator, and behind the smooth, dark curve of his sunglasses, the blue eyes glittered with irritation.

Damn!

And damn Kate Connors! Damn all women with eyes which invited so blatantly, and bodies just made to commit sin with.

He shook his head in denial, as if that could dispel the unmistakable ache of desire that had kept him teetering close to the hot edge of excitement since he had first seen the blaze of her fiery hair.

He wanted nothing more to do with her! And yet, even now he was speeding towards her flat. So why in the name of God was he carrying out his reluctant mission?

Because his godmother had asked him to, that was why. And all because the witch had left her Filofax behind. Again his mouth tightened. It was a laughably obvious ploy! She might as well have dropped her handkerchief to the ground in front of him. Or her panties, he found himself thinking and was cruelly rewarded with the hot, sharp stab of desire.

She must have known that his godmother would insist on his returning it, even though he had shaken his head unequivocably when she had first asked him.

'I cannot, Elisabeth,' he had told her.

'But, Giovanni, the poor girl will be lost without it! It's the size of an encyclopaedia!'

'Then why not post it to her?' he had suggested evenly.

'Because she'll need it,' said Lady St John with all the stubbornness of a woman who had spent her whole life getting her own way. 'And you virtually have to drive past her flat on your way back to the hotel, don't you? What time is your flight tonight?'

'At eight,' he admitted, resigning himself to the fact that he respected his godmother's wishes enough to back down on this. Though if any of his business colleagues had been there, they would have been very surprised to see him without his usual ruthless streak of determination.

'Well, then—you've got *hours*!' said his godmother brightly. '*Please*, Giovanni?'

'*Sí, sí, Elisabeth,*' he sighed, and held his immaculately manicured hand out with a rare smile. 'I will return it to her.'

He should have dropped the damned thing off on the way back to his hotel, but he didn't. Maybe if he had done that...

But instead he took a long, cool shower and changed from his suit into casual trousers and a fine shirt of purest silk that whispered like a woman's fingertips over his skin. And he shaved, and touched a musky-lemon scent to the pure, clean line of his jaw, though not for one moment did he ask himself why.

Nor why he went down to the bar and ordered a single malt whisky, then sat gazing at it, untouched, as though it contained poison.

He left for her flat just before six. That would just give him time to drop the Filofax off and then to drive straight to the airport. No time to linger. No time for coffee or the inevitable offer of a drink. Just a wry smile as he handed the Filofax over, a smile which told her that he knew exactly what her game was. And that he was far too experienced to fall for it.

But his pulse was hammering like a piston as he approached the turn off for her flat.

Kate left Lucy's flat and went upstairs to her own, where for once the glorious colour scheme failed to soothe her jangled senses.

She felt restless as she removed her cotton jacket. Itchy. Like a cat on a hot tin roof. As if there was a gaping hole somewhere deep inside her.

She changed from her hot and itchy clothes into one of her favourite outfits—a tiny green skirt and cashmere vest. It flattered her figure enormously, and as she stared into the mirror she found herself wondering what Giovanni Calverri would think of *that*!

No! This is just becoming *madness*, she told herself when she was back in the sitting room. With a shaking hand she poured herself a glass of wine and she had gulped down half of it before staring at the glass in a stupefied way that was completely alien to her.

She *never* drank on her own! Never!

She put the glass back down, with a hand that was no steadier, and walked through the sitting room into the small study which led directly off it, and sat down at her brand-new computer.

She logged on to the Internet and began tentatively pressing keys, until she reached the site she didn't even realise she was looking for, and one word flashed up on the screen in front of her, mocking her with memories of his lean, beautiful body.

Sicily.

On the screen in front of her, the island unfolded before

her eyes with the aid of the electronic equipment she now took for granted, and she printed out all the information available on the harsh beauty of a land which was known as 'Persephone's Island'. And then, with an odd thundering in her heart, and a prickling sense of expectation, she settled down and began to read.

Soon she was lost in tales of a bloody past, discovering the complex and stormy history of the sensual European island which lay so close to North Africa. Sicilians were the heirs of the ancient Greeks, Carthaginians, Arabs and Normans, she read. No wonder that Giovanni looked more spectacularly different from any other man she had ever met.

She was only disturbed by the insistent ringing of the doorbell and she blinked, and put the sheets of paper down.

Lucy, probably. She wasn't expecting anyone else—and in London no one ever seemed to call on anyone else unexpectedly. In fact, she had planned a quiet night as she always did at the end of a job. The celebration of its successful completion would come at the weekend, when they could lie in until late the next morning. They would go to their local bistro and eat chicken and drink a carafe of French country wine.

The doorbell rang again.

OK, she thought, I'm on my way! And if she hadn't been sure it was her sister she might have felt mildly irritated as she unplugged the Internet connection, but left the picture of Sicily still on the screen.

The ear-splitting sound had just invaded her ears for the third time, and her frown changed to one of worry. What was all the urgency?

With a wrench she pulled the door open, and her heart very nearly stopped.

It was him. Giovanni Calverri.

There.

On her doorstep, with the blue blaze from his eyes nearly

blinding her. Briefly she wondered whether those unbelievable, unusual eyes were a throwback to when the island had been invaded by the Greeks, centuries ago, but she had no time to wonder more, merely note the look of derision which was hardening the luscious mouth.

'Y-you,' she breathed in a stunned kind of disbelief.

'But of course it is,' he concurred sardonically. 'Weren't you waiting for me?'

'Waiting for you?' She prayed for logic and some kind of strength to seep into her addled brain, but all she could think about was his beauty. A hard, cold kind of beauty unlike anything she had ever seen in her life. 'Why should I be waiting for you?'

So she wanted to play games.

And, suddenly, so did he, damn her!

'Didn't you forget something?' he purred.

Right at that moment, she would be hard-pressed to remember her name. She felt a shivering awareness of him as she shook her head distractedly. The lemony, musky scent of him had invaded her nostrils like some kind of raw pheromone and she could sense the warm, male heat radiating off him.

'I don't know what you're talking about.' She frowned.

Part of him wanted to ram the accusation home. To tell her that he had no need of women who lacked such subtlety. Predatory women with hungry green eyes. But that part of him seemed to be fast on the wane and some alien emotion was in the ascendancy.

Until he reminded himself that emotion had no place in what was happening between them. He didn't know her. Or particularly like her. Certainly didn't respect her. He just wanted her, it was as simple and as complicated as that.

His lips parted to say with soft venom, Oh, yes, you do, but some interloper had stolen the words from his mouth. He raised his dark eyebrows questioningly and the hand which had been partially concealed by the hard shaft of his thigh suddenly withdrew and he held out the overstuffed black leather diary towards her. 'This is yours, I believe?'

'My Filofax!' Kate stared at it in astonishment. Why, she depended on it as she would her lifeblood—and she had been in such a state that she hadn't even noticed it missing! 'I didn't even realise I'd left it behind!'

She was a good actress, he would say that for her! For a moment her surprise looked almost genuine. But her reaction to him told him the true story. Should he taunt her with it? Let her know that he could see through her schoolgirl games? 'You mean you hadn't missed it?' he mocked.

Kate stiffened, and indignation took the place of surprise. 'You think I left it behind on purpose?' she asked, her voice rising with incredulity.

He shrugged, and the blue eyes glittered a challenge at her. 'Didn't you?'

She raised her eyebrows, scarcely believing what she was hearing. 'Presumably just so that you would return it, I suppose?'

'If that was your intention.' He gave a coolly beautiful smile. 'Then you have succeeded, mmm, *cara*?'

She almost laughed aloud at his arrogance. 'Maybe such a scenario happens to you all the time *Mr* Calverri—'

'Giovanni,' he corrected softly, unable to stop himself even though the distant clamour of his conscience told him not to enter into this delicious game of flirtation.

'Maybe women *do* throw themselves at you—'

'They do,' he agreed gravely, and was rewarded with a renewed look of outrage, though was unprepared for the stealthy acceleration of his pulse as her sinful lips pursed themselves together.

'Well, for your information—' she drew a deep breath, slightly aware of behaving a little hypocritically since she *had* been sitting here obsessing about him, hadn't she? '—if

I was *that* interested in a man I wouldn't resort to such transparent tactics, I would...would...'

Dark brows were raised in query as her words tailed off. 'You would...?'

Well, why not tell him the truth? 'I would have asked you out,' she said in a matter-of-fact voice.

Giovanni knew a moment of intrigue. Women *had* asked him out before, particularly English and American women, and he had always felt a sizzling disdain for such forward behaviour. Though a modern man in terms of accomplishments, he remained a staunch traditionalist at heart. The island of his birth defined the rôles of the sexes far less markedly than in centuries past. But at its root still lay a machismo society where the man pursued the woman, and not the other way round.

And yet he found himself wondering if the unquestionably strong desire she had aroused in him might have enticed him enough to accept.

'But you didn't,' he stated softly.

Her eyes met his fearlessly. 'No, I didn't.'

But she had thought about it, he realised with a start. Mulled over the possibility and decided against it. He felt his interest flicker again, for wasn't that a kind of rejection?

His eyes narrowed. It was an entirely new sensation for him. No woman had ever rejected him, in any way, shape or form, and Giovanni felt the renewed leap to his senses as the first dull flush of the inevitable made him shrug in wry recognition.

'I will try not to be too offended at such a blow to my ego,' he murmured.

'Oh, thank heavens for that!' came her sardonic retort. 'I wouldn't have been able to sleep nights if you had!'

He almost smiled, acknowledging that something unknown and forbidden and dangerous was pulsing in the air around them. And that, instead of getting out of here as quickly as possible, he lanced through her emerald gaze with a cool look of challenge. 'So, aren't you going to ask me inside, *cara*?' And then realised just how shockingly and beautifully potent that question sounded.

'Inside?' she repeated slowly, and her mind started to play outrageous tricks on her as she imagined the reality of that simple, one-word request which suddenly sounded like the most erotic proposition imaginable. And didn't *cara* mean...darling?

He heard her momentary hesitation, knew what had prompted it and felt himself grow hard—so hard that he felt he might die with wanting her. But he pinned a lazy smile onto his mouth instead. A smile he didn't really mean, because the only thing that had any meaning at that precise moment was the need to possess her. A need he knew he should ruthlessly resist, and yet...yet...

'For a drink?' He shrugged, as though he could take it or leave it. 'As a reward for having come out of my way to see you.'

Some of the tension left her. Some but not all. She forced herself to open the door to him.

Forced! Just who did she think she was kidding? Why, if she gave into her true feelings right then she would have dragged him in by taking a great swathe of that silk shirt in her fist and drawing him close to her. So close that he would not be able to resist her.

But he *had* done her a favour. And wasn't she in danger of letting this all get a little out of hand? She should invite him into her home and expose herself to a little more of his own distinctive air of arrogance—*that* was the way to get him right out of her system! 'A drink?' She flashed him a bright, polite smile. 'Of course. Sure. Come in.'

He walked into her flat and it was as stunning as he had anticipated. He had known that her home would be exquisite, and it was. More than exquisite, it was distinctive. Like her.

Strong, bold colours which somehow managed to blend instead of grating on the eye. A mix and match which pleased and excited the senses. Again, like her.

She had changed, he noted, not for the first time—and now wore an indecently short skirt which showed off her long legs. A little vest-top in cool green cashmere emphasised the firm swell of her breasts and the way her torso tapered down to a delicious, tiny waist.

He swallowed and his eyes travelled almost with relief to a small table, where a half-drunk glass of wine rested. His mouth curved, he felt glad of the opportunity to disapprove of her again.

Kate noticed the tiny elevation of the jet-dark brows, felt his disapproval as surely as if it were shimmering in waves of heat off him. He didn't say anything—but, there again, he didn't have to. It was written clearly all over the autocratic features.

Some small inkling of who she really was came seeping back and she tried to catch hold of it, fast. Not some simpering schoolgirl, but a woman. His *equal.* 'Is something wrong, Giovanni?' she asked sweetly.

He shrugged. 'You drink alone?'

For one quietly hysterical moment she felt like saying that yes, yes, she *did* drink alone. That a bottle of vodka would leave her untouched and unsatisfied. Because she could tell from the unmarred perfection of his face and body that here was a man to whom excess would be anathema. Except perhaps for excess in one thing…

What could she say? That she never drank alone, but that he had unnerved her so much that she felt that wine might bring some warmth and some life back into her cold and bewildered veins?

'Rarely,' she conceded with an answering shrug, not caring whether he believed her or not.

Every instinct in his body was clamouring at him to get

the hell out. Telling him that here lay danger, a hot and inexplicable danger far beyond any he had ever encountered. Giovanni had never known a moment's fear in all his thirty-four years, but in that instant his flesh shivered with trepidation at something quite outside his experience.

And yet he was known for his worldliness—his refusal to be cowed by anybody or anything. So what spell was this witch casting on him? Which honeyed chains were denying him an exit from this enchanted place of hers? His head was ordering him to leave and leave now, even as his body bluntly refused to listen to such requests.

Kate saw the fevered glittering in his blue eyes. Take control, she thought. Take control. She drew a deep breath. 'What would you like to drink, Giovanni?' His name felt delicious on her lips—so wickedly bewitching that just to say it flooded her with the unturnable tide of desire.

He had asked for a drink and now that it was offered knew that he must refuse it. And yet, like some disbelieving watcher of his own self, he heard himself murmuring that yes, yes—he would like a glass of wine very much indeed.

And then he lowered himself onto one of the sofas, and watched her while she poured, his eyes following her closely, intensely aware of every movement she made, bewitched by her as he was rarely bewitched by a woman. The little skirt she wore skimmed her thighs as she bent over, drawing attention to the heart-stopping length of her legs.

Knowing that he watched her, Kate willed her hands not to tremble as she slopped red wine into a simple-stemmed glass of crystal and handed it to him.

'Thank you,' he said gravely and his pupils grew as dark and as wide as a jungle cat's as she stood in front of him as though she didn't quite know what to do next. 'Aren't you going to sit down and join me, Kate?' he murmured.

How could such a mundane request sound like the most erotic invitation she had ever heard? She perched on the edge of the chair opposite him, and wrapped her fingers around the crystal glass.

He noticed the prim way that she had glued her knees together, and a pulse beat deep in his throat. He ran the tip of his finger thoughtfully around the rim of his glass. 'So what shall we drink to?'

For one mad moment, she thought that she saw humour lurking in the depths of those ocean-blue eyes, but the image dissolved almost before it had appeared and a cold hunger had taken its place once more.

'Hmm, Kate?' he prompted silkily. 'A toast to what?'

'I don't know,' she said tonelessly, thinking that her name could sometimes sound like a hard, shotgun sound, but the way that he curved his lips around it made it sound as soft and as beguiling as a caress. 'What do you usually drink to in Sicily?'

He smiled, but it was a smile without heart and now, at least, totally without humour. 'Why, we drink to the same things that people drink to all the world over, *cara mia*. To health. And to happiness,' he murmured, and raised his glass to her in a mocking gesture.

Leaving Kate wondering why the toast sounded such an empty one.

CHAPTER THREE

KATE drank her wine more quickly than she had intended, or was used to. Not enough to be drunk—but enough to make her feel very slightly reckless.

But why not? She was committing no crime, was she? This man, whilst unknown to her, came with the excellent pedigree of being Lady St John's godson. He was an attractive man who fascinated her. So why not just enjoy the drink for what it was worth?

What did she think was going to happen?

That was the trouble—she just *didn't know*!

'It's very good of you to come out of your way,' she said, thinking how stilted her words sounded.

Giovanni opened his mouth to tell her that he was on his way to the airport and that the detour had been a minor one, but some instinct made the words remain unsaid. 'No problem,' he said obliquely.

'Shall I...shall I put some music on?'

Dismissively he shook his dark head and sipped at his wine, allowing his bright blue gaze to sweep around the airy room to where the reflection of light bouncing off the river dappled in pale gold waves across one wall.

'This is a very beautiful place you have,' he observed.

'Thank you.'

'And in an extremely desirable area.'

'Thank you again!'

His eyes narrowed. 'You must have done extremely well,' he observed thoughtfully, 'to be able to afford to live somewhere like this at your age.'

She wondered if she was imagining the inference behind

his casual statement. That maybe some *man* had set her up here? 'My success has so far outstripped my wildest dreams,' she told him truthfully. 'Perhaps in the same way as your own business fortunes? I expect you must be expanding all the time?'

He shook his head impatiently. 'No, we are not!'

'No?' she queried in disbelief. 'When your company's name is synonymous with the world's finest silverware? I'm not an expert—'

'No, you're not,' he agreed coolly.

'—but aren't you missing out on an opportunity?' she persisted, refusing to be cowed by his rudeness.

He shrugged as he acknowledged the compliment, noting almost reluctantly the way that her hair rippled in a fiery waterfall down over her breasts.

'Our company's success is based on traditional methods,' he told her softly. 'Over-expansion would be unwise—or so my father always maintained. We have never been a mass-market company, instead we make a limited number of very beautiful products. It is a lengthy and highly specialised process, and one of which my family is justifiably proud.' He thought how passionate his voice sounded. How he rarely gave so much of himself away to a stranger. Danger.

His fervour drew her irresistibly in and she found herself leaning forward, clasping her hands on her knees. 'How very romantic!'

Her face was earnest and the green eyes were huge and shining in her heart-shaped face. She looked, he thought with a sudden lurch of his heart, as eager and as animated as a child at Christmas. 'It is a little,' he agreed, with a slow smile. 'Though sometimes I have a battle to rein in my ambitions.'

'Beware of ambition which overreaches itself, Giovanni,' she chided softly, without thinking.

'Shakespeare,' he observed. '*Macbeth*.'

'You know the play?' She couldn't keep the surprise from her voice, and then saw the dangerous answering glitter of his eyes. 'I'm sorry, I didn't mean—'

He gave a wry smile. 'Oh, yes, you did,' he contradicted silkily. 'You'd placed me in your stereotypical little box, hadn't you, Kate? The sophisticated veneer merely masking the Sicilian peasant who lies beneath? More familiar with the Mafiosi than with any kind of literature? Is that what you thought?'

Her lips opened to deny it, but the harsh way he had spoken *had* stripped away the urbane sophistication of this elegant man who sat opposite her.

And suddenly she saw someone quite unlike any other who had come into the safe confines of her London life. She saw centuries of pride and of striving encapsulated in that lean, hard body, and that proud and beautiful face.

She could not tear her eyes away from him, observing him with the intense preoccupation she usually gave to a house she was about to decorate.

The muscles which rippled beneath the silk shirt were not the pretty-precious muscles of a man who worked out with weights at the gym every morning. This was a man as men were meant to be. Tough and sometimes harsh, and totally uncompromising.

And she found herself wondering how a man like this would treat a woman.

He saw the dull flush of awareness which had spread rosy wings across her high, pale cheekbones and he rose from the sofa before the dull ache of temptation grew stronger. 'May I use the bathroom?'

'But of course!' Thank heavens she had cleaned the sink that very morning! 'It's along the corridor—the third door down.'

Once there, he spurted icy water onto his wrists, as if doing that could subdue his heated blood. The eyes that stared back at him from the mirror looked like a stranger's eyes with their hectic glitter transforming blue to black.

She is just a woman, he told himself. A very beautiful woman, but a woman all the same. And he had resisted many, many women over the years.

On his way back to the sitting room he passed what was obviously her study. He noted that she had left her computer on, and then he heard a loud buzzing, like the muted sound of a dentist's drill, and saw a wasp as it battered uselessly at the window-pane.

He imagined its sting piercing her pale, smooth flesh and moved towards the insect, his mouth thinning as he acknowledged an inappropriate sense of protectiveness towards her. He raised the flat of his hand to crush the insect, and then relented, flicking the handle so that the window opened, and in that moment the wasp flew free.

As he shut the window he looked down at the scattered papers littered over the desk, and when an instantly familiar word leapt out at him he frowned.

Sicily.

His olive fingers flicked over the sheets and a warmth stole over him as he gazed at the familiar shape of the island. So she *was* interested in him! Interested enough to bother to come straight back here and look up the land of his birth.

In that one moment he knew that he could have her. Recognised and rejected the tantalising idea before it had a chance to move from mind to body.

He went back into the sitting room.

'It's time I was leaving,' he said abruptly.

Her heart lurched with disappointment, and Kate sprang to her feet. He looked so very right here, in her home—with his proud, dark beauty silhouetted against the golden backdrop of the light-dappled wall. Suddenly, she wanted him to stay.

'No, don't go! Not yet!' She saw him raise his eyebrows,

as if such demonstrativeness was faintly distasteful, but her desire not to lose him overrode any sense of maintaining an air of dignity.

'Please,' she continued, some instinct spurring her on as she put her hand out to rest in conciliatory fashion on his arm, and she shivered, for the muscle beneath was as honed as she had imagined it would be. Brazenly, she let the hand stay right where it was, her fingers curling around the curved, hard contour in a gesture which was most definitely possessive.

Their eyes met in a moment which was pure electricity, and she read the question that glittered so provocatively from the sapphire depths.

'I certainly didn't mean to offend you just now when I seemed surprised by your knowledge of literature,' she told him softly. 'Or to stereotype you. I've been very ungracious and you have been very kind.'

Giovanni narrowed his eyes as her words were made incomprehensible by her touch. But then wasn't touch the most irresistible of all the senses? He looked down at where her hand rested lightly on his arm—a gesture at once so innocent and yet so profoundly sensual. He felt the almost imperceptible sting where her nails touched him and the blood begin to roar in his ears, because it was what he had wanted since the first moment he had set eyes on her.

To touch her.

No, more.

Much more than that. He wanted the most fundamental communion of all.

He felt the pull of temptation as something primitive flared into life inside him, like a dark, compelling fever which had taken over his body. And it had overtaken her, too—of that he was certain. He could see from the blackened pools which almost obscured the emerald of her eyes that she wanted him.

Really wanted him. In the space of a heartbeat he made his decision.

She would have him!

Very slowly and very deliberately he lifted his hand, and cupped her face in his palm as if he had every right to do so, grazing an arrogant thumb over the lush outline of her lips which trembled into immediate and urgent response.

Kate's knees turned unfamiliarly to water, her stomach warm and melting as desire flooded hotly through her veins and her hand fell redundantly to her side.

'Giovanni!' She swallowed, trying to tell herself that all he was doing was *touching her lips*, for heaven's sake!

His gaze was full-on, the blue eyes blazing with careless question. If she said no, then he would stop immediately. 'What is it, *cara mia*?' he purred, his accent as pronounced as it was persuasive. The pad of his thumb traced slowly around the quivering Cupid's bow of her mouth. 'What is it that you want from me?'

She trembled violently, unable to pull away, wondering just who *was* this new and over-responsive Kate? Must he think her a brazen fool? A woman who reacted so compliantly to a man she had just met. But suddenly, she *didn't care*! She shook her head, her mouth as dry as dust, as she struggled for words which would make sense of her reaction.

'Tell me.'

'It's a little difficult to say anything,' came her muffled response, 'when you're touching my lips like that.'

'You want me to stop touching them? Is that it?'

Her eyes met his with a fierce, burning look.

'No,' he answered, his accent deepening to one of soft reflection as his gaze dropped downwards, and he watched the flowering of her nipples through the cashmere vest. 'That is the very last thing you want, isn't it, *cara*? So tell me what you *do* want?'

What? Admit that she felt she would die if he didn't replace his thumb with his mouth, and kiss her? She opened her mouth to speak, but no words came, only the sudden erotic entry of his thumb between her lips, and she imprisoned it there with a fierce little suck, just like a baby.

'Or are you afraid to tell me?' He swallowed as he felt the moist plumpness of her mouth encasing his thumb.

For reply she sucked again, hard. She saw his responding shudder, heard the sigh which was very nearly a groan as he muttered a harsh imprecation in what she presumed was Sicilian.

She lifted her eyes to his. Afraid? All she knew was that she had never wanted a man so much and so unequivocably. She always played the respectable game. The getting-to-know-you-and-then-we'll-see game. Except that most times the getting-to-know-you bit had been enough to kill any desire stone-dead. And she always played by the rules, too—rules which Giovanni Calverri seemed hell-bent on redefining.

'Such an independent woman,' he teased, but there was a dark undertone to his taunt. 'With her fantastically successful company. Everything she wants, except the one thing she really, really wants—'

'You,' she breathed, the words coming out as thick and sweet as honey before she could stop them, 'I want you.'

His triumph at her admission was fused with despair. He had expected resistance—an appalled, outraged resistance. Not eager compliance so thinly disguised.

In the moment before he claimed her mouth he knew how doomed sailors must have felt, lured to their fate by sirens who tempted as this woman now tempted him.

He forgot his flight, forgot all about his reasons for flying home to Sicily. He felt the burst of desire which would not, could not, now be denied, and with a small angry growl he pulled her into his arms and began to kiss her.

In the dark heat of longing, she opened her mouth to his,

feeling the tension in his hard body. One taste and she knew that she was lost—it was that complete and that immediate.

'Oh, my God,' she moaned as his tongue began to trace a moist circle inside her lips.

'Your prayers will not help you now, *cara*,' he mocked, still with that slight edge to his voice. But as he felt her body melt closely into his he responded with a raw hunger which drove the last lingering traces of guilt away.

It seemed forever since he had kissed a woman, and these were new lips. Erotic lips. Lush and scented with wine. He groaned and plundered deeply, his hands tightening around the small indentation of her waist, unable to resist the curve of her hips and the cup of her bottom. He pushed up her skirt until the flat of his hands were exploring the cool globes laid bare by the thin, lacy thong she wore, and he felt that he might explode. 'You dress to kill,' he shuddered.

And she felt like she was dying. With need. And with pleasure. She felt her arms snake instinctively around his neck as her hips melded into the rocky power of him, thinking that it was too long since she had been in a man's embrace like this. She pressed her breasts against him, and he groaned, turning her in his arms and pushing her up against the wall, one lean, muscular thigh prising its way authoritatively between hers, and she felt the pooling of desire as it slicked against her thong.

She pushed him away from her, but only so that her fingers could fly to the buttons of his fine silk shirt, clumsily freeing them from their confinement, and he replied by swiftly unclasping and unzipping her skirt. It fell to her ankles immediately, and she stepped over it, wearing nothing now but a cashmere vest and a lacy thong.

With another small, angry growl of desire, Giovanni feasted his eyes on the front of the white thong, where the faint red triangle of hair tempted him from behind the flimsy lace. Her fingers were now scrabbling at his belt, and they were turning and touching like a pair of demented dancers, clothes falling free as they frantically kissed their way out of the sitting room.

He felt his hardness grow explosive, aware that their frenzied path had brought them to a door which he assumed must be to her bedroom.

Unprepared and unwilling to accept a moment's more delay, he scooped her up into his arms.

'Giovanni—' she gasped.

The blue-black eyes glittered obdurately. 'What?'

'Where are you taking me?' As she spoke the words, she knew that it was a foolish and redundant sentence, and his abstract, almost cynical smile told her that he felt exactly the same way.

'To bed,' he ground out, and kicked the door open.

CHAPTER FOUR

GIOVANNI carried Kate straight over to the bed and put her into the centre of it, and, his eyes still holding hers with their icy glitter, began to unzip his trousers.

'You are protected?' he asked, as matter of factly as if he were asking her for a cup of coffee.

She shook her head. 'No.' Pointless to tell him that she had been single for over two years. He did not want a history of her love-life, he just wanted a practical answer to his question.

His eyes narrowed and he nodded almost thoughtfully as he withdrew a packet of condoms from his pocket, and Kate found herself wondering slightly wildly whether he was always so well prepared.

She lay there watching him. She knew that she ought to feel some sense of shame at what was happening. What she was allowing to happen to them, but her only sensation was one of glorious expectation. Even when his mouth twisted in another faint, cynical smile as he eased the zip carefully over his erection.

Wearing nothing but a pair of dark blue silken boxer shorts, he arrogantly kicked the trousers away from him and Kate heard herself gasping with unashamed pleasure as the boxers followed.

Greedily she ran her eyes over his naked body, focusing on the gleaming olive skin and a tight, taut torso. His shoulders were broad and his hips sensuously narrow, whilst the long, hard thighs were unbelievably lean and muscular.

He saw her watching him, and he deliberately touched himself. Saw the way that her eyes dilated as he stroked his finger arrogantly along his aching hardness, provocatively sliding on the sheath and turning practicality into eroticism. And then she lifted one pale, smooth thigh in unconscious invitation, and he could play that particular game no longer. 'You are wearing far too much, *cara*,' he told her softly as he climbed onto the bed next to her.

On an instinct she bent her head forward and licked luxuriously at the Adam's apple that curved at his throat, and felt him shudder beneath her tongue. 'Am I?' she whispered, transfixed by the hungry gleam in his eyes as he glittered a hungry gaze over her body.

'Much, much too much,' he murmured, his accent deepening. He peeled the cashmere vest over her head and felt the pounding of his heart as he caught his first sight of her breasts. So full and so pale. Encased in virginal white lace. His mouth twisted at the irony of that, but his thoughts were banished by the need of his body.

'*Matri di Diu!*' he muttered thickly, and dipped his head to her breast, unable to stop the quick flick of his tongue against the nub which strained so frantically through the delicate white lace.

'Oh!' The pleasure of his touch was so intense that it was almost like pain. No, not pain—because if this was pain, then how to define pleasure, pure and sweet? Her head fell back helplessly against the pillow as he flicked his tongue again.

'You like that, don't you, *cara*?' he enquired almost idly, watching the way that her hips moved against the bed in a frantic little circle, and the heat of his own longing almost made him lose his mind. 'Don't you?' he repeated harshly.

'Yes!'

He unclipped the bra and her breasts fell free, and once more he bent his head, taking the whole nipple greedily between his lips, and sucking on it hard, in an erotic imitation of the way she had sucked his thumb earlier, and Kate very nearly passed out with pleasure.

'Giovanni...' Her head moved from side to side on the pillow, as if in denial. No, not denial. She could deny this man nothing. Not a thing.

'*Sí?*' he whispered softly, but words failed her because he had moved his hand between her thighs and parted them.

She licked her lips feverishly as he moved his middle finger inside her thong.

And Giovanni's breath escaped him on a long, almost helpless shudder as he felt the syrupy desire of her slicking against his skin, feeling her shudder beneath his touch, hearing her moan his name once more. Was she like this for every man? he wondered for one hot and fevered moment.

He moved his finger experimentally against her. And again. And again. Her moans increased, and the sound of her helpless little cries made him grow even harder, almost unbearably so.

'I want you,' she whispered.

He gave an almost cruel smile as he lifted his dark head to look down at her. He would make her beg. Women liked to beg. 'Not yet,' he told her, on a silky taunt.

'Please.'

He shook his head. 'Not yet,' he repeated, on a low, provocative growl.

He wasn't going to stop what he was doing, Kate realised...

He wasn't going to stop...

And, to her utter disbelief, Kate felt the inexorable onslaught of fulfilment. The great tearing warmth of...of...

'Giovanni!' She said his name urgently. 'Oh!' She opened her eyes very wide. 'This is the best!' she gasped in astonishment. 'I'm coming...'

He could see that for himself from the sudden stiffening of her limbs, the way her back arched, the increased slick against his fingers, and then the slow, shuddering spasms which made her cry out loud.

He waited until she was nearly done, and then he straddled her, two taut thighs on either side of her hips, and thrust into her while her body was still pulsing with pleasure.

Her eyes flew open at the renewed sensation. He was so very big. So huge that he filled her completely. But, more than that, it felt so right to have him inside her. As though all her life her body had been yearning to have Giovanni Calverri make love to her like this.

He moved. Over and over. And as he moved he kissed her, and she gave herself up to the sweetness of those kisses, not thinking, not even caring about whether this was right or wrong, because nothing had ever felt this good.

He wanted to prolong it, to make it last forever. He had always been able to do that. Even as a teenager, when the newness of physical pleasure had threatened to overwhelm him. But now he felt the stealthy steal of orgasm come to claim him before he was prepared for it. He tried to fight it. For a moment he almost managed it. But when he felt her begin to pulse around him once more he knew that he was lost.

'Kate,' he said almost brokenly, the first and only time he had said her name since their bodies had joined with such bitter-sweet communion.

And Kate wept with some strange, deep emotion against his bare shoulder as she came again, feeling him begin to shudder deep inside her, arms closing around him tightly as she wished that this night could never end.

Giovanni awoke to unfamiliar shadows, his senses leaping into perception in a split-second as he tried to work out just where he was.

Dear God!

There was a sleeping woman beside him, which in itself was not strange, but he knew immediately that this was different. Her scent was different. The long red hair which the night had made dark was different.

And the sex had been different, too. Beautifully and irrevocably different.

Ruthlessly he quashed the memory as his body betrayed him once more with the stirring of desire, and he slipped silently from the bed.

He was of a race that understood secrecy. And stealth—and he had no difficulty moving without sound around the silent room to locate his clothes and shoes, which he carried from the room.

In the bathroom he dressed, glancing only once in the mirror, but once was enough. The wild glitter in his eyes told its own story. As did the darkened contours of his mouth, where she had kissed him as if she were drowning, as if she couldn't get enough of him.

His mouth twisted with self-contempt as he let himself noiselessly out of the flat into the crispness of the moonless summer night, and to where the black car was sitting reproachfully just as he had left it.

He looked up at the unlit windows of the flat as he turned the key and the engine flooded into powerful life, wondering whether she would appear, clutching a sheet perhaps, bewitching him with that pale and glorious body as she watched him drive away.

But the window remained empty, and relief coursed hotly through his veins, just as desire had heated them only hours earlier.

Two o'clock.

His flight to Sicily had long since departed. And there would be nothing now until the early morning. Night flights were banned—their intrusion into the quiet, sleeping skies around Heathrow not allowed.

He thought about what options lay open to him.

He could go to the airport and wait. Drink some unspeakable coffee while he contemplated his impetuous folly, and thought through the inevitable conclusion of what he had done.

But he shook his dark, gleaming head as if in answer to his unspoken question.

Inactivity would lie too heavily on his conscience.

And on his heart.

He accelerated as if he was aiming for some invisible finishing barrier and headed west.

He drove like a man on a mission—though he was cautious enough to observe the speed limit, but only just, even though the roads were empty of police cars. He had played the devil with fate once already tonight, and a speeding ban would end this remarkable night on an even more bitter note.

His body was still pulsing with the remembered warmth of her body and he uttered a soft curse in Sicilian as he felt the renewed ache of desire. But he forced it away, because the time for passion was now at an end, and he must address the consequences of his actions.

He had betrayed Anna with a woman he scarcely knew—so what did that say about him? More importantly, what did it say about their relationship?

He gave a sigh of regret mingled with anger. He had thought that his life with Anna had been happy—hell, it *had* been happy, but now for the first time he was compelled to acknowledge that something was missing from their life together, something which had never occurred to him was lacking until he had found it with someone else.

Passion.

The question was whether he was prepared to forgo passion and to cherish instead everything he had shared with Anna.

Or whether Anna deserved better.

He continued to drive though he did not know where, only that the miles eaten up by the machine did nothing to ease his sense of wrongdoing. And it was only when daylight began to break in purest gold shot with rose-pink over the horizon that he slowed down and began to follow the signs back towards the airport.

Unfamiliar light woke her. The cold, clear light of dawn as it flooded through the uncurtained windows.

Kate blinked, her body warm and aching, her mind drifting in and out of sweet, remembered places, and then her eyes flew wide open to greet the pale and brilliant light of early morning as memory slipped sharply into focus, at the same time as did one monumental and heartbreaking fact.

He had gone! Giovanni had gone!

Her heart clenched painfully in her chest and she closed her eyes. Please, please, please…let him still be here, she beseeched in silent prayer.

She held her breath, but the flat remained utterly silent save for the almost imperceptible ticking of the bedside clock whose illuminated face showed that it was almost five in the morning.

She shivered as she remembered what she had done. What *they* had done. Without thought. And without shame, she told herself fiercely. Maybe it had not been textbook relationship behaviour as taught to her by her mother, but she could not—and would not—regret it.

She pushed the rumpled sheet back and found herself staring with helpless longing at the indentation of where his head had lain on the pillow. She ran the flat of her hand over it, as if that faint touch could magic him back again. And she found herself understanding why women sometimes kissed the pillow on which their lover had rested his head.

She shuddered a breath as hope flared foolishly in her heart. Maybe he *was* in the bathroom.

But a closer glance around the room killed that hope stone-dead. Only *her* discarded clothes lay scattered wantonly all over the carpet of the bedroom.

Her cheeks flushed.

It had been beautiful. Passionate and profound. She had felt proud to love him, and had imagined that the feeling had been mutual. A man and a woman sent spinning out of orbit by the power of their mutual attraction.

But if that was the case, where was he now?

She licked at her dry lips distractedly. He had been on his way back to Sicily, she reasoned. Perhaps his business had been of a particularly urgent nature, and he had not wanted to disturb her. Because some unshakable instinct told her that Giovanni Calverri was far too fastidious a man to ever indulge in the transient pleasures of a one-night stand. Why, she had certainly never done anything like it herself!

Which meant that he would almost certainly have left a note.

Her heart was beating very fast as she went from room to room, switching on every light as she did so, so that no surface would go unsearched.

Until she was forced to admit to herself the ghastly, horrible truth.

That Giovanni had left without a trace.

And that was when pain began to metamorphosise into anger…

Giovanni lifted his eyes to the dark-haired stewardess, and frowned, barely noticing the overt look of admiration she was slanting at him. 'What?' Automatically, he had lapsed into Sicilian.

Her eyes flashed excitedly as she heard the distinctive dialect, but she was only able to answer him in Italian. 'I asked whether you would like a cup of coffee before take-off?' she said in a smooth, practised voice.

What he wanted was for the damned plane to be touching down on the soil of his homeland—and certainly not a flight which involved a changeover in Rome while he waited for a connection.

For half a moment he had considered chartering a private jet to take him on from Rome, but another sharp jab of his conscience had stopped him. Was he really about to start rewarding his outrageous indiscretion with a flamboyant gesture of extravagance?

'Please,' he said shortly.

She prettily offered him a tray of pastries but he waved them away with an impatient hand, and spent the rest of the flight forcing himself to go through a batch of papers which could easily have waited.

But he needed something to occupy his mind. Something to try to stop him remembering the red blur of her hair and the emerald gleam of bewitching eyes.

You're going home, he told himself. With all that that entails.

In Rome, he forced himself to eat a little something, reminding himself that he had had nothing since yesterday's lunch. But the food tasted bland, and he pushed the half-touched plate away as his flight was announced.

The minutes ticked by like hours as Kate prowled around the flat, her initial sense of desolation gradually being replaced by a feeling of outright fury.

How dared he?

How *dared* he?

By such a cold and uncaring rejection he had reduced a wonderful night to the bitter realisation that she had indulged in a classic one-night stand.

And then been dumped!

She felt her cheeks stain with shame. They were both mature and consenting adults. OK, he might have decided that he didn't want to see her again, but at least he could have done her the courtesy of going through the motions of civilised behaviour. It wouldn't have killed him to have breakfast with her, surely? Or to have made love to her when she woke up? prompted the hungry voice of her senses. He could have taken her telephone number and said that he would ring her, even if he hadn't meant it.

Bastard!

She couldn't sleep, eat, or concentrate on anything. She ran a bath and afterwards threw on a pair of jeans and a T-shirt—and the more she thought about Giovanni's behaviour towards her, the more her fury grew and grew. But fury seemed to hurt less than shame—and far less than the pang of realising that she would probably never see him again.

She couldn't understand it. Had she misread everything?

He had been the best lover she had ever had, and she was certain that the experience had been as wonderful for him as it had been for her. She had seen that almost dazed sense of wonder on his face as their bodies had joined together.

So why creep out like a thief into the night and destroy what they had shared? Why leave her with the bitter taste of rejection and confusion?

Several times that day she reached her hand out to the telephone, then decided against using it when she reminded herself that men like Giovanni Calverri had it much too easy.

How would he ever learn that he couldn't just go around taking what he wanted without showing a little more consideration in the process? Unless somebody actually had the nerve to tell him?

And the unthinkable notion that she might just be one in a long line of broken-hearted international conquests was enough to make up her mind.

Resolutely, Kate reached her hand towards the telephone again, only this time she picked it up.

'International directories, please,' she said crisply.

* * *

Giovanni drew to a halt in front of the Calverri headquarters, and wondered why everything felt different.

Why *he* felt different.

Yet outwardly nothing had changed. Heat sizzled off the parched earth and the sky was a dazzling blue as he stared at the huge, old, cloistered villa set in a magnificent piece of land where his family's silver business was housed. Here, artisans who had been with the company for most of their working lives lovingly created silver heirlooms using traditional methods which had never been bettered.

And every spring students would flock from all over the world to learn their craft at the hands of experts. From these students would be drawn fresh blood and talent which would keep the Calverri business running long into the next century.

Giovanni sighed as he made his way to his secretary's office. His heart was heavy, and the burden of guilt weighed down on him like lead. Soon he was going to have to face Anna and he just didn't know what he was going to say to her.

His secretary looked up as he came in, and her eyes widened with pleasure.

'Giovanni, you're late!' she exclaimed, her smile of welcome dying on her lips as she saw the look on his face. 'What has happened?' she questioned. 'Is something wrong?'

Was it that apparent, then? What had happened to his ability to hide his feelings—to present a cool, remote kind of demeanour—so that people never knew what he was thinking?

'A long journey,' he said, and shrugged, picking up a handful of documents in a gesture designed to guard against further intrusion. 'What needs to be gone through? I had better catch up on whatever is urgent, and then I must go and see Anna.'

His secretary smiled. Once she had entertained romantic notions about Giovanni herself, but then reality had set in.

He was her boss—an untouchable god of a man. And she adored Anna. Everyone did.

'Did that order go off to Texas?' he quizzed.

'As scheduled.' She nodded.

'And what of the Scandinavian project?'

'Better than expected.' She smiled back.

His satisfied nod was more automatic than genuine, and he worked away with a quiet determination until all the backlog was cleared and he knew he could put off the moment of truth no longer. He rose to his feet.

'I will see you tomorrow, Gabriella.'

His secretary narrowed her eyes in silent question, but said nothing other than, '*Sí*, Giovanni.' And she sat watching as he left the office, disturbed only by the sudden intrusion of the telephone, which she picked up.

'*Pronto*!'

On the other end of the line, Kate felt her nerve nearly fail her, but some dogged determination drove her on. 'Do you…do you speak English?' she enquired falteringly.

'But of course!' There was a slight pause. 'Who do you wish to speak to?'

Kate drew a deep breath, and the name came out in a gush. 'Giovanni Calverri! Is he there, please?'

'Who is calling?'

Kate thought how frosty the voice had become. Should she leave her name? 'Is he there, please?' she asked again.

There was a loud, undisguised sigh, as if the person at the other end of the line had scant patience with unknown women who refused to say who they were.

'No, he is not here!'

'And are you expecting him back?'

'Not today.' There was a pause. 'Signor Calverri has been in England.'

I *know*! Kate bit the words back.

'And has only just arrived back.' Another pause. 'So obviously, the very first thing on his mind was to go and see his fiancée.'

His *fiancée*? 'Oh, I see,' said Kate faintly, as, with a slow, sinking pain in her heart, she put the receiver down without another word.

CHAPTER FIVE

GIOVANNI watched the woman who walked alongside the pool towards him.

She was the epitome of elegance—her pure silk dress in a buttery-cream colour setting off the raven-dark hair and the huge, black-fringed brown eyes. Her face was serene, on her lips a smile of calm acceptance—an easy pleasure at seeing once more the man she had known for all her adult life.

He felt the deep, sharp pain of regret.

'Giovanni!'

'Hello, Anna.'

She moved straight into his arms, but he could not bring himself to hold her other than awkwardly, as if she were composed of some brittle substance, and his touch might contaminate her. She pulled away, her brow criss-crossing in a frown.

'What is it, *caro*?' she demanded.

What way to tell her? Though the notion of *not* telling her was even more unthinkable.

He knew that most men of his acquaintance would put the whole experience down to a fleeting temptation of the flesh, not worth confessing to because of the consequences of such a confession. But Anna was the woman he knew. The woman he had always intended to marry.

'Giovanni!' She was looking at him now in alarm. 'What has happened to make you look this way? Is someone sick? Has something happened to the business?'

He met her stare without flinching, and it was perhaps because she knew him so well, and had known him for so long, that a horrified look of comprehension began to dawn in her dark eyes.

Her voice grew faint. 'Tell me!'

He had no desire to hurt her, but hurt was an irrevocable repercussion of his actions. His mouth hardened. 'I met someone—'

He heard her pained intake of breath, and he flinched as he saw the hurt that clouded her eyes.

'And…' He hesitated, trying to pick out the least wounding words of all.

'And what? The truth, Giovanni!' she demanded, in as furious a tone as he had ever heard.

'*I slept with her!*'

There was a short, shocked silence before she spoke.

'How many times?'

Her question astonished him. 'What?'

'You heard me! How many times did you sleep with her?'

'Once,' he answered heavily. 'Just the once.'

'Only once?' She frowned at him in disbelief.

'*Once!*' he emphasised bitterly, his blood heating his veins with shameful pleasure.

She shook her head and let her eyelids flutter down to conceal her eyes. 'Oh, why did you have to tell me?' she whispered.

His heart beat strong with the burden of guilt. 'You needed to know the truth.'

But she shook her head once more. 'No, Giovanni,' she said acidly. 'You needed someone to share the burden with, didn't you? To ease your conscience! Most men would have filed it away under an experience never to be repeated—especially if, as you say, it was just the once.'

But her words leapt out at him like tiny barbs. *If, as you say…* She would never trust him again. He knew that. The rest of her life would be spent watching him. Waiting for him to slip. Always wondering…

'Anna, I'm sorry—'

'No!' she retorted furiously. 'You have offloaded your guilt—please spare me your need for forgiveness!' She sank down on one of the wrought-iron benches that stood in the shade of a cypress tree. Then looked up at him with hurt, bewildered eyes.

'Who is she?'

'No one!'

'*Yes! Somebody!*'

'A girl. Just a girl I met in England and—'

She cut across him icily, 'Was she the first?'

He stared at her incredulously and then his eyes narrowed dangerously. 'Of course she was the first!'

'There's no "of course!" about it!' She studied the engagement ring on her finger, then looked up at him, her gaze very steady. 'The first? And only?'

Giovanni could see the hurt in her eyes, but there was, he realised, no surprise whatsoever. Almost as if she had been *expecting* him to stray. His mouth hardened as he thought of all the women he had turned down over the years. One misdemeanour, and you were scarred by it forever. And he had only himself to blame.

And Kate, of course, he thought with a kick of something akin to both hatred and desire. Kate with those smooth, pink nails which had curled around his arm so possessively, enchaining him with the sweet seduction of her touch.

'The first,' he agreed quietly. 'And the only.'

'Oh, why did you have to tell me, Giovanni?' she whispered sadly and again he felt the sharp pang of remorse as she saw the white glitter of the diamond which sparkled on her finger. 'Most men would have tried to get away with it.'

'Because I could not bear to live a lie with you, Anna,' he told her softly, and a muscle worked in his cheek as he silently cursed the day his path had crossed with that of Kate Connors.

* * *

Back in London, Kate sat staring at the telephone as if it were an alien just landed from Mars.

Engaged, she thought in a frozen kind of disbelief, starting as the doorbell began to ring, and she remembered the last time it had rung like that.

Like a zombie, she walked out to answer it, some stupid hope making her wish that history could repeat itself and that Giovanni would be standing there, telling her that there was no fiancée. That she had made a terrible mistake.

But it was Lucy, her copper hair pulled back into a ponytail, and not a scrap of make-up on her face—but that didn't matter, thought Kate. Not when your eyes were like emeralds sparkling in such a pale, clear face.

'Hello, Lucy,' she said, and then her voice began to tremble.

Lucy swept her a swift, assessing look and her face took on a mixture of concern and anger. 'You've seen him, haven't you?'

'Who?'

'Giovanni Calverri!' Lucy spat the name out.

'Seen him?' Kate very nearly laughed, but tears were much too close to the surface to allow her the luxury of laughter. 'Yes, you could say that I've seen him.'

Lucy came into the flat and shut the door behind her. 'And?'

Kate bit her lip. Who else could she tell? Who else could she bear to tell? Someone who loved her enough never to judge her. And Lucy did.

She tried to recount the whole sorry story matter-of-factly. 'He turned up yesterday after I'd been to see you.'

Lucy nodded. 'Go on.'

'He… I… We…' Kate shook her head and tried again. There was no pretty way to phrase it. 'We went to bed,' she said simply.

'You *what*?' breathed Lucy.

'You sound shocked,' commented Kate drily.

'That's because I am! Oh, no,' she amended suddenly as Kate's lips began to tremble again, 'not because of what you did—but because it's just not like you!'

'I know it isn't.'

'You're the kind of woman who plays safe, Kate. Gosh, I remember when you were going out with Pete—he used to say that you'd virtually interviewed him on at least the first four dates before you would even let him *kiss* you!'

Kate nodded. 'Yep. That's me. Safe, sensible Kate.'

Lucy knotted her fingers together. 'So what happened? What was so different?'

'He was,' said Kate quietly. She walked over to the window and stared unseeingly at the river before she turned round to face the soft consternation in her sister's eyes and tried to explain the inexplicable. 'It was an attraction like no other I'd ever felt. Ever.'

'And he must have felt the same way too, presumably?'

'That's what I thought,' agreed Kate tonelessly, and realised that she couldn't give Lucy only half the story. Didn't want to, either. And who would she be protecting if she kept the horrible, hurtful truth to herself? Only a man who didn't deserve one vestige of protection. 'But he disappeared in the middle of the night.'

Lucy's face fell. 'He did a runner?'

'He certainly did.'

Lucy thought for a moment, then she shrugged awkwardly. 'Maybe he had a good reason—'

'Oh, a very good reason!' Kate gave a hollow laugh. 'Like the fact that he's engaged to be married—that's reason enough!'

Lucy winced. 'You *are* joking?'

Their eyes met.

'I'm sorry, Kate, I didn't mean to be flippant. As if you'd

joke about something like that. But how do you know? I mean, you surely didn't—'

'You think I went to bed with him *knowing* that he was going to be married to someone else?'

Lucy shook her head. 'Of course I didn't!'

'*He should have told me*,' whispered Kate. 'He should have told me that he was promised to someone else!'

'How on earth did you find out?'

This was the humiliating part. Kate swallowed. 'I was angry—angry with him for having left without even so much as a goodbye, and angry with myself for having behaved so *outrageously*. I decided that he needed to be told he just couldn't do something like that—if not for my sake, then maybe he might just think about it with the next poor girl he bowls over with his charm!'

'So you rang him?'

Kate nodded. 'In Sicily. I got some snotty secretary who told me smugly that he had gone off to see his fiancée—'

'Maybe she was lying,' said Lucy hopefully.

Kate put her head to one side as she looked at her sister. 'Oh, sure! Why would she do a thing like that?'

'Because some secretaries are madly in love with their bosses themselves, and so they take it on themselves to be as beastly as possible to other women!'

'Nice try, Lucy, but I don't believe she was lying.' There had been other clues, too. She should have given them more thought. The way that the attraction he had undoubtedly felt towards her had held the unmistakable trace of antipathy. His reluctance to stay once he had dropped off her Filofax. His offensive arrogance in assuming that she had left it behind deliberately. Believing that she wanted to lure him. And her behaviour towards him had probably seemed as though she *had* wanted to lure him here.

What man would pass up on an offer like that?

'So what will you do?' Lucy's face crumpled. 'Oh, God—Kate, you couldn't be...*pregnant*, could you?'

Kate shook her head, because even *that* hurt to tell. 'Oh, no,' she said bitterly. 'No chance of that. Signor Calverri conveniently had a packet of condoms on him! No doubt always prepared for the unexpected!'

'It's a rather good thing, under the circumstances,' observed Lucy drily. 'The last thing you need in a situation like this is an unwanted pregnancy.'

Kate's mouth crumpled. 'I don't know what to do,' she admitted, thinking that for a man who was little more than a stranger the pain he had caused seemed to be disproportionately intense.

'Nothing you can do,' said Lucy in a determinedly bright voice. 'Except carry on working and waiting for Mr Right and put it all down to experience.'

'There's no such thing,' said Kate bitterly.

'What, as experience?'

She swallowed, trying to smile and to lighten up. Maybe tomorrow. Or the next day. But just now her sense of shame and humiliation was too strong for her to be able to resist cynicism. 'As Mr Right,' she said tightly. 'Now, are we going out tonight?'

'You want to?'

Kate shrugged. 'We always do at the end of a job, don't we? I can't sit around here moping for the rest of my life!'

Once Lucy had gone, she made a determined effort to dress up, even though her heart wasn't in it. She nearly wore black, but that seemed like a psychological admission of defeat. So she put on white linen trousers instead—with a glittery little top in silver-spangled white, because the summer night was warm and sultry.

At just past eight she and Lucy set off for the Italian restaurant, stopping off at the pub on the way as they always did.

It was a typical London pub—packed and noisy—so they sat outside on a wall next to a big pot of daisies and drank their lager and enjoyed the river view.

'I've never seen you look so fed-up, Kate,' said Lucy, watching her sister stare miserably into the foamy top of her drink.

'I guess I've been very lucky in the heartbreak stakes,' said Kate lightly. 'Up until now.' Her infrequent love affairs had tended to become friendships more than the mad kind of passionate romances which broke your heart. She had never been the type to sob into her pillow over a man.

So how come one brief and beautiful encounter had left her feeling as though a part of her had been torn out and thrown into the gutter? Her eyes glimmered with unshed tears, and she forced herself to take another sip of beer.

'Come on, Kate,' said Lucy gently. 'Let's go and eat.'

CHAPTER SIX

AT LEAST Kate had her career. That was what she kept telling herself over and over again, in an attempt to convince herself that in work lay some kind of refuge from her problems. The only difficulty being that her particular career was that it was such a solitary occupation.

When she decorated a house she liaised with the owners to discover exactly what it was they wanted her to create. She then went about finding paints and fabrics and *objets d'art* from various suppliers.

But there was no regular daily interaction with workmates. No one to sit and drink coffee with and talk.

Though maybe that was a blessing in the circumstances. Workmates might ask her why her eyes were ringed with great black shadows. Why eating seemed to be an intolerable effort. And why it took all her energy just to summon up a fraction of her usual enthusiasm.

She was now refurbishing a dining room in north London—a sprawling great Edwardian house belonging to a television actor and his presenter wife. Money was no object, and they had seen some of her work at friends' houses and given her a free rein. The dream scenario, really. But this time the smile she pinned to her face each morning felt like an effort, and she hoped that her mood wasn't transmitting itself to her employers.

On Friday, when the walls had been painted in a rich, dark green, she returned to her flat in Chiswick and thought unenthusiastically about the weekend ahead. She needed to keep active. To fill her time, so that the memory of Giovanni and his bright blue eyes and delicious body would fade far away into the distance.

She thought about going to visit her parents. No. That was a crazy idea. Her mother would take one look at her gaunt face and demand to know exactly what was wrong—and how could you tell your mother something like *that*?

The phone began to ring and aimlessly she reached out her hand and picked up the receiver, trying to inject enthusiasm into her voice. 'Hello?'

There was a click as the line was disconnected and she stared at it for a moment, then replaced it uninterestedly, secretly pleased that no one had spoken. The last thing she had felt like doing was having a conversation, having to pretend that everything was all right, when everything in her heart felt all wrong.

The heat of the summer day was still intense, and so she drew herself a bath and soaked in it for ages, until the water was merely lukewarm and the tips of her fingers had shrivelled into pale little starfish. Then she put on a long satin robe and padded barefoot into the sitting room.

She would order in some pizza. She winced. No, definitely not pizza. The Italian connection would be much too great to contemplate. A curry, then. And a glass of wine. With maybe a sad old movie afterwards, which would allow her to shed tears legitimately.

She painted her toenails and had just let them dry, when the doorbell rang, and she hoped it might be Lucy. She didn't want to hassle her sister with her problems, and so she hadn't suggested getting together with her. But maybe Lucy fancied a little company as well.

But it wasn't Lucy who stood on the doorstep, it was Giovanni, and Kate stared at him, her mouth drying, her heart beginning to thunder as she met a hard blue gaze.

'You!' she breathed.

'Me,' he agreed sardonically.

Her mouth had difficulty forming the words. 'Wh-what are you doing here?'

His mouth thinned. What did she think he was doing here? His gaze moved slowly from her face to her body, and the lush swell of her breasts straining against silver-grey satin drove the dull ache of suppressed desire into a heated beat against his temple. He chose his words carefully. 'I had business to see to in England.' His eyes mocked her. 'And I thought I might drop by, as I was passing.'

She knew exactly what he was implying. Oh, the arrogance! The unmistakable predatory assumption of the man! Kate leaned on the door and composed her face into a calm, unperturbed mask made false by the sustained thundering of her heart. 'So here you are,' she observed coolly.

Her haughty demeanour stirred his senses more than it had any right to. Had he expected that she would simply fall into his arms? 'Here I am,' he agreed levelly. He paused deliberately, and his voice deepened into a silky question. 'Are you not going to invite me in, *cara*?'

She supposed that some women might have shouted a few home truths before slamming the door in his face, but her curiosity was aroused. And not just your curiosity, taunted the remorseless voice of her conscience with chilling accuracy. Despairing of the fact that the last thing she wanted was for him to simply walk away, she shrugged nonchalantly.

'Why not?' She opened the door wider, telling herself that it was necessary to see him. To talk to him. What did they call the kind of conversation they needed to have together? Closure, that was it. Common sense told her that she would never completely be free of his memory unless they achieved some kind of closure. That was all it was. She gestured for him to come inside.

Silently he expelled the breath which he hadn't even realised he had been holding, and followed her into the sitting room, his eyes mesmerised by the swaying thrust of each buttock as it moved provocatively against the satin while she walked.

Her heart was beating fast. His presence was like a light, filling the room with some unbearable, shimmering promise. And that was an illusion, she told herself fiercely as she turned to face him, wondering whether her face betrayed the fact that she wanted him.

He was wearing some unspeakably elegant suit in a soft dove-grey. And a thin white shirt through which she could just discern the faint shadowing of the hair which she had scraped her fingernails against at the moment of orgasm. A tie of sapphire almost as blue as his eyes had been loosened, and it exposed a gleaming little triangle of olive flesh. There was nowhere to look but at him, and she forced herself to swallow down desire, and to remind herself instead of the true situation.

But the words still hurt to say. 'So what about your fiancée, Giovanni?' she enquired deliberately. 'Does she know you're here? With me?'

The memory of Anna, and the hurt he had caused her, filled Giovanni with heated regret. But something else heated him too—the same accursed reason which had brought him to her bed in the first place.

'Ex-fiancée,' he corrected icily.

'Oh, dear—I'm so sorry! Still, I guess it's better she found out about you sooner rather than later.'

He stilled, then raised dark brows, and the insult freed him, made what he was about to do seem ridiculously simple. 'Found out about me?' he echoed silkily. 'And just what is that supposed to mean, *cara*?'

He made the word *cara* sound like a profanity. 'What do you think it means?' she demanded, remembering how he had whispered that word to her over and over. 'I'm not flattering myself to think that I was the first little dalliance you'd had on the side!'

Tension tightened his tall, dark frame. His voice was velvet, edged with steel. 'You think that I am the kind of man to regularly commit infidelity, do you, Kate?'

'How should I know? I hardly know a thing about you!' But as soon as the words were out of her mouth she realised that she had dug her own grave of shame.

'No, you don't,' he agreed, and his eyes gave an insolent glitter. 'But that didn't stop you being as intimate with me as it is possible for any woman to be!'

Kate flinched as if he had struck her. But how right he was. She recalled the way she had touched him. Licked him. Sucked him in a place where she had sucked no other man. She felt the colour rush to her cheeks as pride made her construct her own defence against the accusation.

'Do you really think I would have…would have…' she struggled to find the least offensive way to describe what had happened '…would have slept with you if I'd known that you were engaged to be married?'

Her question brought the night back into sharp focus with exquisitely arousing clarity. 'We had very little sleep that night, as I remember, *bella*—you were delightfully eager to repeat the experience over and over again.'

'So were you!'

'Who would refuse such an offer when it was so enticingly offered?' He shrugged. 'But how could I possibly make a judgement about your morality? This bizarre situation is entirely mutual—and, as you just so sweetly pointed out, we barely know each other. At least, not in the conventional sense.'

But the assumption was crystal-clear. Kate flicked angry fingers through the red fall of her hair, only succeeding in making it even more dishevelled than it already was. 'You think I'm some sort of tramp who gives her body to any man who comes along?'

'Not any man,' he corrected, with a shake of his dark head.

'I recognised that you had exquisite taste, right from the beginning. I cannot condemn you for your choice of partner, Kate.'

It took a moment for his words to sink in. 'You're very arrogant.'

He shook his head. 'No. Just honest.'

'But not honest enough to tell me at the time that you were engaged?'

'I wasn't thinking very straight at the time.'

'No.' She stared at him, shocked by how much she wanted to touch him. Wondering just what she would do if he touched *her*. 'Just what *are* you doing here, Giovanni?'

He caught the blinding green question in her eyes, and a pulse began to hammer at his temple. 'I think you know the answer to that very well, *cara*,' he said softly.

There was silence, save for the deafening thunder of her heart. Yes, she knew. She had known ever since she had opened the door to him and seen the predatory glitter in his eyes. Just as she had known the last time, too.

And there didn't have to be a repeat performance.

She lifted her chin and said with surprising calm, 'You think I'm going to fall into bed with you again?'

He thought that bed had nothing to do with it. To do it right there where they stood would do fine to begin with. 'Why not?' He gave a slow, cold smile. 'You know you want to.'

His assessment quite literally took her breath away. But only for a moment. 'You rate yourself very highly as a lover, don't you, Giovanni?'

The smile was now edged with ice. 'You told me so yourself. In fact, you gave me the very highest recommendation—*you said that I was the best*.'

He spoke nothing more than the truth. She remembered her frantic little pleas, the sighed pleasure, and the indolent little murmurs of praise she had whispered into his ear just after she had…had…

'I didn't know then that you were engaged—'

'Would you have cared?'

'Of course I would have cared!'

He shook his head. 'I don't think so. You just wanted me,' he taunted. 'Very badly. As badly as I wanted you.' Still want you. 'You curled your fingers around my arm and I knew then that you would not have been satisfied until I had pleasured you as no other man had before.'

'That was just a touch!' she protested. 'An innocent touch! I hardly started removing my clothes in front of you, like some kind of temptress!'

The ache intensified. 'Don't be so naïve! It is never ''just'' a touch. And never, ever innocent! How could it have been, when the chemistry between us was so strong? You were fascinated by me. Intrigued by me.'

'You can't know that!' she said inadequately.

'Can't I?' He paused. 'I saw the print-out from your computer.'

She stared at him with a look of incomprehension. 'What print-out?' she said blankly.

'You'd been doing your homework on me, hadn't you, Kate?'

Still she didn't get it.

'And reading up about Sicily,' he told her in a soft, taunting voice. 'You clearly wanted to know something of my land and its people—presumably to learn a little more about me. You wanted as much background on me as you could and I cannot deny that I wasn't flattered.'

'I don't believe I'm hearing this!' she declared. 'You'd been positively *insulting* about the fact that I knew nothing about Sicily—and just because I wanted to fill in a few gaps in my knowledge you make it sound like I had some kind of master-plan to ensnare you!'

'You didn't need a master-plan, Kate,' he told her starkly. 'Your eyes ensnared me from the first moment I looked into them.'

She was very nearly beguiled by the velvet caress of his compliment, until she reminded herself that he had betrayed his fiancée, and in a way he had betrayed *her*, too. If, as he had acknowledged, the chemistry between them had been so strong, then why had he asked to come in for a drink in the first place? He must have recognised that he was placing himself in a dangerous situation.

And her.

Unconsciously she tightened the belt of her satin robe around her waist, but the flicker of his eyes as he followed the movement of her fingers told her that it was entirely the wrong thing to do. He was staring at her as if he would like to undo what she had just done, and to…to…

'I think you'd better leave now,' she told him huskily.

Leave? An earthquake would not have budged him. He shook his head and moved towards her, and she was frozen with wanting and longing.

'No,' she whispered. 'Giovanni, no.'

'Oh, yes,' came the silky contradiction. 'Yes, Kate.'

She shook her head, but it was too late, and he was pulling her into his arms and bending his head to hers and she supposed that she could have stopped him. Should have stopped him. But no power in the world could have prevented her lips from parting in a sharp little gasp of remembered pleasure as he drove his mouth down like a man who had been starved of kisses.

She swayed within the circle of hands which impatiently drew her in towards the hard cradle of his desire, and felt the immediate flowering of need as his tongue licked its way inside her mouth.

He tried to tell himself that kissing her was the only way to ensure her capitulation, but that was only a part of it because he could not seem to stop himself. Was dazed by it. A kiss that had started out hard and hungry became luxuriant and soft—the erotic brushing together of two tongues intent on some slow, sensual exploration. And it sparked off an inevitable chain of reaction which could have only one conclusion.

Impatiently he pulled at the belt of her robe so that it parted for him, allowing him to reach one hand inside and cup the swollen globe of her breast, and he heard her make some sound midway between a purr and a protest.

'Look down,' he instructed softly, and she obeyed the order instantly, watching his fingertips as they began to softly encircle each tight, rosy nipple, and seismic little shocks of pleasure began to ripple over her.

She reached blindly for the belt of his trousers. Then her fingers scrabbled down like those of a woman possessed as she urgently eased the zip down, feeling the great power of him in the palm of her hand as he sprang free. And she curled her fingers possessively around his silky hardness.

'*Matri di Diu!*' he gasped out, and lowered her gently onto the carpet, unable to wait or to risk moving—like a schoolboy on his first ever encounter with a woman. He began to fumble in the pocket of his trousers.

She could feel him sliding a condom on and then pushing his trousers down, but only down, and she knew then with an erotic certainty which aroused her far more than it shocked her, that he wasn't even going to take them off. That he was going to take her…take her…

Oh, lord—here! *Here!* Distractedly she turned her head to the side as he lowered himself on top of her. The floor-to-ceiling windows were uncurtained, and it was broad daylight. Someone might see!

'Giovanni,' she husked, from a mouth which suddenly felt as dry as sandpaper.

He paused from tugging at her breast with his mouth, teeth

nipping and grazing in an action which veered tantalisingly between pain and pleasure. '*Chi?*' He saw her look of confusion, and realised that he had spoken in Sicilian. 'What is it?' he questioned feverishly.

With a finger which was shaking she pointed at the window, through which strolling couples could be seen ambling along the towpath in the golden summer evening. 'Someone might see us,' she whispered.

Some madness almost made him cry out that he didn't care—such was his urgent need to possess her. But he had never approved of voyeurism.

With a groan he eased himself away from the honeyed lure of her body, and used the opportunity to kick his trousers away, his modesty maintained by the silken shirt which skimmed the tops of his thighs. His shoes and socks followed, and Kate sucked in a frantic breath which did nothing to quell the acceleration of her heart.

He moved around the side of the room, so that he could not be seen from the outside, and drew the curtains together, and in the few short steps back to where she lay, her eyes dark with hunger and excitement, he unbuttoned his shirt halfway and pulled it over his head.

She lay watching him, saw how proud and aroused he was. Pale light filtered through the curtains and transformed him into a glorious dark and golden silhouette, and she thought that she might pass out if he didn't come back to her quickly.

For one moment he towered above her, unsmilingly surveying the beautiful bounty of her body as she stretched out on the backdrop of silver satin.

She thought how cold his face suddenly looked, inappropriately cold considering how much he obviously wanted her, and she felt the skittering fingers of foreboding icing her skin. But she could not stop him. Not now. Certainly not now. She sensed that he still blamed her for seducing him, but none of that seemed to matter. In fact, nothing seemed to matter other than to have him here with her again…

He sank down and edged the robe completely free, easing it off the pale curves of her shoulders, until she was as naked as he was.

He jerked his head arrogantly towards the window. 'Is that private enough for you, *cara*?'

Her desire for him made her ignore everything—even the sardonic tone in which he had asked the question. Greedily her hands went up to his shoulders. And where her fingers led her mouth followed as she anointed the soft olive gleam of his skin with eager, tiny kisses.

She was wild! Giovanni was deadly sober, but he felt almost drunk with a cold, hard power as he parted her legs and touched her syrupy warmth, so that she bucked with pleasure beneath his fingers.

'Oh!' The single syllable came out in an ecstatic little moan.

He reined in his own needs, wanting to see her even more in his power. His hand stilled. 'Oh, what?'

Kate very nearly wept with frustration. 'Please,' she breathed.

'Please what?' he questioned cruelly.

Her pride now vanquished by the clamour of her senses, she whispered, 'Please do it some more,' and was rewarded with a sure instinctive touch that took her to the very edge.

He could make her come right now, beneath his fingers like last time, he thought with a grim kind of satisfaction. But pleasure was all the more intense when it was prolonged. He moved his hand away, unbearably excited by the sulky little pout of her lips.

'Oh!'

'No, no, no, *cara*,' he murmured, enjoying the way she writhed frustratedly beneath him. 'A little while longer. Why not try…*this* instead…?' and without warning he slipped inside her, seeing her eyes dilate as their flesh joined and he filled her.

He moved, slowly at first. Long, deep, agonisingly slow thrusts, and Kate felt so full of him that she felt as though her heart might burst.

He was playing with her, she thought almost bitterly. Demonstrating his control over her, while she, like a puppet, submitted willingly to the orchestrations of his body.

He did not kiss her. Just watched the mindless flutter of her eyes, the way the breath escaped from her parted lips in frenzied little sighs.

'Open your eyes,' he instructed softly.

She did, then almost wished she hadn't—because there was not a single scrap of tenderness etched on that dark, beautiful face. Just a primitive kind of hunger, which she could see he was reining in with an effort. But succeeding. Oh, yes, he was certainly succeeding.

'You have beautiful eyes,' he whispered.

Was he trying to punish her, by making her wait? To pay her back for what he obviously blamed her for—getting him into bed in the first place?

'Tell me what it feels like,' he instructed softly, and thrust deep inside her once more.

'Heaven!' she burst out, before she had time to think about the wisdom of her reply.

He gave a laugh then, a low, soft, mocking sound of triumph, but the triumph backfired on him when she began to move beneath him, changing the pace so irrevocably that he was caught up on an inexorable ascent towards mindless pleasure.

He gave a small moan as he felt power slip away from him, but the unwillingness of his surrender was quickly replaced by the stealthy warmth of abandonment.

Abandonment?

No, even stronger than that. He was a man who had always

lived his life by rules. And structure. So what was happening to him now?

The feeling which rocked him took him completely off-guard, and her own corresponding gasps of pleasure as she spasmed around him made him tip his head back in a disbelieving kind of wonder as he came and came and came, his seed spilling uselessly into the condom.

And then he rolled off her and gazed unseeingly at the ceiling.

He hadn't known it could feel quite like that.

CHAPTER SEVEN

GIOVANNI must have slept—fallen into an unusually deep, and dreamless, interlude. Only with consciousness did reality begin to chase strange images across his mind.

Red hair and green eyes, and a body which had taken him to paradise and back again. A feeling of powerlessness as he had climaxed. And that, inexplicably, he had found himself actually *resenting* the protection he wore. Had wanted no barrier between him and her slick, beguiling warmth.

He expelled a sigh and stirred, but he did not open his eyes. He needed to realign his thoughts. To work out just where he went from here.

Beside him Kate was awake, though pretending not to be. She had kept watch over him while he slept, like an anxious mother night-watching a fevered child. Only in sleep had his face relaxed. And in orgasm, she reminded herself as a dull warmth began to seep into her satiated blood.

In sleep she had been able to study him with an intensity she was certain he would not have tolerated had he been awake. And the sight of him had been endlessly fascinating.

The hard mouth had softened into a half-smile, giving his face an unthinkable illusion of vulnerability. The dark lashes which framed those dazzling blue eyes had been like two soft, ivory curves brushing the seamless olive of his skin. His jaw held more than a trace of darkness and she found herself wondering if he was the kind of man who had to shave morning *and* evening. Very probably.

She had resisted the desire to stroke a wondering fingertip all over the hard contours of his face—it was so beautiful in repose. She sighed, a sadness washing over her as she closed her eyes with a hopeless kind of yearning.

Giovanni's eyes snapped open and he turned to look at her, unprepared for her wanton loveliness as she lay stretched out on her side facing him, her head pillowed on her arm, with the rich hair spilling all over the pale flesh of her upper body.

So glorious in her nakedness, he thought with a wrench. The long limbs and the tiny waist and the breasts which were so startlingly lush and heavy. Their rosy centres were peaking and he had to stifle the urge to reach out to cup one and gently circle the flat of his hand there. When he touched her he could not think straight, and he needed to think straight.

'Kate?' he said softly.

She effected to stir, and to stretch, carefully composing her face so that he would not see a woman who had been enslaved—by a man who treated her in such cavalier fashion. 'Hello,' she said, her voice as soft as his, as her eyelids fluttered open.

His blood pounded. *Diu!* One word and he wanted her all over again! All his good intentions fell by the wayside. 'You want that we go to bed?' he asked her lazily, his English unusually fractured by the stir of his senses. 'Or shall we stay here?'

Either, or both. That was what she wanted. Or anything else he cared to offer her. But Kate knew that she badly needed to assert some kind of control over her behaviour. She had been wayward. Overly compliant. He was a proud and arrogant man, who, so far, had only to snap his fingers for her to accede to his will. And wouldn't that only make him prouder, more arrogant still?

She sat up, as much to escape that horizontal scrutiny as to assert herself. 'I need to take a shower,' she said crisply, conveniently neglecting to mention that she had been soaking in a long bath just before his arrival. But that had been before he…before he…

He saw her sudden, swift rise in colour and knew that he could make her change her mind. He sat up, too—so that he was facing her.

'Together?' His voice grew husky. 'I could do with a shower myself.' He felt the urgent throb of need, and looked down at himself, peeling the spent condom off his renewed hardness. 'See what you do to me?' he questioned ruefully.

Oh, yes, she saw. Just what was he planning? she wondered angrily. Another frantic bout of sex in the shower before he disappeared from her life again? She supposed that she should be grateful he hadn't left immediately, and then wondered whether that was why she had kept watch over him—to ensure that he didn't.

No. The reason had been much more fundamental and primitive than an urge to check that he didn't desert her. She had wanted nothing more than to drink in his beauty and to revel in the power of a strong, virile body—which had moved her in a way that no man ever had done before.

She met the provocative taunt in his eyes. 'Boasting, Giovanni?'

She looked proud at that moment, he realised. Proud and defiant as she tilted her chin at him, the green eyes flashing emerald fire. The ache grew. 'I don't need to boast, Kate,' he mocked. 'And if there is any boast to be made then it should be yours, not mine—for you are the one responsible for my growing desire, *cara*.'

'Because I'm here?' she challenged, deliberately averting her eyes from just how much his desire was growing. 'Would any woman do if I wasn't?'

'Much as I do not wish to pander to your ego,' he retorted softly, 'it might flatter you to know that I have never been unfaithful before.'

'Flatter me?' She let out a short laugh. 'Isn't flattery supposed to include terms of endearment? And you're a little short on those, Giovanni.'

'I never say anything I don't mean,' he answered insolently. 'And extravagant compliments aren't paramount in my mind right now.'

Kate was unprepared for the sharp tang of pain which contracted her heart. 'Thanks a bunch.'

Giovanni looked at her thoughtfully. He had angered her—and what point was there in angering her when he still wanted her so badly? He had put his own anger on hold for that very reason. His disbelief, too—because if he stopped to think about how he had detonated the whole structure of his life because of his inexplicable need for this woman…

No, not need, he told himself fiercely. Desire was not the same as need. 'I told you that you had very beautiful eyes,' he remarked, with a slow smile.

He had also said some fairly comprehensive things about her breasts and her long legs—but shuddered comments about her physical attributes at the height of passion did not constitute endearment. Not in Kate's book. 'Quickly! Let me go and write it down before I forget!' she said sarcastically, and then her senses flared into life again as he reached his hand out to cup her chin.

'Kate,' he said softly. 'Why are we arguing after what we have just shared together?'

She bit her lip. Should she be silent and passive? Or let him know what was *really* on her mind? Thinking that she didn't have a lot to lose, she said quietly, 'We've shared very little except for sex, Giovanni—'

'Exceptionally good sex,' he demurred.

The best. The very best—but sex wasn't what she was talking about. She wanted more than that, unrealistic though it might be. 'Sex isn't everything.'

'No, but it's a pretty big part of everything.' And it had

taught him just what he had been missing… 'What else did you have in mind?' he countered coolly.

She saw his face close and heard his voice become remote. The very last thing she wanted was to come over as some clinging vine. She had given herself to him freely, so she had no right to play the blushing virgin now.

She gave a shrug, as though she hadn't really thought about it, as though she didn't really care one way or the other. 'To sit and have talked over dinner some time might have been nice.'

He didn't know what he had been expecting, but her use of the past tense both intrigued and tantalised him. He had come here today wanting this. Knowing that she would give him this. And had thought that one more time in her arms would be enough. That afterwards he would be able to think of her as nothing more than a bitter-sweet memory. But he had been wrong. It hadn't been enough—no way near enough. 'You're making it sound as though it's over, Kate.'

'Over?' She stared into his blue eyes with genuine surprise. 'Oh, come on, Giovanni—it never really began, did it?'

'Not in the most conventional of ways, no,' he agreed, and Anna's pain swam uncomfortably into the forefront of his mind. 'But surely that doesn't rule out it carrying on?'

'But you live in Sicily, and I live in London,' she pointed out, even as some kind of delirious kind of hope flared into life inside her.

His eyes narrowed imperceptibly. Surely she couldn't be *that* naïve? She was an independent woman who was clearly at ease with her own sexuality; surely she must know how these things worked?

'I wasn't talking about dating,' he said roughly.

The flare of hope was extinguished, but she kept her expression of interest quite steady. 'Oh? Then how are we supposed to "carry on", as you put it?'

'I could take a couple of weeks off work,' he told her softly. 'Call my secretary and have her cancel all my engagements.'

And maybe in a way it would be best to absent himself from Sicily. Before he had left for London he had told Anna to damn his name as much as it gave her satisfaction to do so. He knew that he deserved it. But Anna had shaken her smooth, dark head and looked at him with sad eyes as she told him that she would say nothing bad about him. That a man she had loved and wanted to share the rest of her life with could not have suddenly become a villain overnight.

That had been the worst part of all. He had seen her attitude change from one of bitter hurt to one of sweet generosity and an attempt at understanding and forgiving what had happened. And he had recognised in that moment just what had motivated the change. Anna didn't want it to be over, he realised. She was telling him what she thought he wanted to hear, in the hope that he would go back to her. Tacitly, she was telling him that many, many women turned a blind eye to their men's transgressions, and many men revelled in this and exploited it. But Giovanni had just discovered he was not one of them.

He had betrayed Anna, and in so doing, it had made him realise what was missing from his relationship. He had also betrayed the fundamental trust on which their relationship had been based. And the relationship had floundered.

And all because of the naked woman who sat before him, her smooth, high bottom resting indolently on silver satin. She had tempted him and he had succumbed. She had offered him forbidden fruit and he had eaten it. A pulse began to patter at his temple.

'So how about I do that?' he murmured, trying by sheer force of will to deny the heat in his loins. 'Stay around for a couple of weeks and you can show me London.'

Two weeks! He certainly wasn't offering her anything in

the way of permanence, was he? She saw how one hard, hair-roughened thigh had come up to shield his manhood from her, but not before she had seen how aroused he had become. She thought women weren't supposed to get turned on by that kind of thing, but Kate found that she was. Very.

'You want me to show you London?' she asked unsteadily.

She must know how these games were played. He doubted if she would want to hear the unvarnished truth—that he wanted to lose himself in her body for just as long as it took for the fire to leave his veins.

'I'd love you to show me London,' he smiled.

It was the smile that did it. The first real smile she had ever seen curve his lips into an irresistible invitation. If he smiled like that he could ask her to show him around a municipal car-park and she would have thoroughly enjoyed every minute of it.

'I think that can be arranged.' She smiled back at him prettily. 'Where are you staying?'

He frowned. Again, so naïve—or was that all some kind of act? She was, he guessed, around twenty-seven, though she seemed to have honed her sexual prowess to resemble a woman in her forties.

He went for broke. 'Usually I stay at the Granchester—unless you're offering me a bed here, Kate?'

Then she understood what he was getting at. This was a game to be played, an erotic and exciting game. She pretended to consider it, while her heart raced. 'It would make more sense, certainly,' she said slowly. 'Otherwise, I'd just have to pick you up from the hotel every morning, wouldn't I?'

His blue eyes flashed. 'Of course it all depends…'

'On what?'

Another smile. A more predatory smile this time. Much more predatory. 'On how many bedrooms you have.'

She struggled to adopt an insouciant air, even as she felt the honeyed rush of desire. 'Just the one.' She swallowed.

'Oh. That decides it, then. I'll arrange to have my bags sent over from the hotel.' He gave a dark smile which sent shivers down her spine. 'But let us waste no more time talking of accommodation, Kate,' he murmured. 'Didn't you say something about taking a shower?'

She framed her lips to say 'alone', then shut them again. He was here. For two weeks. As her lover. She gave a shiver of anticipation. Why bother denying herself what she most wanted?

She rose elegantly to her feet and stared down at him, the raw look of approbation which he washed over her making her revel in her nakedness. 'Will you wash my back for me, Giovanni?' she questioned innocently.

Heat flooded him, and he snaked his hand around her ankle, whispered his fingertips up behind her knee to her inner thigh, and then found her where she was still as molten moist as before. Kate's knees gave way and she sank back down to the carpet.

'The shower?' she said weakly and she saw the look of dark intent on his face as he reached for the packet of condoms once more.

'Will wait,' he growled, and began to kiss her.

CHAPTER EIGHT

KATE got her shower in the end, and so did Giovanni, because he joined her, just as he had said he would, and she found herself wondering whether this was a man who always got exactly what he wanted.

She had never had a shower like it in her life and she had never given herself so freely to a man before. It was as though she was powerless to do anything other than to react to the mastery of his body.

He slowly soaped every bit of her—indecently slowly, so that she heard herself moaning in protest beneath his touch. His fingers lingered on her breasts, and on the tiny swell of her belly, before sliding in between her thighs to bring her to a shuddering orgasm right there in the shower.

Then it was her turn. She stroked her way over his firm flesh, heated by a renewed need herself as he sprang into vibrant life beneath her fingertips.

His eyes glittered as he realised what she was trying to do. 'No,' came the silken rebuttal, before he lifted her up to thrust into her over and over again, while her legs straddled him, her soft thighs pressing into the hard jut of his hips.

'Giovanni!' she gasped.

'That's my name,' he agreed in a grim kind of voice, uncharacteristically feeling himself teetering on the brink of control, and resenting it even as he gloried in it. His mouth hardened as he reined in his desire.

Kate had never been made love to in a shower before, and the contrast between his hot, hard entry and the gushing water that flooded down on them only seemed to intensify her pleasure. She would have liked him to kiss her, but the confined space made kissing difficult. Maybe he liked that, she thought with a sudden wave of sadness—because kissing brought with it a certain kind of tenderness; but then he drove into her even harder and thought gave way to pure, beautiful sensation.

She opened her mouth at the moment of fulfilment and warm water rained into it, at the very same time as Giovanni dissolved with a low, rasping moan of completion.

His face looked darkly serious as he lifted her away from him, the blue eyes giving nothing away.

'Are you always this generous a lover, *cara*?' he asked sombrely, the deep voice sounding almost shaken.

She hid her face by bending to pick up the soap, which had flown from someone's grip—hers or his, she couldn't remember. His question seemed to imply that she carried on like this with hundreds of men—oh, if only he knew how small was the number of lovers in her life!

'I hope so,' she prevaricated, and saw his mouth tighten.

He wondered why it filled him with the white-hot heat of fury to imagine her like this with another man. Why should he have unrealistic expectations of a woman like this?

Anna had been a virgin, had known only him as her lover, and he had always held back just a little, for fear of shocking her.

Yet with Kate he was at his most inhibitedly rampant. He couldn't seem to get enough of her. Novelty value, he told himself angrily, that was all it was. Two weeks of non-stop sex should be able to cure him of *that*.

But, in the meantime, they had run out of certain essential supplies.

'Let me wash your hair for you, *cara*,' he coaxed in velvet entreaty. 'And then...''

'Then?' The question came out breathlessly, because, supper forgotten, all she wanted to do was to take him to her bed. What on earth was happening to her?

'We need to go out.'

'Out?' she pouted.

He gave a low laugh, and ran his finger over the swollen contours of her mouth, the laugh becoming one of delight when she nipped at the tip with her teeth like a tiny animal. 'Yes, out, my beautiful, wanton Kate.'

'Are you hungry?'

'Very,' he answered truthfully, because he had skipped lunch.

'Well, I have plenty of food in. Champagne, too,' she added hopefully, as an incentive.

He gave an almost imperceptible shake of his head. He did not want to drink champagne with her. Why celebrate a fundamental flaw in his character, which he was only just discovering? That this woman had a certain power over him, that she had taken something from him which he had not intended to give? 'But there is one vital provision we have run out of,' he told her softly.

'What?'

For answer he took her hand and guided it between his legs until it touched the silky surface of the rubber which was still in place.

'We have used three already,' he told her, on a silken boast.

She felt a detached feeling of disappointment as she let her head rest on his wet shoulder. Of course that was all he was thinking of—that was all they had ever shared, wasn't it? 'The chemist it is, then,' she said, her voice muffled against his skin.

But he heard the disappointment, and frowned. He lifted her face and looked down into it, thinking how curiously vulnerable her bare, wet face seemed—and what a contrast to the firebrand she had been in his arms. 'You want to have dinner, don't you?' he said softly. 'So go and get ready. We'll buy what we need and then I'll take you out to eat.'

And Kate was unprepared for the great leap of excitement in her heart as she pulled the shower door open.

It isn't a date, she told herself fiercely as she wrapped a towel round her and walked through to the bedroom. It's just a meal—the fuel we need for what is doubtless going to be a marathon bout of delicious sensation.

But she dressed as if she was going on a date.

The first time she had met him she'd been working—and on the two occasions she had seen him since she had been surprised by him at the flat. Tonight she had been wearing nothing but a satin robe and there had been no opportunity to prepare herself, to make sure that she looked her best.

Now was her opportunity to pull all the stops out. To dazzle and beguile him. He might only be here for two weeks, and he might only want her as his temporary lover—but he would see her looking her very best!

She pulled a black dress from her wardrobe, a dress she rarely wore—because it always seemed a little too 'grown-up' for her. But tonight she wanted to feel grown-up—a real woman, in the company of a real man.

It was the simplest dress imaginable—a shift of jet linen—and the beauty was all in the cut. It had cost her a small fortune, and it showed—especially when she scraped her hair back into an almost severe chignon, which meant that her face looked all eyes, fringed with an extravagant lashing of mascara.

She wore no jewellery—the moonstones seemed all wrong, somehow, and she possessed no 'real' jewellery. With her long, slim legs encased in dark silk stockings, the final touch was a pair of outrageous little black shoes with kitten heels.

Giovanni sat waiting for her in the sitting room, his hair still damp from the shower. She saw that he had brought up his bags from the car, and was wearing a snowy-white shirt and some dark, amazing trousers, and the blue eyes were watching her every movement as she swayed into the room.

He pursed his lips and let out an exaggerated long, low whistle of appreciation.

'Mmm,' he murmured. '*Bella.*'

But if she had hoped for kisses now she was to be disappointed, for he made no move to touch her.

He didn't dare. His swallowed down his desire. She looked absolutely breathtaking in a dress that would have looked outstanding in any company. With her hair off her face like that, she looked almost icy. Unapproachable. And again, the contrast to the woman who had straddled him in the shower minutes earlier was quite devastating. If he touched her he knew exactly what would happen—and what would be the use of removing such a beautiful garment from her body before dinner?

Something in the way he was looking at her made Kate feel suddenly unsure of herself. This really was the most bizarre situation, she thought. She had been more intimate with him than she had with any other man, and yet she didn't have a clue what was going on in his mind. 'You like it, then?' she asked him unnecessarily.

A muscle flickered at his cheek. 'You know I do.'

But still he kept his distance. She pinned a bright smile onto her mouth. 'It's getting late; shall we go?'

'Sure.'

Outside, the evening sun danced golden on the river, and they began to walk towards the shops and restaurants.

'Shall we eat first?' he asked.

At least he had given her the choice. It seemed almost too clinical to go and stock up at the pharmacy while they walked side by side as if they were two strangers. Intimate strangers. 'Yes, please,' she answered gratefully.

He heard the relief in her voice. 'And where are you going to take me?'

'I haven't decided yet.'

She didn't take him to her favourite restaurant. They knew

her by name there, and she had no desire for them to get to know Giovanni, too. They might jump to all kinds of the wrong conclusions and think that he was a proper boyfriend. And she wasn't sure she could face the awkward questions which would be bound to arise when he disappeared from her life as suddenly as he had entered it.

Instead, they found a small Indian eaterie which had received rave reviews in the national Press. The place was teeming and a table looked unlikely, but the *maître d'* took one glance at the imposing Sicilian and the pale-faced woman at his side and immediately summoned them in to a small table in one corner of the room.

It was, Kate realised as she sat down to face him, the first time that they had done anything 'normal' together—unless you counted that first, awkward lunch at his godmother's. It didn't help that her hands were shaking as she took the menu, but how could she not feel a trembling bag of nerves? He looked *adorable*. Outrageously good-looking and confident.

She couldn't miss the side-looks which most of the other female diners gave him, followed by envious glances in *her* direction. I don't want to adore him, she told herself. An emotion like that would be wasted on a relationship that wasn't going anywhere past the bedroom.

'I hope you like Indian food?' she questioned conventionally.

His appetite, peculiarly, had deserted him, but he forced a bland smile. 'I'm not familiar with it.' The sapphire gaze captured her. 'Perhaps you would like to order for me?'

She nodded, suspecting that he rarely let a woman take control. 'OK.' She scanned the menu with uninterested eyes.

She didn't have a clue what she was ordering, even though she loved Indian food with a passion. She just jabbed her finger indiscriminately at the menu and hoped for the best.

'We should drink beer with curry,' she told him when she had ordered the drinks.

'So you've changed your mind about champagne?' he drawled.

She looked up from the menu, her heart thudding painfully in her chest. 'We haven't really got anything to celebrate, have we?'

Was it another sudden look of vulnerability that made him say it? 'Except for the most erotic afternoon of my life,' he answered softly.

'Mine, too,' she admitted helplessly.

'So far,' he added, and the soft blue gleam from his eyes set her pulses racing.

She stared at him, trying to see beyond the dark glamour of his looks and the lazy sophistication he exuded. 'Listen,' she sighed, 'we can't spend the whole evening talking about sex, can we?'

He laughed. 'Well, we *can*.... I think what you mean to say is that it could become rather wearing.'

'Thanks for the language lesson,' she responded drily, taking a sip from the glass of lager which the waiter put on the table in front of her.

'What do you want to talk about?' he murmured. 'You want to tell me a little something of your life?'

Again she tried to pretend that this was a normal first date, but her words came out in a stilted list of facts. 'My parents live on the outskirts of London. One older sister. Her name is Lucy.'

'And where is she?'

'She lives in the flat below mine.'

He raised his eyebrows. 'So, two successful, affluent sisters living close to one another—how pleased your parents must be.'

'Yes. They are.' But she didn't want to talk about herself—she wanted to learn about this man to whom she had given herself so freely. She looked at him curiously. 'Your English is absolutely brilliant.'

'There you go again,' he murmured, recognising a deliberate attempt to change the subject. 'Stereotyping me.'

'I wasn't!' she protested.

'Yes, you were!' His faint accent became suddenly exaggerated and pronounced, like a caricature of a foreign accent. 'You want me to talk like *theese, cara*?'

She laughed, but the stupid thing was that his voice sent shivers up and down her spine, no matter *which* way he talked.

She shook her head. 'Tell me where you learnt to speak it so well.'

'In America.'

So *that* explained the accent. *And* the fluency.

'I lived there—for a year in between leaving college and starting work in the company,' he explained, shrugging his shoulders in answer to the question in her eyes. 'My father thought it wise to become completely fluent before I did so. It can be such a disadvantage to have to negotiate in a foreign language unless you are completely familiar with it. People can try to take you for a fool,' he finished, on an odd kind of note.

'I can't imagine anyone trying to take *you* for a fool,' she said slowly.

His eyes glittered. He wondered if she had any idea just how irresistible her mouth was. 'If that was a compliment, then I thank you.'

'Just an observation,' she returned lightly and put her glass of lager down. 'So what was life like in America?'

He sighed. He had worked hard and partied hard, and during the process had come into contact with many beautiful women who had made no secret of their attraction for the tall, lean Sicilian with the disconcerting blue gaze. But despite the attractions not once had he succumbed to any of *their* undoubted charms.

He had been dating Anna since his third year in college,

and had recognised that in her he had found a woman who would make him the perfect wife. Through the many years which had followed, that certainty had never wavered. And yet he had thrown it all away for Kate Connors.

'It was exactly as you would expect,' he said coolly. 'Very vast and very different to the land I had grown up in.'

She heard the edge to his tone and wondered wildly whether a getting-to-know-you dinner had been such a good idea after all. Were they destined only to be compatible when they were horizontal? How about the easy conversation she *usually* managed to achieve when she was in the company of an intelligent, attractive man? She struggled for the right, light touch, even as she despised her own eagerness to please him. 'But you liked it?'

He shrugged. 'It was a new experience—and experience is always useful.'

She gave him a frozen smile. 'And is that how you categorise me, Giovanni? As a useful experience?'

He gave her question a moment's consideration. 'Not just as a useful experience, no.' His eyes mocked her as he lifted his glass in a toast. 'More as a rather beautiful and enjoyable one. Wouldn't you agree?'

But it sounded more of a boast than a tribute, and Kate was glad that their food arrived at that precise moment, and that the ladling out of rice and chicken and lentils occupied their hands as well as meaning that she could drop her eyes from that unsettling gaze.

She wanted to ask him more about his life in order to find out more about the man, but she was scared of what it might reveal. His history would inevitably include details of his engagement, now broken—which instinct told her he bitterly regretted and blamed her for, at least in part. Because, despite his outwardly relaxed air, there was an unmistakable tension about him, a repressed kind of anger which he was only just managing to conceal.

She forced herself to eat a mouthful of curry, while he seemed to have no such reservations, eating his food with a sensual enjoyment, which was a pleasure to watch. And she found herself wishing that she had not been so compliant from the outset, wondering if she had applied her usual brakes something more enduring than a two-week affair might have come of it.

He glanced up to find her looking at him. She had barely touched a thing. 'You're not hungry?'

She made a play of eating a piece of chicken, then put her fork down. 'Not really.'

'You want to leave?'

'When you've finished.'

He ate a last mouthful of rice, his blue eyes fixed thoughtfully on hers. Then he put his own fork down and reached his hand across the table to take hers. 'You're not having second thoughts, are you, Kate?' he questioned softly, unprepared for the sudden jolt of disappointment as he imagined her saying yes.

Of course she was. But even third or fourth thoughts wouldn't make her change her mind. Not now. She gave her head a little shake, even managing a little smile. 'Of course not,' she told him serenely as he raised his hand to call for the bill. It was a little late for that!

Outside, he took her hand as they walked slowly back to the flat, stopping off at the pharmacy on the way.

And Giovanni looked at her with an expression of bemusement lighting his blue eyes when he had seen her rise in colour as he had taken his wallet out to pay for his purchase.

'Why, Kate,' he observed softly, running a fingertip across her hot cheek, 'you're blushing.'

She wanted to tell him that this wasn't the kind of thing she normally did—but what was normal any more? He probably wouldn't believe a word of it, and why should he? 'They know me in this shop,' she said drily, by way of explanation.

'Then they will know that you choose your lovers wisely,' he returned with an irresistible glitter of his eyes.

And all her doubts were driven away at the first hungry touch of his lips once the door of her flat had closed behind them.

'I want you,' he told her unsteadily.

'I'm right here,' she whispered back.

The next morning Kate rang downstairs and had Lucy clear her diary for the next two weeks, and launched whole-heartedly into a fairy-tale, unreal romance.

It was her first experience of living with a man—though the term 'living' had a sort of permanence about it which didn't quite ring true in this case.

She set aside a shelf in the bathroom for him, and cleared a space in her wardrobe for his suits. She learned that he liked nothing more than black coffee for breakfast, that opera pleased him more than any other kind of music and that whatever emotions he had—and sometimes she wondered—he kept them firmly locked away on the inside. For Kate had only ever seen him angry—or passionate when he took her in his arms. The cool Giovanni who accompanied her to restaurants and art galleries—he gave nothing away.

Two days after he had first moved in, he met Lucy.

Kate had been dreading the meeting, without really knowing why, but one look at the disapproval which Lucy iced at him was enough to tell her that her fears had been justified.

'Your sister doesn't like me,' he observed after Lucy had said a stilted hello and refused coffee.

'She doesn't know you,' answered Kate brightly.

'OK, she doesn't approve of me, then.' He paused and looked at her. 'And why should that be, Kate?'

She supposed that there was no point in lying. She sighed. 'She knows about you, and the fact that you were engaged when we first met,' she added, in answer to the questioning look in his eyes.

'And your sister, being such a paragon of virtue, naturally disapproved, did she? What does she do for a living, just out of interest—other than glare at your houseguests?'

Kate suppressed a shudder at his choice of word. Houseguest. You couldn't get any more coldly unemotional than that, could you? 'She works for me. She takes and makes bookings, does my accounts, answers the phone—that kind of thing. And there's no need to make it sound as though I have houseguests like *you* all the time!'

'And do you?' he drawled insolently, but the knife-edge of jealousy twisted itself sharply in his gut.

Bitter reproach sparked green fire from her eyes. 'What do you think?'

He drove the jealousy away and forced himself to stay calm. 'I'd like to think that this was a one-off situation,' he told her steadily. 'For you as much as for me.'

'For your ego's sake, I suppose?' she questioned heatedly.

He shook his dark head. 'No, Kate, more for my pride's sake.'

'Oh, really?'

'And yours too, of course.'

'Oh, you're…you're…'

He gave a soft laugh as he acknowledged her fire. 'What am I, *cara*?'

'Impossible!' she declared, without really knowing why. Or maybe she did. Maybe her rage was directed more at the fact that he would never really be hers to have—other than in a particularly satisfying, but curiously empty, sexual sense. Angrily she turned away from him, but he reached a lazy hand out and stopped her, pulling her, still resisting, into his arms. She struggled a little. 'Go away!' she stormed as he bent to brush his lips against hers.

'You know you don't mean that,' he murmured, feeling their velvet surface begin to tremble at that first contact.

'Yes, I do…. *Oh!*'

He kissed her in earnest then, and she went under, only to gaze up at him dazedly when eventually he stopped the kiss. 'That wasn't fair,' she whispered as she met the question in his eyes.

'What wasn't?'

'You say outrageous things to me and then think you can just kiss them better!'

'So what do you want me to stop doing, *cara*—saying the outrageous things, or kissing them better?'

His cajoling tone coaxed her lips into an unwilling smile. 'What do you think?' she asked, and he tipped her face up to trap her in a blinding blue stare, a different kind of question in his eyes this time.

'I think we'd better go back to bed and make up properly, don't you?' he questioned unsteadily.

'But we've only been up an hour!' Her protest sounded feeble even to her own ears, and the look of hungry intent on his face had her babbling at him like a tour-guide, watching in reluctant fascination as he smiled the smile of a man who knew he had won the battle. 'And we were going to go to visit the Tower of London today, remember?'

'It's been standing there for centuries; it'll wait for a few more hours,' he told her arrogantly, and led her back towards the bedroom.

CHAPTER NINE

'I THINK that's everything.' Giovanni clicked shut his suitcase, and turned to look at where she stood, silently surveying him, her face impassive, and he wondered what thoughts were going through that beautiful head of hers.

So far, at least, there had been no word or demonstration that Kate was going to miss him, after a fortnight spent almost exclusively together—save when she had made an excuse to go downstairs to see her sister to discuss work.

And Kate watched him with a dull ache in her heart. Intellectually she had known that this moment would come, and emotionally she had prepared herself for the inevitable pain it would bring. But the reality was far worse than even her worst imaginings.

'What time does your plane leave?'

He flicked a glance at his watch, and then again at her. 'In two hours.' If it had been at any other time during the past two weeks then he might have tried to make love to her one more time. But this goodbye was turning into something he hadn't quite anticipated, and to take her into his arms to lose himself in that mindless pleasure would, he knew, somehow devalue what they had shared together.

'Would you like some coffee before you go?'

More in an attempt to dissolve the brittle atmosphere than because he really wanted a cup, he nodded in agreement. 'Please.'

She busied herself in the kitchen. Best cups. Best coffee. Some outrageously expensive chocolate biscuits she had once been given and which there had never been a right time to open. Before now.

She spooned coffee into the cafetiére and stared sightlessly out of the window. Would she ever have agreed to this arrangement if she had known that the inevitable parting would prove so painful?

When she carried the tray back into the sitting room he was half sitting, half lying on the sofa watching her, and her heart leapt as it always did at the sight of him.

'Smells good,' he remarked.

'Mmm.' She wished he would *say* something, other than make those bland comments which could have come from a stranger, and not the man who had shared her life for the past fortnight. She handed him a cup and then took her own over to the opposite side of the room and placed it on a small table beside her.

The distance between them seemed to be the size of a tennis court.

'Kate,' he said suddenly. 'Come and sit next to me.'

Her eyes narrowed and she felt the lurch of disappointment. Physical closeness meant only one thing where they were concerned. 'There isn't time, Giovanni,' she told him dully, unprepared for the tightening of his mouth in response.

'You think that the only reason I want you beside me is so that I can make love to you one more time before I go!' he accused hotly. 'Is that it?'

'There's no need to sound so outraged! That's what it always *does* mean where you're concerned!' she told him. 'And we've hardly been behaving like saints for the last couple of weeks, have we?'

'No.' He put his coffee down untouched, and got up to look out of the window, his hands thrust deep inside his pockets as he stared out at the river which was made silvery-grey by the rain today.

Kate watched the tense set of his shoulders and then he turned round, his face looking as though he was fighting some kind of inner war with himself.

'It doesn't have to be over you know, Kate.'

It was her wildest dream become glorious reality. 'What do you mean?' she questioned slowly, and her heart seemed to deafen her with its pounding.

'You know that I come back to England from time to time?' Kate stilled as his words began to make immediate sense.

'Go on,' she said in a strangled kind of voice. 'Explain exactly what it is I think you're suggesting.'

He was trying to think logically about what would work best. For both of them. He gave a slow smile, captivating her with that mocking blue stare. 'I can make sure that business brings me here on Friday—maybe I could stay over until Sunday. Here, with you.' The smile grew lazier. 'How does that sound, *cara*?'

She thought of snatched weekends of bliss with him. Perfect, but never enough. It never *could* be enough. She would be transformed into one of those bloodless women who lived their whole lives from phone call to phone call. The odd visit would dominate her life, until the rest of it grew indistinct and she would become one of those 'nearly' women. Nearly living, but not quite.

She shook her head. 'Thanks, but no, thanks.'

He felt a flicker of irritation only marginally greater than the one of surprise. He had been confident enough in his power over her to expect her to accept. 'Not even a moment to consider it, Kate?' he questioned sardonically.

'I don't need to consider it.'

'May I ask why?'

'It's not what I want from a relationship, Giovanni.'

'What exactly do you object to?' he drawled.

It hurt that he couldn't see. 'All the highs of infrequent passion aren't enough.' She shrugged. 'It isn't *real*, don't you see?'

A muscle began to pulse in his cheek. 'I haven't heard you doing any complaining!'

She withered him a look. 'That was different. That was never planned to be anything other than short-term, was it? The terms were laid out very carefully at the beginning. Surely you can't have forgotten?'

But he had been certain that he would want to let go by now, and he had been wrong. For a man who was rarely wrong it had been a salutary experience. His anger had been spent, but not so his passion for her—that raged like the fierce storm it had always been. He drew a deep breath, knowing that this was as close to conciliation as he would get.

'Look, just what do you want, Kate?' he said evenly. 'We still haven't known each other very long. Surely you're not holding out for living together—'

Her sharp, outraged intake of breath halted him.

'I am *not*,' she said icily, 'holding out for *anything*! My life is not a game show, Giovanni—even though sometimes it's felt weird enough to be one during the last couple of weeks—'

'And just what is *that* supposed to mean?' Now it was his turn to sound icy.

How could she tell him that whatever he gave her, it was never enough? That she wanted more, and more still. She needed to go deeper with him than the great sex and the lunches and dinners and trips around London. She wanted more than a surface relationship, and she could not have it, she realised. Not with him.

'Nothing, Giovanni.' She gave a weary sigh as she raked her fingers to pull the fall of hair back from her face, and looked at him sadly. 'I knew it had to end, and so did you. I just don't want it to end on a bad note.' She hesitated. 'But neither do I want to try to sustain something we both know isn't sustainable.'

'So that's it?'

'It doesn't have to be this way. We can say goodbye, and enjoy the memories of what we had.'

His face grew even more shuttered. 'As you wish.' He walked across the room and picked up his bags. 'But you'll forgive me if I don't hang around.'

'Of course,' she said stiffly, but she followed him out to the front door all the same, opening it for him and praying that he would kiss her. One last kiss to remember him by.

And, looking down at her, he knew what she wanted. Oh, yes. They had kept areas of their lives out of bounds for necessary reasons of survival. They had not discussed Anna, or the man she herself had been briefly engaged to. Those topics would have caused pain and jealousy and recriminations.

But her physical needs he knew inside out. He knew her body and her desires almost better than he knew his own. Not to kiss her would be to punish her, and a cruel and ruthless streak badly wanted to punish her for her rejection of him. Except that he needed that kiss just as badly as she did.

Something to remember her by.

He dropped the bags and drew her into his arms, and her eyes closed as though she could not bear to read what was in his face.

He kissed her. Softly at first, and then with a growing ardour which he knew he must quell, and when he pulled away from her, almost violently, they both gave ragged little sighs of regret.

As her eyelids fluttered open she was unsurprised by the hard and uncompromising set of his features, knowing that he could offer her nothing more than the very bare essentials.

She heard her lips framing a question she had not intended to ask. 'And will you see…Anna?'

She wanted a reassurance that he was unwilling or unable

to give her. What the hell did she expect him to do? Renounce all others out of some inappropriate loyalty to a woman who had just said she didn't want to see him again?

'Of course,' he said, quietly and truthfully, and saw how she tried not to let her pain show. 'Sicily is a small island. We share many friends—it is inevitable that I shall see her.'

She wanted to ask him whether he would rekindle his engagement, whether absence had changed his feelings about Anna, but she didn't dare. She was afraid of what the answer might be. She nodded instead. 'Goodbye, Giovanni,' she whispered.

'*Ciao, bella*,' he gritted and swung out of the door before he could change his mind.

He fumed all the way to the airport, and thought how ironic it was that he remained angry, when he had sought her out precisely to rid himself of that emotion. And for two weeks he had existed in a state which had pushed that anger to the recesses of his mind, but now it was back, and with a brand-new focus.

So why was he angry now? Because she had told him that she had no wish to continue the affair? Wasn't his Sicilian pride wounded more than his heart?

Very probably.

It was purely physical, he told himself grimly as he returned his car to the hire company and picked up his bags. All it ever was and all it ever could be.

He followed the signs to the departure lounge, telling himself that he would fly home and forget all about her.

'Can I get you anything, sir?'

'Mmm?' He looked up absently.

'Some coffee perhaps? Or something else?'

The stewardess flashed him the kind of smile which told him that there was more than coffee on offer, should he so desire.

Enjoy your freedom, he told himself. *Enjoy* it!

'Coffee would be perfect,' he drawled in Italian, and allowed the corners of his mouth to lift in a smile which made the woman's eyes dilate with undisguised pleasure.

And he sank down into the comfort of the First Class lounge, while the stewardess fussed round him like a hen.

After he had gone, Kate behaved like a woman bereaved—not wailing or crying, but going from room to room to try to hang on to what she had left of him before it disappeared forever.

The scent of him on her pillow, and on the towel which she fished out of the laundry basket. Even his half-drunk cup of coffee she foolishly felt like preserving. But soon the pillowcase and the towel would go into the washing machine, and the cup in the dishwasher and then there would be no trace at all left of him—save the red roses he had bought her last week, and which were already beginning to wilt.

She buried her face in the flowers. Their bloom was fast-fading but the petals were still velvety-soft, and there remained the last sweet, lingering trace of scent. She breathed in deeply, as though that could bring new life to her, but the pleasure she gained was only fleeting, and she wondered how long the dull ache in her heart would last.

She sat staring at the bouquet for a long, long time, and only when she thought that the threat of wayward tears was safely at bay did she pick up the telephone to speak to her sister.

'Hello?'

'Kate?' Her sister's voice immediately filled with concern. 'What's happened?'

'Oh, Lucy,' she said, in an odd, flat voice which didn't sound like her voice at all. 'He's gone.'

'I'm on my way up!' said her sister grimly.

Determinedly Kate stripped the bed while she waited for her sister, and assigned all the temptations of the dirty linen to the laundry basket—because what good would it do her to mope around after him and keep reminding herself of him? That would have only served a purpose if he was coming back.

And he wasn't.

When Lucy arrived, she frowned. 'Are you OK?' The frown deepened. 'Stupid question. Of course you're not OK.'

Kate bit her teeth into her bottom lip. 'Is it too early for wine, do you think?' she asked huskily.

'Nope! In fact you look as though you could use a drink,' said Lucy and followed her out into the kitchen. 'So tell,' she said, still in that same grim voice, 'just what your Sicilian stud had to say for himself before he left!'

'Please don't call him that,' said Kate crossly as she took a bottle of white wine from the fridge and pulled the cork out.

Lucy glared. 'Still protecting him, are you, Kate—even though he's treated you like a concubine for the past fortnight?'

Kate shook her head. 'He has treated me beautifully over the past fortnight,' she defended, her voice softening with memory. 'And I walked into it with my eyes wide open. I wanted it just as much as he did.'

'Well, I hope it was worth it,' said Lucy, accepting the proffered glass.

Kate sipped and thought about it. Had it been? 'I don't know,' she said honestly. 'All I know is that I couldn't resist it—him—at the time, and yet it wasn't enough to carry on with.'

'But you weren't given that option, were you?'

Kate gave a small, rather bitter laugh. 'Actually, I was. Giovanni offered to carry on the affair—with him taking the occasional trip to England and us making a weekend of it.'

'The *bastard*!'

Kate shrugged. 'Not really; you can't blame him for trying—'

'Kate, will you stop being so damned *understanding*?'

Kate put her glass down with a shaking hand and turned to look at her sister with tears threatening to spill out of her eyes. 'What alternative do I have?' she whispered. 'At least this way I can remember it with fondness. If I call him every name under the sun—won't that just make everything that we shared seem worthless?'

Lucy shot her a look of understanding. 'You seem to really *like* him.'

Kate shook her head. 'I don't know if *like* is a word you would use in connection with Giovanni—he isn't a man it's easy to get close to. I don't know if there's a word in the dictionary to describe the way I feel about him.'

'Well, if that's the case, why *didn't* you plump for what he was offering you?'

Kate bit her lip. It wouldn't make sense if she told her sister he would lose all respect for her if she opted for the continuation of the affair—because Lucy probably thought that Giovanni had zero respect for her anyway. And she couldn't blame her. Viewed from the outside, she must look like the world's biggest fool—letting a man like that into her home and her life and her heart on a purely temporary basis.

Because something *had* happened during that brief, blissful stay. He had been reluctant to leave, and had shown it this morning, and she wanted to treasure his reluctance for the rest of her life. Surely she must have touched a tiny part of him, for him to have behaved like that?

But she knew that a long-term affair with a man like Giovanni would eventually end, and end bitterly, too—of that she was certain. And she would have her heart broken completely—whilst at the moment it felt only slightly wounded.

Her emerald eyes were brimming with fresh tears as she looked at her sister. 'The affair just wouldn't have been enough,' she told her simply, and Lucy nodded in comprehension.

'Oh, I see,' she said slowly. 'Now I *do* see.' She gave a wry smile. 'But you were wrong, you know, Kate.'

Kate stared at her. 'What are you talking about?'

'There *is* a word in the dictionary to describe the way you're feeling about him.'

Kate's look remained blank.

'It's called love, my darling,' she said gently.

CHAPTER TEN

THE envelope was waiting for her when she arrived home from work, the writing on it unfamiliar, but with a lurch of her heart Kate guessed exactly who it was from. The elegant, lazy script could only have been penned by one person. She stared at it as if it were an unexploded bomb.

Open it, a voice inside her said. Or would a more self-protective woman simply have hurled it into the bin?

She picked it up and slit it open with trembling fingers, and saw that she had been right. Inside was an airline ticket to Barcelona, and a brief, almost insultingly curt note.

> —Have three months been enough to change your mind, *cara*? Why not join me in Spain—and we can take up where we left off?

It was signed, 'G'.

She slammed the note down on the table, resisting the stupid urge to read and reread it, to run her eyes hungrily over the two stark sentences again and again.

''Take up where we left off, *indeed*!'' And where was that? In bed? Swallowing down her anger and her temptation, she told herself that she would telephone him and tell him exactly what he could do with his ticket.

No. She would ignore it completely—that would be far more effective a refusal. His honour would be outraged! And she wouldn't be susceptible to the honeyed persuasion of his voice.

She kicked her shoes across the sitting room as the telephone started ringing and her heart began to pound uncomfortably. Don't be *crazy*, she told herself. It could be absolutely anyone.

But it wasn't.

She seemed to sense that it was him even before he spoke. There was an infinitesimal, irresistible pause, before she heard him murmur, '*Cara?*'

Sweat broke out in icy pinpricks on her brow. 'I am not your darling!' she snapped.

'No. Not my anything. Not any more,' he agreed mockingly. 'When you will not see me.'

The hardest decision she had ever had to make, but she had stuck by it. 'I meant what I said, Giovanni.'

He sighed. 'I know you did.'

'So why send me a ticket to join you?'

'You know exactly why.' A pause. 'I want to see you.'

'And you're a man who is used to getting what he wants,' she observed.

He didn't answer that. 'Have you missed me?'

'Like a hole in the head!'

There came the sound of soft laughter. 'I don't believe you.'

'That's your prerogative,' she said, but her casual air did not quite come off.

'So you have!'

Yes, she had missed him. Of course she had. She wondered what had ever occupied her mind before she had met Giovanni, because now he seemed to haunt her thoughts constantly. Three months of being away from him, when the minutes and the hours had ticked away with excruciating slowness.

'I'm not coming—'

'Mmm?' he interrupted, on a teasing little note of provocation. 'That cannot be much fun for you, Kate, but I can soon change that, I assure you!'

Her cheeks flamed. 'Giovanni, will you *stop* it!'

'I'm not doing anything,' he protested.

'Yes, you are!'

'What am I doing, *cara*?' he questioned softly.

He was tempting her. Unbearably. Reminding her of how much she had loved being with him, being part of him—even though it had been only a very tiny part. 'I'm going to put the phone down in a minute!' she threatened.

'Wait!' He hesitated, thinking that it was never simple with this woman, and wondering why he did not have the sense to put the phone down himself. 'Come and see me, Kate. Please.'

It was the 'please' that did it—it crept into a heart which she had determinedly steeled against him. Yet that one little word brought all her defences tumbling down like a house of cards. Admit it, she thought to herself—just hearing his voice again was like a soothing balm on a soul which had been tortured and troubled without him.

What was the point of existing in a dull state of misery, when she had the means to make herself happy? Maybe not one hundred per cent happy—but since when did anyone get that? Surely even a little happiness was better than this aching anguish which now seemed second nature to her.

'OK.' Had she *really* said that?

He wondered if he had heard her properly. 'Was that a yes?' he demanded.

'No. It was an OK,' she repeated stubbornly.

He smiled, unseen. *Very* lukewarm, he thought. Almost verging on the sullen—but it was still the surrender he had been intent on. He bit down an instinctive little murmur of triumph, because he sensed that she had been very close to saying no to him. And he wanted her far too much to risk that, though his desire for her still confused him.

Why did her memory persist in possessing him like a fever? he asked himself in silent frustration, as he had been asking himself since he had touched down in Sicily that day three months ago.

He had tried applying logic to a situation where logic seemed redundant. She was beautiful, yes—but he had seen women more beautiful than her.

So was it simply her skills as a lover?

For a while he had tormented himself with the idea that she must have had many, many lovers to be that sensational in bed. To think of her as a whore would make it easy to disregard her. And yet the image had stubbornly refused to stick and, for the life of him, he could not work out why.

'Good,' he said softly. 'You won't regret it, *cara*.'

'I think I'm regretting it already.'

'The flight touches down at eight. I'll be waiting for you, Kate.'

'OK,' she said again, and put the phone down.

She was almost frightened about telling Lucy what she had agreed to, expecting her sister to rage against her and tell her that she must be the most stupid woman on the planet—a sentiment which Kate herself could have sympathy with.

But Lucy surprised her.

'I don't blame you,' she said quietly.

'You *don't*?'

'Uh-uh.'

'Why?'

Lucy shrugged. 'I can see his obvious appeal; men like Calverri don't come along more than once in a lifetime—if you're lucky.'

'Lucky?' echoed Kate, with hollow sarcasm.

'And you've been as miserable as sin since he went away—'

'I haven't—'

'Oh, I know you've *tried* not to be. You've been almost

ridiculously cheerful at times—throwing yourself into your work even more than you usually do, which is saying something! But you've had an air of sadness about you which hurts me to see. So if you're going for a chance of lasting happiness with him—then go for it wholeheartedly.'

But Kate shook her head. 'Not lasting happiness, no—it will be purely temporary. I know that. I'm realistic enough to see that there's no future in it.'

'Then you might ask yourself whether you're just setting yourself up for an even bigger hurt by going. You might be better trying to wean yourself off him for good.'

But she couldn't *not* go—that was the trouble. The thought of seeing him again was making her feel half-mad with the sense of being really and truly alive once more. Just the thought of flying to meet him in Barcelona was like landing in bright sunlight after three months of existing in some kind of shadowland.

She blew a small fortune on new clothes for the trip, telling herself that a shopping expedition was long overdue—she hadn't had the enthusiasm for new clothes since he had gone away. She phoned up the travel agent who told her that the weather would be very warm, but not oppressive.

The flight was smooth and uneventful, but Kate's heart was in her mouth as she walked towards Arrivals, a sudden and debilitating insecurity making her wonder what she would do if Giovanni hadn't bothered to turn up…

She needn't have worried. He was there—of course he was—eclipsing every other person in the vicinity with his presence. Tall and striking, leaning lazily against the barrier. Blue eyes were trained on her like blazing guns, though his expression was as dark and as shuttered as she remembered it.

Kate tried to keep her face calm as she walked towards him, but it wasn't easy—not when she wanted to run at full speed and hurl herself into his arms and tell him how much she had missed him…wanted him…

He was wearing a dark coat of the softest leather imaginable, and it made him look very, very European. More as a distraction from the fact that she didn't know what to say, or how to greet him—for where was the rule-book in a situation like this?—Kate ran her finger along the cuff of the expensive coat.

'This is new,' she observed.

He shimmered his fingertip along the lapel of a sage-green silk jacket, thinking that he had not been expecting such a cool reunion. 'So is this,' he said softly.

His words drew her eyes to his, and once they were locked there she seemed unable to break the gaze.

'Hi,' he murmured.

'Hello,' she said breathlessly.

Her big green eyes drove all conventional greetings clean out of his mind. Oh, what the hell? he thought savagely, and bent his head to kiss her.

'G-Giovanni!' The suitcase fell uselessly from her hand and her fingertips went straight up to his shoulders, biting into the sensually scented leather with an abandon which gathered momentum with each thrust of his tongue as he kissed her with shameless abandon.

'Kate,' he murmured into her mouth, his hand straying irresistibly to the firm swell of her breast, and briefly cupping it in his palm. Until he remembered that they were in a public place, and with an effort he tore his mouth and his hand away.

'*Matri di Diu!*' he swore softly, staring down into the hectic glitter of her eyes. 'I think that we had better go straight to the hotel, don't you, *cara*? Before we are arrested for indecent exposure,' he added, with a low, slightly incredulous laugh.

She supposed that she should be relieved that he wasn't

being hypocritical. Not bothering to dress up the true reason for this weekend together. Straight back to the hotel for two whole nights and very probably two whole days of sensational sex, then back on the plane to London.

And if she had wanted more than what he was offering her she should never have come.

'Sounds wonderful,' she agreed evenly.

Outside the air was warm and soft, and the sky a canopy of indigo velvet, punctured by starlight. He glanced at her as they walked out towards the car. 'You've lost a little weight,' he noticed.

'I needed to.'

'No, you didn't.' He had thought her quite perfect before, but now there was an angular edge to her appearance which made her look like some high-profile model. He saw the side-looks she was getting from the taxi drivers who stood waiting for fares, and instead of feeling a swagger of masculine pride in her beauty he found himself wanting to go and verbally threaten them.

'You're saying that I'm too thin now?'

'A little.' He smiled. 'It will give me enormous pleasure to feed you up, *cara*.' One of many pleasures he anticipated during the days to come.

He settled her into the car, and placed her bags in the back, but thought that she seemed tense as he drove out of the airport towards the hotel.

'Are you OK?' he asked softly.

'Mmm! Just fine,' she answered brightly.

He didn't want her brittle; he wanted her fiery in his arms again. 'Ever been to Barcelona before?' he enquired conversationally as he raced the car towards the city.

She shook her head. 'No, never.' She peered out of the window. 'Do you know it well?'

'Well enough to find my way around without a map.'

Her nerves were making breathing difficult. 'And you're here on business?'

'That's right. A big deal has been concluded.' He shot her a glance, reading nothing in her shadowed profile. 'I have to have dinner with some people tomorrow night. I've known them for years and years.' He indicated right. 'I thought you might like to come along, too?'

'Well, unless you're planning to leave me alone in the hotel for the evening!' she joked, but she felt a surge of satisfaction before reprimanding herself. Just because he wanted to take her out to meet some people he was doing business with didn't mean that they were conducting a normal relationship.

No, her role had been defined from the very beginning: she was his mistress—she gave him pleasure.

And you? mocked an inner voice. Does he give you pleasure, too?

She stole a glance at the hard, dark profile. Of course he did, though she suspected that it had been without any effort on his part. She was almost completely smitten *now*—so imagine what it would be like if he was *trying* to impress her…if he were courting her in a traditional way! But why bother wishing for what she couldn't have? That way led only to disillusionment and heartache.

So snap out of it, she told herself. There was no point in agreeing to come here if she was just going to mope around and wish for the impossible.

She glanced out of the window again. 'So come on, Giovanni,' she murmured, 'let's have the guided tour.'

'My pleasure,' he murmured back, unwittingly echoing her thoughts as he began to tell her about each majestic building they passed.

The hotel was in the Ramblas, close to the enchanting Gothic Quarter of the city, and suitably impressive. He checked her in and then they rode up in the lift towards his suite, but the presence of other guests meant that they stood on opposite sides of the confined space, as awkwardly as strangers.

But the moment he had shut the door behind them, he took her into his arms and began to kiss her, and—whilst part of her wished that he might have waited—she gave herself up to the glory of that kiss. Three months without him became a distant memory as his hard mouth danced sensation all over her skin, and she was shaking and dazed when he finally lifted his head to stare down at her.

'So *did* you miss me?' he questioned silkily.

As a mistress, surely she could be as truthful as she liked. 'I missed *that*,' she admitted.

His mouth hardened. 'And nothing else?'

'My coffee bill has been halved,' she joked and saw the narrowing of his eyes. 'What do you want me to say, Giovanni?' she provoked, half in exasperation. 'That I sat around weeping into my little handkerchief, dreaming of you night after night?'

In her way, her lack of sentiment made it easier to do what he had been almost beside himself with the thought of doing since he had driven away from her flat that morning. His planned offer of a drink forgotten, he ran his hands possessively down the sides of her body, feeling her responding shiver.

'This is how I dreamt of you,' he purred, and shrugged the silk jacket from her shoulders, before tossing it over the back of a chair. 'Like *this*.' With one fluid movement he slid the zip of her skirt down, and as it fell to the floor with a whisper he let out a small, impatient groan when he saw what she was wearing beneath.

A scarlet thong and a matching scarlet garter belt, holding up stockings of creamy white which clung silkenly to the tantalisingly long legs.

'*Matri di Diu!*' he muttered hoarsely.

'You like it?'

'Is it new?' he breathed.

'Mmm.' Kate did her flirty little pirouette, and heard him suck in a ragged breath. She turned round to face him, unprepared for the look of dark, unspoken anger on his face.

'You *don't* like it,' she observed in surprise.

'Who bought it for you?' he demanded.

'What?'

'You heard what I said! A woman does not buy these kind of garments for herself. A man buys these for his mistress!'

'So?' she interjected furiously. 'That's exactly what I am, isn't it?'

'Kate—'

She shook her head in anger. 'Just what *are* you suggesting, Giovanni—that as soon as you got on the plane back to Sicily I replaced you with another stud in my bed?'

Just the thought of it filled him with a murderous rage. 'And did you?'

She very nearly slapped him round the face. 'The fact that you feel the need to ask makes me wonder why I ever agreed to come here,' she told him icily, stooping to retrieve her skirt, but he stayed her, placing his hand on her elbow and gently levering her back up to face him.

'Kate—'

'Take your hands off me,' she said, despising herself for the lack of conviction in her voice.

His voice dropped to a placatory caress. 'I should not have said that, *cara mia*—'

'No, you bloody well shouldn't! If you must know—I bought it...' her voice faltered as she wondered about the wisdom of admitting this '...for you!'

'For me?'

Truthful she was allowed to be, but only up to a point. No need to tell him that if she was going to play the part of mistress then she would play it with a vengeance. And a mistress being reunited with her Sicilian lover would surely wear the finest and flimsiest silk and satin to clothe her body. Delicate garments which she had imagined him slowly or not-so-slowly removing. Garments which would guarantee another invitation for another weekend…

'I'll go and get some big knickers and a plain navy bra if that will make you feel better!' she declared, but he shook his head, and his blue eyes looked almost luminous as he lifted her chin with the tip of his finger.

'Nothing will make me feel better than having you back in my arms again, Kate,' he told her gently. 'Come. Come to me.'

And with a helpless little moan she did exactly that.

He laced his fingers into the thick abundance of her hair and drew her into his body, her warm scent drifting over his senses and igniting their fire. 'I've missed you,' he murmured.

'Honestly?'

'Of course. Do you imagine that you are easy to forget?'

She felt his hands slide from her hair to cup the smooth globes of her bottom, and she gave a little cry. She had missed him, too—but she certainly wasn't going to tell him how much.

Because mistresses did not make such statements of ardour and commitment. That tended to scare the object of their affection away. Instead, she began to unbutton his shirt. 'There's a time for talking,' she said shakily.

'And that time isn't now,' he agreed, his eyes closing as her questing fingers found his nipples and began to stroke enticing little circles.

It took him precisely ten seconds to remove her clothes.

'You've hardly noticed all my new finery!' she complained as the bra slithered off to join the skirt.

'Another time! I want to see you naked,' he ground out,

his breath hot and urgent as it sucked on one tight and hungry breast and she gave a sharp gasp of pleasure.

Her fingers faltered with the buckle of his belt as she felt him slide the thong right off, his hands lingering suggestively on her bottom, and sliding briefly against the cool flesh of her inner thighs, until she was left wearing nothing but a pair of emerald-green high-heels.

He threw his shirt off and stepped out of his trousers and underpants just as Kate bent over to unstrap her shoes.

His eyes darkened. 'On second thoughts, I want to see you nearly naked. Leave those on,' he instructed softly, pointing to the shoes, as he led her across to the bed.

Now this really *was* mistress-like, Kate thought, torn between anticipation and self-consciousness, as the cool linen of the duvet whispered against her back. Having your dark, beautiful lover tower over you in a foreign bedroom, with you wearing nothing but a pair of very sexy, green shoes.

'You look like my every fantasy come to life,' he whispered, his voice deepening.

'How?' she whispered back.

'Wicked. Abandoned. And…'

She heard his hesitation, was intrigued by it. 'And what?'

'Here,' he admitted. 'Now. On my bed after too long. Waiting for me to make love to you over and over again.'

She closed her eyes, so that he wouldn't read the regret there. *Making love*. It was nothing but a turn of phrase. What they were about to do was a lot more basic than that. 'Then don't keep me waiting too long,' she said shakily.

Wait? Why, he could barely contain himself enough not to thrust straight into her as soon as his hands began to explore her. But she was as ready and as turned on as he was and it was only moments before he was poised against her.

Provocatively she parted her legs for him and then engaged in intimate capture, teasing him, edging him against her enticingly until he was completely in her power, and she in his.

It all happened so quickly. Too quickly, she thought as regret was dissolved by wave after wave of gut-wrenching pleasure by an orgasm which exploded into instant life.

'Giovanni!' she sobbed.

There was a long silence afterwards while they struggled for breath, and it was a long moment later before he looked down into her face, his dark brows criss-crossing as he saw the tears which slid from beneath her closed eyes.

'Why are you crying?' he asked quietly.

Because this was the only place she could find happiness, locked in the embrace of a man motivated only by desire. Hopeless.

'Because it was beautiful,' she answered, and that was no lie.

He pushed a damp strand of hair from her cheek. 'The best,' he agreed softly. 'The very best.'

'Thank you.'

'Don't mention it,' he said gravely, and then smiled. 'You want to stay here, or do you want to go out and eat?'

'It's too late, surely?' she protested.

'They eat very late in Spain. Didn't you know?'

'I don't know if I can be bothered to get dressed.' She yawned, unwilling to leave this room, to shatter the curious air of intimacy which had somehow evolved between them.

'Then I can ring down for Room Service?'

'Mmm. That sounds better.'

She feasted her eyes on him as he walked naked across the room to the telephone, and heard him issue a number of requests in what sounded—to her untutored ears—like fluent Spanish.

When he turned around he saw her watching him, her eyes alive and on fire, and then saw her face close, as if she was keeping something secret from him. For a man brought up in a culture where secrecy was second nature, it was oddly disconcerting.

'You're happy?' he asked suddenly.

'Of course.' She drew in a deep breath and looked at him. She had to know. 'Did you…did you…see Anna?'

He turned away, but not before she had seen the dark look of regret which haunted his eyes, and it stabbed straight through her heart.

'Isn't this a rather strange time to ask me a question like that?' he returned in a harsh, cruel voice.

She had to know where she stood. She *had to*. 'Did you?' she persisted.

'Yes. Yes, of course I did.' There had been two tense, fraught meetings before Anna had realised that the clock could not be put back. He had told her sincerely that he wanted her to find happiness with someone who deserved her quiet devotion. She had told him to go to hell and somehow that had made him feel better.

'How is she?'

He turned back again. 'Do you really care?' he demanded.

'Of course I care! Do you think I feel good about what happened?'

'I feel a lot worse about it than you do, *cara*, let me assure you.' He gave a short laugh. 'The last I heard, she had cut her hair and was flying to stay with her sister in Rome, who is promising to give her the time of her life.'

Still, there was something else she needed to know. 'So there is no chance of a reconciliation?'

'Kate,' he said dangerously, 'if this was troubling you then should you not have asked me before you agreed to come out here?'

'I suppose so—'

'But you didn't?'

'No.' She bit her lip as she recognised the truth, that she had wanted to see him to the exclusion of all else—of pride…even of common decency.

He shook his head as if in quiet disbelief. 'Did you really imagine that I would betray her for a second time with you?'

'Is that all I am to you?' she said bitterly. 'A betrayal?'

In a sense, yes, she was, but she was more than that. His reaction to her had illuminated the fact that he did not have the steely control he had once thought defined his character. She was his weakness, too.

'Would you be here tonight if I thought that?' he grated.

'It might have been easier if you had found yourself a different bed-partner,' she said stiffly. 'Someone who didn't have such tainted associations as I clearly do.'

'But I didn't want another bed-partner. I wanted you.' His eyes were luminously blue as he came to sit on the edge of the bed, his finger ruefully tracing the tremble of her mouth. 'I wanted to see you again,' he said starkly. 'I had to see you again.'

But she thought that he made her sound like an addiction he couldn't wait to be rid of. 'Can I have a drink now, please?' she asked him as a diversion.

'You can have anything you want,' he smiled.

Except his heart.

'*Magara mia*,' he whispered.

'What's that?' she whispered back.

There was more regret in his face as he shrugged. 'My witch.'

But witches could work magic, and there was no spell she could put on Giovanni to make him love her as she loved him. Lucy had been right all along, Kate realised. Because from unconventional beginnings had grown a feeling which now consumed her.

He gave her a robe to wear, and put one on himself, and then opened champagne just as the food arrived—tiny little tapas which he laid out on a table overlooking the glittering city.

Kate forced herself to forget her useless longings, to enjoy the view and the food and the man who sat before her, enchanting her with little looks of longing as he fed her morsels of delicious food with his fingers.

CHAPTER ELEVEN

KATE had rarely felt so nervous as she dressed for dinner the following evening—and her nerves were compounded when she emerged in her towelling robe from the shower to have Giovanni casually drop a large, flat beribboned box onto the still-rumpled bed.

'What's that?' she asked him.

His eyes glittered. 'Why not open it, and see?'

Beneath the layers of tissue paper lay the most beautiful lingerie she had ever seen—silver silk-satin and filigree lace. Bra. Camiknickers—and a wisp of a garter belt. Kate swallowed as she pulled each delicate item out of the box. 'It's...'

He heard the strained quality in her voice, and frowned. 'You don't like it?'

'How could I not like it?' she questioned shakily. 'It's utterly beautiful.'

But her reaction had not been the delight he had anticipated. 'Will you wear it tonight, *cara*?' he instructed silkily. 'For me?'

She slid the garments onto her still-damp skin, aware that his eyes were devouring every trembling movement she made. The silk felt unbelievably light and delicious as it clung fluidly to every curve, but she couldn't rid herself of an unreasonable sensation of disappointment.

Because as he himself had pointed out the fripperies were such a typical gift of a man to his mistress that she felt almost as if *she* was being stereotyped by the man who had once accused her of the same thing. And now she was being cast into a one-dimensional role from which there could be no escape.

She forced herself to smile as she turned slowly for her captive audience. 'How's that?'

A pulse beat deep within his groin, and he wished that he could cancel the dinner. 'Exquisite,' he murmured throatily. 'It seems a pity that you have to cover them up.'

'You mean that you'd like other men to see me like this?' she demanded wildly.

Jealousy—hot and dark and potent—flooded over his skin. 'They are for my eyes only,' he told her dangerously, but something in the reproachful tremble of her lips made him adjust his tone. 'Just the image of you wearing them will sustain me through dinner, and I will imagine myself removing them later,' he promised.

She wore one of her new dresses—a deceptively simple robe, cut on the bias, which skimmed the floor. Its plain, almost stark cream colour provided the perfect foil to the living fire of her hair, which she clipped back at the sides and let tumble to her waist.

He murmured his approval as she stood in front of him.

And Giovanni looked exquisite, too—in the beautifully cut black dinner suit and a snowy silk shirt. Formality suited him, she thought, but then, in a way, he was almost old-fashionedly formal in his outlook.

His behaviour towards her, as his mistress, was exemplary. He had flown her to a beautiful city and bought her fine underwear. He was the most skilled and considerate lover, and now he was taking her out to a fancy restaurant to meet business colleagues of his.

If only there could have been a little more *warmth* in his attitude towards her—but warmth implied emotion, didn't it, and there was precious little where he was concerned? Which made it imperative that she keep her own feelings hidden.

The restaurant was crowded and had the lively buzz of success about it. The others were already seated and

Giovanni introduced her to Xavier and Juan, and Juan's wife, Rosa.

Very Spanish, with their dark, flashing-eyed looks, Kate thought that both men were attractive, but Xavier especially so. His eyes narrowed appreciatively as she walked in at Giovanni's side, and he made a great play of bending to kiss her fingertips in an impossibly chivalrous manner.

'Giovanni did not tell me that *you* would be *quite* so beautiful,' he murmured in perfect English.

Giovanni took Kate's hand to his lips and let it linger there in an action which was decidedly possessive. 'And I did not tell Kate that *you* were quite so presumptuous! Be careful, *cara*—Xavier has quite a reputation with women!'

Kate laughed, enjoying his territorial display. 'I'll heed your warning,' she told him.

Rosa was not so forthcoming, and her polite smile at Kate was undoubtedly iced with frost, though Kate doubted whether any of the men had noticed.

They drank expensive wine and ordered food, and Rosa subjected her to a gentle little grilling, which to the outside world must have sounded like genuine interest. But the look in her brown eyes told a different story.

'You have known Giovanni long, Kate?' she asked quietly.

How to answer this? She had *known* him for about three and a half months, but the reality boiled down to about fifteen hot and steamy days. Kate turned her eyes desperately to Giovanni for assistance.

'We met at my godmother's house, back in July,' he said smoothly.

'Oh!' Rosa's plucked eyebrows shot upwards in two delicate arcs. 'You are a friend of Giovanni's godmother?'

Don't let her intimidate you, thought Kate. 'Our relationship is a working one,' she said staunchly.

'You *work* for her?' quizzed Rosa.

She was making her sound like Lady St John's *cleaner*,

thought Kate indignantly. 'In a sense. I decorate her homes for her.' She smiled, with an effort.

'*Oh!*' said Rosa again, and curved her lips into a smug, little smile.

The fish course was brought, and Kate felt as if she were ploughing through sawdust, but she finished most of it, washed down with the occasional mouthful of white Rioja.

Across the table, Giovanni watched her. Outwardly, she was completely at ease in the luxurious surroundings, and her table-manners were a delight to observe, and yet she seemed unaccountably *nervous*, and he wondered why.

Surely the sight of Xavier looking as though he would like to devour her for courses one, two, three and four was not making her look almost self-conscious—a quality he had never associated with Kate. He sent Xavier a searing look, and this was interpreted with a rueful shrug.

Before the dessert, Kate got up to use the powder room, and Rosa got to her feet at the same time.

'Let's go together,' she said prettily. 'And then the men can talk about us while we're away!'

'We'll be talking football, I can assure you,' said Giovanni mockingly.

In the powder room, all pretence slid away as Rosa turned to Kate, an undisguised look of hostility on her face.

'So,' she observed slowly, 'you are the woman responsible for the breaking up of Anna and Giovanni's engagement.'

The mention of Anna's name made Kate's cheeks flush hot and she thought that it must look like an admission of guilt. 'You know Anna, do you?'

'But of course.' Rosa shrugged. 'She and Giovanni were together for such a long time—'

'How long?' asked Kate, without thinking about the folly of asking such a question.

'You don't *know*?' The smile grew superior. 'No, I suppose you wouldn't. Well, my dear, they were together for eight years.'

Kate felt all the blood drain from her face and had to grip onto the handbasin to stop herself swaying. Eight years! That long!

'You *do* look guilty,' observed Rosa, her soft tone unable to disguise the barb in her voice. 'I expect that I would feel exactly the same—but then I can never imagine doing what you have done to another woman.'

Kate wanted to cry out and defend herself. To tell this woman that she had not known of Anna's existence. That Giovanni had not told her. But something stopped her—and she wasn't sure whether it was loyalty to Giovanni, or a sinking worry about whether she would have behaved differently even if she *had* known about Anna.

Instead, she fixed a bland smile onto her lips. 'I think we'd better get back now, don't you—or the men will wonder where we are?'

Somehow she got through the rest of the meal without letting her smile slip, aware that Giovanni was watching her closely.

And once they were back in the car he didn't start the engine, just turned to look at her. 'What is the matter with you?' he demanded. 'You've been acting strangely all evening!'

She wasn't going to blab. She pretended to search in her handbag for a tissue she didn't really want. 'Nothing.'

'Yes, there is something,' he contradicted. 'Look at me! Something was wrong tonight, Kate, and I demand to know what it is!'

She looked up and glared at him. 'You lay no claim on me! You cannot demand *anything* of me, Giovanni!' she told him proudly. 'Nothing!'

He almost smiled at her defiance, but he remained resolute. 'Was something said?'

Kate sighed, recognising a persistence and a determination about his character which was very similar to her own. Giovanni would push and push and push until she gave him the answers he required. Better, she supposed, to give in gracefully now, rather than ruin the rest of their last precious night together.

She stared out at the night. 'Rosa spoke of Anna—'

An abrasive word was torn from his lips. 'She had no right! It is not her business!' he snarled, and then his voice grew softer. 'What did she say?'

Kate shifted uncomfortably in her car-seat. 'It doesn't matter.'

'Kate,' he said, on a dark note of warning, and she stared unhappily into his glittering eyes. 'It matters.'

'I had no idea that you had been together for so *long*!' she said despairingly. 'Eight years! That somehow makes it all the worse!'

Her pain affected him more than it had any right to. 'It is the custom in Sicily,' he told her gently, 'for engagements to be long ones.' His face altered into a grim mask. 'I will speak to Rosa,' he said in a voice of deadly venom.

'No, Giovanni! You mustn't!'

'*Mustn't?*' he repeated imperiously, as if he had never been forbidden to do something by a woman in his life. 'Don't forget, you lay no claim on me either, Kate.'

'But what point is there in saying anything—it'll only cause trouble?' she asked him urgently. 'You've known Rosa and her husband for years and years—you can't fall out, just because of me!'

'Thank you for your consideration, Kate,' he said implacably. 'But I will say a few quiet words. Don't worry, *cara mia*,' he tilted her face upwards and coaxed a smile, 'we will not fall out.' He wasn't going to tell Kate that Rosa was probably jealous of her, and that the wife of one of his oldest associates had been giving him the come-on for the past year. Giovanni's mouth hardened. It was time he warned her off.

'Kate?'

'What?'

He bent his head forward and planted a soft kiss on her lips, smiling as he watched her eyes flutter helplessly to a close. 'Let's make the most of our last few hours in Barcelona,' he whispered urgently. And he wasn't talking sightseeing.

He drove as if demons were at his heels, and, back in the hotel room, he stripped her clothes from her body with such slow, sensuous care that she wanted to beg him to hurry up.

But the waiting and the anticipation more than compensated for her mounting need for him, and only when she was lying in the beautiful silver undergarments on the bed did he remove his own clothes and come to lie on top of her.

She saw the look of dark hunger on his face and gestured to the camiknickers she still wore, a question in her eyes.

'I want to leave them on,' he whispered. 'I want to do this.' And he pushed aside the panel which shielded the very core of her femininity, his finger coming away coated with the syrup of her longing and he groaned and positioned himself and thrust into her long and slow and deep.

The sensation of the silk still against her skin, and then the silk of him inside her skin was almost too much too bear, and frantically she clung to him as he kissed her, and rocked her with the oldest rhythm of all.

And then it was too late, it was happening all over again, and this time she had to concentrate very hard to keep her emotions in check.

Because this time she was determined not to cry.

Kate felt subdued as she stood close to the departure lounge, but she hoped that she achieved the right kind of grown-up expression. The kind of look which would tell him that she had enjoyed herself—though she guessed he must have known that. A look which would tell him she had no expectations about the future.

She wondered what he would say. Just a goodbye, and then a brief, poignant kiss, maybe?

Giovanni looked down into eyes as green as the cypress trees which dotted the hills around the place of his birth, and touched his mouth to hers.

'So did you enjoy your visit to Barcelona, Kate?' he murmured.

To be honest, they could have been in any city in the world, for all the sightseeing they had done, but then sightseeing hadn't been number one on their agenda. She knew that and he knew that.

She nodded, and smiled, her smile masking the thought that this might be the last time she would ever see him. 'You know I did.'

'Mmm. I thought so, *magara mia*!'

'I am *not* your witch!'

His eyes narrowed. 'Your Sicilian is improving by the day!'

Her flight announcement was called for the second time, and he swore softly beneath his breath. Had two days really passed with such indecent speed?

'Giovanni, I really *must* go—'

He halted her with a forefinger placed softly over her lips. 'Listen, I'm going to Roma in a few weeks' time. Would you like to come and join me there?'

Her heart leapt, even while she registered how casually he broached the question. She pretended to give the question careful consideration, determined not to seem too eager.

'To Rome?' she repeated, and then she smiled. 'Do you know, Giovanni?' she said, taking care to keep her voice as casual as his. 'I've always wanted to visit Rome.'

* * *

Rome. Paris. Prague. Vienna. New York. She joined him in one luxurious hotel after another—and in between times Kate threw herself into her work in an attempt to consume her thoughts with something other than her dark Sicilian lover. But it wasn't easy.

Christmas came and went, but she didn't see him. He spent it with his parents in Palermo, while Kate and Lucy went to their own family home.

Giovanni sent her a package which she dared not put beneath her parents' Christmas tree, imagining more of the exquisite lacy undergarments he had made a habit of buying for her—and she could just imagine what her father would say about *that*.

But he surprised her with a Sicilian-English dictionary with a mocking foreword written in his distinctive hand: 'Learn something new each day, *cara*—and then teach me what you have learned.'

She devoured it during the holiday—oblivious to the sounds of carols or the lure of mince-pies and turkey—memorising as many words as she thought might be appropriate to relate when next she saw him…and resolutely casting aside the word 'love'.

'You're still crazy about him, aren't you?' asked Lucy one morning in late January, when she and Kate had been going through her expenses.

Kate had flown in from New York the evening before, still glowing from Giovanni's lovemaking, a box of matching yellow lace underwear hidden away inside her suitcase.

'Not more?' she had asked him, her mouth curving into a slow smile as she had taken another outrageous wisp of nothing from the box. 'You've bought me enough already, surely?'

He had shaken his head as she began to pull the camiknickers up her long, long legs, knowing that very soon he would be pulling them off her again. 'Never enough, *cara*,' he told her huskily. 'You should have something different for every day of the year.'

And Kate found herself working out how many weekends she would have with him to enable him to be able to provide *that*.

She had taken a Thursday and Friday off work and had flown into Kennedy Airport on Thursday evening, to find Giovanni looking tense and strained, and she had teased him about it.

'You don't want me here?'

'I couldn't wait for you to arrive,' he admitted huskily and took her into his arms and kissed her with an urgency which thrilled her.

'Then why the long face?' she asked in the cab on the way to their hotel.

'Oh, some—' He said some vehement word in Sicilian. 'Some mix-up over a big consignment which was meant to arrive from Sicily last week, but didn't.'

She crossed one leg over the other, hearing him draw in an unsteady breath as he was treated to the briefest glimpse of lacy stocking-top beneath a creamy-white thigh. 'Shame,' she murmured.

And he laughed. What the hell did it matter—what did any of it matter—when he had her here, like this? 'A terrible shame,' he agreed gravely, as he reached for her in the darkened intimacy of the car.

They spent the next morning in bed and then travelled to Liberty Island, where the queues for the statue seemed to go on forever.

Giovanni's mouth tightened. 'Let's skip it for today,' he said roughly, thinking that all he wanted was to be alone with her again.

But Kate shook her head. 'Queuing will do you good,' she said firmly.

'Oh, really?'

'Yes. Really! We'll people-watch and then over dinner we can see if we agree or disagree.'

'On what?' he asked, mystified.

'Oh, who's brought their wife. Who's brought their mistress—that kind of thing!'

'Mistress is a very old-fashioned word,' he growled, inexplicably offended by the term.

She batted her eyelashes at him. 'It's a very old-fashioned occupation, darling—didn't you know?' But inside she was on a high. In these cities—foreign to both of them—she could be exactly what she wanted to be, and, more than anything else, she felt as if they were on equal terms.

That weekend—like all the others which had preceded it—passed all too quickly, and Giovanni seemed reluctant to let her go.

'I'm sick of departure lounges!' he declared vehemently, sliding his hands around her waist, and locking them possessively in the small of her back.

Well, so was she—but she was determined that his last memory of her would be a sunny smile.

'I'm not overfond of them, myself,' she whispered. 'But there you go! Now, Giovanni, that's the third and final call, so will you *please* let me go?'

He had complied, reluctantly, but stood watching her retreating back until long after she had disappeared from view.

'Aren't you?' asked Lucy.

'Mmm?' Lost in a dreamworld dominated by Giovanni and only Giovanni, Kate looked up at her sister absently. 'Aren't I what?'

'Crazy about him? Even more than before.'

There was a moment of silence. 'I guess I am.' How could she not be? 'He's gorgeous,' she sighed, then shrugged, as if it didn't really matter. 'Though I guess it's easy for him to be gorgeous—the situation is very beautiful, but very false.

We meet in glamorous destinations, we stay in glamorous hotels. We eat delicious meals and make delicious love, and then I come home again.' She looked at her sister candidly. 'I guess that's what it's like—being a mistress.'

'Yes,' said Lucy thoughtfully, 'I suppose it is. You're intimate in so many ways, and yet not intimate at all. You get the sex and the glamour—but none of the ordinary stuff that makes for companionship.'

Kate tried to make light of it. 'What, like washing his socks, you mean?'

'Something like that.' Lucy's green eyes were piercing. 'And he never says he loves you?'

'Never.'

'Nor express any desire for a bit more…permanence?'

'Never.' Kate saw the expression on her sister's face and sprang to his defence, as though her pride expected her to. 'He hasn't long come out of a broken relationship, remember? He's hardly going to want to leap straight back into another.'

'And you're happy for things to continue this way, are you, Kate—the long-term mistress?'

'Happy enough.' Because what was the alternative? Life without him was a million times worse than these snatched moments of bliss; she had already tried that.

'And what's he like, during these weekends?' persisted Lucy.

'Perfect,' answered Kate simply. 'Absolutely perfect.'

'Not mean or moody any more?'

'No.' Kate looked at her sister with an air of defiance. 'I may be besotted with the man, but I'm not into masochism, you know, Lucy. And what would be the point of spending time with him if he continued to be angry with me?'

That much, at least, had changed.

These days, they had almost as much conversation as sex, and Kate wanted that. She wanted shared experiences which she would be able to store up in her memory. She wanted to learn more about *him*.

And she had.

He had told her about his parents and his younger brother, and the house he had grown up in, in the hills outside Palermo. The brother was now ensconced in Rome, running that branch of the Calverri empire.

He described the beautiful villa he had bought for himself and Kate had wondered wistfully if she would ever see it. He had spoken about his early life, and the Sicilian culture, and its proud, aloof people, and Kate had nodded in comprehension, remembering the print-out from her computer.

For Giovanni epitomised the Sicilian man. Proud, yes. And aloof—yes, more than a little. He gave so much, but that was all. She knew as much of him as he would allow her to know, and yet at times she felt as though she knew him better than she knew herself.

But maybe that was because physically, at least, they were so perfectly in tune with one another.

He called the following week, when Kate was feeling out-of-sorts, even though she knew that she should be feeling delighted, because he had just suggested coming to London. But she had been feeling off-colour for days now, and was beginning to wonder whether she had eaten something which disagreed with her. Or whether it was a mild form of jet lag.

'London?' she questioned weakly as little spots danced before her eyes.

'That's right.' Giovanni frowned at the telephone. He had thought she would be pleased. 'What's the matter, Kate—have you grown too used to room service?' he teased. 'I don't have to stay at your place, you know, *cara*. We can always go to a nice hotel, and you can pretend to be a tourist in your own city!'

She took a deep breath and sank down onto the sofa, wondering why her legs felt as though they were made of cotton wool. 'No, that's fine—I'd love you to stay here. When are you arriving?'

He paused, his heart beating hard with excitement. He had things he needed to tell her. 'Tomorrow,' he told her.

A wave of nausea washed over her. 'Tomorrow?' she repeated feebly.

'This is not the rapturous response I expected,' he murmured drily. 'Don't tell me you're becoming bored with me, *cara*?'

Never! Not as long as there were planets edging around the skies! But Giovanni expected playful teasing, she knew that. Just as she knew how much the truth would send him spinning out of her orbit.

'I'll tell you when I see you,' she teased back.

'I can't wait.'

And normally, neither could she. Normally she would be counting the hours and then the minutes until he would be back in her arms again.

Only this time she did so for a different reason entirely.

Kate shivered as she heard his peremptory ring on the doorbell, and walked to answer it from the kitchen, where she had been making supper—even though eating was the very last thing she felt like doing.

She opened the door to him, as always unprepared for the glorious shock to her senses which his presence always seemed to invoke. But this time the sensation was all too fleeting. This time...

She bit her lip. 'Hello, Giovanni,' she said slowly. 'Come in.'

He frowned as he dropped his bags on the floor of the hall and shut the front door behind him.

'No kiss?' he accused softly.

'Let's go into the sitting room,' she said nervously. 'It's warmer in there.'

His eyes were watchful as he followed her. There was something different about her tonight. What was it? She seemed tense. Not herself at all. And pale, he thought—much paler than usual.

'Come to Giovanni, Kate,' he instructed softly.

How could she resist him? she wondered helplessly. How could she *ever* resist him? She went into the circle of his arms, raising her head so that he could kiss her.

Her body melted into his, and he felt the first heavy pulse of desire. 'That's better,' he purred when he eventually lifted his head. 'You seemed a little tense back there, *cara*.' He drifted the palm of his hand around the curve of her chin, a question in his eyes. 'What's the matter, Kate? Hmm? Busy week at work?'

Kate hoped that her bright smile did not look like a ghastly grimace. 'Er, yes. It *was* pretty hectic.'

'So now you relax. With me.'

Oh, God—she couldn't let him make love to her. Not now! Not yet! 'I've been preparing supper,' she told him wildly.

Supper? His obdurate expression hid his surprise. Usually food was remembered halfway through the evening as something of an afterthought. He surveyed her again, even though he went through the action of sniffing the air, in a parody of a hungry man returning home. 'I can tell,' he said indulgently. 'Smells good.' And then he frowned. More than smelling good, it smelt *familiar*. He frowned again. 'What is it, *cara*?'

She forced herself to inject some enthusiasm into her voice. After all, hadn't she spent hours preparing for what was supposed to be the surprise to end all surprises? Until…

'Can't you tell?' she asked him, her heart beating very fast with fear and foreboding.

He strode straight through into the kitchen, where it quickly became clear what she had done—the ingredients gave it away. He saw a pile of pasta and he peered at what lay within the simmering pot. Fresh sardines. And wild fennel. Currants and pine nuts and saffron. A slow smile dissolved his frown.

And very nearly dissolved her, too.

'*Pasta con le sarde*,' he murmured. 'Sicily's most typical dish. Oh, Kate, *cara mia* Kate—do you do this because you know that the way to a man's heart is through his stomach?'

Fear gripped her. If only he hadn't said that! As if she was trying to manipulate some kind of permanence with him. It was just a teasing, throwaway comment, but in view of the bombshell she was shortly to drop…

'Shall we eat?' she questioned hoarsely.

He told himself that she was nervous because she had obviously gone to a lot of trouble preparing this dish. He told himself that the timing was important—it could not be left to sit and spoil; its beauty was in its freshness and crispness.

But somewhere deep inside him there remained the disquiet that something was not quite as it should be.

She had laid the table carefully, as if her life depended on it. With napkins and candles and fresh flowers.

'This looks very welcoming,' he observed as she struck a match and lit the candles. 'The perfect supper.'

The last supper, she thought, with a sudden shiver of apprehension. 'Sit down, Giovanni,' she said huskily as she hovered in the kitchen doorway.

Almost imperceptively he raised his brows. Was she *deliberately* staying far away from him physically, he wondered, or was he simply imagining it? 'Shall I open some wine?'

Not for me, she was about to say, until something made her bite the words back. 'That would be lovely,' she said weakly. 'And after that you could unpack, couldn't you—while I throw it all together?'

'Sure,' he said impassively, with an almost imperceptible elevation of his dark brows as he put the opened bottle of Sicilian red on the table to let it breathe.

He hung his clothes up, and placed a package for her on the bed and when he returned she was dishing the meal out. He sat down at the table and poured them both a glass of wine.

Kate sat down opposite him, glad for the relief thrown on their faces by the flickering candlelight. At least he wouldn't be able to read her expression.

He raised his glass to hers. '*Saluti!*' he said softly.

But she merely brushed her lips against the crimson liquid, she did not drink. Even the smell of it was making her stomach clench once more.

Giovanni ate his food, noticing that she did little but move hers around on the plate, arranging it in little piles, in order, he guessed, to appear as if she had actually eaten some of it.

He wondered whether she now saw the role of mistress as too submissive. His independent Kate. Had she decided that this kind of relationship was not for her? And how would he respond if she did? Would it be easy just to let her go?

He sighed and put his fork down, his news forgotten. 'Do you want to tell me about it?' he questioned.

She stared at him. 'Tell you about *what*?' she whispered hoarsely.

He noted her surprise, and its implication irritated him. 'You think I don't know you well enough to know when something is wrong, Kate?' he demanded. 'You think that all I notice is the way you are when I make love to you? That I am completely obtuse as a man?'

She shook her head. 'Giovanni…' She couldn't say it; she couldn't.

'*Matri di Diu!*' he swore as he saw the increased whitening of her face. 'What is it, Kate? Tell me!'

There were only words now. Bald, bare words—because nothing could disguise or cushion the unpalatable fact she was about to tell him.

'I'm pregnant,' she said flatly.

CHAPTER TWELVE

FOR a moment, Giovanni's world imploded. He thought he heard the loud beating of a clock, but there was no clock in Kate's dining room, so it must have been the thundering of his heart.

He stared across the table at her. 'What did you just say?' he asked in a voice which was dangerously calm.

She had thought that she had seen his face in almost every guise. She had thought that she had seen his anger before, but the anger which darkened and hardened his features now was truly monumental. She tried to tell herself that he was shocked. Naturally, he was shocked.

She tried again. 'I'm pregnant.'

There was a loud crash and at first Kate thought that it was the sound of his chair being scraped back, and of Giovanni rising menacingly to his feet. But the crash had been the glass of wine he had knocked over. The glass had not broken, but the wine had spilt out and seeped all over the white damask table-cloth like a puddle of blood, and neither of them made a move to stop it.

His heart was pounding in his ears. 'It cannot be my baby,' he told her with cold emphasis. 'Can it?'

The indignity and the implication made her cheeks sting. 'Of course it's your baby!' she declared, and she trembled her way to her feet, facing him, her breath ragged, as if they were two combatants in a boxing ring. 'Whose could it be if not yours?'

'I have always made absolutely sure that you could not become pregnant,' he said, still in that cold, deadly voice. 'You know that!' He approached her round the table with all the dangerous stealth of a jungle cat, while a hot rage burned inside him. 'Has there been someone else, Kate? Some man who wasn't quite so careful while I was away? You are a highly sexed and very responsive woman, we both know that. Tell me the truth, Kate, and I promise not to judge you.'

Judge her? He might as well have torn her heart from her chest. There was a ringing smack as the flat of her hand connected with his cheek, but he did not flinch, merely raised his own hand in lightning-fast reaction to imprison her wrist and to haul her close to him. So close that she could feel his warm, angry breath—see the furious black glitter of his eyes.

'Whose is it?' he demanded.

'Yours! Yours! Yours! *Yours!*'

Her mouth taunted her victory at him. The oldest trick in the book. Damn her! Damn her! And his anger transmuted into something else—something which was about as earth-shattering as he could imagine. The realisation that something of him would now be carried on into the next generation. His own little piece of immortality. She was carrying his child! His!

'Mine?' he questioned, but now there was a wondering note to his voice. 'Mine, *cara*?'

'Yes.'

With a dazed look in his eyes, he lowered his mouth irresistibly down on hers and began to kiss her in a kiss which was very close to tender.

But the kiss went the way of all their kisses, and the tenderness—was it real or imagined? wondered Kate heatedly—swiftly became desire, pure and sharp and undiluted.

She told herself not to respond, to push him away as he deserved to be pushed after the hideous accusations he had made, but her body would not heed her. It was too finely tuned to his sensual mastery to be able to do anything other than to spring into instant and urgent life beneath his touch. This was the father of her child, she thought weakly—the man who had created this new life growing within her, who could create all life in her.

'Giovanni!' The word came out in an exultant little whisper as he kissed her with a fervour which surpassed his normal kisses. And it was easy to forget the cruel things he had said to her when he kissed her like that.

Her thready little moan excited him even more, and without warning it was suddenly about much more than kissing. He was beyond thought, beyond reason, pursuing some blessed communion with her.

'Giovanni,' Kate breathed in disbelief, because now his hands were rucking up her skirt, and his fingers were snapping at the delicate lace of her panties, so that they fell uselessly to the floor. And with his other hand he was unzipping himself. 'Giovanni!' she whimpered, but the word sounded more like a plea than a protest, and it was. God, help her—it *was*!

He found himself driven on by a life-force so primeval that he could barely think, barely hear—all he could do was feel…feel *her*. He looked down at her mockingly as his fingers flicked enticingly against her molten heat. 'You want me to stop, *cara*? I don't think you do, but tell me yes, and I will.'

'Yes! Yes! *Oh*, no!' she sobbed as he touched her again, oh, so intimately, and she squirmed with excitement. 'No, don't stop! Please, don't stop! Do it! Do it! Do it to me! Now!'

Her words incited him almost as much as the frantic movements of her hips and he pushed her against the wall and levered her legs up around his waist, gasping aloud as he entered her, thrusting into her again and again, losing himself in pursuit of that sweet destination.

This might be the very last time that the man she had grown to love might take pleasure in her arms, she realised.

Heartache ripped through her, but somehow he banished it with every insistent movement of his strong, virile body.

Briefly she opened her eyes to see what a decadent picture the pair of them made—his trousers at his ankles, her skirt pushed up to her waist. How could he ever respect a woman who let him do something like this? But then she began to dissolve in the familiar ecstasy, and her greedy body began to convulse about his. She heard his helpless moan as he spilled his seed into her, and then let his head fall against her shoulder, his lips against her neck.

Kate closed her eyes. What had she done? She had let him take her like that, after his sickening reaction to her momentous news. Had she no shame where this man was concerned? No pride?

She let her feet slide to the floor and pushed him away, tired now. And weary. Impossibly and hopelessly weary. She was aware of the irony of what had just happened. The first time that he had ever made love to her without using any protection. Though it was a little late in the day for protection now.

She stumbled from the dining room and collapsed on the sofa, praying that he would just go. Go away and leave her alone with her fate, and she need never see him again.

She didn't hear him come back into the room, the first time she became aware of his presence was when she found him standing in the doorway, studying her, his face shadowed. And grave. As if he had just received some very bad news, which, in a way, she supposed he had.

'Are you all right?' he questioned, but he made no move towards her.

All right? How could he ask her a question like that at a time like this? 'I'm fine,' she said, still with that flat, tired note in her voice. 'Under the circumstances.'

'Kate, we shouldn't have…' His voice tailed away, and it

was the first time Kate had ever seen him look remotely uncomfortable.

'Shouldn't have what, Giovanni?'

His eyes narrowed. 'Made love like that, of course!'

'That wasn't called making love,' she told him scornfully. 'That was having wham-bam sex up against the wall!'

His mouth hardened. 'Is that why you begged me to do it to you?'

Shuddering at the memory, Kate raked a hand to scoop the damp red hair which had fallen over her face. 'It's irrelevant now, anyway. It's happened.' It's over, she thought, with a certainty which ached at her heart.

'Yes.' He found himself staring down at her flat belly. 'How far gone are you?'

She stared up at him as she considered his reasons for asking this. 'I'm going to keep the baby!' she declared wildly. 'You can't stop me from having it!'

For a moment the import of her words remained unclear to him, and when he understood their true meaning he stared at her with a look of furious distaste. 'Do you really think I would try?' he asked.

Relief flooded through her, and she shook her head slowly. 'No,' she said. 'No, I don't.'

'Then why say it?' he demanded. 'To hurt me? To insult me?'

'We all say things under pressure,' she returned. 'You said a few pretty wounding things yourself.'

'Yes.' He narrowed his eyes as he looked at her, unexpectedly vulnerable in her new-found condition. 'Kate—'

'I want you to know that this isn't some kind of trap to get you to commit to me,' she interrupted proudly, before he had the chance to make the accusation himself. 'Unless you think I somehow punctured one of the condoms with my fingernails when you weren't looking!'

'Of course I wasn't suggesting that!' he exploded. 'I was

just…shocked…taken off-guard. I didn't know what I was saying.'

'We're both shocked. Naturally.'

He studied her pale features and wanted to take her into his arms and smooth away the troubled look on her face, but her body was stiff with tension. She did not want him near her, he acknowledged—and who could blame her? He forced out the unbelievable words. 'You still haven't told me how pregnant you are.'

There was a pause. 'Eight weeks.' She watched him doing sums in his head. 'It must have happened in Rome,' she added.

Giovanni nodded. Yes, Rome.

He remembered her arrival. She had not been nervous, as she had been initially during that first trip to Barcelona. She had been the independent and confident Kate of their very first meeting, and he had been swept away by her.

Her beauty had been almost incandescent—like a fiery light which had surrounded her, and he had bathed in it. So had he been careless? So eager to lose himself in her that he had neglected to protect himself properly?

Kate watched him. 'But it doesn't really matter where or when or how, does it?' she asked heavily. 'The fact remains that it happened. Is happening,' she emphasised painfully, and placed the palm of her hand on a still-flat stomach.

'Yes,' he said, for what else was there for him to say? That he was delighted? No. She would scent his hypocrisy immediately—she was far too perceptive to be given platitudes which disguised his true feelings.

Kate sucked in a breath as she saw his expression of disquiet. She must tell him that she was not planning to use this situation to imprison him in a life not of his choosing. Her gaze was very level as she looked at him. 'Listen, Giovanni. I want you to know that I'm going to go ahead with the pregnancy. I'm going to have the baby and bring it up myself.'

'And me?' he questioned savagely. 'You've got it all worked out, haven't you? Don't I feature in this whole scenario? Or are you planning to exclude me from this baby's life, Kate?'

She tried to play fair, even though her heart told her how difficult it would be to cope with the occasional paternal visit from him. 'You shall have as much or as little of this baby's life as you choose to have,' she said carefully.

'And that's what you want, is it?'

She didn't answer that, not straight away. Of course it wasn't what she wanted! What she wanted was the impossible—the happy little trio of a real family, with Giovanni the doting partner and the doting father at her side. But he hadn't offered that, had he? Nor shown any sign of wanting it—certainly not before her announcement today—and even if he offered it now she could not contemplate a life with Giovanni staying beside her simply because it was his *duty*.

'In the circumstances, there isn't a lot else I can do,' she answered quietly.

Her cheeks looked so translucent, as if her skin were made of rice-paper, and he felt his heart lurch as he realised how traumatic this all must have been for her. First of all finding out, and then having to tell him, fearing his wrath. And oh, he had given it, hadn't he? Attacked her and blamed her when, in reality, she was blameless. 'I'll make you some coffee.'

'I don't want any coffee—'

'You need something,' he insisted forcefully. 'You look terrible!'

She didn't have the energy or the inclination to make a joke about that, and if the truth were known she *felt* terrible. Sick and troubled—and weren't pregnant women supposed to feel glowing and radiant?

Maybe pregnant women whose futures did not look like some unknown black, gaping hole they were being forced to leap into.

He was in the middle of heaping coffee into the pot when he heard her strange, muffled cry, and the spoon fell unnoticed from his fingers—some terrible fear, some awful foreboding telling him that something here was very, very wrong.

He ran into the sitting room to find her doubled up, clutching at her abdomen, and rocking to and fro with tiny fraught cries coming from her lips.

'Kate!' He was by her side in an instant, and as she looked up at him he saw pain in her eyes. And terror. 'Kate!'

He crouched down to her level. 'What is it, *cara*?' he questioned with soft urgency. 'Is it the baby?'

'I'm…' Her fingers waved awkwardly to where she could feel the unmistakable warm flood of blood against her thighs. 'Giovanni—there's a pain! A bad pain!' She reached out and clutched onto his arms, because right at that moment he seemed like the only sure foundation in her disintegrating world. 'Help me, Giovanni,' she whispered. 'Please, help me.'

Her plea smote at his heart, and gently but swiftly he disengaged her fingers and went to the telephone, where he made a rapid call.

She lifted her head painfully. 'What are you doing?'

'Phoning the hospital.'

'I don't need to go to hospital—'

'Kate, yes, you *do*,' he denounced sternly. 'And, what is more, you *will* go!' He began speaking and gave the address, looking round at her as he did so, wishing that he could obliterate that look of agony etched all over her delicate features. He replaced the receiver. 'The ambulance is on its way. Do you want me to tell your sister?'

Through the mists of pain she hesitated. Sometimes she and Lucy felt more like twins than sisters. She nodded. 'Yes.'

'And does she know? About the baby?'

'What baby?' she cried hysterically. 'There isn't going to *be* a baby, is there? But no, I haven't told her.' She hadn't told anyone, as if by not doing that could make it not seem real.

Lucy arrived at the same time as the paramedics, who were carrying a stretcher. She took one wild look of disbelief at Kate lying huddled miserably on the sofa, with Giovanni stroking a cool cloth at her brow, and her mouth fell open in horror.

'What's happened?' she demanded, her eyes flying accusingly to Giovanni. 'What have you done to her?'

He flinched, but he stood up to face the venom on her face quite calmly. 'Your sister is pregnant,' he said quietly.

'You bastard,' hissed Lucy, so that only he could hear.

'Lucy!' called Kate weakly, and she looked up into her sister's face, her green eyes swimming with the unbearable reality of what was happening to her.

She was losing Giovanni's baby.

'Oh, Kate, darling! Darling! What is it?'

'I think I'm having a miscarriage,' whispered Kate brokenly, and saying the hateful word made the first tears come—they slid freely down her cheeks and she made no move to dry them.

'We'll lift you onto the stretcher,' said the paramedic.

She shook her head. 'No, I'll walk.'

'Kate, either you go on the stretcher or I will carry you out to the ambulance myself,' said Giovanni grimly. 'Which is it to be?'

She heard the implacable note in his voice, and allowed herself to be lifted on.

'And will your partner—' the paramedic looked at Kate, and then to Giovanni '—be coming in the ambulance with you?'

Kate stared up into the blue gleam of his eyes, unable to

read any emotion in that shuttered expression. She thought about how babies *should* be conceived. Planned. With love. And preferably within the confines of a happy marriage. Not as the result of a matter-of-fact affair during a passionate weekend when contraception had somehow failed.

Giovanni did not want to be a father, nor her to be a mother. He certainly did not want her to carry *his* baby—so why subject him to the indignity of seeing this brief, precious life come to a premature end? Why should he be witness to a heartbreak he would be unable to understand?

'No,' she said huskily. 'I want my sister with me.'

He flinched again at the ultimate rejection. 'Very well, Kate,' he said flatly. 'I will wait here.'

He kept a vigil, only just preventing himself from ignoring her request and tearing down to the hospital to sit there and wait, and to interrogate the doctors and the nurses until he had news that she was safe and out of danger.

But Kate had expressly said that she did not want him to accompany her, and he came from a culture which treated a pregnant woman as a jewel above all others.

Except, as he reminded himself bitterly, that the chances were that she was no longer a pregnant woman.

Resisting the urge to smash something, Giovanni sucked in a hot, dry breath of pain. She was losing his baby, he thought, unprepared for the wave of despair which rocked him.

He kept himself busy by clearing away the remains of their meal. He winced as he imagined her making his country's most famous dish. Imagined her shopping for all the ingredients, knowing all the while what she had to tell him.

And what an unforgivable bastard of a man he had been.

He lifted the wine-stained tablecloth from the table and put it in the laundry basket, and settled down to wait.

He waited all night and well into the next morning.

He rang the hospital to be told that she had been 'taken to Theatre' and that her condition was 'stable'. He had wanted to shout down the phone at that point, to ask what on earth such a bland word could possibly mean when applied to a woman who had had a new life torn from her body.

He assumed.

He allowed himself a brief fantasy. That her pain and the blood—for he had seen the hideous blush of crimson for himself—had all been some kind of false alarm. Nature's way of warning her to take things easy. Perhaps the pregnancy was still viable.

But, in his heart, he feared the worst.

They would tell him nothing more. He was not a relative. She had not named him as her next-of-kin—that honour had gone to her sister. In the bureaucratic world of hospitals, he did not have a role in Kate's life.

She came home the following morning at eleven, accompanied by an even whiter-faced Lucy. The facts were stark and were spelt out to him by Lucy in the kitchen, whilst Kate slept fitfully.

There had been a baby, yes, but no more. The 'spontaneous miscarriage'—more hospital jargon, he thought grimly—had been followed by a routine operation to remove all traces of the pregnancy from her womb.

'*Routine?*' he questioned incredulously.

'That's what they said,' answered Lucy.

He saw how much she disliked him, and perhaps in a way he could not blame her, but, whatever the hospital thought and whatever Lucy thought, he *did* have a role in Kate's life. If no longer as her lover, then certainly as the man responsible for bringing her to this.

'I'll look after her now,' said Lucy fiercely.

He shook his head. 'No.' His voice was implacable. 'I will stay with Kate until she recovers.'

In the bedroom, Kate stirred and his words penetrated her

consciousness. *Until she recovers.* Then she heard Lucy speaking.

'You think it's that easy for her?' Lucy was saying. 'To recover from something like this?'

Kate pulled the duvet over her head to blot out the sounds of their voices. She felt weak and bereft as it was; she couldn't even begin to contemplate that Giovanni was planning to leave her.

Giovanni looked at Lucy. 'I will not share my thoughts with you, Lucy—they are for Kate's ears and Kate's ears alone.'

'And you really think that she *wants* you here?'

He looked deep into her eyes. 'Has she told you she doesn't?'

'How long will you be staying?'

He noted that she hadn't answered his question. 'Until her physical strength is such that she can fly,' he said quietly.

Her sarcasm showed on her face. 'What? Fly away from you?'

'To Sicily,' he said in a voice which brooked no argument. 'I intend taking her there to recuperate.'

Lucy stared at him. 'Are you completely out of your mind?'

He was tempted to tell her that it was none of her business, but—of course—it was. Kate was her sister and she was simply being protective.

'I appreciate your concern,' he said softly. 'But I do not intend to discuss it with you, Lucy.'

'I have never met a more stubborn man!' she exclaimed, shaking her head in frustration. 'Well, I'd better go. Please tell Kate I'm here whenever she needs me.'

'I'll tell her.'

After Lucy had gone, Giovanni went into the bedroom and stood looking down at her, and his face darkened as he saw her white features and shadowed eyes. He had done this to her!

Her eyes fluttered open as if she had sensed he was there. For a split-second she forgot why she was in bed at noon, with Giovanni observing her with such a tense, tight face, and then she remembered. 'Oh,' she cried, and she felt the hot well of tears behind her eyes.

He wanted to reach out to her, but she looked like a hunted animal, and so he sat on the edge of the bed instead.

'Kate,' he said softly, 'we have to talk about it.'

'Not now,' she said, and shut her eyes again, keeping them tightly closed, in a vain attempt to stop the tears streaming out.

CHAPTER THIRTEEN

KATE woke early the following morning, with the warmth of sunshine piercing her senses, and the dull ache inside where her baby had been. She bit back the sob which had clawed at the back of her throat, and turned to stare at the wall.

'Kate?'

The smell of coffee wafted into the room and drifted towards her nostrils, and Kate turned over to see Giovanni standing in the doorway, a tray of coffee in his hands.

'Hello,' he said, but his voice was as sombre as his face.

'Hello.' She sat up in bed, forcing a smile.

'Here.' He put the coffee down on the dressing table and plumped up the pillows behind her back, and she settled against them comfortably.

'Thank you.'

He wondered what she was thanking him for, when he…he… A muscle moved at his mouth as he poured two cups of coffee and took one over to the bed and gave it to her. He let her drink some and saw a corresponding colour creep into her cheeks before he spoke.

'Kate, there is something I have to say to you.'

Through her mind shot a catalogue of statements she might expect now. Kate, it's over. Kate, it's been wonderful. Kate, Kate, Kate…

'Kate.' He saw her give a ghostly glimmer of a smile and wondered why. 'The miscarriage—'

'Please, don't!' she winced on a whisper.

'I caused it,' he said flatly. 'It was my fault.'

She stared at him with bewildered eyes and put the cup

down before she dropped the scalding remains of her coffee. '*What?*'

'When I made love to you.'

'What are you talking about?'

'Do you think....?' For the first time in his life he was having difficulty forming a sentence. 'Do you think the fact that the...the...sex we had was quite—?'

Her pain made her want to hurt him, too. 'Quite what, Giovanni?'

'Quite forceful? Do you think that was what caused the miscarriage? *I need to know!*'

She stared candidly into his blue eyes, knowing that he was seeking absolution and knowing that she would have given it, had it been within her power. But it was not, and her own guilt overwhelmed her. 'I don't know,' she said honestly, and he buried his face in his hands.

'*Matri di Diu!*' he muttered hoarsely. 'What have I done?'

Part of her wanted to reach out and comfort him, but how could she when she was so badly in need of comfort herself? She closed her eyes wearily and lay back against the pillows.

They stayed there in silence for a little time, and then Giovanni stood up.

'I'll make you breakfast—'

'I don't want any—'

'Oh, yes,' he said grimly, 'you do. Or rather your body does. You will grow no paler than you already are, Kate, and you will eat it if I have to mash it with a fork and feed you like a baby. Is that understood?'

And, whilst the normal Kate might have rebelled against such high-handedness, this frightened and hurting Kate was glad to have him there, making her decisions and helping make her well again.

She ate breakfast, then soaked in the bath that he had run for her, and forced herself to dress—or, rather, she compromised at dressing. A long, silky caftan which Lucy had bought her for her twenty-first birthday, and the familiar light, loose garment was a little like wrapping herself in a security blanket.

When she walked into the sitting room Giovanni was sitting there and he stood up.

'Come and sit down. What can I get you?'

She shook her head. 'Nothing. You don't have to keep fussing over me, Giovanni.'

'I want to.'

She remembered his words to Lucy. He would stay until she recovered—so presumably he wanted her recovered in the shortest time possible.

He noted her silence, her normally mobile face grown inert, as if the life had been sucked out of it. And it had, he thought with a sudden fierce pain. It had. 'I want to take you back to Sicily with me,' he said suddenly.

How she had once longed to hear him say that! In her wildest fantasies she had imagined her clinging onto his arm, Giovanni's girl, the woman he had finally professed love to. 'You can't do that,' she said tiredly.

'Why not? You need to rest. You need the sun to warm your skin.'

She stared at him as though he was crazy. 'What about your family?'

'What about them?'

'What will they think of you bringing an English girl to their home—?'

'I have my own villa,' he interrupted gently, and, when he saw the expression on her face, added, 'with my own live-in housekeeper, so your reputation will not be tarnished.'

'Do they know about the baby?'

He shook his head. 'How can they, when I only found out myself the day before yesterday?'

'And what about Anna? Won't she want to come and find me and tell me exactly what she thinks of me?'

His shoulders tensed, the news which had seemed so important now totally insignificant in the light of what had happened. 'Anna is still in Roma.'

But would his family hate her? See her as the reason why his relationship with Anna had come to an end?

'Kate,' he said, in the gentlest voice she had ever heard him use, 'my family do not interfere. They know that I am a man, and expect me to make my own judgements about my life. They will respect you as my guest.'

'I don't know,' she said weakly.

'Well, I do. I am taking you to Sicily. I will look after you.'

Until she recovered. And then?

But she had no energy left to fight him. Nor any inclination, if the truth was known—and in a way it was rather a relief to let him take over everything. She did not see herself as passive, merely weary—and he seemed to have strength enough for the two of them.

And Kate knew that her willingness to go with him was about more than Giovanni's tenacity. She needed someone to look after her—but Lucy's partner was back—and as he was so often away, how could she ask Lucy?

She certainly couldn't go to her parents without explaining the circumstances, and she wasn't prepared to put them through that kind of hurt and disappointment. And, although the doctors had said she could start working as soon as she felt like it, the fact was that she felt completely empty inside. As though she had been blasted clean of all feelings bar one—that, no matter how useless she knew it to be, her feelings for Giovanni still burned as strong as ever.

'Well?' The blue eyes blazed into her.

'OK,' she nodded, and drifted back into a fitful sleep.

He stood and watched her for a time, until her breathing grew more even and her strained expression had relaxed with the onset of deep sleep. And only then did he lean over her to plant the lightest of kisses on her forehead. Then he moved silently from the room, his face dark with loss and pain.

Giovanni hired a plane the following day. He would not countenance the thought of the noise and bustle of airports, with Kate having to change planes and wait for connections. She was still pale, he noted with a pang—and quieter than he had ever known her.

She forced a smile. 'I'd better pack—'

'No, *I'll* pack some clothes for you,' he said.

'I'm not an invalid,' she protested.

Her wan little face made mockery of her words, and his heart clenched. 'I know that,' he agreed quietly. 'But I intend to look after you, Kate.'

It was ironic that the things she had always wanted to hear him say were now hers for the taking. Until she remembered that he didn't mean them—not long-term, anyway. He was falling into a role which he seemed to suit very well—that of macho protector. But it was only a temporary role, and one which he would relinquish once he was satisfied that she had recovered from her ordeal.

They flew out from the grey of a wintry English day and arrived to the warm, sensual air of a Sicilian spring. Kate hadn't known what to expect, and as the plane came in to land she could see hills awash with green—greener than she could ever have imagined.

He saw the surprise in her eyes. 'It is springtime,' he explained softly as the plane kissed the runway. 'And the very best, most beautiful time of all. You should see it in the summer when it gets diabolically hot, and the land becomes parched and brown and the harsh, unremitting wind they call the sirocco blows all around. Then Sicilians hide themselves indoors and away from the sun as much as they can.'

He had a car waiting, which he drove himself after carefully settling her into the back seat, a light cashmere rug tucked around her knees.

'But—'

'I know. You're not an invalid. Just enjoy it, won't you, Kate?' he added in what came pretty close to a plea—and how could she ever resist that?

The car began to mount the hills outside Palermo, where wild flowers of every imaginable hue studded the green hills. It was as pretty as anything she had ever seen, and Kate felt a great tug of something like longing. The land of his birth, she thought, and bit her trembling lip.

Towards the very top of the hill the car passed through wrought-iron electronic gates which slid silently open and closed behind them, just as silently and a beautiful long, low villa awaited them.

They were greeted at the villa by an elderly woman, dressed in a plain black dress, her face openly curious as she opened the door to them.

'This is Michelina, Kate.' He switched rapidly to Sicilian, and the woman inclined her head at Kate as Giovanni introduced them.

'Michelina has worked for my family in some capacity for many years,' he explained as he showed her along a shady passageway and into a luxurious marble-floored bedroom. Its windows were shuttered against the light of the day, and a large bed covered with an exquisitely embroidered cover loomed large in her vision. She turned to look at him with a silent question in her eyes, knowing that here lay another potentially painful moment of truth.

'This is where you will sleep,' he said abruptly, wondering if she was trying to test his resolve with that dewy-eyed look at him.

He felt the quickening of his heart. Was she trying to break him? To see whether he would repeat his outrageous behaviour of that terrible night when he had made such passionate love to her? Trying to break a man driven solely by his baser instincts, who could not nurture the woman who carried his child within her?

'And you?' she questioned, because she needed to know.

His mouth hardened. 'I will be along the corridor.'

So that was that. Looking after her would not include holding her in the night, and she must force herself to recognise—and to *accept*—that that side of their lives had come to a natural end. Perhaps it was for the best—at least this way she would be able to wean herself off him slowly.

Kate dressed for dinner that evening, wondering if she could bear it, and questioning her own sanity. For how could she possibly make a complete recovery if inside her heart was breaking?

But Michelina's presence meant that outwardly, at least, she was forced to behave as the perfect guest, and it quickly became tolerable for her to actually *feel* that way. She praised the wonderful food—though it was rather ironic that the housekeeper had chosen to present her with *pasta con le sarde* for her first evening.

'It is our national dish,' she told Kate with a smile, in her faltering English.

And Giovanni had glimmered a look across the table at her. 'Kate has heard of it,' he smiled.

'It's delicious,' she said, and it was. She had eaten barely anything of her own attempt at making the dish. She resolutely pushed that particular thought away, since looking back would not help her.

'You have many gastronomic feasts in store for you, Kate,' murmured Giovanni as he poured her a glass of wine. 'Sicilian food comes hotter, spicier and sweeter than the rest of Italy.' He gave a rueful smile. 'For which we must thank our Arab conquerors.'

She was yawning over the coffee Michelina had left them, when Giovanni stood up with an air of determination.

'You need to go to sleep now,' he instructed softly. 'Come with me.'

Outside her door, she wanted him to touch her—not in a sexual way, but in a comforting kind of way, to enfold her in his strong embrace and take some of the aching away, but he kept his distance.

Their physical closeness seemed like a distant dream as he quietly shut the bedroom door behind him, and she heard him moving off down the corridor.

But the sun was shining the next day and he drove her through the mountains to a resort along the Tyrrhenian coast called Cefalú, which he promised her was spectacular, and from the moment she saw the fishing village, squeezed between a long, curving sweep of sand and a massive peak known as the Rocca, Kate fell in love with it.

Giovanni slowed the car down, and pointed to the Rocca. 'What does that resemble?'

It was like one of those games you played with ink-spots, trying to make sense out of a random shape. Except that this shape seemed very clear to Kate.

'It looks like a head?' she guessed.

He laughed in delight. 'Clever girl! That's exactly what the ancient Greeks who came here thought, too. And kephalos is the Greek word for ''head''—hence Cefalú.'

Kate sat back in her seat, pleased at her perception and even more pleased by his smiling praise. At times like this, it was easy to forget her reason for being here—and easy to imagine that they were just like any other couple, enjoying the sights and relaxing in each other's company.

But they weren't, she reminded herself. They weren't.

She turned her head quickly to look out of the window. Too often in the past had she wished for the impossible and now it was time to change the game-plan.

Side by side, they walked down to the Norman cathedral and Giovanni gave her his linen jacket to wear.

'Women must cover their arms in this holy place,' he told her gravely as they stepped inside its cool, dim interior.

She felt as though she was being swept up into Sicily's stormy past as they walked around the majestic building in silence, and she studied her guidebook avidly. She insisted on lighting a candle, but her lips began to tremble as she did so, and her face was very pale when they re-entered the warm spring sunshine.

His eyes were assessing as he looked at her, but now was not the time nor the place for analysis. 'Lunch, I think,' he said firmly.

They found a restaurant whose sheltered terrace overlooked the fishermen's beach, and Giovanni ordered swordfish for them both. And, when the waiter had left them with their water and basket of bread, he turned his gaze intently on her.

'Kate, we have to talk about it,' he said gently.

She wilfully misunderstood him, because surely it was too painful to contemplate the truth. 'The cathedral?'

'The baby.'

She shook her head, and her red hair flailed wildly around her shoulders. 'Who *says* we do? It was nothing, was it? An accident which happened, which mercifully—'

'*No!*' His negation was low, but savage—and his face burned with the intensity of conflicting emotions. 'Don't say that!' he grated. 'Don't you ever say that!'

'But it's the truth, isn't it? And for you it must have been…' she bit the words out painfully '…a relief.'

He shook his head and his words were quiet, almost bleak. 'How could something so negative ever be described in a positive way?'

She swallowed. 'Because we *didn't plan it*!'

'Out of all babies born, how many do you think are planned, Kate?'

Did she imagine the sadness in his voice, or did she simply

want to hear it there, to wish that he had wanted that baby just as much as she had? 'That's different, and you know it!' she responded fiercely. 'You didn't want a baby, Giovanni—so don't for heaven's sake now start saying that you did!'

He pondered her accusation in silence for a moment, knowing that she spoke the truth. 'And for you, Kate? Was it a relief for you, too?'

His gaze was so intense—as blue as the sea beneath them, and she could not insult him, or herself, by pretending that it had been nothing.

'Women feel differently about these things,' she told him haltingly. 'They may not have planned a baby, nor wanted a baby—but, once that baby is there, something primitive takes over—something outside all their control. Something that defies all logic!'

'Tell me,' he prompted softly.

'It's a protective thing, I guess. Nature's way of ensuring the survival of the species. A woman feels proud, and…sort of…*special*, when she knows she's carrying a child.' Especially the child of the man she loved.

'Well, you weren't acting proud and special the night you told me about it,' he observed.

'Oh, for heaven's sake, Giovanni!' She stared at him across the table. 'What did you expect? I anticipated your reaction…' She saw the look of remorse which darkened his features and she knew she could not bear him to feel she was attacking him. 'I *understood* your reaction,' she told him softly. 'The pregnancy came out of the blue. We had made no plans to commit—on the contrary, in fact—and it must have looked like the oldest trick in the book, from your point of view.'

He acknowledged her generosity and her understanding, even though he felt he did not deserve it, and knew then that he owed her nothing less than the truth himself. 'That's exactly what I felt at the time,' he admitted.

'I know. That's human nature,' she murmured. But oddly, now that it was out in the open, his admission had lost something of its sting.

His mouth hardened and he stared angrily down at the boats which bobbed on the water. 'And is it human nature to make love to a woman so violently—?'

'No!' she corrected, so fervently that he turned his head to stare deep into her emerald eyes, seeing forgiveness there. 'Not violently, Giovanni—*passionately*, and yes, there *is* a difference.'

'I shouldn't have done it!' He shook his head as he remembered the fever which had devoured him, a fever more intense than anything he had ever experienced.

'*You* didn't do anything, or, rather, you did—but I did it, too. I wanted you just as much as you wanted me. It felt…' She struggled to put it into words that would not make him feel trapped still, only this time by the strength of her unrequited feelings for him, rather than an unwanted baby. 'It felt primeval,' she said slowly. 'As though it had to happen, as if something had *compelled* it to happen.'

'Snap,' he murmured, and then his face darkened again as reality made its presence known. 'Except that our passion lost us the baby, Kate, didn't it?'

She wanted to take the hurting from him—because when he was hurting she was hurting, too. 'You can't know that!'

'I won't ever know, will I?' he questioned darkly.

But then the waiter arrived with their food and half a bottle of white wine, and as if by an unspoken mutual agreement the subject was suspended while they each tried to lose themselves in the beauty of their surroundings and the taste of the fresh fish.

She was sleepy after lunch, and he insisted on taking her back to the villa.

'Don't you want to sightsee some more?' She yawned.

He smiled. 'You forget—I know the island like I know my own face. These trips are for *you, cara mia.*'

Telling herself that it was merely habit now that made him call her that, she opened her mouth to object. 'But—'

'No buts, Kate. Now you take a siesta,' he ordered.

She couldn't have resisted that tone of voice even if she had wanted to. It seemed deliciously decadent to be going to bed in the middle of the afternoon, but it was not decadent at all, because Giovanni gave her a brief, terse goodbye, and left her at the door of her room once more.

The shutters were drawn and the room was a cool haven, but her heart was heavy as she sank down onto the bed. It wouldn't have killed him to hold her in his arms, surely? To give her the physical comfort and reassurance she badly needed right now.

But no, Giovanni was no hypocrite. He recognised that she was in a weakened state. He would not wish to be cruel to her by raising her hopes, only to dash them again. She must be strong, for the sake of her pride and her sanity.

And then the embrace of sleep claimed her, and she went willingly into its arms.

CHAPTER FOURTEEN

THE midday sun streamed gold into the airy interior of the sitting room, and Giovanni lounged on the sofa as he waited for Kate to finish dressing for lunch. He gave a small groan as he shifted his position. Wanting her never got any easier, he thought. His body seemed to be in a permanent state of arousal.

They had spent the morning in Palermo, and he had taken Kate to the Calverri offices. His secretary had been polite—just—but he could see the naked curiosity in her eyes, wondering what this red-haired Englishwoman meant to her boss.

And now would come her baptism of fire, for within the hour—he glanced at his watch—his parents and his two aunts would be arriving for lunch. They had expressed a wish to meet her, and Kate had reluctantly agreed.

'But why do they want to?' she had asked.

'Kate,' he had replied patiently, 'you've been here for almost two weeks and they're rather curious about you, that's all.'

That's all. She had nodded. 'Oh, I see.'

'And I've never brought a woman to Sicily before.'

Well, of course he hadn't—there had never been any need to. He had had Anna—the fiancée whose name was never mentioned—the fiancée she secretly feared he was gearing up to go back to, which would account for his attitude towards her since they had arrived.

Oh, his behaviour had been impeccable—almost *too* impeccable. How aloof he had sometimes seemed as he had kept a courteous but definite distance.

Or maybe the miscarriage had killed all his desire for her.

Why else would he have gone so far out of his way to avoid any kind of physical contact with her?

'I bet your parents won't like me,' she moaned.

'Rubbish! Of course they will.'

But to Kate his voice sounded forced.

'And how will I speak to them? I only know about fifty words in Sicilian!'

'That's because I have taught you a new word every day,' he murmured. 'It seems we must increase your lessons, *cara*.'

Please don't flirt with me, her eyes told him silently.

He acknowledged the reproach with a narrowing of his eyes. 'And, besides, they speak perfectly good English—all my family do.'

'OK,' she had sighed. 'You win!'

But there was no taste of victory in his mouth, and he still had something he needed to tell her.

He looked up as she walked into the room, her bright hair newly washed and gleaming, a soft-green dress he had never seen before making the most of her tall, slim figure and those heart-stopping legs. Her skin was glowing with a light tan and the good food had filled out her hollow cheeks a little. She looked good enough to eat and, God, how he wanted her!

He couldn't seem to tear his eyes away from her, which wasn't doing his heart-rate any good whatsoever. 'You look...*spectacular, cara*,' he said carefully.

Well, make the most of it, she thought, hoping that her eyes held no trace of her unhappiness. Because soon she would be gone from here and gone from Giovanni's life for good.

'Thank you,' she said calmly.

'Come and sit down.' He patted the space beside him, then wished he hadn't, as she perched beside him, sliding her knees decorously together. 'Can I get you anything?'

She shook her head. 'No, I'm fine.' Which she supposed

she was. Well, physically, at any rate. The rest and the recuperation had made her feel whole again. The warm sunshine and the good food had worked their simple magic, as had the island itself, which Giovanni had shown her with the loving pride of the true Sicilian.

It had been all too easy to suspend disbelief. To imagine that this could go on and on—her and Giovanni, a happy couple, to all intents and purposes.

Because once she had resigned herself to the fact that he didn't want to share her bed any more it had—perversely—allowed her to relax. Sex had always dominated their time together, and it had only been here that true companionship had entered the arena.

That didn't stop her wanting him, of course—she doubted whether anything could ever put a stop to that, but at least the absence of him in her bed was preparing her for a life without him when she returned to England.

'What time are your family getting here?'

'In about an hour.' He paused. 'Kate, there's something I need to tell you before they arrive.'

She looked up quickly, something in his voice warning her that he wasn't about to start discussing what was on the lunch menu. 'Oh?'

'It's about Anna.'

Her heart deafened her with a sickening thunder. 'I rather thought it might be.'

He stared at her. Was she reading his mind now? 'You did?'

Say it first, she urged herself. That way you emerge with your pride and your dignity intact. Force yourself to congratulate him and then he might remember you with at least a modicum of respect.

'You're getting back with her,' she stated dully.

'*What?*'

'She's going to marry and become Mrs Calverri...'

There was a moment of stunned silence, and then he laughed. 'Yes. Yes, she is.'

How bloody insensitive could a man be? The smile she had intended feeling more like a grimace, she said stiffly, 'I hope you'll both be very happy.'

The laughter stopped. 'Do you, Kate?' he asked softly. 'Do you really?'

She was fast discovering that she wasn't *that* good a liar. She shifted right up to the other end of the sofa and glared at him. 'What do *you* think?' she demanded. 'Do you think I have no feelings?'

'You keep your feelings very well-hidden,' he commented.

'That's pretty rich—coming from you!'

'I am a Sicilian,' he drawled arrogantly. 'What's your excuse?'

'Well, you must be a grandmaster at concealment—if you've been playing the perfect host to me, whilst all the while...all the while...you...you...' Her words petered out; they had to—much more of this and she would be bursting into howling sobs of hurt.

'Kate—'

She shook her head. 'Perhaps I deserve it! After all, it's no worse than what I did to her—'

'No, what *I* did to her,' he corrected fiercely. 'It was my relationship and my responsibility. You were right, you know, Kate—you knew nothing of her existence. I should not have blamed you for my own weakness.'

There it was again, that hateful word. *Weakness*. Well, she would show him just how strong she could be! Fighting on every reserve she possessed, she pulled herself together with a steadying breath. 'I don't know if I can face having lunch with your parents—won't they see this as a conflict of interests? And what about Anna? Won't she be furious?'

'I doubt it,' he said slowly.

She stared at him in disbelief. 'What, her future in-laws fraternising with your secret lover?'

He frowned over the phrase and then his mouth twisted contemptuously. 'Never describe yourself like that again!'

'Well, I am, aren't I?'

This had gone far enough. He wanted to reach out and take her hand, but her arms were crossed so firmly across her chest that he didn't even try. 'Kate, Anna is getting married to my brother.'

She froze. Stared at him, wild hope being squashed by all-consuming insecurity. 'Say that again.'

'Anna is getting married to my brother.'

'Your *brother*?'

He heard the incredulity in her voice and understood perfectly—because his own reaction had been very similar. 'He's been working in Roma. Remember, I told you? Anna met him there, and…' He shrugged, a rueful smile playing about his lips. 'It now emerges that Guido is the man for her, that she is happier with Guido than she has ever been in her whole life,' he finished drily.

Wild hope—which had briefly triumphed—now lost out to insecurity. Just because he wasn't getting back with Anna didn't mean he wanted *her*, did it? You had only to look at his behaviour to know that he didn't.

'When did you find out?' she asked quietly.

His gaze was very steady. 'The night I arrived in London, the night…' His words tailed off. He had been feeling like a man free of chains that night. Anna's new-found happiness had given him a heady sense of freedom that he had been longing to convey to Kate. And new and very different chains had locked themselves around his heart.

'And was your pride wounded?' she asked flippantly, because a flip remark seemed the only way that she could push the memory of that night away.

He raised his eyebrows at her defiant pout, and the ache

intensified. He contemplated punishing her with a hard, sweet kiss, but at that moment there was a loud ringing at the front door.

'Saved by the bell,' he murmured resignedly.

Kate stood up hastily, smoothing down imaginary creases in her dress with hands which were suddenly clammy and she didn't know if that was a reaction to what he had just told her or apprehension about meeting a group of people she was still convinced would dislike her.

But in that she was wrong. True, his mother scrutinised her intently when they first shook hands, as did his two aunts. His father took one look at her and murmured something softly in Sicilian to his son, who gave a small smile in response.

Kate was seated between Giovanni's father, and his father's sister—an absolute delight of a woman named Maria. Giovanni had told her that she was his favourite aunt and she had a very dry sense of humour. And a way of asking questions which really made you want to answer them, though some questions were just too difficult to answer…

They ate *pasta alla Norma*—eastern Sicily's favourite pasta and supposedly named after Bellini's opera, or so Giovanni told her, pouring some wine for his aunt with a smile which nearly broke Kate's heart.

'And I believe that you know Lady St John?' asked Giovanni's mother.

Swallowing a mouthful of water nervously, Kate nodded. 'That's right. I decorated her house for her—and her London flat last year.'

Mrs Calverri nodded. 'She speaks very highly of you,' she said.

So Giovanni's mother had been talking to Lady St John, had she? Why on earth would she do that? Kate wondered. 'She told me that she'd met you when she was travelling around Europe,' she ventured.

'Indeed. Her father was at the embassy in Rome and my uncle was on the local staff there.' Mrs Calverri gave a smile that bordered on the wistful. 'Such a summer we girls had!'

Mr Calverri muttered something in Sicilian and his wife batted her eyelashes at him. 'Don't be jealous, *caro*. It was a long time ago!'

They ate cannoli for dessert—pastry tubes filled with fresh ricotta, bits of chocolate and candied fruit—and Michelina had left them with their coffee, when Giovanni's aunt Maria turned to her nephew.

'Will you show me your beautiful garden, Giovanni? It is so long since I have seen it.'

Kate looked nervously at Giovanni.

'Put some music on for Mama and Papa,' he said softly, and another pang of guilt hit him, hard, as he noted the anxiety which clouded her green eyes. What had he ever done for Kate, other than bring her unhappiness and loss? he asked himself in despair.

His aunt slipped her arm through his and they wandered outside, where the pale sunshine was warm on their skin.

The garden of the villa was beautiful and the pride of an old man who tended to it every day except Sunday and who had known Giovanni since he had been a baby.

Blue-green cypress trees pointed elegant spires skywards and lush, fleshy shrubs contrasted with the bright blooms of the semi-tropical flowers which spilled in such abundance on the edges of a perfect green lawn.

And in February the lawn was strewn with the white petals from the almond tree. 'Like confetti,' Giovanni had told Kate, and she had turned away from him, and he had guessed that the memory of her baby was still with her. And always would be with her, he thought now, his heart heavy.

Aunt Maria bent and fussed over the flowers, and pointed at the trees, and when they had reached the far end of the garden she stopped and spoke to him in Sicilian.

'Something is wrong, I think, Giovanni?'

His eyes narrowed. 'Wrong?'

'Something is troubling you,' said Aunt Maria perceptively. 'I can tell.'

His aunt was a wise and insightful woman, he thought, but he said nothing.

'Something which is threatening your happiness,' mused Aunt Maria, and she stooped to remove a dead flower.

'Happiness is too precarious not to be continually threatened,' he said quietly.

Aunt Maria straightened up, faded blue eyes, which must have once been just like his, narrowing as they regarded him.

'You and Anna were never right for one another, you know,' she said firmly. 'You are far too much your own man to be constrained by tradition. I told your father so. If you send a man to America at such a tender age, I said, you must be prepared for him to break against convention when he comes back.'

'I loved Anna,' he said, and his voice broke into a sigh. 'I never wanted to hurt her.'

'Of course you loved her!' declared his aunt passionately. 'But there is love, and there is love. Sometimes I thought you seemed more like brother and sister.' She regarded him thoughtfully. 'And a man like you needs real love; passionate love.'

'Oh, Zia Maria,' he said in a tone which was half-mocking.

The look she threw him back was equally mocking. 'You think that because I am of the older generation, that because I am old, I cannot understand passion?'

He shook his head, vigorously. '*Never!*' he declared fervently. 'Passion has no sell-by date.'

His aunt's eyes narrowed, and then she nodded thoughtfully. 'Sicilians are by nature and necessity the most secretive of people. Our culture and our history has always required our silence.'

'But not you?' queried Giovanni wryly. 'You're not like that?'

She laughed. 'No, you are right—I am not like that! My mother used to despair of my loose tongue!' She paused for a moment before she spoke. 'I think that your Kate means a very great deal to you?'

For a moment he didn't speak; he was not a man who unburdened his soul, nor one who bared his thoughts for others. And yet the weight of his guilt was an intolerably heavy one. He gave a heavy sigh.

'I think that, whatever my feelings for Kate, it may be too late for us now.'

Aunt Maria frowned. 'Too late? How can it be too late? Why is she here with you if it is, as you say, too late?'

A torrent of emotion seemed to well up like a tide inside him and his mouth twisted with pain.

'Tell me, Giovanni,' prompted his aunt softly. 'Tell me.'

There was a long, painful pause. 'She was having my baby!' he burst out at last. 'My *baby*, Zia Maria.'

Aunt Maria went very still. '*Was?*' she questioned quietly.

He nodded. 'I had only just found out. She told me, and I was…' His words tailed off.

'What were you, Giovanni?' she prompted quietly.

'I was so *angry*!' he bit out. 'Angry with her, and with myself—we had not planned a baby, you see!'

'That *is* the way these things sometimes go.' She smiled gently, but then her face grew serious. 'What happened?'

Could he bring himself to tell his aunt? To confess to his sin? 'I made love to her,' he said, in a cold, empty kind of voice. 'And within the hour she…she lost the baby.'

'And you blame yourself—is that it?'

'*Jesu*, Maria! Of course I blame myself!' he exploded. 'If I hadn't done that then she would still be pregnant!'

Aunt Maria shook her head. 'Oh, Giovanni, don't be ridiculous!' Her face was very candid as she laid a hand gently on his arm. 'Giovanni, think about this logically. Do you imagine that once a woman is pregnant, she and her partner never make love again until the baby arrives?'

'Of course not!'

'Well, then…what happened happened, and no one is to blame. It could well be,' she hesitated, 'that she would have lost the baby anyway. It would have occurred whether you made love to her or not. Sex does not cause miscarriages.'

'I've made her so unhappy!' he declared hotly.

'And yourself, by the look of you,' observed his aunt. 'The question you must ask yourself is whether you are going to let this ruin what you have between the two of you.'

And what *did* they have between them? He didn't know. He had never got around to asking her. Or telling her. He had been locked into a part-time relationship which was full of passion, but low on commitment. He had imagined that things would continue in their sweet, blissful way—but nothing ever remained the same, he realised now. Especially feelings. His own had changed somewhere along the way, but had hers?

'You must talk to her!' declared his aunt urgently. 'You must!'

'I know I must,' he echoed quietly.

The following morning he drove her into central Sicily, and Kate tried very hard to concentrate on the scenery and not the count-down happening inside her head as the hours before going home slowly ticked away. Tomorrow she would be on a flight back to England—her stay with Giovanni nothing but a bitter-sweet memory.

She had spent nights aching with the anticipation of how this moment might feel. She had imagined pain—a harsh, intense pain—but in that she had been wrong, because she felt numb. As if nothing could touch her. Please let me stay this way, she prayed, let me be strong when we say our goodbyes.

At least the scenery was spectacular enough to take her breath away as they drove up through the narrow, tortuous bends of the mountain roads. She saw forbidding rows of terracotta-roofed villages which seemed to hang in the air, and she shivered.

'They were built up there to keep out invaders from long ago,' mused Giovanni as he shot a glance at her frozen profile.

Kate thought that their very isolation and aloofness must be successful at discouraging modern-day tourists, too.

'Where are we going?' she asked.

'To Lake di Pergusa,' he said, and paused. 'The very spot where Persephone was abducted, all those years ago.'

Memories of the famous Sicilian myth came drifting back to her as he skirted the lake which was, rather disappointingly, skirted by a motor speedway. And the lake itself was noisy with waterskiers and motorboats.

He switched off the ignition, and they sat there for a moment or two in silence, while Kate's heart thudded with dread.

'So what do you think of my island, Kate?' he asked softly, wishing that she would look at him instead of presenting him with that unfathomable profile.

She tried hard not to imagine what this would be like if it was the beginning and not the end, but it took some doing. Resolutely, she kept her eyes fixed on the lake and tried to think what the old Kate would have said.

'Well, the circumstances of how I came to be here wouldn't have been my first choice,' she managed drily.

He recognised just what it must have cost her to say that, and his heart turned over. 'And are you recovered now?' he murmured. 'At least a little?'

Until she recovers. Like a bad dream, the words came back

to haunt her, but her heartbreak was her burden to carry, not his.

She nodded. 'More than a little. You see—I barely had time to realise I was pregnant, before…' Her voice wobbled, and she took a deep breath before she spoke again. 'Maybe that helped a bit.'

He felt the knife-twist of bitter regret. 'I wish I could undo the past, Kate.'

She turned to him then and her green eyes were huge in her face. Her words came out on a tremble. 'What, all of it?' Was he saying that he wished he had never met her, was that it?

He shook his head. Had she misunderstood him so badly, or had his actions caused her to do so? 'The bad bits—the times when I was angry, when I spoke so harshly to you.' His eyes imprisoned hers with their blue fire.

Something akin to hope flared in her heart, and, no matter how hard she tried to quash it, it stubbornly refused to die. 'And the good bits?' she asked tremulously. 'What of those?'

He had spent a lifetime keeping his feelings hidden, locked away inside his secret Sicilian nature, but suddenly he found himself wanting to tell her—*needing* to tell her. 'I would relive them over and over and over again,' he said softly. 'The very first time I saw you, what I felt for you—'

'Lust,' she forced herself to say, and bit her lip.

He saw the uncertainty on her face and shook his head. 'Passion,' he corrected gently. 'Not lust, *cara*, but passion. Something which had never entered my life before I met you.'

'Not even with Anna?' The words were out before she could stop them.

'Not even with Anna.' He sighed, knowing that he owed her everything, but the most important thing of all was the truth. Even if she did not want him, he owed her that.

'Anna and I had all the right ingredients for a relationship.

We had mutual liking and respect, and we both wanted a perfect marriage, I guess.' He shrugged. 'But life doesn't always conform to the ideals you set yourself. The moment I met you, my subconscious must have been telling me that there are emotions which go beyond reason, beyond understanding, even.'

Her heart began to thud. 'And what emotions are they?' she questioned painfully.

There was a long pause, and his blue eyes were luminous as he looked at her. 'Why, love, of course, *cara mia*. Just love.'

Just love? *Just* love? She stared at him, her heart not daring to believe the words he had just said to her.

'I love you, Kate. *Ti vogghiu beni*. I want you and I need you…by my side, and in my heart. Forever.'

'Oh, Giovanni.' Words she had longed for, prayed for. Tears began to slide down her cheeks. 'Giovanni,' she said brokenly.

'Don't cry, *cara mia*,' he beseeched. 'Why are you crying?'

'Because…' She thought of his honesty and at last allowed her own true feelings to come flooding out, like a river which had burst its banks. 'Because I thought you didn't want me any more—'

'Not *want* you?' he demanded incredulously. 'Not *want* you?'

'You haven't come near me since…'

'Since the baby?' he prompted painfully, his mouth twisting. 'You want to know why? Because I blamed myself! If I hadn't made love to you—'

'But it could have happened anyway!' she told him fiercely.

'I know that. Now.'

Tenderly he wiped the tears from her cheek and she looked up into his face. 'You d-do?'

He nodded. 'My aunt Maria helped me see things in perspective.'

'You told her?' asked Kate in surprise.

His eyes narrowed. 'You don't mind?'

How could she mind about something that had absolved his guilt? It was just the thought of her aloof Giovanni confiding in something as personal as that to his aunt!

He saw her look of confusion.

'Aunt Maria realised that I was hurting,' he told her. 'And she also realised that what you and I had between us was strong—much too strong to be broken. She made me realise that some things happen just because they are meant to. That men have been making love to pregnant women since time began—and there was no earthly reason why we shouldn't have done the same.'

'I shouldn't have let you shoulder the burden of guilt,' she told him falteringly. 'But I was hurting too much to be able to reach out and help you—and you seemed so proud and remote. You wouldn't come near me afterwards—you wouldn't even touch me.'

'I thought that you would push me away,' he admitted. 'As well as feeling I didn't deserve to touch you.'

Kate shook her head wonderingly. 'And I thought that you just didn't want my help. Or my body.'

He gave her a searingly honest look of total capitulation. 'I want everything you're prepared to give me,' he said simply.

'Then you'd better have my love, Giovanni—because it's yours.' Her voice trembled with emotion. 'Only yours.'

He was filled with the urgent need to kiss her, but he wanted to vanquish all the remaining shadows that lingered between them.

'Does it still hurt?' he asked in a low voice. 'About the baby?'

She nodded. The truth was painful, yes, but out of pain

grew healing, and a new kind of maturity. 'A little. But it gets easier day by day.'

'I want to give you more babies,' he whispered. 'As many as you want. And I want to marry you. *Mi vo spusari, cara?*'

She didn't need to speak fluent Sicilian to understand what he had just said. '*Sí, caro. Sí.*' Her eyes grew misty as she gently ran her fingertips lovingly around the hard, proud line of his jaw, just as she had been longing to for days and days.

'Now kiss me, please,' she said shakily, and he took her in his arms and held her for a long, restoring moment and then did exactly that.

EPILOGUE

THE lusty cries had abated at last, and Kate slanted Giovanni a rueful smile as she sank down onto the sofa next to him.

'He has lungs, our baby!' she murmured.

'He will sing opera one day,' predicted Giovanni with the kind of expansive pride he always used when talking about his son.

'I thought he was going into parliament?' teased Kate.

'Maybe.' He reached his arm out and pulled her close to him, absently and tenderly kissing the top of her head. 'Shall I make dinner now?' he murmured.

'Oh, if only your mother could hear you say that!' she giggled. 'She once told me that you had never set foot inside the kitchen in your life!'

'Ah, but that was before I married my independent Kate who taught me everything I know. Well, *nearly* everything!' His blue eyes glittered as he planted another kiss on top of her fragrant red hair.

'Two years ago tomorrow we've been married,' she said wonderingly. 'Can you believe it?'

Two years? They might as well have been two minutes, they had swept by with such sweet, glorious abandon. A wife, and now a son. Giovanni closed his eyes. Contentment and passion—an unbeatable combination, and one which seemed just as easy as breathing, such was his life with Kate.

Their time together had not been completely without some tensions—but then life was never like that. During the early stages of her pregnancy, he had treated her as he would have a delicate piece of porcelain, and Kate had not objected, not once. As each week had passed, they had breathed sighs of relief that the baby was growing safely, and as her body had burgeoned with the new life, so had their love for each other. Deeper and deeper, so that some mornings she had felt she really ought to pinch herself.

The wedding had been in London and afterwards there had been a big post-wedding party in Sicily for all Giovanni's family and friends. Kate had met Anna for the first time, then already pregnant by Guido. She and Giovanni's brother had been married the previous summer, and their happiness was evident for all to see.

Anna had sought Kate out in what had proved initially to be a rather nervous meeting on both sides, but all bitterness had been forgotten when her new sister-in-law had admired Kate's wedding band.

'It's very beautiful,' she had said. 'I understand that Giovanni designed it?'

'Yes.' Kate's smile had faltered, knowing that she must say something about the past. 'Anna, listen, I'm sorry—'

'No!' The dark-haired beauty had shaken her smooth head firmly. 'It is all in the past and the only memories I have of Giovanni are good ones. I am happier now than I could have ever been with him; I realise that now. Guido,' she had added, with a slow, luminous smile, 'he is the right man for me—and I am the right woman for him.'

Guido and Anna were installed in their home in the hills outside Palermo, Guido having taken over the running of the factory, whilst Giovanni now masterminded the international side of the business from his brand-new offices in central London.

He and Kate had decided not to settle in Sicily—the dramatic change in culture would not have suited his wife, he had decided. Nor him. His aunt had been right—his trip to America had made him truly cosmopolitan—although in his heart he would always be a Sicilian.

Instead, he and Kate would spend as many holidays as

possible in his homeland, and especially in springtime, which held such tender memories for them both.

'Kate?'

She turned her head up to look at him lazily, basking as always in the glow of love from his eyes. 'Mmm?'

'Do you want your anniversary present now?'

'Shouldn't I wait?'

'Have one today, and something else tomorrow,' he said, smiling as he remembered the glittering diamond cross which lay in a small box in his sock drawer. 'Look over there.'

She followed the direction of his gaze to a low table that stood in the window of their airy town-house and saw a small box standing next to the fruit bowl. Why hadn't she noticed it before?

She walked over and picked it up, and turned to face him, a soft smile curving her lips. 'You buy me too many presents,' she protested, but only halfheartedly.

He shook his head, admiring the way her silk skirt clung to the slim swell of her bottom. His beautiful Kate! 'Never enough,' he murmured indulgently.

She flipped the box open, and inside was a ring—a circlet of bright, glittering diamonds—and she stared at him. 'Oh, darling,' she whispered. 'It's exquisite.'

'Come over here,' he instructed throatily. 'And let me put it on.'

She walked towards him, almost dazzled by the blaze of love from his eyes, perching next to him on the sofa, aware of the warm male scent of him, and of how much she wanted him. Always wanted him.

He slipped the ring onto her finger above the plain wedding band she wore and it fitted perfectly, as she had known it would.

There had been no engagement ring—they had both quietly decided that to have one would be disrespectful to Anna.

'It's an eternity ring,' he told her softly. 'It means that you are mine for all eternity, *cara*—as I am yours.'

She sighed with pleasure. 'Oh, Giovanni, you say the most beautiful things—promise me you'll never stop saying them!'

'Never!' He smiled as he watched her hold her hand up to the light and the ring threw off rainbow rays. 'The first time I saw you I wanted to see you in diamonds,' he admitted.

It was like a fairy story she could never hear too often. 'What else?' she questioned throatily.

'I wondered if you wore silk next to your skin.' His voice was husky now and his eyes alight with promise as they lazily scanned her body with proprietorial air. 'And now I know that you do.'

'Mmm.' The promise in his eyes was reflected in her own. 'And do you know what I thought the first time I saw you?'

He loved this game. 'What?'

She gave him a smile which was pure provocation. 'How much I'd like you to undress me.'

His eyes glittered. 'Did you?'

'Mmm.'

'Then I think I'd better fulfil your every wish, don't you, *cara*?' he murmured, and pulled her into his arms.

IN THE SPANIARD'S BED

by

Helen Bianchin

Helen Bianchin was born in New Zealand and travelled to Australia before marrying her Italian-born husband. After three years they moved, returned to New Zealand with their daughter, had two sons, then resettled in Australia. Encouraged by friends to recount anecdotes of her years as a tobacco sharefarmer's wife living in an Italian community, Helen began setting words on paper and her first novel was published in 1975. An animal lover, she says her terrier and Persian cat regard her study as much theirs as hers.

Don't miss Helen Bianchin's exciting new novel *The Marriage Possession* out in April 2007 from Mills & Boon Modern Romance™

CHAPTER ONE

'I'M ON my way.' Cassandra released the intercom, caught up her evening purse, keys, exited her apartment and took the lift down to the foyer where her brother was waiting.

At twenty-nine he was two years her senior, and he shared her blond hair, fair skin and blue eyes. Average height in comparison to her petite frame.

'Wow,' Cameron complimented with genuine admiration, and she responded with an affectionate smile.

'Brotherly love, huh?'

The ice-pink gown moulded her slender curves, its spaghetti straps showing silky skin to an advantage, and the diagonal ruffled split to mid-thigh showcased beautifully proportioned legs. A gossamer wrap in matching ice-pink completed the outfit, and her jewellery was understated.

'Seriously cool.'

She tilted her head to one side as she tucked a hand through his arm. 'Let's go slay the masses.'

Tonight's fundraiser was a prestigious event whose guests numbered among Sydney's social élite. Held in the ballroom of a prominent city hotel, it was one of several annual soirées Cassandra and her brother attended on their father's behalf after a heart attack and stroke two years ago forced him into early retirement.

Guests were mingling in the large foyer when they arrived, and she summoned a practised smile as she acknowledged a few acquaintances, pausing to exchange a greeting with one friend or another as she selected iced water from a hovering drinks waiter.

Observing the social niceties was something she did well. Private schooling and a finishing year in France had added polish and panache. The Preston-Villers family held a certain social standing of which her father was justly proud.

While Cameron had been groomed to enter the Preston-Villers conglomerate from an early age, Cassandra chose to pursue gemmology and jewellery design, added the necessary degree, studied with a well-known jeweller and she was now beginning to gain a reputation for her work.

Mixing and mingling was part of the social game, and she did it well.

Committee members conferred and worked the room in a bid to ensure the evening's success. The hotel ballroom was geared to seat a thousand guests, and it was rumoured there had been a waiting list for last-minute ticket cancellations.

'There's something I need to discuss with you.'

Cassandra met Cameron's gaze, examined his expression, and restrained a faint frown as she glimpsed the slight edginess apparent.

'Here, now?' she queried lightly, and waited for his usual carefree smile.

'Later.'

It couldn't be anything serious, she dismissed, otherwise he would have mentioned it during the drive in to the city.

'Darling, how are you?'

The soft feminine purr evoked a warm smile as she turned to greet the tall, slender model. 'Siobhan.' Her eyes sparkled. They'd attended the same school, shared much, and were firm friends. 'I'm fine, and you?'

'Flying out to Rome tomorrow, then it's Milan followed by Paris.'

Cassandra uttered a subdued chuckle in amusement. 'It's a hard life.'

Siobhan grinned. 'But an interesting one,' she conceded. 'I have a date with an Italian count in Rome.'

'Ah.'

'Old money, and *divine.*'

The musing twinkle in those gorgeous green eyes brought forth a husky laugh as Cassandra shook her head. 'You're wicked.'

'This time it's serious,' Siobhan declared as Cassandra's smile widened.

'It always is.'

'Got to go. The parents are in tow.'

'Have fun.'

'I shall. In Italy.' She leaned forward and pressed her cheek against Cassandra's in a gesture of affection.

'Take care.'

'Always.'

Soon the ballroom doors would be open, and guests would be called to take their seats. There would be the introductory and explanatory speeches, the wine stewards would do their thing, and the first course served.

Speaking of which, she was hungry. Lunch had been yoghurt and fruit snatched between the usual weekend chores.

Cameron appeared deep in conversation with a man she presumed to be a business associate, and she sipped chilled water from her glass as she debated whether to join him.

At that moment she felt the warning prickle of awareness as her senses went on alert, and she let her gaze skim the guests.

There was only one man who had this particular effect on her equilibrium.

Innate instinct? An elusive knowledge based on the inexplicable?

Whatever, it was crazy. Maddening.

Maybe this time she had it wrong. Although all it took was one glance at that familiar dark head to determine her instinct was right on target.

Diego del Santo. Successful entrepreneur, one of the city's nouveau riche…and her personal nemesis.

Born in New York of Spanish immigrant parents, it was reported he'd lived in the wrong part of town, fought for survival in the streets, and made his money early, so it was rumoured, by means beyond legitimate boundaries of the law.

He took risks, it was said, no sensible man would touch. Yet those risks had paid off a million-fold several times over. Literally.

In idle fascination she watched as he turned towards her, then he murmured something to his companion and slowly closed the distance between them.

'Cassandra.'

The voice was low, impossibly deep with the barest trace of an accent, and possessed of the power to send tiny shivers feathering the length of her spine.

Tall, broad-framed, with the sculptured facial features of his Spanish ancestors. Dark, well-groomed hair, dark, almost black eyes, and a mouth that promised a thousand delights.

A mouth that had briefly tasted her own when she'd disobeyed her father and persuaded Cameron to take her to a party. Sixteen years old, emerging hormones, a sense of the forbidden combined with a desire to play grown-up had proved a volatile mix. Add her brother with his own agenda, a few sips too many of wine, a young man who seemed intent on leading her astray, and she could easily have been in over her head. Except Diego del Santo had materialised out of nowhere, intervened, read her the Riot Act, then proceeded to show her precisely what she should be wary of when she heedlessly chose to flirt. Within minutes he had summoned Cameron and she found herself bundled into her brother's car and driven home.

Eleven years had passed since that fateful episode, ten of which Diego had spent in his native New York creating his fortune.

Yet she possessed a vivid recollection of how it felt to have his mouth savour her own. The electric primitiveness of his touch, almost as if he had reached down to her soul and staked a claim.

Diego del Santo had projected a raw quality that meshed leashed savagery with blatant sensuality. A dangerously compelling mix, and one that attracted females from fifteen to fifty.

Now there were no rough edges, and he bore the mantle of power with the same incredible ease he wore his designer clothes.

In his mid-to-late thirties, Diego del Santo was a seriously rich man whose property investments and developments formed a financial portfolio that edged him close to billionaire status.

As such, his return to Australia a year ago had soon seen him become an A-list member of Sydney's social élite, receiving invitations to each and every soirée of note. His acceptance was selective, and his donations to worthy charities, legend.

Preston-Villers' involvement with similar charity events and her father's declining health meant they were frequently fellow guests at one function or another. It was something she accepted, and dealt with by presenting a polite façade.

Only she knew the effect he had on her. The way her pulse jumped and thudded to a rapid beat. No one could possibly be aware her stomach curled into a painful knot at the mere sight of him, or how one glance at his sensual mouth heated the blood in her veins in a vivid reminder of the way it felt to have that mouth possess her own.

The slow sweep of his tongue, the promise of passion, the gentle, coaxing quality that caught her tentative response and took it to an undreamt-of dimension.

Eleven years. Yet his kiss was hauntingly vivid…a taunting example by which she'd unconsciously measured each kiss that followed it. None matched up, no matter how hard she tried to convince herself imagination had merely enhanced the memory.

There were occasions when she thought she should dispense with her own curiosity and accept one of his many invitations. Yet each time something held her back, an innate knowledge such a step would put her way out of her depth.

His invitations and her refusals had become something akin to a polite game they each played. What would he do, she mused, if she surprised him by accepting?

Are you *insane?* a tiny voice queried insidiously.

'Diego,' Cassandra acknowledged coolly, meeting his compelling gaze with equanimity, watching as he inclined his head to her brother.

'Cameron.'

For a millisecond she thought she glimpsed some unspoken signal pass between the men, then she dismissed it as fanciful.

'A successful evening, wouldn't you agree?'

Tonight's event was a charity fundraiser aiding state-of-the-art equipment for a special wing of the city's children's hospital.

Without doubt there were a number of guests with a genuine interest in the nominated charity. However, the majority viewed the evening as a glitz-and-glamour function at which the women would attempt to outdo each other with designer gowns and expensive jewellery, whilst the men wheeled and dealed beneath the guise of socialising.

Diego del Santo didn't fit easily into any recognisable category.

Not that she had any interest in pigeon-holing him. In fact, she did her best to pretend he didn't exist. Something he seemed intent on proving otherwise.

He could have any woman he wanted. And probably did. His photo graced the social pages of numerous newspapers and magazines, inevitably with a stunning female glued to his side.

There was a primitive quality evident. A hint of something dangerous beneath the surface should anyone dare to consider scratching it.

A man who commanded respect and admiration in the boardroom. Possessed of the skill, so it was whispered, and the passion to drive a woman wild in the bedroom.

It was a dramatic mesh of elemental ruthlessness and latent sensuality. Lethal.

Some women would excel at the challenge of taming him, enjoying the ride for however long it lasted. But she wasn't one of them. Only a fool ventured into the devil's playground with the hope they wouldn't get burnt.

Eluding Diego was a game she became adept at playing. If they happened to meet, she offered a polite smile, acknowledged his presence, then moved on.

Yet their social schedule was such, those occasions were many. If she didn't know better, she could almost swear he was intent on playing a game of his own.

'If you'll excuse me,' Cassandra ventured. 'There's someone I should catch up with.' A time-worn phrase, trite but true, for there were always a few friends she could greet by way of escape.

Cameron wanted to protest, she could tell, although Diego del Santo merely inclined his head.

Which didn't help at all, for she could *feel* those dark eyes watching her as she moved away.

Sensation feathered the length of her spine, and something tugged deep inside in a vivid reminder of the effect he had on her composure.

Get over it, she chided silently as she deliberately sought a cluster of friends and blended seamlessly into their conversation.

Any time soon the doors into the ballroom would open and guests would be encouraged to take their seats at designated tables. Then she could rejoin Cameron, and prepare to enjoy the evening.

'You had no need to disappear,' Cameron chastised as she moved to his side.

'Diego del Santo might be serious eye candy, but he's not my type.'

'No?'

'No.' She managed a smile, held it, and began threading her way towards their table.

'Do you know who else is joining us?' Cassandra queried lightly as she slid into one of four remaining seats, and took time to greet the six guests already seated.

'Here they are now.'

She registered Cameron's voice, glanced up from the table...and froze.

Diego del Santo and the socialite and model, Alicia Vandernoot.

No. The silent scream seemed to echo inside her head.

It was bad enough having to acknowledge his presence and converse for a few minutes. To have to share a table with him for the space of an evening was way too much!

Had Cameron organised this? She wanted to rail against him and demand *Why?* Except there wasn't the opportunity to do so without drawing unwanted attention.

If Diego chose the chair next to hers, she'd scream!

Of course he did. It was one of the correct dictums of society when it came to seating arrangements. Although she had little doubt he enjoyed the irony.

Cassandra murmured a polite greeting, and her faint smile was a mere facsimile.

This close she was far too aware of him, the clean smell of freshly laundered clothes, the subtle aroma of his exclusive cologne.

Yet it was the man himself, his potent masculinity and the sheer primitive force he exuded that played havoc with her senses.

A few hours, she consoled herself silently. All she had to do was sip wine, eat the obligatory three courses set in front of her, and make polite conversation. She could manage that, surely?

Not so easy, Cassandra acknowledged as she displayed intent interest in the charity chairperson's introduction prior to revealing funding endeavours, results and expectations.

Every nerve in her body was acutely attuned to Diego del Santo, supremely conscious of each move he made.

'More water?'

He had topped up Alicia's goblet, and now offered to refill her own.

'No, thank you.' Her goblet was part-empty, but she'd be damned if she'd allow him to tend to her.

Did he sense her reaction? Probably. He was too astute not to realise her excruciating politeness indicated she didn't want anything to do with him.

Uniformed waiters delivered starters with practised efficiency, and she forked the artistically arranged food without appetite.

'The seafood isn't to your satisfaction?'

His voice was an accented drawl tinged with amusement, and she met his dark gaze with equanimity, almost inclined to offer a negation just to see what he'd do, aware he'd probably summon the waiter and insist on a replacement.

'Yes.'

The single affirmative surprised her, and she deliberately widened her eyes. 'You read minds?'

The edge of his mouth curved, and there was a humorous gleam apparent. 'It's one of my talents.'

Cassandra deigned not to comment, and deliberately turned her attention to the contents on her plate, unsure if she heard his faint, husky chuckle or merely imagined it.

He was the most irritating, impossible man she'd

ever met. Examining why wasn't on her agenda. At least that's what she told herself whenever Diego's image intruded…on far too many occasions for her peace of mind.

It was impossible to escape the man. He was *there,* a constant in the media, cementing another successful business deal, escorting a high-profile female personality to one social event or another. Cameron accorded him an icon, and mentioned him frequently in almost reverent tones.

Tonight Diego del Santo had chosen to invade her personal space. Worse, she had little option but to remain in his immediate proximity for a few hours, and she resented his manipulation, hated him for singling her out as an object for his amusement.

For that was all it was…and it didn't help that she felt like a butterfly pinned to the wall.

Cassandra took a sip of wine, and deliberately engaged Cameron in conversation, the thread of which she lost minutes later as the waiter removed plates from their table.

She was supremely conscious of Diego's proximity, the shape of his hand as he reached for his wine goblet, the way his fingers curved over the delicate glass…and couldn't stop the wayward thought as to how his hands would glide over a woman's skin.

Where had that come from?

Dear heaven, the wine must have affected her

brain! The last thing she wanted was any physical contact with a man of Diego del Santo's ilk.

'Your speciality is gemmology, I believe?'

Think of the devil and he speaks, she alluded with silent cynicism as she turned towards him. 'Polite conversation, genuine interest,' she inclined, and waited a beat. 'Or an attempt to alleviate boredom?'

His expression didn't change, although she could have sworn something moved in the depths of those dark eyes. 'Let's aim for the middle ground.'

There was a quality to his voice, an inflexion she preferred to ignore. 'Natural precious gemstones recovered in the field by mining or fossiking techniques are the most expensive.' Such facts were common knowledge. 'For a jewellery designer, they give more pleasure to work with, given there's a sense of nature and the process of their existence. It becomes a personal challenge to have the stones cut in such a way they display maximum beauty. The designer's gift to ensure the design and setting reflect the stone's optimal potential.' A completed study of gemmology had led to her true passion of jewellery design.

Diego saw the way her mouth softened and her eyes came alive. It intrigued him, as *she* intrigued him.

'You are not in favour of the synthetic or simulants?'

Her expression faded a little. 'They're immensely popular and have a large market.'

His gaze held hers. 'That doesn't answer the question.' He lifted a hand and fingered the delicate argyle diamond nestling against the hollow at the base of her throat. 'Your work?' It was a rhetorical question. He'd made it his business to view her designs, without her knowledge, and was familiar with each and every one of them.

She flinched at his touch, hating his easy familiarity almost as much as she hated the tell-tale warmth flooding her veins.

If she could, she'd have flung the icy contents of her glass in his face. Instead, she forced her voice to remain calm. 'Yes.'

A woman could get lost in the depths of those dark eyes, for there was warm sensuality lurking just beneath the surface, a hint, a promise, of the delights he could provide.

Sensation feathered the length of her spine, and she barely repressed a shiver at the thought of his mouth on hers, the touch of his hands...how it would feel to be driven wild, beyond reason, by such a man.

'Have dinner with me tomorrow night.'

'The obligatory invitation?' Her response was automatic, and she tempered it with a gracious, 'Thank you. No.'

The edge of his mouth lifted. 'The obligatory refusal...because you have to wash your hair?'

'I can come up with something more original.'

She could, easily. Except she doubted an excuse, no matter how legitimate-sounding, would fool him.

'You won't change your mind?'

Cassandra offered a cool smile. 'What part of *no* don't you understand?'

Diego reached for the water jug and refilled her glass. The sleeve of his jacket brushed her arm, and her stomach turned a slow somersault at the contact.

It was as well the waiters began delivering the main course, and she sipped wine in the hope it would soothe her nerves.

Chance would be a fine thing! She was conscious of every move he made, aware of the restrained power beneath the fine Armani tailoring, the dangerous aura he seemed to project without any effort at all.

Another two hours. Three at the most. Then she could excuse herself and leave. If Cameron wanted to stay on, she'd take a cab home.

Cassandra drew a calming breath and regarded the contents on her plate. The meal was undoubtedly delicious, but her appetite had vanished.

With determined effort she caught Cameron's attention, and deliberately sought his opinion on something so inconsequential that afterwards she had little recollection of the discussion.

There were the usual speeches, followed by light entertainment as dessert and coffee were served. Never had time dragged quite so slowly, nor could she recall an occasion when she'd so badly wanted the evening to end.

To her surprise, it was Cameron who initiated the desire to leave, citing a headache as the reason, and Cassandra rose to her feet, offered a polite good-night to the occupants of their table, then preceded her brother out to the foyer.

'Are you OK?'

He looked pale, too pale, and a slight frown creased her brow as they headed towards the bank of lifts. 'Headache?' She extended her hand as he retrieved his car keys. 'Want me to drive?'

CHAPTER TWO

MINUTES later she slid behind the wheel and sent the car up to street level to join the flow of traffic. It was a beautiful night, the air crisp and cool indicative of spring.

A lovely time of year, she accorded silently as she negotiated lanes and took the route that led to Double Bay.

Fifteen, twenty minutes tops, and she'd be home. Then she could get out of the formal gear, cleanse off her make-up, and slip into bed.

'We need to talk.'

Cassandra spared him a quick glance. 'Can't it wait until tomorrow?'

'No.'

It was most unlike Cameron to be taciturn. 'Is something wrong?' Her eyes narrowed as the car in front came to a sudden stop, and she uttered an unladylike curse as she stamped her foot hard on the brakes.

'Hell, Cassandra,' he muttered. 'Watch it!'

'Tell that to the guy in front.' Her voice held unaccustomed vehemence. Choosing silence for the remaining time it took to reach her apartment seemed a wise option. The last thing she coveted was an argument.

'Park in the visitors' bay,' Cameron instructed as she swept the car into the bricked apron adjacent to the main entrance.

'You're coming up?'

'It's either that, or we talk in the car.'

He didn't seem to be giving her a choice as he unbuckled his seat belt and slid out from the passenger seat.

She followed, inserted her personalised card into the security slot to gain entry into the foyer, and used it again to summon a lift.

'I hope this won't take long,' she cautioned as she preceded him into her apartment, then she turned to face him. 'OK, shoot.'

He closed his eyes, then opened them again and ran a hand through his hair. 'This isn't easy.'

The tension of the evening began to manifest itself into tiredness, and she rolled her shoulders. 'Just spit it out.'

'The firm is in trouble. Major financial trouble,' he elaborated. 'If Dad found out just how hopeless everything is, it would kill him.'

Ice crept towards the region of her heart. 'What in hell are you talking about?'

'Preston-Villers is on a roller-coaster ride to insolvency.'

'What?' She found it difficult to comprehend. *'How?'*

He was ready to crumple, and it wasn't a good look.

'Bad management, bad deals, unfulfilled contracts. Staff problems. You name it, it happened.'

She adored her brother, but he wasn't the son her father wanted. Cameron didn't possess the steel backbone, the unflagging determination to take over directorship of Preston-Villers. Their father had thought it would be the making of his son. Now it appeared certain to be his ruination.

'Just how bad is it?'

Cameron grimaced, and shot her a desperate look. 'The worst.' He held up a hand. 'Yes, I've done the round of banks, financiers, sought independent advice.' He drew in a deep breath and released it slowly. 'It narrows down to two choices. Liquidate, or take a conditional offer.'

Hope was uppermost, and she ran with it. 'The offer is legitimate?'

'Yes.' He rubbed a weary hand along his jaw. 'An investor is prepared to inject the necessary funds, I get to retain an advisory position, he brings in his professional team, shares joint directorship, and takes a half-share of all profits.'

It sounded like salvation, but there was need for caution. 'Presumably you've taken legal advice on all this?'

'It's the only deal in town,' he assured soberly. 'There's just a matter of the remaining condition.'

'Which is?'

He hesitated, then took a deep breath and expelled it. 'You.'

Genuine puzzlement brought forth a frown. 'The deal has nothing to do with me.'

'Yes, it does.'

Like pieces of a puzzle, they began clicking into place, forming a picture she didn't want to see. 'Who made the offer?' Dear God, no. It couldn't be…

'Diego del Santo.'

Cassandra felt the blood drain from her face. Shock, disbelief, anger followed in quick succession. 'You can't be serious?' The words held a hushed quality, and for a few seconds she wondered if she'd actually uttered them.

Cameron drew in a deep breath, then released it slowly. 'Deadly.' To his credit, Cameron looked wretched.

'Let me get this straight.' Her eyes assumed an icy gleam. 'Diego del Santo intends making this personal?' His image conjured itself in front of her, filling her vision, blinding her with it.

'Without your involvement, the deal won't go ahead.'

She tried for *calm,* when inside she was a seething mass of anger. 'My *involvement* being?'

'He'll discuss it with you over dinner tomorrow evening.'

'The *hell* he will!'

'Cassandra—' Cameron's features assumed a

grey tinge. 'You want Alexander to have another heart attack?'

The words stopped her cold. The medics had warned a further attack could be his last. 'How can you even say that?'

She wanted to rail against him, demand why he'd let things progress beyond the point of no return. Yet recrimination wouldn't solve a thing, except provide a vehicle to vent her feelings.

'I want proof.' The words were cool, controlled. 'Facts,' she elaborated, and glimpsed Cameron's obvious discomfiture. 'The how and why of it, and just how bad it is.'

'You don't believe me?'

'I need to be aware of all the angles,' she elaborated. 'Before I confront Diego del Santo.'

Cameron went a paler shade of pale. 'Confront?'

She fired him a look that quelled him into silence. 'If he thinks I'll meekly comply with whatever he has in mind, then he can think again!'

His mouth worked as he searched for the appropriate words. 'Cass—'

'Don't *Cass* me.' It was an endearing nickname that belonged to their childhood.

'Do you have any idea who you're dealing with?'

She drew in a deep breath and released it slowly. 'I think it's about time Diego del Santo discovered who *he* is dealing with!' She pressed fingers to her throbbing temples in order to ease the ache there.

'Cassandra—'

'Can we leave this until tomorrow?' She needed to *think.* Most of all, she wanted to be alone. 'I'll organise lunch, and we'll go through the paperwork together.'

'It's Sunday.'

'What does that have to do with it?'

Cameron lifted both hands in a gesture of conciliation. 'Midday?'

'Fine.'

She saw him out the door, locked up, then she removed her make-up, undressed, then slid into bed to stare at the darkened ceiling for what seemed an age, sure hours later when she woke that she hadn't slept at all.

A session in the gym, followed by several laps of the pool eased some of her tension, and she re-entered her apartment, showered and dressed in jeans and a loose top, then crossed into the kitchen to prepare lunch.

Cameron arrived at twelve, and presented her with a chilled bottle of champagne.

'A little premature, don't you think?' she offered wryly as she prepared garlic bread and popped it into the oven to heat.

'Something smells good,' he complimented, and she wrinkled her nose at him.

'Flattery won't get you anywhere.' Lunch was a seafood pasta dish she whipped up without any fuss, and accompanied by a fresh garden salad it was an adequate meal.

'Let's eat first, then we'll deal with business. OK?'

He didn't look much better than she felt, and she wondered if he'd slept any more than she had.

'Dad is expecting us for dinner.'

It was a weekly family tradition, and one they observed almost without fail. Although the thought of presenting a false façade didn't sit well. Her father might suffer ill-health, but he wasn't an easy man to fool.

'This pasta is superb,' Cameron declared minutes later, and she inclined her head in silent acknowledgement.

By tacit agreement they discussed everything except Preston-Villers, and it was only when the dishes were dealt with that Cassandra indicated Cameron's briefcase.

'Let's begin, shall we?'

It was worse, much worse than she had envisaged as she perused the paperwork tabling Preston-Villers slide into irretrievable insolvency. The accountant's overview of the current situation was damning, and equally indisputable.

She'd wanted proof. Now she had it.

'I can think of several questions,' she began, but only one stood out. 'Why did you let things get this bad?'

Cameron raked fingers through his hair. 'I kept hoping the contracts would come in and everything would improve.'

Instead, they'd gone from bad to worse.

Cassandra damned Diego del Santo to hell and back, and barely drew short of including Cameron with him.

'Business doesn't succeed on *hope.*' It needed a hard, competent hand holding the reins, taking control, making the right decisions.

A man like Diego del Santo, a quiet voice insisted. Someone who could inject essential funds, and ensure everything ran like well-oiled clockwork.

There was sense in the amalgamation, and as Cameron rightly described, it was the only deal in town if Preston-Villers was to survive.

'Shall I contact Diego and confirm you've reconsidered his dinner invitation?'

'No.'

Disbelief and consternation were clearly evident. 'No?'

'My ball. My play.' Something she intended to take care of tomorrow. She stood to her feet. 'I need to put in an hour or two on the laptop before leaving to have dinner with Dad.' She led the way to the door of her apartment. 'I'll see you there.'

'OK.' Cameron offered an awkward smile. 'Thanks.'

'For what?' She couldn't help herself. 'Lunch?'

'That, too.'

It was after five when Cassandra entered the electronic gates guarding Alexander Preston-Villers' splendid home. Renovations accommodated wheelchair usage, and a lift had been installed for easy access between upper and lower floors. There was a resident housekeeper, as well as Sylvie, the live-in nurse.

Cassandra rang the bell, then used her key to enter the marble-tiled lobby.

It tore at Cassandra's heart each time she visited, seeing the man who had once been strong reduced to frail health.

Tonight he appeared more frail than usual, his lack of motor-skills more pronounced than they had been a week ago, and his appetite seemed less.

She looked at him, and wanted to weep. Cameron seemed similarly affected, and attempting to maintain a normal façade took considerable effort.

There was no way she'd allow *anyone* to upset Alexander. Not Cameron, nor Diego del Santo.

She made the silent vow as she drove back to her apartment. The determined bid haunted her sleep, providing dreams that assumed nightmarish proportions, ensuring she woke late and had to scramble in order to get to work on time.

Confronting Diego del Santo was a priority, and given a choice she'd prefer to beard him in his office than meet socially over a shared meal.

Which meant she'd need to work through her lunch hour in order to leave an hour early.

Cassandra found it difficult to focus on the intricate attention to detail involved with the creative-design project for an influential client.

Diego del Santo's image intruded, wreaking havoc with her concentration, and consequently it was something of a relief to pack up her work and consign it to the security safe before freshening her make-up prior to leaving for the day.

Del Santo Corporation was situated on a high floor of an inner-city office tower, and Cassandra felt a sense of angry determination as she vacated the lift and walked through automatic sliding glass doors to Reception.

'Diego del Santo.' Her voice was firm, clipped and, she hoped, authoritative.

'Mr del Santo is in conference, and has no appointments available this afternoon.'

She made a point of checking her watch. 'Put a call through and tell him Cassandra Preston-Villers is waiting to see him.'

'I have instructions to hold all calls.'

Efficiency. She could only admire it. 'Call his secretary.'

A minute...Cassandra counted off the seconds...a woman who could easily win secretary-of-the-year award appeared in Reception. 'Is there a problem?'

You betcha, Cassandra accorded silently, and I'm it. 'Please inform Diego del Santo I need to see him.'

A flicker of doubt. That's all she needed. Yet none appeared. Was his secretary so familiar with Diego's paramours, she knew categorically that Cassandra wasn't one of them?

'I have instructions to serve drinks and canapés at five,' his secretary informed. 'I'll mention your presence to him then.'

It was a small victory, but a victory none the less. 'Thank you.'

Half an hour spent leafing through a variety of glossy magazines did little to help her nervous tension.

Staff began their end-of-day exodus, and she felt her stomach execute a painful somersault as Diego's secretary moved purposely into Reception.

'Please come with me.'

Minutes later she was shown into a luxurious suite. 'Take a seat. Mr del Santo will be with you soon.'

How soon was *soon?*

Five, ten, thirty minutes passed. Was he playing a diabolical game with her?

Nervous tension combined with anger, and she was almost on the point of walking out. The only thing that stopped her was the sure knowledge she'd only have to go through this again tomorrow.

Five more minutes, she vowed, then she'd go in search of him...conference be damned!

The door swung open and Diego walked into the room with one minute to spare.

'Cassandra.'

She rose to her feet, unwilling to appear at a disadvantage by having him loom over her.

'My apologies for keeping you waiting.' He

crossed to the floor-to-ceiling plate-glass window, turned his back on the magnificent harbour view, and thrust one hand into his trouser pocket.

Her expression was coolly aloof, although her eyes held the darkness of anger. 'Really? I imagine keeping me waiting is part of the game-play.'

Sassy, he mused, and mad. It made a change from simpering companions who held a diploma in superficial artificiality.

'If you had telephoned, my secretary could have arranged a suitable time,' Diego inferred mildly.

'Next week?' she parried with deliberate facetiousness, and incurred a cynical smile.

'The very reason I suggested we share dinner.'

'I have no desire to share anything with you.' She paused, then drew in a deep breath. 'Let's get down to business, shall we?' She indicated the sheaf of papers tabled together in a thick folder. 'I have the requisite proof, and a copy of your offer. Everything appears to be in order.'

'You sound surprised.'

Cassandra swept him a dark glance. 'I doubt there's anything you could do that would surprise me.'

'I imagine Cameron has relayed the deal is subject to a condition?'

Her eyes glittered with barely repressed anger. 'He said it was personal. *How* personal?'

'Two separate nights and one weekend with you.'

She felt as if some elusive force had picked her

up and flung her against the nearest wall. 'That's barbaric,' she managed at last.

'Call it what you will.'

It took her a few seconds to find her voice. 'Why?'

'Because it amuses me?'

Was this payback? For all the invitations he'd offered and she'd refused...because she could. Now, her refusal would have far-reaching implications. Did she have the strength of will to ruin her father, the firm he'd spent his life taking from strength to strength?

'An investment of twenty-three million dollars against all sage advice, allows for—' he paused deliberately '—a bonus, wouldn't you say?'

She didn't think, or pause to consider the consequences of her actions. She simply picked up the nearest thing to hand and threw it at him. The fact he fielded it neatly and replaced it down onto his desk merely infuriated her further.

'Who do you think you are?' Her voice was low, and held a quality even she didn't recognise.

Stupid question, she dismissed. He knew precisely who he was, what he wanted, and how to get it.

'I'd advise you to think carefully before you consider another foolish move,' Diego cautioned silkily.

Her eyes sparked brilliant blue fire. 'What did you expect?' Her voice rose a fraction. 'For me to fall into your arms expressing my undying gratitude?'

She didn't see the humour lurking in those dark

depths. If she had, she'd probably throw something else at him.

'I imagined a token resistance.'

Oh, he did, did he? 'You realise I could lay charges against you for coercion?'

'You could try.'

'Only to have your team of lawyers counter with misinterpretation, whereupon you withdraw your financial rescue package?'

'Yes.'

'Emotional blackmail is a detestable ploy.'

'It's a negotiable tool,' Diego corrected, and in that moment she hated him more than she thought it possible to hate anyone.

'No.' Dear God, had she actually said the verbal negation?

'No, you don't agree it's a negotiable tool?'

'I won't have sex with you.'

'You're not in any position to bargain.'

'I'm not for sale,' Cassandra evinced with dignity.

'Everything has its price.'

'That's your credo in life?'

He waited a beat. 'Do you doubt it?'

She'd had enough. 'We're about done, don't you think?' She tried for calm, and didn't quite make it as she hitched the strap of her shoulder bag as she turned towards the door.

Damn Cameron. Damn the whole sorry mess.

'There's just one more thing.'

She registered Diego's silky drawl, recognised the

underlying threat, and paused, turning to look at him.

'Cameron's homosexuality.'

Two words. Yet they had the power to stop the breath in her throat.

Diego del Santo couldn't possibly know. No one knew. At least, only Cameron, his partner, and herself.

Anxiety meshed with panic at the thought her father might catch so much as a whisper...

Dear God, *no.*

Alexander Preston-Villers might find it difficult to accept Cameron had steadily sent Preston-Villers to the financial wall. But he'd never condone or forgive his son's sexual proclivity.

An appalling sense of anguish permeated her bones, her soul. Who had Diego del Santo employed to discover something she imagined so well-hidden, it was virtually impossible to uncover?

How deep had he dug?

No stone unturned. The axiom echoed and re-echoed inside her brain.

It said much of the man standing before her, the lengths he was prepared to go to to achieve his objective.

'I hate you.' The words fell from her lips in a voice shaky with anger. She felt cold, so cold she was willing to swear her blood had turned to ice in her veins.

Diego inclined his head, his eyes darkly still as

he observed her pale features, the starkness of defeat clearly evident in her expression. 'At this moment, I believe you do.'

He'd won. They both knew it. There was only one thing she could hope for...his silence.

'Yes.' His voice was quiet. 'You have my word.'

'For which I should be grateful?' she queried bitterly.

He didn't answer. Instead, he indicated the chair she'd previously occupied. 'Why don't you sit down?'

He crossed to the credenza, extracted a glass, filled it with iced water from the bar fridge, then placed the glass in her hand.

Cassandra didn't want to sit. She preferred to be on her feet, poised for flight.

Diego moved towards his desk and leaned one hip against its edge. 'Shall we begin again?'

Dear heaven, how did she get through this? With as much dignity as possible, an inner voice prompted.

'The ball's in your court.'

Did she have any idea how vulnerable she looked? The slightly haunted quality evident in those stunning blue eyes, the translucence of her skin.

He remembered the taste of her, her fragrance, the soft, tentative response... He'd sought to imprint her with his touch, unclear of his motivation. A desire to shock, to punish? A lesson to be wary of men whose prime need was sex?

Instead, it had been she who'd left a lingering memory, unexpectedly stirring his soul…as well as another pertinent part of his anatomy. A pubescent temptress, unaware of her feminine power, he mused, wondering at the time how she'd react if he took advantage of her youth.

Sixteen-year-old girls were out of bounds. Especially when this particular sixteen-year-old was the cherished daughter of one of the city's industrial scions. Her brother, the elder by two years, should have known better than to bring her to a party where drinks were spiked and drugs were in plentiful supply. A fact he'd cursorily relayed before bundling brother and sister out of the host's house, then following in their wake.

Relationships, he'd had a few. Women he'd enjoyed, taking what was so willingly offered without much thought to permanence. As to commitment…there hadn't been any woman he'd wanted to make his own, exclusively. Happy-ever-after was a fallacy. Undying love, a myth.

For the past year one woman had teased his senses, yet she'd held herself aloof from every attempt he made to date her, and he'd had to content himself with a polite greeting whenever their social paths crossed.

Until now.

'As soon as our personal arrangement has satisfactorily concluded,' Diego drawled, 'I'll attach my signature to the relevant paperwork and organise for funds to be released.'

Cassandra registered his words, and felt her stomach contract in tangible pain. 'And when do you envisage our *personal arrangement* will begin?'

'Anyone would think you view sex with me as a penance.'

'Your ego must be enormous if you imagine I could possibly regard it as a pleasure.'

'Brave words,' Diego drawled, 'when you have no knowledge what manner of lover I am.'

The mere thought of that tall, muscular body engaged intimately with hers was enough to send heat spiralling from deep inside.

Instinct warned he was a practised lover, aware of all the pleasure pulses in a woman's body, and how to coax each and every one of them to vibrant life with the skilled touch of his mouth, his hands.

It was there, in the darkness of his gaze…the sensual confidence of a man well-versed in the desires of women.

A tiny shiver started at the base of her spine, and feathered its way to her nape, settled there, so she had to make a conscious effort to prevent it from appearing visible.

'Wednesday evening I'm attending a dinner party. I'll collect you at six-thirty. Pack whatever you need for the night.'

The day after tomorrow?

An hysterical laugh rose and died in her throat. So soon? Oh, God, why not? At least then the first night would be over. One down, one and a weekend to go.

'The remaining nights?' Dear heaven, how could she sound so calm?

'Saturday.'

She felt as if she were dying. 'And the last?'

'The following weekend.' His gaze never left hers. 'One million dollars will be deposited into the Preston-Villers business account following each of the three occasions you spend with me. Monday week, Preston-Villers' creditors will be paid off.'

'A *condition*, tenuously alluded to in the documentation as "being met to Diego del Santo's satisfaction", doesn't even begin to offer me any protection. What guarantee do I have you won't declare the offer documented as null and void on the grounds the *condition* hasn't been met to your satisfaction?'

'My word.'

She had to force her voice to remain steady, otherwise it would betray her by shattering into a hundred pieces. 'Sorry, but that won't cut it.'

'Do you know how close you walk to the edge of my tolerance?'

'Don't insult my intelligence by detailing a *condition* that has so many holes in it, even Blind Freddie could see through them!'

'You don't trust me?'

'No.'

He could walk away from the deal. It was what he *should* do. Twenty-three million dollars was no small amount of money, even if in the scheme of things it represented only a very small percentage of his investments.

He enjoyed the adrenalin charge in taking a worn-down company, injecting the necessary funds and making it work again.

'What is it you want?'

It was no time to lose her bravado. 'Something in writing detailing those nights, each comprising no more than twelve hours spent in your company, represents my sexual obligation to you, as covered by the term *condition*, and said obligation shall not be judged by my sexual performance.' She took a deep breath, and released it slowly. 'The original copy will be destroyed when you release funds in full into the Preston-Villers business account.'

She watched as he set up a laptop, keyed in data, activated the printer, proofread the printed copy, then attached his signature and handed her the page.

Cassandra read it, then she neatly folded the page and thrust it into her shoulder bag. Un-notarised, it wouldn't have much value in a court of law. But it was better than nothing.

The melodic burr of his cellphone provided the impetus she needed to escape.

Diego spared a glance at the illuminated dial, and cut the call. He moved to the door, opened it, then he led the way out to the main foyer and summoned the lift.

'Six-thirty, Wednesday evening,' he reminded as the electronic doors slid open.

It nearly killed her to act with apparent unconcern, when inside she was a quivering mess. 'I won't say it's been a pleasure,' Cassandra managed coolly as she depressed the appropriate button to take her down to ground level.

As a parting shot it lacked the impact she would have liked, but she took a degree of satisfaction in having the last word.

Two weeks from now she would have fulfilled Diego del Santo's *condition*.

Three, no, four nights in his bed. She could do it…couldn't she, and emerge emotionally unscathed?

CHAPTER THREE

Two evenings later Cassandra stood sipping excellent champagne in the lounge of a stunning Rose Bay mansion.

Guests mingled, some of whom she knew, and the conversation flowed. However, the evening, the venue, the fellow guests…none had as much impact on her as the man at her side.

Diego del Santo exuded practised charm, solicitous interest, and far too much sexual chemistry for any woman's peace of mind. Especially hers.

Worse, she was all too aware of the way her nervous tension escalated by the minute.

She didn't want to be here. More particularly, she didn't want to be linked to Diego del Santo in any way.

Yet she was bound to him, caught in an invisible trap, and the clock was ticking down towards the moment they were alone.

Even the thought of that large, lithe frame, naked, was enough to send her heartbeat into overdrive.

'More champagne?'

His voice was an inflected drawl as he indicated her empty flute, and he was close, too close for comfort, for she was supremely conscious of him, his fine tailoring, the exclusive cologne, and the man beneath the sophisticated exterior.

'No,' she managed politely. 'Thank you.' There was some merit in having one drink too many in order to endure the night. However, the evening was young, dinner would soon be served, and she valued her social reputation too much as well as her self-esteem to pass the next few hours in an alcoholic haze.

Choosing what to wear had seen her selecting one outfit after another and discarding most. In the end she'd opted for a bias-cut red silk dress with a soft, draped neckline and ribbon straps. Subtle make-up with emphasis on her eyes, and she'd swept her hair into a careless knot atop her head. Jewellery was an intricately linked neck chain with matching ear-studs.

Packing an overnight bag had been simple...she'd simply tossed in a change of clothes and a few necessities. A bag Diego had retrieved from her hand as she emerged from the foyer and deposited in the trunk of his car.

Quite what she expected she wasn't sure. There had been nothing overt in his greeting, and he made no attempt to touch her as he saw her seated in his stylish Aston Martin.

During the brief drive to their hosts' home he'd

kept conversation to a minimum...presumably influenced by her monosyllabic replies.

What did he expect? For her to smile and laugh? Act as if this was a *date*, for heaven's sake?

He'd made her part of a deal, and she hated him for it. Almost as much as she hated being thrust among a coterie of guests for several hours.

Guests who were undoubtedly curious at Diego's choice of partner for the evening. Or should that be curiosity at *her* choice of partner?

Had whispers of Preston-Villers' financial straits begun to circulate? And if they had, what context was placed on Cassandra Preston-Villers appearing at Diego's side? Would gossip allude the amalgamation had moved from the boardroom to the bedroom?

Cassandra told herself she didn't care...and knew she lied.

Dinner. Dear heaven, how could she *eat*? Her stomach felt as if it were tied in knots, and primed to reject any food she sent its way.

'Relax.'

Diego's voice was a quiet drawl as they took their seats at the elegantly set table, and she offered a stunning smile. 'I'm perfectly relaxed.'

There were numerous courses, each a perfect complement served with the artistry and flair of a professional chef.

Compliments were accorded, and Cassandra

added her own, painfully aware her tastebuds had gone on strike.

She conversed with fellow guests, almost on autopilot, playing the social game with the ease of long practice. Although afterwards she held little recollection of any discussion.

Diego was *there*, a constant entity, and the build-up of tension accelerated as the evening progressed. The light brush of his hand on hers succeeded in sending her pulse into overdrive, and she almost forgot to breathe when he leaned close to refill her water glass.

She began to pray for the evening to end, to be free from the constraints of polite society. At least when they were alone she could discard the façade and fence verbal swords with him!

Somehow she made it through the seemingly endless meal, and it was a relief to retreat to the lounge to linger over coffee.

Diego seemed in no hurry to leave, and it was almost eleven when he indicated they bid their hosts goodnight.

The short drive to nearby suburban Point Piper was achieved in silence, and Cassandra felt her body stiffen as he activated the electronic gates guarding the entrance to a curved driveway illuminated by strategically placed lights leading to a large home whose architecturally designed exterior and interior had featured in one of the glossy magazines soon after its completion.

The Aston Martin eased beneath electronic garage doors and slid to a halt as the doors closed behind them with an imperceptible click.

Trapped.

Take me home. The words rose as a silent cry, only to die unuttered in her throat.

You have to go through with this, a silent voice prompted pitilessly. Think of Alexander, Cameron.

But what about *me*?

Diego popped the trunk, then emerged from behind the wheel and retrieved her bag as she slipped out of the passenger seat.

In silence she preceded him indoors, then walked at his side as he moved into the main foyer.

With a sense of increasing desperation she focused on the generous dimensions, the gently curving staircase with its intricately designed balustrade leading to the upper floor. A crystal chandelier hung suspended from the high ceiling, and solid mahogany cabinets added to the Spanish influence. Art graced the walls, providing an ambience of wealth.

Had he personally chosen all this, or consulted with an interior decorator?

Diego deposited her bag at the foot of the staircase, then he indicated a door on his right. 'A nightcap?'

Cassandra watched as he crossed the foyer and

revealed a spacious lounge. The thought of exchanging polite conversation and playing *pretend* was almost more than she could bear.

The entire evening had been a preliminary to the moment she'd need to share his bed. Drawing it out any further seemed pointless.

'If you don't mind, I'd prefer to get on with it.'

She was nervous. He could sense it in her voice, see the way her pulse jumped at the base of her throat, and he took pleasure from it.

'Cut to the chase?'

His query was a silky drawl that sent an icy feather sliding down her spine. 'Yes.'

Diego gave an imperceptible shrug as he closed the door and indicated the staircase. 'By all means.'

Was she *mad*? Oh, for heaven's sake, she chided silently. He's only a man, like any other.

They'd have sex, she'd sleep, he'd wake her at dawn for more sex, then she'd shower, dress, and get a cab to work.

How big a deal could it be?

The way the blood fizzed through her veins, heating her body was incidental. The rapid thudding of her heart was merely due to nervous tension. Stress, anxiety…take your pick. A direct result of the sexual price she'd agreed to pay with a man she told herself she didn't like.

Together they ascended the curved staircase, then

turned left, traversing the balustraded gallery to a lavishly furnished master suite.

Cassandra entered the room, only to falter to a halt as uncertainty froze her limbs. *Think,* she silently cajoled. Slip off your stiletto-heeled pumps, remove your jewellery…

The ear-studs were easy, but her fingers shook as she reached for the clasp at her nape.

'Let me do that,' Diego said quietly, and moved in close.

Far too close. She could sense him behind her, almost *feel* the touch of that powerful body against her own. How much space separated them? An inch? If she leant back, her shoulders would brush his chest.

Oh, hell, *should* she, and make it easy for herself? Play the seductress and melt into his arms?

His fingers touched her nape and she unconsciously held her breath as he dealt with the clasp. Then it was done, and she took a step away from him as he dropped the jewellery into her hand.

Cassandra crossed to where Diego had placed her bag and tucked the jewellery into a pouch. When she turned he was close, and her stomach clenched as he reached for the pins in her hair.

His fingers grazed the graceful curve of her neck, and sensation shivered the length of her spine.

'Beautiful.'

His silky murmur did strange things to her equilibrium, and she fought against the almost mesmeric fascination threatening to undermine her defences.

It would be so easy to sway towards him, angle her head, fasten her mouth on his and simply sink in.

Yet to meekly comply meant she condoned his actions, and there wasn't a hope in hell she'd ever forgive his manipulation.

'Let's not pretend this is anything other than what it is.'

Cassandra reached for the zip fastener on her dress, and managed to slide it down a few inches before his hand halted its progress.

'Highly priced sex?' Diego queried in a faintly accented drawl.

'You got it in one.'

She was nervous, and that intrigued him. Any other woman would have played the coquette, and provocatively stripped for his pleasure. Teasing, before undressing *him*, then moving in to begin a practised seduction before he took control.

'If you want to unwrap the package…' Cassandra managed what she hoped was a negligent shrug '…then go ahead.'

Diego's eyes narrowed, and his voice was a husky drawl. 'How could a man resist the temptation?'

He slid the zip fastener all the way down, then lifted his hands to the shoestring straps, slipping them over each shoulder so the gown slithered to a heap on the carpeted floor.

The only garment that saved her from total nudity was a silk thong brief, and she forced herself to stand still beneath his studied appraisal.

Her eyes blazed blue fire as his gaze lingered on her breasts, skimmed low, then lifted to meet the defiant outrage apparent.

With slow, deliberate movements he removed his shoes and socks, shed his jacket, loosened his tie and removed it, then he freed his trousers before tending to the buttons on his shirt.

He was something else. Broad shoulders, lean hips, a washboard stomach, olive-toned skin sheathed an enviable abundance of hardened sinew and muscle. Fit, not pumped, with a sleekness that denoted undeniable strength.

Black silk briefs did little to hide his arousal, and she hated the warm tinge that coloured her cheeks as he swept back the bedcovers.

With unhurried steps he closed the distance between them, and her eyes widened fractionally as he touched a gentle finger to her lips and traced the lower curve. Warmth flooded her body and became pulsing heat as he cupped her face, and a soundless groan rose and died in her throat as he lowered his head down to hers.

Whatever she'd expected, it wasn't the slow, evocative touch of his mouth on her own, or the way his tongue slid between her lips as his hands cupped her face.

She felt his thumbs brush each cheek, and the breath caught in her throat as he angled his mouth and went in deep.

He tugged at her senses and tore them to shreds, destroying the protective barrier she'd built up against him.

Her hands lifted to his shoulders in a bid to hang on, only to rest briefly, hesitantly there as he slid a hand to capture her nape while the other skimmed the length of her spine to curve over her bottom and pull her close.

In one fluid movement he dispensed with the scrap of silk, and she gasped as he sought the warm heat at the apex of her thighs.

There was little she could do to prevent his skilled fingers wreaking havoc there. He knew where to touch and how…light strokes that almost drove her wild, and just when she thought she couldn't stand any more he eased off, only to have her gasp as the oral stimulation intensified to another level.

'Let go,' Diego instructed huskily, and absorbed her despairing groan.

Her body might be tempted, but her mind wasn't in sync. Had it ever been? she registered cynically, aware that for her intimacy, while pleasurable, was hardly a mind-blowing experience. Why should it be any different this time?

Fake it, a silent imp prompted. Just…get it over with, then it'll be done. For tonight.

His hands shifted to cup her face. 'Don't.'

Cassandra stilled at his softly voiced admonition, and cast him a startled glance. 'I don't know what you mean.'

He traced the lower curve of her mouth with the pad of his thumb, and saw her eyes flare. 'Yes, you do.'

She could feel the warmth colour her cheeks. What was it with this man that he could lay bare her secrets?

Her previous partners had been so consumed with their own pleasure they hadn't cared about her own.

A strangled laugh rose and died in her throat. It wasn't as if she'd had numerous partners…only two, each of whom had declared undying devotion while fixing an eye on her father's wealth.

'I don't want to be here with you.'

'Perhaps not.' He waited a beat. 'Yet.'

'Are you sure there's enough space in this room for both you and your ego?'

His husky laugh was almost her undoing. 'You doubt I can make you want me?'

'It would be a first.' The words were out before she thought to stop them, and she saw his eyes narrow.

He was silent for what seemed an age, then he released her. In one fluid movement he reached for the bedcovers, restored them to their former position, then he indicated the bed. 'Get in.'

Uncertainty momentarily showed in her features. 'You prefer the bed?'

'It's more comfortable.'

Comfort. It beat tumbling to the carpeted floor. Although somehow she doubted Diego was prone to awkward moves.

'To sleep,' Diego added, watching confusion cloud her eyes.

'Sleep?' She felt as if she was repeating everything he said.

His gaze speared hers. 'For now,' he qualified evenly. 'Does that bother you?'

A stay of execution? She wasn't sure whether to be pleased or peeved. 'A reprieve? Should I thank you?'

'Don't push it, *querida*.' His voice held the softness of silk, but the warning was pure steel.

Capitulation would be a wise choice, she perceived, and crossed to her bag, extracted a large cotton T-shirt and pulled it on, then after a moment's hesitation she joined him in the large bed, settling as far away from him as possible.

Diego pressed a remote module and doused the lights, and Cassandra felt her body tense in the darkness as she waited for the moment he might reach for her.

Except he didn't, and she lay still, aware of the moment his breathing slowed to a steady pace.

Dammit, he was asleep! As easily and quickly as that, he'd been able to relax sufficiently to sleep.

Leaving her to lie awake to seethe in silence. The temptation to fist her hand and *punch* him was paramount! How dared he simply switch off? How *could* he?

She still had the imprint of his hands on her body, and her mouth felt slightly swollen from the touch of his.

Unfulfilled anticipation. Dear heaven, she couldn't be disappointed, surely?

Diego del Santo was someone she intensely disliked, *hated,* she amended. Just because there was an exigent chemistry between them didn't alter a thing.

How could she *sleep*, for heaven's sake? He was *there*, his large, powerfully muscled body within touching distance.

Was it imagination, or could she feel his warmth? Sense the heat of his sex, even in repose?

It was madness. Insane. She closed her eyes and summoned sleep, only to stifle the groan that rose and died in her throat.

Her limbs, her whole body seemed stiff, and she'd have given anything to roll over and punch her pillow, then resettle into a more comfortable position.

Yet if she moved, she might disturb Diego, and that wasn't a favoured option.

Cassandra counted sheep…to no avail. She concentrated on an intricate jewellery design she was working on, visualised the finished item and made a few minor adjustments.

How long had she been lying in the dark? Ten, twenty minutes? Thirty? How long until the dawn? Four, five hours?

There was a faint movement, then the room was bathed in soft light, and Diego loomed close, his upper body supported on one elbow.

'Can't sleep?' His voice was a husky drawl that curled round her nerve-ends and tugged a little.

Her eyes were large, and far too dark, her features pale.

'I didn't know you were awake.' He must sleep like a cat, attuned to the slightest movement, the faintest sound.

'Headache?'

It would be so easy to acquiesce, but she wasn't into fabrication. 'No.'

He lifted a hand and trailed gentle fingers across her cheek. 'Waging an inner battle?'

There was nothing like the witching midnight hour to heighten vulnerability. 'Yes.'

His mouth curved into a musing smile. 'Honesty is a quality so rarely found in women.'

'You obviously haven't met the right woman.'

Was that her voice? It sounded impossibly husky. *Sexy,* she amended, slightly shocked, and flinched as his fingers traced a path to her temple and tucked a swathe of hair behind her ear.

There was a sense of unreality in the conversation. She was conscious of the room, the bed...then the man, only the man became her total focus.

The pad of his thumb traced her lower lip, depressed its centre, then slid to her chin, holding it fast as he fastened his mouth on hers, coaxing in a prelude to the deliberate seduction of her senses.

The subtle exploration became an evocative sensual possession that took hold of her inhibitions and dispensed with them...far too easily for her peace of mind.

She should withdraw and retreat, protest a little. Except his touch held a magic she couldn't resist, and she groaned as his hands caressed her breasts, shaped the sensitive flesh, then tantalised the burgeoning peaks.

Heat flooded her veins, filling her body with sensual warmth as she arched against the path of his hand, and he absorbed her soft cry as he caught hold of her T-shirt and tugged it free.

For several long seconds she bore his silent appraisal, glimpsed the vital, almost electric energy apparent, and knew instinctively that intimacy would surely take place.

The intention, the driven need was there, clearly

evident, and sensation spiralled through her body at the thought of his possession.

All her skin-cells came achingly alive, acutely sensitive to his touch as he lowered his head over her breast and suckled its tender peak. Then she cried out as he used his teeth to take her to the brink between pain and pleasure.

Cassandra slid her fingers through his hair and tugged, willing him to cease, only to gasp as he trailed a path to her waist, paused to circle her navel with his tongue before edging slowly towards the apex of her thighs.

He couldn't, wouldn't...surely?

But he did, with brazen disregard for her plea to desist. The level of intimacy shocked her, and she fought against the skilled stroking, the heat and thrust of his tongue as he sent her high. So high, the acute sensory spiral tore a startled cry from her throat.

Just as she thought the sensation couldn't become more intense, it came again, so acutely piercing it arrowed through her body, an all-consuming flame soaring from deep within.

Dear heaven. The fervent whisper fell from her lips as an irreverent prayer as Diego shifted slightly and trailed his lips over her sensitised flesh to possess her mouth in a kiss that took her deep, so deep she simply gave herself over to it and shared the sensual feast.

Somewhere in the deep recesses of her mind an alarm bell sounded, and she stilled. 'Protection?'

'Taken care of.'

Cassandra felt him nudge her thighs apart, the probe of his arousal as he eased into her, and her shocked gasp at his size died in her throat.

His slick heat magnetised her, and she felt her muscles tense around him, then relax in a rhythm that gradually accepted his length. He stilled, his mouth a persuasive instrument as he plundered at will, sweeping her high until all rational thought vanished.

Then he began to move, slowly at first, so slowly she felt the passage inch by inch, and just as she began to think he intended to disengage, he slid in to the hilt in one excruciatingly sensual thrust, repeating the movement as he increased the pace. Until the rhythm became an hypnotic entity she had no power to resist.

Mesmeric, urgent, libidinous...it became something she'd never experienced before. An intoxicating captivation of her senses as he swept them high to a point of magical ecstasy.

She had no memory of the scream torn from her throat, the way her nails raked his ribs, or how she sought his flesh with her teeth. She was a wild wanton, driven beyond mere desire to a primitive place where passion became an incandescent entity.

Diego brought her down slowly, gently, soothing her quivering body until she stilled in his arms.

There were tears trickling down each cheek, and he felt his heart constrict at her vulnerability.

She felt exposed. As if this man had somehow managed to see into her heart, her soul, and that everything she was, all her secrets were laid bare.

There was little she could gain from his expression, and her mouth shook as he carefully rolled onto his back, taking her with him.

His gaze held hers in the soft light, and she couldn't look away. There were no words, nothing she could say, and the breath hitched in her throat as he lifted both hands to her breasts.

With the utmost care he tested their weight, then traced the gentle swell, using his thumb pad to caress the swollen peaks.

Her skin felt sensitive to his touch as he cupped her waist, then slid to her hips.

Cassandra felt her eyes widen as he began to swell inside her, and a soundless gasp parted her lips as he began a slow, undulating movement.

Again? He was ready for more?

She caught the rhythm and matched it, enjoying the dominant position, and what followed became the ride of her life…and his, for there was no doubting his passion, or the moment of his climax as it joined with her own.

Afterwards he drew her down against him and

cradled her close until her breathing, his own, returned to normal.

She could have slept right there, her cheek cushioned against his chest, and she began to protest as he disengaged and eased her to lie beside him.

Then she did voice a protest as he slid from the bed and swept her into his arms.

'What are you doing?' Her faintly scandalised query held an edge of panic as he crossed to the *en suite* and entered the spacious shower cubicle.

'We can't share a shower,' Cassandra protested, and earned a husky laugh.

'We just shared the ultimate in intimacy,' Diego drawled as he picked up the soap and began smoothing it over her skin.

So they had, but this…this was something else, and she put a hand to his chest in silent remonstrance.

'No.'

He didn't stop. 'Afterwards we sleep.'

She pushed him. Or at least she tried, but he was an immovable force. 'I can take care of myself.'

'Indulge me.'

'Diego—'

'I like the sound of my name on your lips.'

'Please!' His touch was a little too up close and personal, and he was invading her private space in a way no man had done before.

'You get to have your turn any minute soon,' he

drawled with amusement, then had the audacity to chuckle as she took a well-aimed swipe at his shoulder.

'If you want to play, *querida*, I'm only too willing to oblige.'

'I'm all played out.' It was the truth, for exhaustion was beginning to overpower her, combined with the soporific spray of hot water, heated steam and lateness of the hour. Plus she hurt in places she'd never hurt before.

He finished her ablutions, then set about completing his own. Within minutes he turned off the water, snagged a bath towel and towelled her dry before applying the towel to his own torso.

Seconds later he led her into the bedroom and pulled her down onto the bed, settled the covers, then doused the light.

With one fluid movement her gathered her in against him and held her there, aware of the moment tiredness overcame her reluctance and she slept.

CHAPTER FOUR

CASSANDRA woke slowly, aware within seconds this wasn't her bed, her room, or her apartment. Realisation dawned, and she turned her head cautiously...only to see she was the sole occupant of the large bed.

Of Diego there was no sign, and she checked the time, gasped in exasperated dismay, then she slid to her feet, gathered fresh underwear and day clothes from her bag and made for the *en suite*.

Fifteen minutes later she gathered up her bag and moved down to the lower floor. She could smell fresh coffee, toast...and felt her stomach rumble in growling protest as she made her way towards the kitchen.

Diego stood at the servery, dressed in dark trousers, a business shirt unbuttoned at the neck, and a matching dark jacket rested over the back of a chair with a tie carelessly tossed on top of it.

He looked far too alive for a man who'd spent the greater part of the night engaged in physical activity, and just the sight of him was enough to shred her nerves.

'I was going to give you another five minutes,'

he drawled. 'Then come fetch you.' He indicated the carafe. 'Coffee?'

'Please.' She felt awkward, and incredibly vulnerable. 'Then I'll call a cab.'

Diego extracted a plate of eggs and toast from a warming tray. 'I'll drive you home. Sit down and eat.'

'I'm not hungry.'

He subjected her to a raking appraisal, saw the darkened shadows beneath her eyes, the faint edge of tiredness. 'Eat,' he insisted. 'Then we'll leave.'

Any further protest would be fruitless, and besides, the eggs looked good. She took a seat and did justice to the food, sipped the strong, hot black coffee, and felt more ready to face the day.

As soon as she finished he pulled on his tie and adjusted it, then shrugged into his jacket.

She began clearing the table with the intention of doing the dishes.

'Leave them.'

'It'll only take a few minutes.'

'I have a cleaning lady. Leave them.'

Without a word she picked up her bag and followed him through to the garage.

The distance between Point Piper and Double Bay amounted to a few kilometres, and Cassandra slid open the door within seconds of Diego drawing the car to a halt outside the entrance of her apartment building.

There wasn't an adequate word that came to

mind, and she didn't offer one as she walked away from him.

The cat gave an indignant miaow as she unlocked her door, and she dropped her bag, put down fresh food, then took the lift down to the basement car park.

Minutes later she eased her vintage Porsche onto the road and battled morning peak-hour traffic to reach her place of work.

Concentration on the job in hand proved difficult as she attempted to dispel Diego's powerful image.

Far too often she was reminded of his possession. Dear heaven, she could still *feel* him. Tender internal tissues provided a telling evidence, and just the thought of her reaction to their shared intimacy was enough to bring her to the point of climax.

As if last night wasn't enough, he'd reached for her in the early dawn hours, employing what she reflected was considerable stealth to arouse her before she was fully awake and therefore conscious of his intention.

Worse, he had stilled any protest she might have voiced with a skilled touch, inflaming her senses and attacking the fragile tenure of her control.

How could she react with such electrifying passion to a man she professed to hate? To transcend the physical and unleash myriad emotions to become a willing wanton in his arms. Accepting a degree of intimacy she'd never imagined being sufficiently comfortable with to condone.

Yet she had. Swept away beyond reason or rational thought by sexual chemistry at its zenith.

Her cellphone buzzed, signalling an incoming text message, and she checked it during her lunch break, then responded by keying in Cameron's number.

'Just checking in,' her brother reassured.

'Enquiring how I survived Act One of the three-act night play?'

'Cynicism, Cassandra?'

'I'm entitled, don't you think?'

'Act Two takes place…when?'

'Saturday night.'

'I appreciate—'

'Don't,' she said fiercely, 'go there.' She cut the connection, automatically reached for the Caesar salad she'd ordered, only to take one mouthful and push the plate aside. Instead, she ate the accompanying Turkish bread and sipped the latte before returning to the workshop.

Mid-afternoon she gave in to a throbbing headache and took a painkiller to ease it, then she fixed the binocular microscope, adjusted the light, and set to work.

Cassandra was relieved when the day came to an end, and she stopped off at a supermarket *en route* to her apartment and collected groceries, cat food and fresh fruit.

Essential provisions, she mused as she carried the sack indoors, unpacked it, then she fed the cat, prepared fish and salad for herself. Television interested her for an hour, then she opened her laptop, double-checked design measurements and made some minor adjustments, then she closed everything down and went to bed.

Within minutes she felt the familiar pad of the cat's tread as it joined her and settled against her legs. Companionship and unconditional love, she mused with affection as she sought solace in sleep.

Difficult, when the one man she resented invaded her thoughts, filling her mind, and invaded her dreams.

Diego del Santo had a lot to answer for, Cassandra swore as the next day proved no less stressful. Her stomach executed a downward dive every time her cellphone rang as she waited for him to confirm arrangements for Saturday night.

By Friday evening she was a bundle of nerves, cursing him volubly…which did no good at all and startled the cat.

Consequently when she picked up the phone Saturday morning and heard his voice, it was all she could do to remain civil.

'I'll collect you at six-thirty. Dinner first, then we're due to attend a gallery exhibition.'

'If you'll advise an approximate time you expect to return home,' Cassandra managed stiffly, 'I'll meet you there.'

'No.'

Her fingers tightened on the cellphone casing. 'What do you mean…*no*?' She felt the anger begin a slow simmer, and took a deep breath to control it. 'You can take someone else to dinner and the gallery.'

'Go from one woman to another?'

He sounded amused, damn him. 'Socialising with you doesn't form part of the arrangement.'

'It does, however, entitle me to twelve hours of your time on two of our three legally binding occasions. If you'd prefer not to socialise, I'm more than willing to have you spend those twelve hours in my bed.'

She wanted to kill him. At the very least, she'd do him an injury. 'Minimising sex with you is my main priority.' Trying to remain calm took considerable effort. 'As I'll need my car for the morning, I'll drive to your place.'

'Six-thirty, Cassandra.' He cut the connection before she could say another word.

Choosing what to wear didn't pose a problem, for she led a reasonably active social life and possessed the wardrobe to support it.

For a brief moment she considered something entirely inappropriate, only to dismiss it and go with *stunning*.

Soft and feminine was the *in* style, and she had just the gown in jade silk georgette. Spaghetti straps, a deep V-neckline, and a handkerchief hemline. Guaranteed *wow* factor, she perceived as she swept her hair into a careless knot and added the finishing touches to her make-up.

It was six-twenty-five when she drew her car to a halt outside the gates guarding the entrance to Diego's home. Almost on cue they were electronically released, and she wondered whether it was by advance courtesy on his part or due to a sophisticated alarm system.

The Aston Martin was parked outside the main entrance, and Diego opened the front door as she slid out from her car.

Cassandra inclined her head in silent greeting and crossed to the Aston Martin.

'A punctual woman,' Diego drawled, and incurred a piercing glance.

'You said six-thirty.' She subjected him to a deliberate appraisal, taking in the dark dinner suit, the crisp white shirt, black bow-tie...and endeavoured to control the sudden leap of her pulse. 'Shall we leave?'

Polite, cool. She could do both. For now.

'No overnight bag?'

'I'll get it.' She did, and he placed it indoors before tending to the alarm.

'You've dressed to impress,' Diego complimented, subjecting her to a raking appraisal that had male appreciation at its base, and something else she didn't care to define.

There was an edge of mockery apparent, and she offered a practised smile. 'That should be...to *kill*,' she amended as he unlocked the car door, saw her seated, then crossed round the front to slide in behind the wheel.

'Should I be on guard for hidden weapons?'

Cassandra shot him a considering glance. 'Not my style.'

'But making a fashion statement is?'

'It's a woman's prerogative,' she responded with a certain wryness. 'Armour for all the visual feminine daggers that'll be aimed at my back tonight.'

'In deference to my so-called reputation?'

'Got it in one.'

The sound of his husky laughter became lost as he ignited the engine, and she remained silent for the relatively short drive to Double Bay, electing to attempt civility as the *maître d'* seated them at a reserved table.

'Australia must appeal to you,' she broached in an attempt at conversation. 'You've been based in Sydney for the past year.'

They'd progressed through the starter and were waiting for the main.

Diego settled back in his chair and regarded her with thoughtful speculation. 'I have business interests in several countries.' He regarded her with musing indolence. 'And homes in many.'

'Therefore one assumes your time of residence here is fairly transitory.'

'Possibly.'

Cassandra picked up her wine glass and took an

appreciative sip. 'Hearsay accords you a devious past.'

'Do you believe that?'

She considered him carefully. 'Social rumour can be misleading.'

'Invariably.'

There was a hardness apparent, something dangerous, almost lethal lurking deep beneath the surface. He bore the look of a man who'd seen much, weathered more...and survived.

'I think you enjoy the mystery of purported supposition.' She waited a beat. 'And you're too streetwise to have skated over the edge of the law.'

'*Gracias.*' His voice held wry cynicism.

The waiter presented their main, topped up their wine glasses, then retreated.

Cassandra picked up her cutlery and speared a succulent morsel. 'Do you have family in New York?'

'A brother.' The sole survivor of a drive-by shooting that had killed both their parents. A shocking event that happened within months of his initial sojourn in Sydney, the reason he'd taken the next flight home...and stayed to build his fortune.

It was almost nine when they entered the gallery. Guests stood in segregated groups. The men deep in discussion on subjects which would vary from the state of the country's economy to the latest business acquisition, and whether the current wife was aware of the latest mistress.

The women, on the other hand, discussed the latest fashion showing, which cosmetic surgeon was currently in vogue, speculated who was conducting a clandestine affair, and what the husband would need to part with in order to soothe the wife and retain the mistress.

The names changed, Cassandra accorded wryly, but the topics remained the same.

Tonight's exhibition was more about being seen than the purchase of a sculpture or painting. Yet the evening would be a success, due to the fact only those with buying power and social status received invitations.

Should nothing appeal, it was considered *de rigueur* to donate a sizeable cheque to a nominated charity.

Uniformed waitresses were circulating proffering trays with canapés, while waiters offered champagne and orange juice.

'Feel free to mix and mingle.'

Their presence had been duly noted, their coupling providing speculation which would, Cassandra deduced, run rife.

Had news already spread about the financial state of Preston-Villers? It was too much to hope it would be kept under wraps for long.

'Let's take a look at the exhibits,' Diego suggested smoothly, and led her towards the nearest section of paintings.

Modern impressionists held little appeal, and she

found herself explaining why as they moved on to examine some metal sculptures, one of which appeared so bizarre it held her attention only from the viewpoint of discovering what it was supposed to represent.

'Diego. I didn't expect to see you here.'

The silky feminine purr held a faint accent, and Cassandra turned to see Alicia move close to Diego.

Much too close.

'Cassandra,' the model acknowledged. 'I haven't seen Cameron here tonight.'

A barbed indication she should get a life, a lover…and not resort to accompanying her brother to most social events? Cameron relied on her presence as a cover, while she was content to provide it. A comfort zone that suited them both. Two previous relationships hadn't encouraged her to have much faith in the male of the species. One man had regarded her as a free ride in life on her father's money; the other had wanted marriage in order to gain eventual chairmanship of Preston-Villers.

'Cameron was unable to attend,' she answered smoothly. It was a deviation from the truth, and one she had no intention of revealing.

Alicia looked incredible, buffed to perfection from the tip of her Italian-shod feet to the elegantly casual hairstyle. Gowned in black silk which clung to her curves in a manner which belied the use of underwear, she was a magnet for every man in the room.

Alicia's eyes narrowed fractionally as a fellow guest commandeered Diego's attention, drawing him into a discussion with two other men.

'You're here tonight with Diego?' The query held incredulous disbelief. 'Darling, isn't he a little out of your league?'

Cassandra kept her voice light. 'The implication being…?'

'He's rich, primitive, and dangerous.' Alicia spared her a sweeping glance. 'You'd never handle him.'

This was getting bitchy. 'And you can?'

The model cast her a sweeping glance, then uttered a deprecatory laugh. 'Oh, *please*, darling.'

Well, that certainly said it all!

She resisted the temptation to tell the model the joke was on her. *Handling* Diego was the last thing she wanted to do!

'In that case,' Cassandra managed sweetly, 'why did Diego invite me along when you're so—' she paused fractionally '—obviously available?'

Anger blazed briefly in those beautiful dark blue eyes, then assumed icy scorn. 'The novelty factor?'

If you only knew! 'You think so?' She manufactured a faint smile. 'Maybe he simply tired of having women fall over themselves to gain his attention.'

Alicia placed a hand on Cassandra's arm. 'Playing hard to get is an ill-advised game. You'll end up being hurt.'

'And you care?'

'Don't kid yourself, darling.'

'Are you done?' She offered a practised smile, and barely restrained an audible gasp as Alicia dug hard, lacquered fingernails into her arm.

'Oh, I think so. For now.'

Anything was better than fencing verbal swords with the glamour queen, and Cassandra began threading her way towards the remaining exhibits, pausing now and then to converse with a fellow guest.

There was a display of bronze sculptures, and one in particular caught her eye. It was smaller than the others, and lovingly crafted to portray an elderly couple seated together on a garden stool. The man's arm enclosed the woman's shoulders as she leaned into him. Their expressive features captured a look that touched her heart. Everlasting love.

'Quite something, isn't it?' a male voice queried at her side.

Cassandra turned and offered a smile. 'Yes,' she agreed simply.

'Gregor Stanislau.' He inclined his head. 'And you are?'

'Cassandra.'

His grin was infectious. 'You have an interest in bronze?' He indicated the remaining sculptures and led her past each of them. He was knowledgeable, explaining techniques, discussing what he perceived as indiscernible flaws detracting from what could have been perfection.

'The elderly couple seated on the stool. It's your work, isn't it?'

He spread his hands in an expressive gesture. 'Guilty.'

'It's beautiful,' she complimented. 'Is it the only piece you have displayed here?'

He inclined his head. 'The couple were modelled on my grandparents. It was to be a gift to them, but I was unable to complete it in time.'

She didn't need to ask. 'Would you consider selling it?'

'To you?' He named a price she considered exorbitant, and she shook her head.

He looked genuinely regretful. 'I'm reasonably negotiable. Make me an offer.'

'Forty per cent of your original figure, plus the gallery's commission,' Diego drawled from behind her, and she turned in surprise as he moved to her side. How long had he been standing there? She hadn't even sensed his presence.

Gregor looked severely offended. 'That's an outrage.'

Diego's smile was superficially pleasant, but the hardness apparent in his eyes was not. 'Would you prefer me to insist on a professional appraisal?'

'Seventy-five per cent, and I'll consider it sold.'

'The original offer stands.'

'Your loss.' The sculptor effected a negligible shrug and retreated among the guests.

'You had no need to negotiate on my behalf,'

Cassandra declared, annoyed at his intervention. 'I was more than capable of handling him.'

Diego shot her a mocking glance, which proved a further irritation. Did he think *blonde* and *naïve* automatically went hand-in-hand?

Wrong. 'He saw me admiring it, figured I was an easy mark, so he spun a sentimental tale with the aim to double his profit margin.' She lifted one eyebrow and deliberately allowed her mouth to curve in a winsome smile. 'How am I doing so far?'

His lips twitched a little. 'Just fine.'

Cassandra inclined her head. 'Thank you.'

'I can't wait to see your follow-up action.'

'Watch and learn.'

'At a guess,' he inclined indolently, 'you'll file a complaint with the gallery owner, who'll then offer to sell you the sculpture at a figure less than its purported value, as a conscience salve for the sculptor's misrepresentation.'

A slow smile curved her mouth, and her eyes sparkled with musing humour. 'You're good.'

Cassandra was discreet. No doubt it helped her father was a known patron of the arts, and the name Preston-Villers instantly recognisable. Apologies were forthcoming, she arranged payment and organised collection, then she turned to find Alicia deep in conversation with Diego.

Nothing prepared her for the momentary shaft of pain that shot through her body. It was ridiculous, and she hated her reaction almost as much as she hated *him*.

Diego del Santo was merely an aberration. A man who'd callously manipulated a set of circumstances to his personal advantage. So what if he was a highly skilled lover, sensitive to a woman's needs? There were other men equally as skilled... Men with blue-blood birth lines, educated in the finest private schools, graduating with honours from university to enter the fields of commerce, medicine, law.

She'd met them, socialised with them...and never found the spark to ignite her emotions. Until Diego.

It was insane.

Was Alicia his current companion? Certainly she'd seen them together at a few functions over the past month or so. There could be no doubt Alicia was hell-bent on digging her claws into him.

'Cassandra—*darling*. I was hoping to find you here. How *are* you?'

There were any number of society matrons in the city, but Annouska Pendelton presided at the top of their élite heap.

The air-kiss routine, the firm grasp of Annouska's manicured fingers on her own formed an integral part of the greeting process.

Annouska working the room, Cassandra accorded silently, very aware of the matron's charity work and the excessively large sums of money she managed to persuade the rich and famous to donate to the current worthy cause.

'How is dear Alexander?' There was a click of the tongue. 'So very sad his health is declining.' There was a second's pause. 'I see you're with Diego del Santo this evening. An interesting and influential man.'

'Yes,' Cassandra agreed sweetly. 'Isn't he?'

Annouska's gaze shifted. 'Ah, Diego.' Her smile held charm. 'We were just talking about you.'

He stood close, much too close. If she moved a fraction of an inch her arm would come into contact with him. The scent of his cologne teased her nostrils, subtle, expensive, and mingled with the clean smell of freshly laundered linen.

'Indeed?' His voice was a lazy honeyed drawl that sent all her fine body hairs on alert.

'You must both come to next month's soirée.' The matron relayed details with her customary unfailing enthusiasm. 'Invitations will be in the mail early in the week.' She pressed Cassandra's fingers, then transferred them to Diego's forearm. 'Enjoy the evening.'

'Would you like coffee?' Diego queried as Annouska moved on to her next quarry.

What I'd like is to go home to my own apartment and sleep in my own bed...alone. However, that wasn't going to happen.

Already her nerves were playing havoc at the thought of what the night would bring.

'No?' He took hold of her hand and threaded his fingers through her own. 'In that case we'll leave.'

She attempted to pull free from his grasp, and failed miserably. 'Alicia will be disappointed.'

'You expect me to qualify that?'

Cassandra didn't answer, and made another furtive effort to remove her hand. '*Must* you?'

It took several long minutes to ease their way towards the exit, and she caught Alicia's venomous glare as they left the gallery.

'Do you mind?' This time she dug her nails into the back of his hand. 'I'm not going to escape and run screaming onto the street.'

'You wouldn't get far.'

'I don't need to be reminded I owe you.'

The Aston Martin was parked adjacent to the gallery and only a short-distance walk. Yet he didn't release his grasp until he'd unlocked the car.

She didn't offer so much as a word during the drive to Point Piper, and she slid from the seat the instant Diego brought the car to a halt inside the garage.

It wasn't late by social standards, but she'd been in a state of nervous tension all day anticipating the evening and how it would end.

Dear heaven, she *knew* what to expect. There was even a part of her that *wanted* his possession. What woman wouldn't want to experience sensual heaven? she queried silently.

So why did she feel so angry? Diego del Santo wasn't hers. She had no tags on him whatsoever. He was free to date anyone, and Alicia Vandernoot was undoubtedly a tigress in bed.

Wasn't that what men wanted in a woman? A whore in the bedroom?

A hollow laugh rose and died in her throat as she preceded Diego into the house.

'Would you like something to drink?' He undid his tie and unbuttoned his jacket.

Cassandra continued towards the stairs. 'Play *pretend*?' She reached the elegantly curved balustrade and began ascending the stairs. 'In order to put a different context on the reason I'm here?'

'A man and a woman well-matched in bed?' Diego countered silkily, and she paused to turn and face him.

'It's just…sex.' And knew she lied.

Without a further word she moved towards the upper floor, aware of the sensual anticipation building with every step she took.

The warmth, the heat and the passion of his possession became a palpable entity, and she hated herself for wanting what he could gift her, for there was a part of her that wanted it to be real. The whole emotional package, not just physical sex.

Yet sex was all it could be. And she should be glad. To become emotionally involved with Diego would be akin to leaping from a plane without a parachute.

Death-defying, exhilarating…madness.

Cassandra made her way along the gallery to the

main bedroom, and once there she stepped out of her stiletto-heeled pumps, removed her jewellery, then reached for the zip fastener of her gown.

She was aware of Diego's presence in the room, and the fact he'd retrieved her overnight bag. Her fingers shook a little as she took it from him and retreated into the *en suite*.

Minutes later she removed her make-up, then she unpinned her hair and deliberately avoided checking her mirrored image.

Showtime.

Diego was reclining in bed, his upper body propped up on one elbow, looking, she perceived wryly, exactly what he was...one very sexy and dangerous man.

She was suddenly supremely conscious of the large T-shirt whose hemline fell to mid-thigh, her tumbled hair and freshly scrubbed face.

The antithesis of glamour. Alicia, or any one of the many women who had shared his bed, would have elected to wear something barely-there, probably transparent, in black or scarlet. Provocative, titillating, and guaranteed to raise a certain part of the male anatomy.

Except she wasn't here to provoke or titillate, and she slid beneath the covers, settled them in place, then turned her head to look at him.

He lifted a hand and trailed fingers across her cheek, then threaded his fingers through her hair.

He traced the delicate skin beneath her ear, then

circled the hollow at the base of her neck as he fastened his mouth over hers.

She told herself she was in control, that this was just physical pleasure without any emotional involvement.

Only to stifle a groan in despair as his hand slid down her body to rest on her thigh.

How could she succumb so easily? It galled her to think she'd been on tenterhooks all evening, waiting for this moment, *wanting* it.

His tongue tangled with hers in an erotic dance as she began to respond. Her T-shirt no longer provided a barrier, and she exulted in the glide of his hands as he moulded her body close to his.

Diego rolled onto his back, carrying her with him, and he eased her against the cradle of his thighs, then shaped her breasts, weighing them gently as he caressed the sensitive skin.

Their peaks hardened beneath his touch, and the breath hissed between her teeth as he rolled each nub between thumb and forefinger, creating a friction that sent sensation soaring through her body.

With care he eased her forward to savour each peak in turn, and she cried out as he took her to the edge between pleasure and pain.

His arousal was a potent force, and he settled her against its thickened length, creating a movement that had the breath hitching in her throat.

Cassandra felt as if she was on fire, caught up in the passion he was able to evoke, rendering everything to a primitive level as he positioned her to accept him in a long, slow slide that filled her to the hilt.

Then he began to move, gently at first, governing her body to create a timeless rhythm that started slow and increased in depth and pace until she became lost, totally. Unaware of the sounds she uttered as she became caught up in the eroticism of scaling the heights, only to be held at the edge…and caught as she fell.

CHAPTER FIVE

IT WAS early when Cassandra stirred into wakefulness, the dawn providing a dull light filtering through the drapes, and she lay there quietly for a while before slipping from the bed.

With slow, careful movements she collected her bag and trod quietly from the room, choosing to dress at the end of the hallway before descending the stairs to the kitchen, where she spooned ground coffee into the coffee maker, filled the carafe with water, then switched it on.

When it filtered, she took down a mug and filled it, added sugar, and carried it out onto the terrace.

A new day, she mused, noting the glistening dew. The sun was just lifting above the horizon, lightening the sky to a pale azure, and there was the faint chirping of birds in nearby trees.

It was peaceful at this hour of the morning. Nothing much stirred. There wasn't so much as a breeze, and no craft moved in the harbour.

'You're awake early,' Diego drawled from the open doorway, and she turned to look at him.

He was something else. Tousled dark hair, hastily donned jeans barely snapped, bare-chested, nothing on his feet…gone was the sophisticated image, instead there was something primitive about his stance.

'I didn't mean to disturb you.'

Diego effected a faint shrug. 'I woke as you left the room.'

The memory of what they'd shared through the night was hauntingly vivid, and she swallowed the faint lump that rose in her throat. 'I'd like to leave soon. I have a few things to do, and I need to spend time with my father.'

'I'll start breakfast.'

'No. Please don't on my account. I'll just finish my coffee, then I'll get my bag.'

Suiting words to action, she drained the mug, then she moved through the house to the front door, collected her bag, and turned to say goodbye.

He was close, and she was unprepared for the brief hard kiss he pressed against her mouth.

Cassandra wasn't capable of uttering a word as he opened the door, and she moved quickly down to her car, slipped in behind the wheel, fired the engine, then she eased the Porsche down the driveway.

There were the usual household chores, and she spent time checking her electronic mail before leaving to visit her father.

His increasing frailty concerned her, and she didn't stay long. He needed to rest, and she conferred with Cameron as to who would contact Alexander's cardiologist.

An early night was on the agenda, and she slept well, waking at the sound of the alarm to rise and face the day.

An early-morning meeting to review the week's agenda, assess supplies and prioritise work took place within minutes of her arrival, then she took position at her workspace and adjusted the binocular microscope to her satisfaction.

It was almost midday when her cellphone buzzed, signalling an incoming text message, and she retrieved it to smile with delight at the printed text. 'home, dinner when, news. Siobhan'

For those with minimum spare time and a tight schedule, text messaging provided easy communication. Brief, Cassandra grinned as she keyed in a response, but efficient.

Within minutes they'd organised a time and place to meet that evening.

Suddenly the day seemed brighter, and she found herself humming lightly beneath her breath as she adjusted a magnification instrument, then transferred to a correction loupe. Using a calliper, she focused on the intricate work in hand.

It was almost seven when Cassandra stepped into the trendy café. Superb food, excellent service, it was so popular bookings needed to be made in advance.

A waiter showed her to a table, and she ordered mineral water, then perused the menu while she waited for Siobhan to arrive.

She was able to tell the moment Siobhan entered the café. Almost in unison every male head turned towards the door, and everything seemed to stop for a few seconds.

Cassandra sank back in her chair and watched the effect, offering a quizzical smile as Siobhan extended an affectionate greeting.

'Cassy, sorry I'm late. Parking was a bitch.'

Very few people shortened her name, except Siobhan who used it as an endearment and fiercely corrected anyone who thought to follow her example.

The clothes, the long blonde flowing hair, exquisite but minimum make-up, the perfume. Genes, Siobhan blithely accorded, whenever anyone enviously queried how she managed to look the way she did. One of the top modelling agencies had snapped her up at fifteen, and she was treading the international catwalks in Rome, Milan and Paris two years later.

Yet for all the fame and fortune, none of it had gone to her head. On occasion she played the expected part, acquiring as she termed it, the *model* persona.

Together, they'd shared private schools and formed a friendship bond that was as true now as it had been then.

Siobhan barely had time to slip into a seat before a waiter appeared at her side, and she gave him her order.

'Mineral water. Still.'

The poor fellow was so enraptured he could hardly speak, and barely refrained from genuflecting before he began to retreat.

Cassandra bit back a smile as she sank back in her seat. 'How was Italy?'

'The catwalk, behind-the-scene diva contretemps, or the most divine piece of jewellery I acquired?'

'Jewellery,' she said promptly, and gave an appreciative murmur of approval as Siobhan indicated the diamond tennis bracelet at her wrist. Top-grade stones, bezel setting…exquisite. 'Beautiful. A gift?'

'From me to me.' Siobhan grinned. 'Otherwise known as retail therapy.'

Cassandra gave a delighted laugh. 'Moving on…tell me about the Italian count.'

'Sustenance first, Cassy, darling. I'm famished.'

It wasn't fair that Siobhan could eat a healthy serving of almost anything and still retain the fabulous svelte form required by the world's top designers to model their clothes.

Cassandra made a selection, while Siobhan did likewise, and another waiter appeared to take their order the instant Siobhan lowered the menu.

'Dining with you is an incredible experience,' Cassandra said with an impish grin. 'The waiters fall over themselves just for the pleasure of fulfilling your slightest whim.'

Siobhan's eyes twinkled with devilish humour. 'Helpful when things are hectic, and I have like—'

she gestured with her glass '—five minutes to take a food break.' Her cellphone rang, and she ignored it.

'Shouldn't you get that?'

'No.'

'O-K,' she drew out slowly. 'You're not taking phone calls in general, or not from one person in particular?'

'The latter.'

Their chicken Caesar salads arrived and were placed before them with a stylish flourish.

'Problems?' Cassandra ventured.

'Some,' Siobhan admitted, and sipped from her glass.

'The Italian count?'

'The Italian count's ex-wife.'

Oh, my. 'She doesn't want you to have him?'

'Got it in one.' Siobhan picked up her cutlery and speared a piece of chicken.

'You're not going to fill in the gaps?'

'She wants to retain her title by marriage.' Siobhan's eyes rolled. 'Lack of social face, and all that crap.'

'You don't care a fig about the title.' It was a statement, not a query.

'They share joint custody of their daughter. The ex is threatening to change the custody arrangements.'

'Can she do that?'

'By questioning my ability to provide reasonable

care and attention while the child is in the paternal home due to my occupation and lifestyle.'

'Ouch,' she managed in sympathy.

'Aside from that, Rome was wonderful. The fashion showing went well…out front,' she qualified. 'Out back one of the models threw a hissy fit, and was soothed down only seconds before she was due to hit the catwalk.' She leaned forward, and made an expressive gesture with her fork. 'Your turn.'

Where did she begin? Best not to even start, for how could she justify complex and very personal circumstances?

'The usual.' She effected a light shrug. 'Nothing much changes.'

'Word has it you and Diego del Santo are an item.'

Ah, the speed of the social grapevine! 'We were guests at a dinner party, and attended the same gallery exhibition.'

'Cassy, this is *me*, remember? Being fellow guests at the same event is something you've done for the past year. It's a step up to arrive and leave with him.'

'A step up, huh?'

'So,' Siobhan honed in with a quizzical smile. *'Tell.'*

'It seemed a good idea at the time,' she responded lightly. It was part truth, and the model's gaze narrowed.

'You're hooked.'

'Not in this lifetime.'

'Uh-huh.'

'You're wrong,' Cassandra denied. 'He's—'

'One hell of a man,' Siobhan finished, and her expressive features softened. 'Well, I'll be damned.'

A delighted laugh escaped her lips as she lifted her glass and touched its rim to the one Cassandra held. 'Good luck, Cassy, darling.'

Luck? All she wanted was for the next week to be over and done with!

They finished their meal and lingered over coffee, parting well after ten with the promise to catch up again soon.

Thursday morning Cassandra woke when the cat began to miaow in protest at not being fed, and she rolled over to check the time, saw the digital blinking, and muttered an unladylike oath. A power failure during the night had wiped out her alarm, and she scrambled for her wrist-watch to check the time...only to curse again and leap from the bed.

It didn't make a good start to the day.

Minutes later she heard the dull burr of the phone from the *en suite* and opted to let the machine pick up, rather than dash dripping wet from the shower.

Towelled dry, she quickly dressed, collected a cereal bar and a banana to eat as she drove to work, caught up her briefcase, and was almost to the door before she remembered to run the machine.

Cameron's recorded voice relayed he had tickets

to a gala film première that evening, and asked her to return his call.

She'd planned a quiet night at home, but her brother enjoyed the social scene and she rarely refused any of his invitations. Besides, an evening out would help her forget Diego for a few hours.

As if.

His image intruded into every waking thought, intensifying as each day went by. As to the nights…they were worse, much worse. He'd begun to invade her dreams, and she'd wake mid-sequence to discover the touch of his mouth, his hands, was only a figment of an over-active imagination.

She cursed beneath her breath as she waited for the lift to take her down to the basement car park. Whatever gave her the idea she could enter into Diego's conditional arrangement and escape emotionally unscathed?

Fighting peak-hour traffic merely added to her overall sense of disquiet, and it was mid-morning before she managed to return Cameron's call.

The workshop prided itself on producing quality work, and there was satisfaction in achieving an outstanding piece. Especially a commissioned item where the designer had worked with the client in the selection of gems and setting.

Software made it possible to assemble a digital diagram, enhance and produce an example of the finished piece.

There was real challenge in producing something

strikingly unusual, even unique, where price was no object. Occasionally frustration played a part when the client insisted on a design the jeweller knew wouldn't display the gems to their best advantage.

It was almost six when she let herself into the apartment, and she fed the cat, watered her plants, then showered and dressed for the evening ahead.

On a whim she selected an elegant black trouser suit, added a red pashmina, and slid her feet into stiletto-heeled sandals. Upswept hair, skilful use of make-up, and she was ready just as Cameron buzzed through his arrival on the intercom.

The venue was Fox Studios, the film's lead actors had jetted in from the States, and Australian actors of note would attend as guests of honour, Cameron informed as they approached the studios.

Together they made their way into the crowded foyer, where guests mingled as waiters offered champagne and orange juice.

The film was predicted to be a box-office success, with special effects advertised as surpassing anything previously seen on screen.

There was the usual marketing pizzazz, the buzz of conversation, and Cassandra recognised a few fellow guests as she stood sipping champagne.

'I imagine Diego will be here tonight.'

'Possibly,' she conceded with deliberate unconcern, aware that if he did attend it was unlikely to be alone.

'Does that bother you?'

'Why should it? He's a free agent.' The truth shouldn't hurt so much. 'I'm just a transitory issue he decided to amuse himself with.'

She didn't want to see him here...or anywhere else for that matter. It would merely accentuate the difference between their public lives and the diabolical arrangement Diego had made in forcing her to be part of a deal.

'He's just arrived,' Cameron indicated quietly.

'Really?' Pretending indifference was a practised art, and she did it well. She told herself she wouldn't indulge in an idle glance of the foyer's occupants, only to have her attention drawn as if by a powerful magnet to where Diego stood.

Attired in an immaculate evening suit, he looked every inch the powerful magnate. Blatant masculinity and elemental ruthlessness made for a dangerous combination in any arena.

Cassandra's gaze fused with his, and in that moment she was prepared to swear everything stood still.

Sensation swirled through her body, tuning it to a fine pitch as she fought to retain a measure of composure.

Almost as if he knew, he inclined his head in acknowledgement and proffered a faintly mocking smile before returning his attention to the man at his side.

It was then Cassandra saw Alicia move into his

circle, and she felt sickened by Alicia's effusive greeting.

With deliberate movements she positioned herself so Diego was no longer in her line of vision, and she initiated an animated conversation with Cameron about the merits of German and Italian motor engineering.

Cars numbered high on his list of personal obsessions, and he launched into a spiel of detailed data that went right over her head.

He was in his element, and she allowed her mind to drift as she tuned out his voice.

Diego didn't owe her any loyalty. If he'd issued her with an invitation to partner him here tonight, she would have refused. So why did she care?

Logic and rationale were fine, but they did nothing to ease the pain in the vicinity of her heart.

Are you crazy? she demanded silently. You don't even *like* him. Why let him get to you? Except it was too late…way too late. He was already there.

'…and given a choice, I'd opt for Ferrari,' Cameron concluded, only to quizzically ask, 'Have you heard a word I said?'

'It was an interesting comparison,' Cassandra inclined with a faint smile.

'Darling, don't kid yourself. You were miles away.' He paused for a few seconds, then said gently, 'Alicia isn't *with* him. She's just trying to make out she is.'

'I really don't care.'

'Yes, you do. And that worries me.'

'Don't,' she advised with soft vehemence. 'I went into this with my eyes open.'

'There's only the weekend, then it's over.'

Now, why did that send her into a state of mild despair?

It was a relief when the auditorium doors opened and the guests moved forward to await direction to their seats.

'Cassandra. Cameron.'

She'd have recognised that faintly accented drawl anywhere, and she summoned a polite smile as she turned towards the man who'd joined them.

'Diego,' she acknowledged, and watched as he shifted his gaze to Cameron.

'If I had known you were attending I could have arranged a seating reallocation.'

'I was gifted the tickets last night,' Cameron relayed with regret.

'Pity.'

Alicia appeared at Diego's side, and curved her arm sinuously through his own. 'Diego, we're waiting for you.' She made a pretence of summoning charm. 'Cassandra, Cameron. I'm sure you'll excuse us?'

Diego deliberately released her arm from his, and Cassandra wondered if she was the only one who caught the dangerous glitter in Alicia's eyes.

To compound the situation, Diego ushered Cassandra and Cameron ahead, and Cassandra felt

Alicia's directed venom like hot knives piercing her back.

'That was interesting,' Cameron accorded quietly as they slid into their seats. 'Alicia is a first-class bitch.'

'They deserve each other,' Cassandra declared with dulcet cynicism, and incurred a musing glance.

'Darling, Diego is light-years ahead of her.'

'Is that meant as a compliment or a condemnation?'

Cameron laughed out loud. 'I'll opt for the former. I'm sure you prefer the latter.'

Wasn't that the truth!

The film proved to be a riveting example of superb technical expertise with hand-to-the-throat suspense that had the audience gasping in their seats.

Eventually the credits rolled, the lights came on, and guests began vacating the theatre.

Cassandra sent up a silent prayer she'd manage to escape without encountering Diego. Except the deity wasn't listening, and the nerves inside her stomach accelerated as he drew level with them in the foyer.

His gaze locked with hers, and she could read nothing from his expression. 'We're going on for coffee, if you'd care to join us.'

Are you kidding? You expect me to sit opposite you, calmly sipping a latte, while Alicia plays the vamp?

'Thank you, no,' she got in quickly before

Cameron had a chance to accept. 'I have an early start in the morning.' She didn't, but he wasn't to know that, and she offered a sweet smile as he inclined his head.

'I'll be in touch.'

Alicia's mouth tightened, and Cassandra glimpsed something vicious in those ice-blue eyes for a timeless second, then it was gone.

Cassandra wasn't conscious of holding her breath until Diego moved ahead of them, then she released it slowly, conscious of Cameron's soft exclamation as she did so.

'Watch your back with that one, darling,' he cautioned. 'Alicia has it in for you.'

She met her brother's wry look with equanimity. 'Tell me something I don't know.'

They reached the exit and began walking towards where Cameron had parked the car. 'If she discovers Diego is sleeping with you...' He left the sentence unfinished.

'I can look after myself.'

He caught hold of her hand and squeezed it in silent reassurance. 'Just take care, OK?'

CHAPTER SIX

'CASSANDRA, phone.'

Diego, it had to be.

Cassandra took the call, and tried to control the way her pulse leapt at the sound of his voice.

'We're taking the mid-morning flight. I'll collect you at nine tomorrow.'

'I can meet you at the airport.' That way her car would be there when they returned.

'Nine, Cassandra,' he reiterated in a quiet drawl that brooked little argument, then he cut the connection.

He was insufferable, she fumed as she returned to her workspace.

The resentment didn't diminish much as day became night, and she rose early, packed, put out sufficient dry food and water for the cat, then a few minutes before nine she took the lift down to Reception.

The Gold Coast appeared at its sparkling best. Clear azure sky, late-spring warm temperatures, and sunshine.

Diego picked up a hire car and within half an hour they reached the luxurious Palazzo Versace hotel complex.

It was more than a year since Cassandra had last visited the Coast, and she adored the holiday atmosphere, the canal estates, the trendy sidewalk café's and casual lifestyle.

The hotel offered six-star accommodation, plus privately owned condominiums and several penthouse apartments.

Why should she be surprised to discover Diego owned a penthouse here? Or that he'd elected to take the extra total designer furnishing package including bed coverings and cushions, towels, china, glassware and cutlery?

The total look, she mused in admiration. Striking, expensive, and incredibly luxurious.

There was a million-dollar view from the floor-to-ceiling glass walls, and she took a deep breath of fresh sea air as Diego slid open an external glass door.

Delightful. But let's not forget the reason he's brought you here, an imp taunted silently.

Bedroom duties. The thought should have filled her with antipathy, but instead there was a sense of anticipation at a raw primitive level to experience again the magical, mesmeric excitement he was able to evoke.

Was it so wrong to want his touch, his possession without any emotional involvement other than the pleasure of the moment?

Don't kid yourself, she chided inwardly. Like it

or not, you're involved right up to your slender neck!

After this weekend her life would return to normal…*whatever* normal meant. Work, she mused as Diego took their overnight bags through to the bedroom. The usual social activities…which would never be quite the same again as she encountered Diego partnering Alicia, or any one of several other women all too willing to share his evening. Dammit, his *bed*.

How would she cope, imagining that muscular male body engaged in the exchange of sexual body fluids? The entanglement of limbs, the erotic pleasure of his mouth savouring warm feminine skin as he sought each sensual hollow, every intimate crevice?

It would be killing, she admitted silently. Perhaps she could retreat into living the life of a social recluse, and simply bury herself in work.

Except that would be accepting defeat, and she refused to contemplate a slide into negativity.

For now, there was the day, and she intended to make the most of it. With or without him. The night he would claim as his, but meantime…

Cassandra heard him re-enter the spacious lounge, and she lifted a hand and gestured to the view out over the Broadwater. 'It's beautiful here.'

Diego moved to stand behind her, and she was supremely conscious of him. Her skin tingled in reaction to his body warmth, and the temptation to lean back against him was almost irresistible.

'Do you spend much time here?' It seemed almost a sacrilege to leave the apartment empty for long periods of time.

'The occasional weekend,' he drawled.

But not often, she concluded, and wondered if and when he took a break to enjoy the fruits of his success. He possessed other homes, in other countries...perhaps he chose somewhere more exotic where he could relax and unwind.

'Lunch,' Diego indicated. 'We can eat in the restaurant here, cross the road to the Sheraton Hotel, or explore nearby Tedder Avenue.'

She turned towards him and saw he'd exchanged tailored trousers for shorts, and joggers replaced hand-tooled leather shoes.

'You're allowing me to choose?'

'Don't be facetious,' he chided gently.

'Tedder Avenue,' Cassandra said without hesitation. 'We can walk there.' Half a kilometre was no distance at all.

One eyebrow rose in quizzical humour. 'You want exercise, I can think of something more athletic.'

'Ah, but my sexual duties don't begin until dark...remember?'

He pressed an idle finger to the lower curve of her lip. 'A sassy mouth could get you into trouble.'

'In that case, I'll freshen up and we can leave.'

His husky laugh curled around her nerve-ends, pulled a little, then she stepped around him and walked through to the master bedroom.

She took a few minutes to change into tailored shorts and blouse, then she snagged a cap, her shoulder bag, and re-entered the lounge.

'Let's hit the road.'

It was a pleasant walk, the warmth of the sun tempered by a light breeze, and they settled on one of several pavement cafés, ordered, then ate with evident enjoyment.

They were almost ready to leave when Diego's cellphone buzzed, and she looked askance when he merely checked the screen and didn't pick up.

'It'll go to message-bank.'

'Perhaps you should take that,' Cassandra said when it buzzed again a few minutes later.

Diego merely shrugged and ignored a further insistent summons.

Within a few minutes Cassandra's cellphone buzzed from inside her bag, and she retrieved it, saw the unfamiliar number displayed, then engaged the call.

'You're with Diego.' The feminine voice was tight with anger. 'Aren't you?'

Oh, lord. 'Alicia?'

'He's taken you to the Coast for the weekend, hasn't he?'

'What makes you think that?'

'Fundamental mathematics.'

'No chance you might be wrong?'

'Darling, I've already checked. Diego picked you up from your apartment this morning.'

Counting to ten wouldn't do it. Hell, even *twenty* wouldn't come close. 'You have a problem,' Cassandra managed evenly.

'*You* in Diego's life is the problem.'

'I suggest you discuss it with him.'

'Oh, I intend to.'

She cut the connection and met Diego's steady gaze with equanimity. 'You owe Alicia an explanation.'

'No,' he said quietly. 'I don't.'

'She seems to think you do.'

The waitress presented the bill, which he paid, adding a tip, then when she left he sank back in his chair and subjected Cassandra to an unwavering appraisal.

'Whatever Alicia and I shared ended several months ago.'

She raised an eyebrow and offered him a cynical smile. 'Yet you continue to date her?'

'We have mutual friends, we receive the same invitations.' He lifted his shoulders in a negligible shrug. 'Alicia likes to give the impression we retain a friendship.'

She couldn't help herself. 'Something she manages to do very well.'

Diego's eyes hardened. 'That bothers you?'

'Why should it?'

Did she think he was oblivious to the way her pulse quickened whenever he moved close? Or feel the thud of her heart? The soft warmth colouring her skin, or the way her eyes went dark an instant before his mouth found hers?

'It's over, and Alicia needs to move on.'

A chill slithered down her spine. As she would have to move on come Monday? What was she *thinking*, for heaven's sake? She couldn't wait for the weekend to be over so she could get on with her life.

A life in which Diego didn't figure at all.

Now, why did that thought leave her feeling strangely bereft?

'Let's walk along the beach,' Cassandra suggested as they stood to their feet. She had the sudden need to feel the golden sand beneath her feet, the sun on her skin, and the peace and tranquillity offered by a lazy outgoing tide.

The ocean lay a block distant, and within minutes she slid off her sandals and padded down to the damp, packed sand at the water's edge.

They wandered in companionable silence, admiring the long, gentle curve stretching down towards Kirra. Tall, high-rise apartment buildings in varying height and colour dotted the foreshore, and there was a fine haze permeating the air.

Children played in the shallows while parents stood guard, and in the distance seagulls hovered, seemingly weightless, before drifting slowly down onto the sand to dig their beaks in in search of a tasty morsel.

It was a peaceful scene which changed and grew more crowded as they neared Surfer's Paradise.

'Feel like exploring the shops?' Diego ventured, and Cassandra inclined her head.

'Brave of you. That's tantamount to giving a woman *carte blanche*.'

'Perhaps I feel in an indulgent mood.'

'Who would refuse?' she queried lightly, and changed direction, pausing as they reached the board-walk to brush sand from her feet before slipping on her sandals.

It became a delightful afternoon as they strolled along an avenue housing several designer boutiques before venturing down another where Cassandra paused to examine some fun T-shirts.

She selected one and took it to the salesgirl, whereupon Diego extracted his wallet and passed over a bill.

'No.' Cassandra waved his hand aside, and shot him an angry glance as he insisted, to the amusement of the salesgirl, who doubtless thought Cassandra a graceless fool. 'Thank you, but no,' she reiterated firmly as she forcibly placed her own bill into the salesgirl's hand.

She was the first woman who'd knocked back his offer to pay, and her fierce independence amused him. There had been a time when he'd had to watch every cent and look to handouts for clothing and food. Nor was he particularly proud he'd resorted to sleight-of-hand on occasion. Very few knew he now donated large sums of money each year to shelters for the homeless, and funded activity centres for underprivileged children.

'Let's take a break and linger over a latte,' Diego suggested as they emerged from the shop.

'Can't hack the pace, huh?' Cassandra teased as she tucked her fingers through the plastic carry-bag containing her purchase.

There wasn't an ounce of spare flesh on that powerful body, and she wondered what he did to keep fit.

A gym? Perhaps a personal trainer?

They took a cab back to the Palazzo as dusk began to fall, and on entering the penthouse Cassandra headed for the bedroom, where she gathered up a change of clothes and made for the *en suite*.

There was a necessity to shampoo the salt-mist from her hair, and she combined it with a leisurely shower, then she emerged from the glass stall, grabbed a bath-towel and she had just secured it sarong-style when Diego walked naked into the *en suite*.

Oh, my, was all that came immediately to mind. Superb musculature, olive skin, a light smattering of dark, curly hair on his chest. Broad shoulders, a tapered waist, slim hips…

She forced her appraisal to halt there, unable to

let it travel lower for fear of how it would affect her composure.

It was difficult to meet his gaze, and she didn't even try. Instead she moved past him and entered the bedroom, sure of his faint husky chuckle as she closed the door behind her.

There was a certain degree of satisfaction in witnessing her discomfort. In truth, it delighted him to know she wasn't entirely comfortable with him, and there was pleasure in the knowledge her experience with men was limited.

His body reacted at the thought of the night ahead. Her scent, the taste of her skin…*por Dios,* how it felt to be inside her.

He hadn't felt quite this sense of anticipation for a woman since his early teens when raging hormones made little distinction between one girl or another.

Now there was desire and passion for one woman, only one. Cassandra.

If he had his way, he'd towel himself dry, go into the bedroom and initiate a night-long seduction she'd never forget.

Soon, he promised himself as he turned the water dial from hot to cold. But first, they'd dine at the restaurant downstairs overlooking the pool. Fine wine, good food.

Cassandra put the finishing touches to her make-up, then she caught up an evening purse and preceded Diego from the apartment.

The classic black gown with its lace overlay was suitable for any occasion. The very reason she'd packed it, together with black stiletto-heeled pumps. A long black lace scarf wound loosely at her neck was a stunning complement, and she wore minimum jewellery, diamond ear-studs and a diamond tennis bracelet.

With her hair twisted into an elegant knot atop her head, she looked the cool, confident young woman. Who was to know inside she was a mass of nerves?

Act, a tiny voice prompted. You can do it, you're good at it. Practised social graces. Taught in the very best of private schools.

The restaurant was well-patronised, and the *maître d'* presided with friendly formality as he saw them seated.

Wine? One glass, which she sipped throughout the meal, and, although they conversed, she had little recollection of the discussion.

For there was only the man, and the sexual aura he projected. It was a powerful aphrodisiac…primitive, *lethal.*

She had only to look at his hands to recall the magic they created as they stroked her skin. And his mouth…the passion it evoked in her was to die for, almost literally.

For she did die a little with each orgasm as he led her towards a tumultuous climax and joined her at the peak, held her there, before toppling them both in glorious free-fall.

The mere thought sent the blood racing through her veins, the quickened thud of her heartbeat audible to her ears as she waited for the moment Diego would settle the bill.

How long had the meal lasted? Two hours, three? She had little recollection of the passage of time.

The apartment was dark when they returned, and Cassandra crossed to the wall of glass to admire the night-scape.

The water resembled a dark mass, dappled by threads of reflected light. Bright neon flashed on buildings across the Broadwater, and there were distant stars dotting an indigo sky.

She sensed rather than heard Diego stand behind her, and she made no protest as he cupped each shoulder and drew her back against him.

His lips caressed the delicate hollows at the edge of her neck, and sensation curled deep within, radiating in a sweet, heated circle through her body until she felt achingly alive.

Diego slid a hand down to grasp hers, and he led her down to the bedroom. He dimmed the lights down low, then slowly removed each article of her clothing until she stood naked before him. With care he lifted both hands to her hair and slowly removed the pins, so its length cascaded down onto her shoulders.

He traced a pattern over her breasts, then drew a

line down to her belly before seeking the moist heart of her.

'You're wearing too many clothes,' she managed shakily, and watched as he divested each one of them.

Then he lowered his head and kissed her, arousing such passion she soon lost a sense of time or place as she became lost in the man, a wanton willing to gift and take sensual pleasure until there could be only one end.

It was then Diego pulled her down onto the bed and ravished her with such exquisite slowness she cried out in demand he assuage the ache deep within.

Afterwards they slept, to wake at dawn to indulge in the slow, sweet loving of two people in perfect sexual accord.

It was an idyllic place, Cassandra bestowed wistfully as they sat eating breakfast out by the pool, and wondered how it would feel to fall asleep in Diego's arms every night, knowing he was *there*. To gift him pleasure, as he pleasured her.

Whoa...wait a minute here. So the sex is great. Hell, let's go with fantastic. But it stops with tonight.

Early tomorrow morning they'd take the dawn flight back to Sydney and go their separate ways.

She should be happy it was nearly over. Instead she felt incredibly bereft.

Given the option of how to spend the day,

Cassandra chose the theme park. Lots of people, plenty of entertainment, and it meant she didn't have much opportunity to dwell on the coming night.

Tigers, baby cubs, the Imax theatre were only a few of the features available, and the hours slipped by with gratifying ease.

'Want to dine out, or order in?' Diego queried as they returned to the penthouse.

'Order in.' It would be nice to sit out on the balcony beneath dimmed lighting, sip chilled wine, and sample food while taking in the night scene out over the marina, where large cruisers lay at berth and people wandered along the adjacent board-walk.

He moved to where she stood and trailed light fingers down her cheek. 'Simple pleasures, hmm?'

Sensation began to unfurl deep inside, increasing her pulse-beat. It was crazy. Think with your head, she bade silently. If you go with what your heart dictates, you'll be in big trouble. Somehow she had the feeling it was way too late for rationale.

'I'll go freshen up.' If she didn't move away from him, she'd be lost.

A refreshing shower did much to restore a sense of normalcy, and she donned jeans and a cotton-knit top, tied her hair back, then added a touch of lip-gloss.

Diego was standing in the lounge talking on his cellphone, and he concluded the call as she entered the room.

'Check the menu while I shower and change.'

Seafood, Cassandra decided as she viewed the selection offered, and chose prawn risotto with bruschetta. Diego, when he re-emerged in black jeans and polo shirt, endorsed her suggestion and added lobster tail and salad.

Diego opened a bottle of chilled sauvignon blanc while they waited for the food to be delivered, and they moved out on the balcony as the night sky began to deepen.

Lights became visible in a number of luxury cabin cruisers berthed close by, and Cassandra stilled, mesmerised, as Diego leant out a hand and freed the ribbon from her hair.

'All day I've resisted the temptation.' He threaded his fingers through its length so it curved down over her shoulders.

The breeze stirred the fine strands, tumbling them into a state of disarray. A warm smile curved his mouth as he leaned in close and took possession of her mouth in an exploratory open-mouthed kiss that teased and tantalised as he evoked her response.

He tasted of cool wine, and she placed a steadying hand to his shoulders and leaned in for a few brief moments until the electronic peal of the doorbell broke them apart.

Diego collected the restaurant food while Cassandra set the small balcony table with fine china and cutlery, and they shared a leisurely meal, offering each other forked morsels of food to sample in a gourmet feast.

The moon shone brightly, and there were myriad tiny stars sprinkling the night sky. Magical, she accorded silently.

They lingered over the wine, and when a fresh breeze started up they carried everything indoors, dealt with the few dishes, dispensed the food containers, and contemplated coffee.

It wasn't late, yet all it took was the drift of his fingers tracing the line of her slender neck, the touch of his lips at her temple, and she became lost.

With one fluid movement he swept her into his arms and carried her down to the bedroom, where dispensing with her clothes, his, became almost an art form.

She wanted to savour every moment, each kiss, the touch of his hands, his mouth, and exult in his possession. To gift him pleasure and hear the breath hiss between his teeth, his husky groan as she drove him to the end of his endurance.

When he reached it, she drew him in, the long, deep thrust plunging to the hilt, and he felt her warm, slick heat, revelled in the way she enclosed him, urging a hard, driving rhythm that scaled the heights with a shattering climax that left them both exhausted.

Afterwards they slept for a few hours, and Cassandra stirred as he carried her into the *en suite* and stepped into the spa-bath.

Dreamlike, she allowed his ministrations, and stood like an obedient child as he blotted the moisture from her body before tending to his own, then he took her back to bed to savour her body in a long, sweet loving that almost made her weep.

All too soon it was time to shower and dress, pack, drink strong black coffee, then drive down to Coolangatta Airport. Check-in time was disgustingly early, the flight south smooth and uneventful.

It was just after eight when they disembarked at Sydney Airport, and it took scant minutes to traverse the concourse to ground level.

'I'll take a cab,' Cassandra indicated as they emerged from the terminal.

Diego shot her a dark look that spoke volumes. 'Don't be ridiculous.'

'I need to get to work.'

One eyebrow slanted. 'So I'll drop you there.'

'It's out of your way.'

'What's that got to do with anything?'

She heaved an eloquent sigh. 'Diego—'

'Cool it, Cassandra. You're coming with me.'

Like a marionette when the puppeteer pulls the string? She opened her mouth to protest, only to close it again as the Aston Martin swept into the parking bay with an attendant at the wheel.

She remained silent during the drive into the city, and she had her seat belt undone with her hand on the door-clasp when he eased the car to a halt adjacent to the jewellery workshop.

'Thank you for a pleasant weekend.' The words sounded incredibly inadequate as she slid from the passenger seat. 'If you pop the trunk I'll collect my bag, then you won't need to get out of the car.'

Except her words fell on deaf ears as he emerged from behind the wheel, collected her bag and handed it to her.

Then he lowered his head and took possession of her mouth in a brief, hard kiss that left her gasping for breath. Then he released her and slid into the car as she walked away without so much as a backward glance.

Could anyone see her heart was breaking? Somehow she doubted it as she got on with the day. She checked with Sylvie, Alexander's nurse, and arranged to share dinner that evening with her father.

At four Cameron rang, jubilant with the news Diego had released the balance of funds.

Mission accomplished, she perceived grimly as she took a cab to her apartment, changed and freshened up, then she drove to Alexander's home.

He looked incredibly frail, and she felt her spirits plummet at the knowledge he'd deteriorated in the short time since she'd seen him last.

His appetite seemed to have vanished, and she coaxed him to eat, amusing him with anecdotes that brought forth a smile.

Cassandra stayed a while, sitting with him until Sylvie declared it was time for him to retire. Then she kissed his cheek and held him close for a few long minutes before taking her leave.

Meeting Diego's demands had been worth it.

Alexander remained ignorant of Cameron's business inadequacies, together with details surrounding his private life.

What about *you*? a tiny voice demanded a few hours later as she tossed and turned in her bed in search of sleep.

CHAPTER SEVEN

THURSDAY morning Cassandra woke with an uneasy feeling in the pit of her stomach. A premonition of some kind?

She slid out of bed, fed the cat, made a cup of tea and checked her emails, then she showered, dressed, and left for work.

There was nothing to indicate the day would be different from any other. Traffic was at its peak-hour worst, and an isolated road-rage incident, while momentarily disconcerting, didn't rattle her nerves overmuch.

Work progression proved normal, with nothing untoward occurring. Cameron rang, jubilant the Preston-Villers deal with Diego was a *fait accompli*, suggesting she join him for a celebration dinner.

So why couldn't she shake this sense of foreboding that hung around like a grey cloud?

It was almost six when she entered the apartment, and she greeted the cat, fed her, and was about to fix something to eat for herself when her cellphone buzzed.

'Cassandra.' Sylvie's voice sounded calm and unhurried. 'Alexander is being transported to hospital by ambulance. I'm about to follow. I've spoken to

Cameron, and he's already on his way.' She named the city's main cardiac unit. 'I'll see you there.'

Cassandra's stomach plummeted as she caught up her bag, her keys, and raced from the apartment. The cardiologist's warning returned to haunt her as she took the lift down to basement level, slid into her car to drive as quickly as traffic and the speed limit would allow.

Hospital parking was at a premium, and she brought her car to a screeching halt in a reserved space, hastily scrawled *emergency* onto a scrap of paper and slid it beneath the windscreen wiper, then she ran into the building.

What followed numbered among the worst hours of her life. Sylvie was there, waiting, and Cameron. The cardiac team were working to stabilise Alexander, but the prognosis wasn't good.

At midnight they sent Sylvie home, and Cassandra and Cameron kept vigil as the long night crept slowly towards dawn.

'Go home, get some sleep,' Cameron bade gently, and she shook her head.

At nine they each made calls, detailing the reason neither would be reporting for work, and took alternate one-hour shifts at Alexander's bedside.

It was there Diego found her, looking pale, wan and so utterly saddened it was all he could do not to sweep her into his arms and hold her close.

Not that she'd thank him for it, he perceived, aware he had no place here. Strict *family only* regulations applied, but he'd managed to circumvent them in order to gain a few minutes to express regret and ask if there was anything he could do.

'No,' Cassandra said quietly. 'Thank you.'

Diego cupped her shoulder, allowed his hand to linger there before letting it fall to his side.

A hovering nurse cast him a telling look, indicated the time, and he inclined his head in silent acquiescence.

'I'll keep in touch.'

'How did he get in here?' Cassandra asked quietly minutes later, and Cameron responded wearily,

'By sheer strength of will, I imagine. It happens to be one of his characteristics, or hadn't you noticed?'

In spades, she acknowledged, then jerked to startled attention as the machines monitoring her father's vital signs began an insistent beeping.

From then on it was all downhill, and Alexander slipped away from them late that evening.

Cassandra lapsed into a numbed state, and both she and Cameron shared a few silent tears in mutual consolation.

'Maybe you should spend the night at my place.'

She pulled away from him and searched for a handkerchief. 'I'll be fine. I just want to have a shower and fall into bed.'

'That goes for me, too.'

They walked down the corridor to the lift and took it down to ground level, then emerged into the late-night air. Cameron saw her to the car, waited until she was seated, then leaned in. 'I'll follow and make sure you get home OK.'

At this hour the streets carried minimal traffic, and as she reached Double Bay a light shower of rain began to fall. She saw the headlights of Cameron's car at her rear, and as she turned in to her apartment building he sounded his horn, then executed a semicircle and disappeared from sight.

Weariness hit her as she stepped out of the lift, and she was so caught up in reflected thought she didn't see the tall male figure leaning against the wall beside her apartment door.

'Diego? What—?'

He reached out and extricated the keys from her fingers, unlocked the door and gently pushed her inside.

'—are you doing?' she finished tiredly. 'You shouldn't be here.'

'No?' He removed her shoulder bag, put it down on the side-table, then led her towards the kitchen. He made tea, invaded her fridge and put a sandwich together.

'Eat.'

Food? 'I don't feel like anything.'

'A few mouthfuls will do.'

It was easier to capitulate than argue, and she obediently took a bite, sipped the tea, then she pushed the plate away. Any more and she'd be physically ill.

'Shower and bed,' Cassandra relayed wearily as she stood to her feet. 'You can let yourself out.' She didn't bother to wait for him to answer. Didn't care to see if he stayed. It was all too much, and more than anything she needed to sleep.

Diego fed the cat, washed the few dishes, checked his cellphone, made one call, then he doused the lights and entered her bedroom.

She was already asleep, and he undressed, then carefully slid beneath the covers. The thought she might wake and weep with grief alone was a haunting possibility he refused to condone.

Cassandra was dreaming. Strong arms held her close, and she felt a hand smoothing her hair. Lips brushed her temple, and she sank deeper into the dreamlike embrace, savouring the warmth of muscle and sinew beneath her cheek, the steady beat of a human heart.

It was comforting, reassuring, and she was content to remain there, cushioned in security, and loath to emerge and face the day's reality.

Except dreams didn't last, and she surfaced slowly through the veils of sleep to discover it was no dream.

'Diego?'

'I hope to hell you didn't think it could be anyone else,' he growled huskily, and met her startled gaze.

'I didn't want you to be alone.'

She tried to digest the implication, and found it too hard at this hour of the morning.

He watched as comprehension dawned on her pale features, saw the pain and glimpsed her attempt to deal with it.

'Want to talk?'

Cassandra shook her head, and held back the tears, hating the thought of breaking down in front of him.

'I'll go make coffee.' It would give him something to do with his hands, otherwise he would use them to haul her close, and while his libido was high, he was determined the next time they made love it would be without redress.

He slid from the bed, pulled on trousers and a shirt, then he entered the *en suite*, only to re-emerge minutes later, wryly aware a woman's razor was no substitute for a man's electric shaver.

In the kitchen he ground fresh coffee beans, replaced a filter, and switched on the coffee maker.

It was after eight, and breakfast was a viable option. Eggs, ham, cheese...ingredients he used to make two fluffy omelettes, then he slid bread into the toaster.

Cassandra dressed in jeans, added a blouse, then tended to her hair. She felt better after cleansing her face, and following her usual morning routine.

Not great, she assured her mirrored image, but OK. Sufficient to face the day and all it would involve.

The smell of fresh coffee, toast and something cooking teased her nostrils, and she entered the kitchen to find Diego dishing food onto two plates.

Her appetite didn't amount to much, but she ate half the omelette, some toast, and sipped her way through two cups of coffee.

'Shouldn't you be wherever it is you need to be at this hour of the morning?'

'Later,' Diego drawled, leaning back in his chair, satisfied she looked less fragile. 'When Cameron arrives, I'll leave.'

Her eyes clouded a little. 'I'm OK.'

One eyebrow slanted. 'I wasn't aware I implied you weren't.'

The cat hopped up onto her lap, padded a little, then settled.

She owed him thanks. 'It was thoughtful of you to stay.'

'I had Cameron's word he'd contact me if you insisted on returning home.'

Diego had done that out of concern? For her?

At that moment the phone rang, and she answered it. Cameron was on his way over.

Cassandra began clearing the table, and they dealt with the dishes together. There was an exigent awareness she was loath to explore, and she concentrated on the job in hand.

When it was done, she used the pretext of tidying the bedroom to escape, and the intercom buzzed as she finished up.

Cameron didn't look as if he'd slept well, and she made fresh coffee, served it, and was unsure whether to be relieved or regretful when Diego indicated he would leave.

The days leading up to Alexander's funeral were almost as bleak as the funeral itself, and Cassandra took an extra day before returning to the jewellery workshop.

Sylvie stayed on at Alexander's home, Cameron flew to Melbourne on business, and Cassandra directed all her energy into work.

Diego rang, but she kept the conversations short for one reason or another and declined any invitation he chose to extend.

A pendant commissioned by Alicia would normally have had all the fine hairs on Cassandra's nape standing on end. As it was, she took extra care with the design, ensuring its perfection.

The ensuing days ran into a week, and Cameron returned to Sydney briefly before taking a flight interstate within days.

'Cassandra, you're wanted at the shop.'

She disengaged from the binocular microscope, ran a hand over the knot atop her head, then made her way towards the retail shop.

A client wanting advice on a design? Soliciting suggestions for a particular gem? Or someone who had admired one of her personal designs and wanted something similar?

Security was tight, and she went through the entry procedure, passed through the ante-room and entered the shop, where gems sparkled against dark velvet in various glass cabinets.

Two perfectly groomed assistants stood positioned behind glass counters, their facial expressions a polite mask as they regarded a tall young woman whose back and stance seemed vaguely familiar.

Then the woman swung round, and Cassandra saw why.

Alicia. Beautifully dressed, exquisitely made-up, and looking very much the international model.

Trouble was the word that immediately came to mind.

'Miss Vandernoot would like to discuss the pendant she commissioned.'

'Yes, of course,' Cassandra said politely and crossed to where Alicia stood. 'Perhaps you'd care to show it to me.' She reached for a length of jeweller's velvet and laid it on the glass counter top.

'This,' Alicia hissed as she all but tossed the pendant down.

It was a beautiful piece, rectangular in shape with five graduated diamonds set in gold. The attached chain, exquisite.

'There are scratches. And the diamonds are not the size and quality I originally settled on.'

It was exactly as Alicia had commissioned. The diamonds perfectly cut and set.

Cassandra extracted her loupe, and saw the

scratches at once. Several. None of which were there when Alicia inspected and took delivery of the pendant. Inflicted in a deliberate attempt to denigrate her expertise?

'My notes are on file,' she began politely, and she turned towards the senior assistant. 'Beverly, would you mind retrieving them? I need to check the original details with Miss Vandernoot.'

It took a while. Cassandra went through the design notations and instructions with painstaking thoroughness, taking time to clarify each point in turn, witnessed and checked with Beverly. By the time she finished, Alicia had nowhere to go.

'There's still the matter of the scratching.'

Cassandra could have wept at the desecration to what had been perfection. 'They can be removed,' she advised quietly.

Alicia drew herself up to her full height, which, aided by five-inch stiletto-heeled sandals, was more than impressive.

'I refuse to accept substandard workmanship.' She swept Cassandra's slender frame with a scathing look.

'If you care to leave the item, we'll assess the damage and repair it at no cost to you.'

'Restitution is the only acceptable solution,' Alicia demanded with haughty insolence. 'I want a full credit, and I get to keep the item.'

Cassandra had had enough. This wasn't about

jewellery. 'That's outrageous and against company policy,' she said quietly.

'If you don't comply, I'll report this to the jewellers' association and ensure it receives media attention.'

'Do that. Meanwhile we'll arrange an expert evaluation of the scratches by an independent jeweller, and his report will be run concurrently.'

She'd called Alicia's bluff, and left the model with no recourse whatsoever. Alicia knew it, and her expression wasn't pretty as she scooped up the pendant and chain and flung both into her bag.

With deceptive calm Cassandra turned towards Beverly. 'I'll see Miss Vandernoot out, shall I?'

It was a minor victory, but one that lasted only until they reached the street.

'Don't think you've won,' Alicia vented viciously. 'I want Diego, and I mean to have him.'

'Really?' Cassandra watched as the model's gaze narrowed measurably. 'Good luck.'

'Keep your hands off him. I've spent a lot of time and energy cultivating the relationship.'

For one wild moment, Cassandra thought Alicia was going to hit her, and she braced herself to deal with it, only to hear the model utter a few vehement oaths and walk away.

Settling back to work took effort, and she was glad when the day ended and she could go home.

Grief sat uneasily on her shoulders, and Alicia's hissy fit only served to exacerbate her emotions. It would be all too easy to rage against fate or sink into a well of tears.

What a choice, she decided as she let herself into her apartment. The cat ran up to her, and she crouched down to caress the velvet ears. A feline head butted her hand, then smooched appealingly before curling over onto its back in silent invitation for a tummy rub.

'Unconditional devotion,' she murmured as she obligingly rubbed the cat's fur, and heard the appreciative purr in response.

She was all alone with no one close to call.

Cameron was in Melbourne, Siobhan had returned to Italy, and she couldn't, *wouldn't* ring Diego.

OK, so she'd feed the cat, fix herself something to eat, then she'd clean the apartment. An activity that would take a few hours, after which she'd shower and fall into bed.

CHAPTER EIGHT

WORK provided a welcome panacea, and Cassandra applied herself diligently the following morning as she adjusted the binocular microscope and focused on the delicate setting. Its intricate design provided a challenge, professionally and personally.

She wanted the best, insisted on it, aware such attention to minuscule detail brought the desired result…perfection.

If achieving it meant working through a lunch-hour, or staying late at the workshop, nothing mattered except the quality of the work.

Yet there were safety precautions in place. Loose stones were easy to fence, and therefore provided a target for robbery. Priceless gems, expensive equipment. Security was tight, the vault one of the finest. Bulletproof glass shielded those who worked inside, and a high-priced security system took care of the rest.

It all added up to a heightened sense of caution. Something she had become accustomed to over the years, and one she never took for granted.

The cast-in-stone rule ensured two people, never one alone, occupied the workshop on the premise that if by chance something untoward happened to one, the other was able to raise the alarm.

In the three years she'd worked for this firm, no one had attempted to breach the security system in daylight.

Oh, for heaven's sake! Why were such thoughts chasing through her mind? Instinct, premonition? Or was it due to an acute vulnerability?

No matter how hard she tried, she was unable to dismiss Diego from her mind. He was an intrusive force, every waking minute of each day.

She could sense his touch without any trouble at all. *Feel* the way his mouth moved on her own. As to the rest of it…

Don't go there. The memories were too vivid, too intoxicating.

Great while it lasted, she admitted. A fleeting, transitory fling orchestrated for all the wrong reasons. Manipulation at its worst.

So why was she aching for him?

The deal was done. Preston-Villers would flourish beneath Diego's management. Cameron retained anonymity in his private life. As to her? She'd fulfilled all obligations and was off the hook.

A hollow laugh sounded low in her throat. Sure she was! She'd never been so tied up in her life!

She barely ate, she rarely slept. Some of it could be attributed to grieving for her father. The rest fell squarely on Diego's shoulders.

The electronic buzzer sounded loud above background music from wall-speakers, and Cassandra glanced up from her work to see a familiar figure holding twin food bags on the other side of the door.

Sally from the café near by with their lunch order.

'Want to take those sandwiches, or shall I?' Cassandra queried, only to see Glen in the throes of heating fine metal. 'OK, I'll get them.'

She laid down her tools, then moved towards the door, released the security lock and reached for the latch.

At that moment all hell let loose.

She had a fleeting glimpse of Sally's terrified expression, caught a blur of sudden movement as Sally catapulted into the workroom, followed by a man whose facial features were obscured by a woollen ski-mask.

A nightmare began to unfold as he whipped out a vicious-looking knife and brandished it.

The drill in such circumstances was clear. Do what you're told...and don't play the hero.

A knife wasn't a gun. She had self-defence training. Could she risk attempting to disarm him?

'Don't even think about it.' The harsh directive chilled her blood as he pulled out a hand gun and brandished it. In one swift movement he hooked an arm round her shoulders and hauled her back against him, then he pressed the tip of the knife to her throat.

Calm, she had to remain calm. Not easy with a

gun in close proximity, not to mention the threat of a knife.

At the edge of her peripheral vision she glimpsed Glen making a surreptitious move with his foot to the panic button at floor level. An action that would send an electronic alert to the supervisor's pager, the security firm and the local police station.

Had the intruder seen it? She could only pray not.

'Empty the vault.' The demand held a guttural quality, and she saw Glen lift his hands in a helpless gesture.

'I don't know the combination.'

He was buying time, and the intruder knew it.

'You think I'm a fool?' the intruder demanded viciously, tightening his hold on Cassandra's shoulders. 'Open it *now*, or I'll use this knife.'

She felt the tip of it slide across the base of her throat, the sting of her flesh accompanied by the warm trickle of blood.

Glen didn't hesitate. He crossed to the vault, keyed in a series of digits, then pulled open the door.

'Put everything into a bag. *Go!*'

Glen complied, moving as slowly as he dared.

'You want me to hurt her bad?'

The knife pressed hard, and Cassandra gasped at the pain.

'I'm being as quick as I can.' And he was, withdrawing trays, tossing the contents into a bag. 'That's all of it.'

'Give it to me!' He released her, and backed towards the workshop door.

She saw what he could not, and she deliberately kept her expression blank as two armed security guards positioned themselves each side of the outer door.

One well-aimed kick, the element of surprise, that was all it would take to disarm the intruder and provide the essential few seconds' confusion to give the guards their opportunity to burst in and take him down.

She went into calculated action, so fast it was over in seconds as her foot connected with his wrist and the gun went flying.

A stream of obscenities rent the air as he lunged for her, and she barely registered the door crashing open, or the security guards' presence as he swung her in against him.

Oh, God. The pressure against her ribs was excruciating, and she had difficulty breathing.

Sally began to cry quietly.

'Let her go.' One of the security guards made it a statement, not a plea, and earned a scathing glare.

'Are you crazy? She's going to be my ticket out of here!'

'Put down the knife.'

'Not in this lifetime, pal.' His snarl was low, primal, and frightening.

What began as a robbery had now become a hostage situation.

Then Cassandra heard it…the distant sound of a siren, the noise increasing in velocity, followed by the diminishing sonorous wail as the engine cut.

Seconds later the phone rang.

'Pick it up!'

The guard's movements were careful as he obeyed, listened, spoke, then he held out the receiver to her captor. 'It's for you.'

'Tell the man I want clear passage out of here and a fifteen-minute start. That's the deal.'

They wouldn't buy it. At least, not without resorting to any one of several psychological ploys in an attempt at negotiation.

The scene was too close to a movie script. Worse, the man holding her was desperate and wouldn't hesitate to hurt her.

Did your life flash before your eyes in a moment of extreme crisis? Cassandra pictured her mother, father. Cameron was there. *Diego.* Oh, hell, why Diego?

She didn't have a future with Diego. Dammit, she might not have a future at all!

'I want all of you out. *Now!*' He was incandescent with rage, and she consciously held her breath.

The guards, Sally and Glen filed out quietly, the door closed, leaving only Cassandra and the madman in the workshop.

'We're going to take a ride together, you and me.' His voice was close to her ear. 'If you're very good,

I just might let you go when we've put in some distance from here.'

Sure. And the sun shone bright at midnight in the Alaskan winter-time.

His hand closed over her breast, and squeezed. 'Or maybe you and me could shack up together awhile, have some fun.'

'In your dreams.'

He pinched her, hard, then thrust her roughly against a work-bench. 'Pick up that damned phone, and tell those bastards to get their act together.'

She could hardly believe they'd let him walk out of here alone. The gems in the vault were worth a small fortune. And there was the matter of her life.

Her hand stung, and she saw blood seeping from a deep cut as she lifted the receiver.

'Stay calm. Do what he says. We've set up road blocks. He can't get far.' The masculine voice was quiet, steady. As if he controlled a hostage situation on a weekly basis. Maybe he did, she thought wildly.

'They make a wrong move, and you're history, y'hear?'

What happened next was a nightmare of action, noise, fear in a kaleidoscope of motion as she was forced to carry the bag of gems, then used as a human shield as her captor hustled her towards his waiting car.

Would they try to take him out? Shoot, or hold their fire?

In those few terrifying seconds out in the open she consciously prepared herself for anything, and it wasn't until he shoved her across the driver's seat and climbed in almost on top of her that she realised he was about to make good his escape.

Taking her with him.

He fired the ignition and surged forward, wheels screeching as he took off at a frightening speed.

Cassandra automatically reached for the dashboard, not that it afforded her any purchase, and heard his maniacal laughter as he swerved in and out of traffic, then he took a hard turn left, only to scream with rage as he saw the road block up front.

She barely had a second to gauge his next move when he swung the car round and roared back down the road to crash through a hastily set-up road block.

The car bounced off another vehicle with a sickening thud of grinding metal before careening off down the road. Car horns blasted, brakes screamed.

Cassandra saw impending disaster a few seconds ahead of contact, and she acted entirely on impulse, throwing open the passenger door and leaping out an instant before the car hit.

There was a moment of searing pain as her body hit the asphalt, a conscious feeling of movement, then nothing.

Cassandra was dreaming. Her body felt strangely weightless, and at some stage she seemed to drift towards consciousness, only to retreat into a non-intrusive comfort zone.

There were voices, indistinguishable at first, then invasive as she came fully awake.

White walls, bustling movement, the faint smell of antiseptic...and a uniformed nurse hovering close checking her vital signs.

Hospital.

She became aware of an intravenous drip, bandages on one arm...and the dull ache of medicated pain. Her head, shoulder, hip.

'Good. You're awake.'

And alive. Somehow that fact held significance!

The nurse spared Cassandra a steady look. 'Multiple contusions, grazed skin, superficial knife wounds. Concussion.'

No fractures, no broken bones. That had to be a plus!

'We have you on pain relief. Doctor will be in soon. Meantime, you have a visitor.' Someone who had descended on the hospital within minutes of the patient being admitted, the nurse acknowledged silently. Insistently demanding the best specialists be summoned, and the patient allocated a private suite. Each attempt to compromise had been met with a steely glare.

'A visitor?'

'If you don't feel up to it, I can have him wait.' It wouldn't hurt to have him cool his heels a little longer. And if he dared upset the patient, she'd have his guts for garters.

Who knew she was here? It was probably a police officer needing her statement.

'It's OK.'

'Five minutes,' the nurse stipulated, and left the suite.

No sooner had she swept through the door, than it swung back and Diego entered. A tall, dark force whose presence seemed to fill the room.

Her surprised expression brought a faint smile to his lips, one that didn't reach his eyes as he advanced towards the bed.

'No *hello*?' He lowered his head and brushed his lips to her cheek.

Not even being pumped up with painkillers stilled the fluttering inside her stomach, nor did it prevent her quickening pulse. 'I'm temporarily speechless.'

'That I should come visit?' He kept his voice light, and wondered if she had any idea what he'd been through in the past few hours. Anger…hell, no, *rage* on being informed what had happened. And fear. Unadulterated fear he could have lost her.

He was still fighting both emotions, controlling them by sheer force of will. Her captor would pay…and pay dearly for putting this woman's life at risk.

'No one could stop me,' Diego drawled, his voice a mix of steel and silk.

Cassandra looked at him with unblinking solemnity. 'Who would dare?' His power was a given. His use of it, unequivocal.

His expression softened, and his eyes warmed a little. 'How are you, *querida*?'

The quietly voiced endearment almost brought her undone. 'As comfortable as can be expected.'

He lifted a hand and trailed gentle fingers along the edge of her jaw. 'Is there anything you need?'

You. Except he wasn't hers to have. 'When can I get out of here?'

The pad of his thumb traced the lower curve of her mouth. 'A day or two.'

She had to ask. 'My abductor?'

Diego's features became a hard mask. 'Arrested and behind bars.'

So there was justice, after all.

The door opened and the nurse returned. 'I must ask you to leave. The patient needs to rest.'

For a moment Cassandra thought he was going to refuse, then he moved in close, lowered his head and covered her mouth with his own.

It was a gentle kiss, and his tongue slid in to tangle briefly with hers. Electrifying seconds that sent a rush of blood to her head. Then he straightened, touched a light finger to her cheek, and vacated the suite.

Flowers arrived late afternoon. A bouquet from the workshop staff, and three dozen red roses with *'Diego'* scrawled in black ink on the attached card, together with a special-delivery package from one of the élite lingerie boutiques.

'Definitely *ah-hh* time,' an attentive nurse declared as Cassandra revealed two exquisite nightgowns and a matching robe. There were also essential toiletries—Chanel. He was nothing if not observant.

Cassandra ate little, endured a short visit from the police, gave a detailed account covering events during and after the robbery.

Then she slept, and she was unaware of Diego's presence in the room as he stood observing her features in repose.

So small, such a petite frame. Porcelain skin, and a mouth to die for.

He wanted to gather her up and take her home. To share his bed and hold her through the night. Just so he could. To protect, and ensure no one ever got close enough to hurt her again.

He, Diego del Santo, who'd bedded any number of women in his lifetime, now only wanted to bed one.

A slip of a thing, whose beautiful blue eyes had captivated him from the start. Without any effort at all she'd slipped beneath his skin and stolen his heart.

Was she aware of the effect she had on him?

The question was what he intended to do about it.

* * *

Cassandra woke early, accepted the nursing ritual and took a supervised shower. This morning the intravenous drip would be removed, and she wanted out of here.

The specialist was less than enthusiastic. 'I'd prefer you remained under observation for another twenty-four hours.'

'Prefer, but it's not essential?'

'Do you live alone?'

Tricky. 'Not exactly.' A resident cat didn't count. But she had the phone, her cellphone, and a caring neighbour.

He checked her vital signs, perused her chart. 'Let's effect a compromise. I'll check on you this afternoon with a view to possible release.' He gave her a piercing look. 'You have someone to collect and drive you home?'

She'd take a cab.

Which she did, arriving at her apartment just after six that evening. The manager produced a spare key and there was a sense of relief in being *home*.

The cat greeted her with a plaintive protest, and she fed her, put down fresh water, then made herself a cup of tea.

The *ouch* factor was very much in evidence, and she swallowed another two painkillers.

A nice quiet evening viewing television followed by an early night. By Monday she should be able to return to work.

Cassandra settled comfortably on the sofa, and

smiled as the cat jumped onto her lap. She surfed the television channels, selected a half-hour comedy and prepared to relax.

The insistent ring of the intercom buzzer was an unwelcome intrusion, and she transferred the cat, then moved to check the security screen.

Diego.

She picked up the in-house phone. 'I'm fine, and I'm about to go to bed.'

'Release the door.' His voice was deceptively mild.

'I'm too tired for visitors.'

'You want for me to get the manager and explain you left hospital under false pretences?'

'I already spoke to him. He gave me a spare key.'

'Cassandra—'

'Leave me alone. Please,' she added, then she replaced the receiver and moved back to take up her position on the sofa.

The cat had just re-settled itself on her lap when her doorbell rang. Her neighbour?

The manager, she determined through the peephole, with Diego at his side.

She unlocked and opened the door. The manager looked almost contrite. 'Your—er—friend expressed concern about your welfare.'

'As you can see, I'm fine.' If she discounted the pain factor.

Diego turned towards the man at his side. 'I'll take it from here.'

He looked momentarily nonplussed. 'Cassandra?'

What could she say? 'It's OK.'

Seconds later she closed the door and turned to face the man who'd managed to turn her life upside-down. 'Just what do you think you're doing?'

He was silent for a fraction too long, and there was something very controlled in his manner. 'You want me to pack a bag, or will you?'

'I beg your pardon?'

'You heard,' Diego said calmly. 'You get to come with me, or I sleep here.' His gaze lanced hers, and there was no mercy in the silkiness of his voice. 'Choose, Cassandra.'

'I don't want you here.' It was a cry from the heart, and her breath hitched at the pain from her ribs.

Diego's eyes went dark, and a muscle bunched at his jaw. Without a word he turned and made for her bedroom.

'You can't do this!' Dammit, he was several steps ahead of her.

'Watch me.'

'Diego...' She faltered to a halt at the sight of him opening drawers and tossing contents into a holdall before crossing to her walk-in wardrobe, where he chose clothes at random. From there he moved into the *en suite* and swept items into a toiletry pouch.

'OK, let's go.'

'I'm not going anywhere with you!'

'Yes, you are. On your feet, or I get to carry you.'

He waited a beat. 'On your feet is the better option.'

Cassandra wanted to hit him...*hard*. 'Just who in hell do you think you are?' she demanded furiously.

Diego sought control, and found it. 'You need to rest, recuperate. I intend to see that you do.'

'I can look after myself.'

'Sure you can.' He closed the zip fastener on the holdall and caught the straps in one hand. 'Next week.'

His gaze seared hers in open challenge. 'Until then, I get to call the shots.'

'And if I refuse?'

'I carry you out of here.'

There was no doubt he meant every word. Dignity was the key, and she observed it in silence as she followed him out into the lobby, then rode the lift down to the entrance foyer.

The Aston Martin was parked immediately outside, and she slid into the passenger seat, then watched as he crossed round to the driver's side.

Minutes later they joined the flow of traffic, traversing the relatively short distance to his Point Piper home.

Cassandra barely held her temper. He was the most impossible man she'd ever had the misfortune to meet. Dictatorial, indomitable, omnipotent.

She could think of several more descriptions, none of which were ladylike.

Diego swept the car along the driveway, activated the modem controlling the garage doors, then eased to a halt and switched off the engine.

Cassandra heard the dull click as the doors closed and made no attempt to exit the car.

'How long do you intend to sulk?'

She threw him a fulminating glare. 'I don't *sulk*.' She drew in a deep breath, and winced. 'I simply have nothing to say to you.'

Whereas he had a lot to say to her about taking risks and being a hero. Dammit, did she have any idea what the outcome could have been?

His blood ran cold just thinking about it.

However, it would have to wait. If she felt anywhere near as fragile as she looked, the only thing she needed right now was some tender loving care.

Diego slid out from behind the wheel and reached for her holdall, then he crossed round to open the passenger door. 'Let's take this inside.' He reached in and released her safety belt.

'I'd prefer to go home.'

'We've already done this.'

So they had, but she was in a perverse mood and uninclined to comply.

'Stubborn.' He slid one arm beneath her knees and lifted her out from the car, then he bent down, caught up the holdall, used one hip to close the car door, and strode through to the foyer.

'I hate you,' Cassandra said fiercely.

'It's a healthy emotion.'

'Put me down.'

He began ascending the stairs. 'Soon.'

'If you intend taking me to bed, I'll *hit* you.'

They gained the gallery, and reached the master suite seconds later, where he lowered her gently down onto her feet. With deft movements he turned back the covers and built up a nest of pillows.

'Get into bed. I'll bring you a cup of tea.'

'I don't need you to play nursemaid.'

Diego loosened his tie and discarded his jacket, and threw both over a nearby chair. 'It's here with me, or the hospital.'

'You're giving me a choice?'

He undid the top few buttons of his shirt. 'I made the choice for you.' He walked to the door, then paused as he turned to face her. 'If you're not in bed when I come back, I'll put you there.'

'Fat chance.' Empty retaliatory words that gave her a degree of satisfaction.

She spared a glance at the bed, and the comfort it offered was sufficient for her to snag a nightshirt and toiletries from her holdall, then retreat with them into the *en suite*.

Every movement hurt, her body ached, and she began to wonder at her wisdom in leaving hospital too soon.

Minutes later she emerged into the bedroom and slid carefully beneath the covers. It would be so easy just to close her eyes and drift off to sleep.

Diego re-entered the room, tray in hand, and quietly closed the door behind him. The snack and hot tea could wait. He could wait.

Just the sight of her lying in repose against the nest of pillows was enough to stop the breath in his throat and send his heart thudding to a faster beat.

He should dim the lights, exit the room quietly and let her sleep.

He did the first, laid down the tray, then settled his lengthy frame into a chair. There was a sense of satisfaction in watching over her.

Here was where she belonged. Where he wanted her to stay.

Diego sat there for a long time, alert to her faintest move, the slightest murmur of pain. In the depth of night he extracted two painkillers, part-filled a glass with water, then had her swallow both.

Only when she slipped effortlessly back to sleep did he discard his clothes and slide carefully in beneath the bedcovers to lay awake until the early pre-dawn hours.

CHAPTER NINE

CASSANDRA drifted through the veils of sleep into wakefulness, aware from the room's shadowed light that night had become morning. Early morning, unless she was mistaken.

Her body tuned into numerous bruises and made her painfully aware that any sudden movement on her part was not going to be a good idea.

The bed, this room…they weren't her own. Then she remembered…and wished she hadn't.

She turned her head slowly and encountered Diego's dark gaze. He lay on his side, facing her, his body indolently at ease as he appraised her features.

An improvement on last night, he perceived, lifting a hand to brush a swathe of hair back from her cheek.

His eyes narrowed at the thin line inches long at the base of her throat. It would heal, and after a while the scar would fade.

'Want to talk about it?'

'A verbal post-mortem?' She tried for flippancy, and failed miserably. 'The facts are in the official report.'

Facts he'd read, assimilated, and dealt with. 'You

didn't follow the book.' He still went cold at the thought of what could have happened.

'Concern for my welfare, Diego?'

'That surprises you?'

It seeded a germ of hope. She attempted a light shrug, and didn't quite pull it off. 'Banking, gem merchants and jewellers are high-risk industries for robbery.'

So they were. But employees were drilled to respond passively, not attack or act with aggression.

'You scared the hell out of me.' He traced the outline of her mouth with a gentle finger. 'Next time don't be a hero, hmm?'

Cassandra didn't answer. No one in their right mind wanted a *next time*.

'What would you have done in a similar situation?'

Diego's eyes narrowed. He'd known the streets in his teens, lived on them for a while, worked them. Taken risks that brought him too close to the law, but never close enough to be caught. He'd carried a knife, but never a gun, studied and practised oriental techniques of combat and self-defence. Techniques that could kill a man with a well-aimed blow from the hand or foot.

In answer to her question, he would have judged the odds and taken a calculated risk. As she had done.

'If you dare tell me it's OK for a man, but not a

woman,' Cassandra said with quiet vehemence, 'I'll have to hit you.'

His eyes darkened and assumed a musing gleam. 'Now, that could prove interesting.'

She could only win if he allowed her to, she perceived, aware there were few, if any, capable of besting him in any arena.

There was much more beneath the surface than he permitted anyone to see. No one, not even the most diligent member of the media, had uncovered much of his past. It made her wonder if the shadows shielded something that didn't bear close scrutiny...and what there had been to mould him into the person he'd become.

'Hungry?'

For food or you? *Both*, she could have said and almost did. Except the former had priority, and was a much safer option than the latter.

Besides, she retained too vivid a memory of what they'd shared together in this bed.

'Shower, then breakfast.' Decisive words followed by smooth action as she slipped out of bed and crossed to the *en suite*.

Cassandra set the water temperature to warm, then she stepped into the glass and marble stall, caught up the shampoo and began with her hair.

There was a need to thoroughly cleanse her skin of her abductor's touch. She hated the memory of his hands, his almost manic expression, and the sound of his voice. It could have been worse, much worse, and she trembled at the thought. Delayed reaction, she determined, and vigorously massaged shampoo into her scalp.

'Let me help you with that.'

She stilled, locked into speechless immobility for a few electric-filled seconds, then she released the pent-up breath she'd unconsciously held. 'I can manage.'

'I don't doubt it,' Diego drawled, as he began a series of slow, soothing, circular movements.

His gaze narrowed as he took in her bruised ribcage, the deep bluish marks on her arms. He wanted to touch his mouth to each one, and he would… soon. But for now he was content to simply care for her.

Dear heaven, Cassandra breathed silently. To stand here like this was sheer bliss…magical. She closed her eyes and let the strength of his fingers ease the tension from her scalp, the base of her neck, then work out the kinks at her shoulders.

He had the touch, the skill to render her body boneless, and an appreciative sound sighed from her lips as he caught up the soap and began smoothing it gently over the surface of her skin.

When he was done, he caught her close and cradled her slender frame against his own, then nuzzled the curve at her neck.

Diego felt her body tremble, and he trailed his mouth to hers in a gentle exploration that brought warm tears to her eyes.

Did he see them, taste them? she wondered, wanting only to wrap her arms round him and sink in. The temptation was so great, it took all her strength to resist deepening the kiss.

With considerable reluctance she dragged her mouth from his and rested her cheek against his chest.

It felt good, so good to be here with him like this. To take the comfort he offered, savour it and feel secure.

Cassandra felt him shift slightly, and the cascading water stilled.

'Food, hmm?' He slid open the door, snatched a towel and began rubbing the moisture from her body before tending to his own.

It took scant minutes to utilise toiletries and clean her teeth before she escaped into the bedroom, where she retrieved jeans and a loose shirt from her bag, then, dressed, she caught up a brush and restored order to her hair.

Diego emerged as she applied pins to secure its length, and her gaze strayed to his reflected image, mesmerised by the smooth flex of sinew and muscle as he donned black jeans and a polo shirt.

She tamped down the warmth flooding her veins, the core of need spiralling deep inside. Crazy, she acknowledged. She was merely susceptible to circumstance…and knew she lied.

He turned slightly and his gaze locked with hers. For a brief moment everything else faded from the periphery of her vision, and there was only the man and a heightened degree of electric tension in the room.

It felt as if her soul was being fused with his, like twin halves accepting recognition and magnetically drawn to become one entity.

Mesmeric, primitive, incandescent.

She forgot to breathe, and she stood still, like an image caught frozen in time and captured on celluloid.

Then the spell broke, and she was the first to move, thrusting her hands into the pockets of her jeans as she turned towards the door.

Had Diego felt it, too? Or was she merely being fanciful?

Coffee. She needed it hot, strong, black and sweet.

Cassandra took the stairs and made her way towards the kitchen, aware Diego followed only a step behind her.

'Go sit down on the terrace. I'll fix breakfast.'

Soon the aroma of freshly made coffee permeated the air, the contents in the skillet sizzled, and minutes later he placed two plates onto the table.

The morning sun held the promise of warmth, the air was still, and the view out over the infinity pool to the harbour provided a sense of tranquillity.

Cassandra ate well, much to her surprise. She hadn't expected to do the meal justice, and she pushed her empty plate to one side with a sense of disbelief.

'More coffee?' It was a token query as Diego refilled her cup, then his own.

She felt at peace, calm after the previous afternoon's excitement.

'I'll call a cab.'

His expression remained unchanged, but there was a sense of something dangerous hovering beneath the surface. 'To go where?'

His tone was deceptively mild…too mild, she perceived. 'My apartment.' Where else?

He replaced his empty cup down onto its saucer with care. 'No.'

'What do you mean…*no*?'

'It's a simple word,' Diego drawled. 'One not difficult to understand.'

She looked at him carefully. 'I don't want to fight with you.'

'Wise choice.'

'But—'

'There has to be a *but*?'

It was time to take a deep breath…except her ribs hurt too much, and she had to be content with *shallow*. 'Thank you for—' She paused fractionally. For what? Taking care of her, bringing her here…caring. Oh, hell, she had to keep it together! 'Looking after me,' she concluded. 'It was very kind.'

He was silent for a few measurable seconds, and his eyes narrowed, masking a hardness that was at variance with the softness of his voice. 'Are you done?'

'Yes.' She waited a beat. 'For now.'

'I'm relieved to hear it.'

He was something else. All hard, muscular planes, and leashed strength as he leaned back in his chair, looking as if he owned the world...and her.

Total power, she accorded silently, and was determined not to be swayed by his sense of purpose.

Cassandra discarded her coffee and rose to her feet, then began stacking empty plates onto a tray, only to have it taken from her hands.

Without a further word she moved from the room and made her way upstairs.

It didn't take much to scoop her belongings into the holdall Diego had thrust them in the previous evening, and minutes later she picked up the bedroom extension, punched in the digits for a cab company, and was in the process of giving instructions when Diego entered the room.

Without a word he crossed to where she stood and cut the connection.

An action which sparked indignant anger as she turned to face him. 'How *dare* you?'

'Easily.'

'You have no right—'

He held up a hand. 'Last night you discharged yourself from hospital against medical advice. Your brother is in Melbourne, and unless I'm mistaken he's unaware of yesterday's escapade. You live alone.' His eyes were dark and held a latent anger that most would shrink from. 'Want me to go on?'

'I don't need a self-appointed guardian.'

'Like it or not, you've got one…for another twenty-four hours at least.'

Her chin tilted. 'You can't force me to stay.'

'It's here, or hospital readmission,' Diego said succinctly. 'Choose.'

She considered punching him, then discarded the idea on the grounds it would inevitably hurt her more than it would him. 'You're a dictatorial tyrant,' she said at last.

'I've been called worse.'

He wasn't going to budge. She could see it in his stance, the muscle bunching at his jaw.

'Who said you get to make the rules?' It was a cry from the heart, rendered in anger.

He didn't answer. He didn't need to.

'I need to feed my cat.' She threw one hand in the air to emphasise the point, then winced as pain shot through her body. 'Dammit.'

Diego swung between an inclination to shake or kiss her, considered the former followed by the latter, then went with rationale. 'So, we'll go feed him.'

'She,' Cassandra corrected. 'The cat's a *she*.'

He collected his keys and moved towards the door, then paused, turning slightly to look at her when she hadn't shifted position. 'You need to think about it?'

She wanted to throw something at him, and would have if there had been something close at hand. Instead she opted for capitulation…reluctantly.

Silence won over recrimination during the short drive to her apartment building, and she cast Diego a hard glance as he slid from behind the wheel.

'You don't have to come up with me.' What did he think she might do? Lock herself in? A speculative gleam lit her eyes…now, there was a thought!

He didn't answer as he joined her at the security area immediately adjacent to the entrance, and she restrained from uttering an audible sigh as he walked at her side to the bank of lifts.

A deeply wounded *miaow* greeted her the moment she unlocked her apartment door, and the cat butted its head against her leg in welcome.

Bite him, Cassandra silently instructed as Diego leant down and fondled the cat's ears.

The cat purred in affectionate response, and ignored her.

Great. Three years of food, a bed to sleep on and unconditional love…for all that I get ignored? There was no accounting for feline taste.

It took only minutes to put down food and fresh water, and Cassandra spared Diego a level look. 'I'm fine. Really.'

One eyebrow rose. 'So…go now and leave me alone?' He examined her features, assessing the pale cheeks, the dark blue eyes. 'We've done this already.'

So they had, but she felt akin to a runaway train that couldn't stop. 'I'm sure you have a social engagement lined up for this evening.' It was, after all, Saturday. 'I'd hate to be the reason you cancelled. Or cause problems with your latest—' she paused momentarily '—date.'

'Are you through?'

'I don't want to be with you.'

He didn't move, but she had the impression he shifted stance. How did he do that? Go from apparent relaxation mode to menacing alert?

'Afraid, Cassandra?'

Yes, she wanted to cry out. Not of you. Myself. For every resolve I make away from you disintegrates into nothing whenever you're near. And I can't, *won't* allow myself to fall to pieces over you.

Too late, a silent imp taunted. You're already an emotional wreck.

Every reason for her to walk away *now*. If only he would leave.

'Of yourself…or me?' Diego queried quietly.

Her chin tilted. 'Both.'

His mouth curved into a soft smile. 'Ah, honesty.' His gaze swept the room. 'If there's nothing else you need to do, we'll leave.'

Her lips parted in protest, only to close again as he pressed a finger against them.

'No argument, hmm?'

On reflection it was a restful day.

Within minutes of returning to Point Piper, Diego

excused himself on the pretext of work and entered the study, leaving Cassandra to amuse herself as she pleased.

She made a few calls from her cellphone, then she browsed through a few glossy magazines. Lunch was a light meal of chicken and salad eaten alfresco, and afterwards she slotted a DVD into the player and watched a movie.

Work took Diego's attention, leaving her with little option but to spend time alone. Restless, she ventured outdoors and wandered the grounds, admiring the garden.

Flowers were in bud, providing a colourful array in sculpted beds. Topiary clipped with expert precision, and a jacaranda tree in bloom, its fallen petals providing a carpet of lavender beneath spreading branches.

She reached the pool area, and she ascended the few terracotta-tiled steps to the terrace, crossed to a comfortable lounge setting beneath a shaded umbrella and sank into a seat.

The pool sparkled and shimmered beneath the sun's warmth, its infinity design providing the illusion its surface melded with the harbour beyond. Subtle shades of blue…pool, harbour, sky.

A sense of peace reigned as she took in the magnificent panoramic view. The city with its tall buildings of concrete and glass, the distinctive lines of the Opera House, the harbour bridge. Not to mention various craft skimming the waters and numerous mansions dotting the numerous coves.

Beautiful position, magnificent home.

And the man who owned it?

Cassandra closed her eyes against his powerful image. Four weeks ago he'd been a man she politely avoided.

Now… Dear heaven, she didn't want to think about *now*. Or what she was going to do about it. Hell, what *could* she do about it?

Loving someone didn't always end with happy-ever-after. And she wasn't the type to flit from one partner to another, enjoying the ride for however long it happened to last.

Tomorrow she'd return to her apartment, and her life as she knew it to be. Whenever her path crossed socially with Diego's, she'd greet him politely and move on. As she had during the past year.

Chance would be a fine thing, she alluded with unaccustomed cynicism. How could she do *polite* with a man with whom she'd shared every intimacy?

And fallen in love.

The to-the-ends-of-the-earth, the depth-of-the-soul kind.

Maybe she should take a leave of absence from the jewellery workshop and book a trip somewhere. A change of place, new faces.

Cassandra must have dozed, for she came awake at the sound of her name and a light touch on her shoulder.

'You fell asleep.' Diego didn't add that he'd kept watch over her for the past hour, reluctant to disturb her until the air cooled and the sun's warmth began to fade.

He was close, much too close. She could sense the clean smell of his clothes, the faint musky tones of his cologne. For a wild moment she had the overwhelming urge to reach up and pull his head down to hers, then angle her mouth in against his in a kiss that would rock them both.

Except such an action would lead to something she doubted she could handle...and walk away from.

His eyes darkened, almost as if he could read her thoughts, then he touched gentle fingers to her mouth and traced its curve.

'There's steak to go with salad. Go freshen up and we'll eat, hmm?'

Ten minutes later she sat opposite him, sampling succulent, melt-in-your-mouth beef fillet, together with crisp fresh salad and crunchy bread rolls.

'You can cook,' she complimented, and met his musing smile.

'That's an advantage?'

'For a man, definitely,' Cassandra conceded.

'Why, in this era when women maintain careers equal to those of men?'

'Do men think hearth and home, *food,* in quite the same way a woman does?' she countered.

'The man works to provide, while the woman nurtures?' He took a sip of wine. 'A delineation defining the sexes?'

'Equality in the workplace,' she broached with a tinge of humour. 'But outside of it, men and women are from two different planets.'

'And not meant to cohabit?'

'Physically,' she agreed. 'The emotional aspect needs work.'

'*Vive la difference,* hmm?'

It proved to be a leisurely meal, and afterwards they viewed a movie on DVD. When the credits rolled she rose to her feet and bade him a polite goodnight.

She couldn't, wouldn't slip into the bed she'd shared with him last night, she determined as she ascended the stairs to the upper level.

It took only minutes to collect her nightwear and toiletries and enter another bedroom. There were fresh sheets and blankets in the linen box at the foot of the bed, and she quickly made up the bed, undressed, then slid beneath the covers.

She was about to snap off the bedside light when the door opened and Diego entered the room.

'What are you doing here?'

'My question, I think,' he drawled as he crossed to the bed and threw back the covers. 'You want to walk, or do I get to carry you?'

'I'm not sleeping in your bed.'

'It's where you'll spend the night.'

Cassandra could feel the anger simmer beneath

the surface of her control. Soon, it would threaten to erupt. 'Sex as payment for you taking on the role of nursemaid?' She regretted the words the instant they left her lips.

'Would you care to run that by me again?' His voice sent icy shivers scudding down the length of her spine.

'Not really.'

Without a further word Diego turned and walked from the room, quietly closing the door behind him. An action that was far more effective than if he'd slammed it.

Dammit, what was the matter with her?

Subconsciously she knew the answer. Fear…on every level.

Ultimately, for losing something she'd never had…the love of a man. Not just any man. Diego del Santo.

Cassandra lay in the softly lit room, staring at the walls surrounding her, and faced the knowledge that life without him would amount to no life at all.

Her eyes ached with unshed tears, and she cursed herself for allowing her emotions free rein.

She had no idea how long it was before she fell into an uneasy sleep where dark figures chased her fleeing form.

At some stage she came sharply awake, immensely relieved to have escaped from a nightmarish dream. Until memory returned, and with it the knowledge she was alone in a bed in Diego's home…and why.

She closed her eyes in an effort to dispel his image, and failed miserably as she accorded herself all kinds of fool.

The admission didn't sit well, and after several long minutes she slid from the bed and crossed to the *en suite*.

There was a glass on the vanity top, and she part-filled it with water, then lifted the glass to her lips, only to have it slip from her fingers, hit the vanity top and fall to the tiled floor, where it shattered into countless shards.

It was an accident, and she cursed the stupid tears welling in her eyes as she sank down onto her haunches and collected the largest pieces of glass.

There was a box of tissues on the vanity top, and she reached for them, tore out several sheets and began gathering up the mess.

It became the catalyst that unleashed her withheld emotions, and the tears overflowed to run in warm rivulets down each cheek, clouding her vision.

'What the hell—?'

Cassandra was so intent on the task at hand she didn't hear Diego enter the room, and her fingers shook at the sound of his voice.

'I dropped a glass.' As if it wasn't self-explanatory.

He took one look at her attempt to gather the shards together, and the breath locked in his throat.

'Don't move.' The instruction was terse. 'I'll be back in a minute.'

He made it in three, and that was only because he had to discard one broom cupboard and search in another for a brush and pan.

In one fluid movement he lifted her high and lowered her down onto the bedroom carpet, then he completed the clean-up with deft efficiency.

Cassandra could only stand and watch, mesmerised by the sight of him in hastily pulled-on jeans, the breadth of his shoulders and the flex of muscle and sinew.

He made her ache in places where she had little or no control, and she turned away, wanting only for him to leave before she lost what was left of her composure.

'Use one of the other bathrooms until morning just in case there are any splinters I might have missed.'

She had difficulty summoning her voice. 'Thanks.' She made a helpless gesture with one hand. 'I'm sorry the noise disturbed you.'

Did she have any idea how appealing she looked? Bare legs, a cotton nightshirt with a hem that reached mid-thigh, and her hair loose and tousled?

No other woman had affected him quite the way she did. He wanted to reach beneath the nightshirt, fasten his hands on warm flesh and skim them over her skin. Touch, and be touched in return in a prelude that could only have one end.

'Are you OK?'

How did she answer that? She'd never be *OK* where he was concerned. 'I'm fine.' An automatic response, and one that took first prize in the fabrication stakes.

'I'll get rid of this.'

The pan, brush and broken glass. She nodded, aware he crossed to the door, and she registered the moment he left the room.

She should get into bed, douse the light and try to get some sleep. Instead she sank down onto the edge of the mattress and buried her head in her hands.

Reaction could be a fickle thing, and she let the tears fall. Silently, wondering if their release would ease the heartache made worse by having crossed verbal swords with the one man who'd come to mean so much to her in such a short time.

It was crazy to swing like a pendulum between one emotion and another. The sooner she returned to her apartment and moved on with her life, the better.

She wanted what she had before Diego del Santo tore her equilibrium to shreds and scattered her emotional heart every which way.

Oh, *dammit*, why did love have to hurt so much?

With a sense of frustration she rubbed her cheeks and smoothed the hair back from her face. It was then she saw Diego's tall frame in the open doorway.

If there was anything that undid a man, Diego acknowledged, it was a woman's tears. He'd witnessed many in his time. Some reflecting genuine grief; others merely a manipulative act.

None had the effect on him to quite the degree as evidence of this woman's distress did.

There were occasions when words healed, but now wasn't the time.

In silence he crossed the room and gathered her into his arms, stilling her protest by the simple expediency of placing the palm of one hand over her mouth.

It took a matter of seconds to reach the master suite, and he released her carefully down onto her feet.

Without a word he skimmed the nightshirt over her head and tossed it onto the carpet, then followed it with his jeans.

'What do you think you're doing?' As a protest it failed, utterly.

His eyes were dark, so dark she thought she might drown in them, as he captured her arms and slid his hands up to cup her face.

'This is the one place where everything between us makes sense,' he drawled as his head lowered down to hers.

She felt the warmth of his breath a second before his mouth took possession of hers in a kiss that liquefied her bones.

A faint moan rose and died in her throat as he

took her deep, so deep she lost track of where and who she was as emotion ruled, transcending anything they'd previously shared.

Somehow they were no longer standing, and she gasped as Diego's mouth left hers and began a slow descent, savouring the sensitive hollow at the edge of her neck before trailing a path over the line at the base of her throat where her captor had pierced her skin with the tip of his knife.

With the utmost care Diego caressed each bruise, as if to erase the uncaring brutality of the man who'd inflicted them.

The surface of her skin became highly sensitised, and her pulse raced to a quickened beat, thudding in unison with his own. She could feel it beneath her touch, the slide of her fingers.

What followed became a leisurely, sweet loving, so incredibly tender Cassandra was unable to prevent the warm trickle of tears, and when at last he entered her she cried out, exulting in the feel of him as warm, moist tissues expanded to accept his length.

Sensation spiralled to new heights, and she wrapped her legs around his waist, urging him deep, thrilling to each thrust as he slowly withdrew, only to plunge again and again in the rhythm of two lovers in perfect unison in their ascent to the brink of ecstasy.

Diego held her there, teetering on the edge, before

tipping them both over in a sensual free-fall that left them slick with sweat and gasping for breath.

The aftermath became a gentle play of the senses, with the soft trail of fingertips, the light touch of lips.

CHAPTER TEN

CASSANDRA stirred, and gradually became aware she wasn't alone in the bed. For her head lay pillowed against Diego's chest, a male leg rested across her own, and his arms loosely circled her body as he held her close.

Diego sensed the quickened heartbeat, the change in her breathing, and brushed his lips to her hair. Tousled silk, he mused, inhaling its fresh, clean smell. A man could take immense pleasure from waking each morning with a warm, willing woman in his arms.

Not just any woman…*this* woman.

'You're awake.'

She heard his quiet drawl, *felt* the sound of it against her cheek, and offered a lazily voiced affirmative.

He trailed the tips of his fingers down the length of her spine, shaped the firm globe of her buttock, then he traced a path over her hip, settled briefly in the curve of her waist before shifting to her breast.

There was a part of her that knew she should protest. To slip so easily into intimacy meant she accepted the current situation…and she didn't.

Dear heaven. She bit back a gasp as he eased her

gently onto her back, then lowered his mouth to suckle at one tender peak.

Seconds later the breath hissed between her teeth as his hand trailed to the soft curls at the apex of her thighs and began a teasing exploration.

She went up and over, then groaned out loud as another orgasmic wave chased the first with an intensity that took hold of her emotions and spun them out of control.

His arousal was a potent force, and just as she thought she'd scaled the heights he nudged her thighs apart, slid in, and took her higher than she'd ever been before, matching her climax with his own in a tumultuous fusion of the senses.

It took a while for their breathing to settle into its former rhythm, and they lay entwined together, spent as only two people could be in the aftermath of very good sex.

Make that incredible, off-the-planet sex, Cassandra amended as she closed her eyes and indulged her mind and body in an emotional replay.

It had, she mused indolently, been all about her pleasure. Soon, she'd seek to even the scales a little.

And she did, later, taking delight in testing his control…and breaking it.

Enjoy, Cassandra bade silently. For within a few hours she'd return to her apartment and a life from which Diego would fade.

Later, much later they rose from the bed, shared a shower, then, dressed, they descended the stairs to the kitchen for a meal that was neither breakfast nor lunch but a combination of both.

Diego's cellphone buzzed as they lingered over coffee, and he checked the caller ID, then rose to his feet.

'I'll have to take this.'

Cassandra lifted a hand, silently indicating he should do so, and she watched as he crossed the terrace.

French, she registered, barely discerning a word or two…and wondered how many languages he spoke.

Business, she determined, and let her gaze drift across the pool to the harbour beyond.

'I have to meet with two business colleagues. Their scheduled stopover was cancelled and they took an earlier flight,' Diego relayed as he returned to the table. 'I'll be an hour or two.' He drained the rest of his coffee, then leant down and took brief, hard possession of her mouth. 'We need to talk.' His lips caressed hers with a soothing touch.

She wasn't capable of saying a word, and he uttered a husky imprecation.

'Cassandra—'

The insistent sound of his cellphone brought forth a harsh expletive, and she saw the flex of muscle at his jaw as he sought civility. 'Dammit.' He raked fingers through his hair.

'It's OK.'

His eyes darkened. It was far from OK. Yet delegation was out of the question. There were only two associates capable of handling the current negotiations, and neither were in the same state.

'I should be able to tie this up within an hour or two.'

'Go,' she managed quietly. 'They,' whoever *they* were, 'will be waiting for you.'

He shot her a piercing look, then turned and made his way through the house, collected his briefcase and keys and entered the garage.

Minutes later Cassandra stood to her feet, cleared the table, then dealt with dishes and tidied the kitchen.

Stay, or leave.

If she stayed, she'd be condoning an affair. And while she could live with that if mutual *love* was at its base, she found it untenable when the emotion was one-sided.

She wasn't an 'it's OK as long as it lasts' girl. Nor could she view hitching up with a man for whatever she'd gain from the relationship.

No contest, she decided sadly as she made her way upstairs.

It didn't take long to pack, or to pen a note which she propped against the side-table in the foyer. Then she crossed to the phone and called for a cab.

The cat greeted her with an indignant sound and a swishing tail. The message light on her answering machine blinked, and she organised priorities by feeding the cat, then she tossed clothes into the washing machine, fetched a cool drink, then she ran the machine.

Siobhan…'Tying the knot in Rome next weekend. Need you there, darling, to hold my hand.'

Cameron…'Flying home Tuesday. Let's do dinner Wednesday, OK?'

Alicia…'Hope you're enjoying the ride. It won't last.'

Cassandra didn't know whether to laugh or cry at the latter. The ride, as Alicia called it, was over.

Keeping busy would help, and when the washing-machine cycle finished she put the clean clothes into the drier.

The contents of the refrigerator looked pathetic, and she caught up her car keys. Milk, bread, fresh fruit and salad headed her mental list, and she took the lift down to the basement car park, then drove to the nearest store.

There was a trendy café close by, and she ordered a latte, picked up a magazine, and leafed through the pages while she sipped her coffee.

It was almost five when she swept the car into the bricked apron adjacent to the apartment building's main entrance, automatically veering left to take the descending slope into the basement car park.

It was then she saw a familiar car parked in the visitors' area. As if there was any doubt, Diego's tall frame leaning indolently against the Aston Martin's rear panel merely confirmed it.

For a few heart-stopping seconds she forgot to

breathe, then she eased her car towards the security gate, retrieved her ID card and inserted it with shaking fingers and drove down to her allotted space, killed the engine, then reached for the door-clasp…only to have the door swing open before she had a chance to release it.

She tilted her head to look at him, and almost wished she hadn't, for his features appeared carved from stone.

'What are you doing here?'

'Did you think I wouldn't come after you?'

She felt at a distinct disadvantage seated in the car. By comparison he seemed to tower over her, and if they were going to get into a heated argument she needed to even the stakes a little.

With careful movements she slid from behind the wheel, then closed and locked the door before turning to face him. 'I don't know what you're talking about.'

'Yes, you do.' His voice resembled pure silk, and she swallowed the sudden lump that rose in her throat.

'Why didn't you stay?'

'There was no reason to,' she managed. 'We don't owe each other a thing.'

'All obligations fulfilled,' Diego accorded with dangerous softness.

It almost killed her to say it. 'Yes.'

'No emotional involvement. Just good sex?'

She was breaking up, ready to shatter. 'What do

you want from me?' It was a cry from the heart that held a degree of angry desperation.

'I want you in my life.'

'For how long, Diego?' she demanded. 'Until either one of us wants it to end?' As it would. 'Nothing lasts forever, and lust is a poor bedfellow for love.'

A car swept close by and slid into an adjacent space. She recognised the driver as a fellow tenant, and she met his concerned glance.

'Everything OK, Cassandra?'

Diego hardly presented a complacent figure. She managed a reassuring smile. 'Yes.'

The tenant cast Diego a doubtful look, glimpsed a sense of purpose in those dark eyes, and chose to move on.

'Let's take this upstairs.'

If he touched her, she'd be lost. One thing would lead to another…

It was better to end it now. 'No.'

Diego barely resisted the temptation to shake her. 'Tell me what we share means nothing to you.'

She couldn't do it. Her eyes clouded, then darkened as she struggled to find something to say that wouldn't sound inane.

Some of the tension eased in his gut as he reached for her. He cupped her nape with one hand and drew her in against him with the other, then his mouth was on hers, moving like warm silk as he took possession.

When he lifted his head she could only look at him.

'You're a piece of work,' he accorded quietly. 'No woman has driven me as crazy as you have.' His lips curved into a warm smile. 'A year of being held at a distance, when you've politely declined every invitation I extended. I've had to be content with brief, well-bred conversations whenever we attended the same social functions.'

Cassandra recalled each and every one of those occasions. The edgy onset of nerves the instant his familiar frame came into view; a recognition on some deep emotional level she was afraid to explore, fearing if she entered his space she'd never survive leaving it.

'Marry me.'

Cassandra opened her mouth, then closed it again. 'What did you say?'

'Marry me.'

She could only look at him in shocked silence.

'Do you really want our children to learn their father proposed to their mother in a basement car park?' Diego queried gently.

This was a bad joke. 'You can't be serious.'

'As serious as it gets.'

'Diego—'

'I want to share the rest of your life,' he said gently. 'I want to be the father of your children and grow old with you.'

There could be no doubt he meant every word. It

was there in the depth of his dark eyes, the heartfelt warmth of his voice, his touch.

Joy began a radiating spiral as it sang through her veins, piercingly sweet and gloriously sensual.

A faint smile lifted the edges of his mouth as he gave the concrete cavern a sweeping glance. 'I'd planned on different surroundings from these.'

Cassandra's lips parted in a tremulously soft smile. 'I don't need soft music, dimmed lights, fine food or wine.'

Diego brushed his fingers along the edge of her jaw, tilting her chin a little as he caressed the curve of her lower lip with his thumb. 'Just the words, *querida*?'

She felt as if she was teetering on the edge of something wonderful. 'Only if you mean them.'

'You're the love I thought I'd never find,' he said gently. 'I want, *need* you. *You*,' he emphasised gently. 'For the rest of my life.'

For a moment she didn't seem capable of finding her voice. It overwhelmed her. *He* overwhelmed her. In an instinctive gesture she pressed her mouth against his palm.

'I didn't want to like you,' Cassandra said shakily. 'I especially didn't want to fall in love with you.' She'd fought him every inch of the way, hating him for forcing recognition their souls were twin halves of a whole.

'Because of my so-called dangerous past?' he queried with teasing amusement.

'It shaped and made you the man you've become.' Providing the tenacity, strength of will and integrity lacking in many men his equal.

He fastened his mouth on hers in a kiss that was so evocatively tender it melted her bones.

Minutes later Diego caught hold of her hand and began leading her towards the lift. 'We need to get out of here.' His smile held the heat of passion overlayed with a tinge of humour. 'Your place or mine?'

'You're letting me make the decision?'

He paused to take a brief, hard kiss, tangled his tongue with hers, and felt the breath catch in her throat. 'You have a sassy mouth.'

'That's a compliment?'

Seconds later the lift doors opened and they entered the cubicle. 'Foyer?' Diego queried as he indicated the panel. 'Or your apartment?'

'There's the cat—'

'Not the foyer.'

The lift began its ascent towards her floor. 'I need clothes,' Cassandra continued.

'The cat will adjust.'

'To what?'

'Her new home.'

She looked at him, and melted. 'I love you.'

'Love me, love my cat?' he quizzed with amusement.

'Uh-huh. She's with me.' The lift slid to a stop, and she preceded him into the lobby.

He took the keys from her hand and unlocked and entered the apartment, then he closed the door behind them.

'I take it that's a *yes*?'

Her expression sobered as she looked at him. The love was there, for her, only her. She doubted anyone had ever seen him so vulnerable, and it moved her more than anything he could have said.

'Yes,' she said simply.

He needed to show her just how much she meant to him…and he did, with such thoroughness the end of the day faded into night, and it was after midnight when they raided the fridge, made an omelette, toast, and washed them both down with coffee.

'Groceries!' Cassandra exclaimed in despair. 'I left them in my car.' She thought of spoiled milk and other comestibles, and shook her head.

'Do you have any specific plans over the next few weeks?' Diego queried idly. She looked adorable, sparkling eyes, warm skin, and gloriously tumbled hair. He reached out a hand and pushed an errant swathe back behind her ear.

'Any particular reason?'

His smile assumed musing indulgence. 'A wedding. Ours.'

There would come a day when nothing he did or said would surprise her…but she had a way to go before that happened.

'Something low-key, in deference to your father. Just family, a few close friends. If you have your heart set on a traditional ceremony, we can reaffirm our vows in a few months.'

'Weeks?' Cassandra reiterated with a sense of stunned amusement. 'I'm due in Rome this weekend for Siobhan's wedding—'

'Perfect. We'll fly in together, spend some time there—'

She put up a hand. 'Whoa! You're going too fast.'

'And arrive back in time to meet our marriage-application requirements,' he concluded.

'The honeymoon before the wedding?' She tried for humour, and didn't quite make it.

'You object?'

How could she, when all she wanted to do was be with him? 'You take my breath away,' she admitted shakily in an attempt to get her head around organising a wedding, travel plans for Rome. Then there was work…

He witnessed her emotional struggle, and sought to ease it. 'All it involves is a series of phone calls. Let me take care of it.'

CHAPTER ELEVEN

ROME was magical, with Siobhan's wedding to her Italian count a glamorous event with much love and rejoicing.

The week that followed became a special time as Diego indulged Cassandra in a tour of the city's galleries, the exclusive jewellery boutiques, with leisurely lunches in one trendy trattoria or another. At night they visited a theatre, or lingered over dinner.

And made love with a passion that was both evocatively sensual and intensely primitive.

They flew in to Sydney three days before their own wedding was scheduled to take place. Days which merged one into the other as Cassandra ran a final check with the dressmaker, the florist, caught up with Cameron, and organised the last remaining items from her apartment to Diego's home.

Sunday dawned bright and clear, and within hours the last-minute touches were being made by various people employed to ensure every detail represented perfection.

Gardeners put finishing touches to the grounds, and florists lined the gazebo with white orchids. An altar was set ready for the marriage celebrant, and the caterers moved into the kitchen.

Cameron arrived ahead of the guests, and Cassandra accepted his careful hug minutes before they were due to emerge onto the red-carpeted aisle that led to the gazebo.

'Nervous?'

'Just a little.'

'Don't be,' he reassured, and she offered a shaky smile as the music began.

Diego stood waiting for her at the altar, and Cassandra's heart skipped a beat as he turned to watch her walk towards him.

Everything faded, and there was only the man.

Tall, dark and attractive, resplendent in a superbly tailored suit. But it was his expression that held her entranced. There was warmth, caring…and passion evident. Qualities she knew he'd gift her for the rest of his life.

In an unprecedented gesture he moved forward and took her hand in his, raised it to his lips, then he led her the remaining few yards to the gazebo.

It was a simple ceremony, with a mix of conventional and personal vows. By mutual consent, they'd agreed to choose each other's wedding ring.

Jewellery design was her craft, and Cassandra had selected a wide gold band studded with a spaced line of diamonds. It was masculine, different, and one of her personal designs.

There had been a degree of subterfuge in Diego's choice, for the ring he slipped onto her finger was a feminine match of his.

'For what we've already shared, what we have now,' Diego said gently, adding a magnificent solitaire diamond ring together with a circle of diamonds representing eternity. 'The future.'

She wanted to cry and smile at the same time, and she did both, one after the other, then gave a choking laugh as Diego angled his mouth over hers in a kiss that held such a degree of sensual promise it was all she could do to hold back the tears.

It was later, much later when they were alone, that she took the time to thank him.

Instead of booking a hotel suite, they'd opted to remain at home. It seemed appropriate, somehow, to spend their wedding night in the bed where they'd first made love.

'You're welcome,' Diego said gently as she slid her arms high and pulled his head down to hers.

'I love you.' Emotion reduced her voice to a husky sound. 'I always will.'

He brushed his lips across her forehead, then trailed a path to the edge of her mouth, angled in and took his time. '*Mi amante, mi mujer,* my life.'

A deliciously wicked smile curved her lips. '*Gracias, mi esposo.*'

Diego gave a husky laugh, and uttered something incomprehensible to her in Spanish.

'Translate.'

He offered a devilish grin. 'I'll show you.'

And he did.

On the edge of sleep he curled her close and held her...aware one lifetime would not be enough.

THE ITALIAN MARRIAGE

by

Kathryn Ross

Kathryn Ross was born in Zambia where her parents happened to live at that time. Educated in Ireland and England, she now lives in a village near Blackpool, Lancashire. Kathryn is a professional beauty therapist, but writing is her first love. As a child she wrote adventure stories and at thirteen was editor of her school magazine. Happily, ten writing years later DESIGNED WITH LOVE was accepted by Mills & Boon. A romantic Sagittarian, she loves travelling to exotic locations.

CHAPTER ONE

'DADDY is getting married.'

The words fell in the drowsy heat of the summer afternoon like an incendiary device.

'Sorry?' Gemma had been pouring a glass of lemonade for her son and it spilt on the picnic rug, flowing over the hem of her floral sundress. 'What did you say, Liam?'

'You've spilt lemonade,' the four-year-old pointed out, reaching to get a chocolate bar from the picnic basket.

'Yes, I know.' Ordinarily, Gemma would have told her son not to eat the chocolate until he'd finished his sandwiches but her mind was in total disarray. 'What did you say about Daddy?' she asked again, trying hard not to sound flustered.

'He's going to get married.' Liam munched on the chocolate and regarded her steadily from dark eyes that were unnervingly like his father's. 'Does that mean I will have two mummys like Annie does?'

'Well...I suppose it does...'

Gemma was at a loss to know what to say. She was still reeling with shock.

It was strange how one moment the world could seem settled and then the next a gaping great hole could open up under your feet. She didn't know why she felt so shocked...or surprised. Marcus Rossini was thirty-eight, spectacularly handsome, and wealthy. He'd had his pick of women for years. With forty looming on the horizon, maybe he thought it was finally time to put his philandering days behind him and settle down.

So who was the woman? she wondered. She'd put bets on it being his childhood sweetheart, Sophia Albani. Women had come and gone over the years but she seemed to have remained in the background—despite the miles that sometimes separated them, despite the fact that Marcus had fathered a child. Sophia had taken it all in her stride and their relationship seemed to have survived, against all odds. Maybe that was the test of true love? For some reason the pain of that thought seared straight through to Gemma's heart.

'Are you sure about this, Liam?' she asked her son gently. 'How do you know Daddy is getting married? Did he tell you himself?'

Liam shook his head and reached into the basket to get a biscuit. 'I was supposed to be in bed but I got up because I had tummy ache and I heard him talking…'

'Was this last night?'

Liam nodded.

Curiosity ate into Gemma. 'Who was he talking to?'

Liam shrugged.

'Do you think it was Sophia? Was she at Daddy's house yesterday?'

'He was talking on the phone.' Liam grasped a packet of crisps and Gemma broke from the trance that had possessed her. Interrogating a four-year-old was not the done thing and Marcus's personal life was nothing to do with her.

'Liam, no more junk food. Eat a sandwich, please.'

Liam wrinkled his nose. 'I don't like them. I don't like that green squishy stuff.'

'It's not squishy, it's cucumber and you love it.'

Liam shook his head mutinously. 'I hate it.'

'Just have one to please me.'

'Daddy doesn't make me eat horrid things.'

Gemma felt a flash of irritation. It was always the same. Liam idolized his dad; she felt that she heard a sentence similar to this half a million times during the day. 'Daddy doesn't make me go to bed this early...Daddy lets me watch this programme on TV...Daddy reads to me when I wake up at night...'

Gemma tried to let it all go over her head without resorting to any sarcastic replies, but sometimes when she was tired or harassed it was more than flesh and blood could stand and she really wanted to say something derogatory—something that would tell Liam that his wonderful daddy wasn't a man you could trust.

But of course she would never, never stoop that low. Because the truth of the matter was that, no matter how much Marcus Rossini had hurt her in the past, or how much she wanted to forget his very existence, he was a damned good dad to Liam and that was all that really counted in the end.

'Please don't argue with me, Liam. Just eat the sandwich. Otherwise I just might have to tell Daddy that you've been naughty when he comes to pick you up tonight.'

She watched as the child hesitated and then dutifully did as he was asked. It always worked, Gemma thought, as she dabbed at the hem of her dress with a tissue to mop up the lemonade. And the irony was that her conversations with his father were as brief as Gemma could possibly make them. She never discussed anything with him except the arrangements for picking Liam up. In fact, she hadn't even seen Marcus for months, because as soon as his car drew up outside she sent Liam out with his bag ready packed, eliminating the need for

Marcus even to walk through her front door. And, when he returned, she had her mother answer the door to them. Gemma found it easier that way. She couldn't converse easily with Marcus—not without reopening lots of old wounds.

Thankfully, Liam was too young to realize this at the moment, but one day, she supposed, the threat of reporting him to his dad wouldn't work quite so easily.

Was Marcus really going to get married? she wondered as she watched Liam. She felt something inside her twist painfully. Not that she cared on a personal level, she told herself firmly; she had long ago resigned herself to the fact that Marcus was not the man for her. She was only concerned about how it would affect Liam.

'Can I go on the swings now?' Liam asked as he finished his sandwich.

'Yes, if you like.'

She watched as he ran the short distance towards the playground, little legs hurtling along in blue jeans like a mini tornado. Then he turned around halfway there and ran back to her, flinging his arms around her and kissing her on the cheek. 'I love you, Mummy,' he said.

'I love you too,' Gemma said, giving him a hug.

'Will you watch how high I can go on the swings?' His dark eyes were filled with an impish excitement.

'I will, darling.'

She watched as he ran off into the playground again, her heart heavy with pride and with love.

Although it was a sunny Saturday afternoon there weren't many people in the park. If it wasn't for the distant roar of the London traffic they could have pretended they were in the midst of the countryside.

Gemma wondered what Marcus was doing today. He usually picked Liam up in the morning and spent the weekend with him, but there had been a last-minute change of plan. He'd had the boy last night instead, dropping him off early this morning, because he said he had something to do today and that he would pick him up again around four-thirty.

Maybe he was seeing Sophia…maybe he was taking her out today to buy an engagement ring?

Gemma put the box of sandwiches away into the basket and settled back on the blanket to watch her son. Marcus could set up a harem for all she cared, she told herself briskly. It was none of her business.

The drone of bees plundering the foxgloves in the flowerbed next to her filled the air. For a second the heat and the tranquillity conjured up the memory of an afternoon when she had lain entwined in Marcus's arms by the banks of a river. His hands had been running possessively and confidently over her body, finding the buttons of her blouse and stealing beneath the material to find the heat of her naked flesh. 'I want to make love to you, Gemma…I want you right now…'

The heat and the urgency of that memory made her go hot inside now, with a renewed surge of longing. And she hated herself for it. It was years since she had slept with Marcus and those feelings were dead, she told herself fiercely. Dead and buried, with a full grieving process very firmly behind her.

'Hi, Gemma.' Marcus's voice coming so coolly and so quickly on top of the steamy memory made her sit bolt upright and turn around.

It was almost as if she had conjured him up, as if he had stepped out from her daydreams and into reality.

'What are you doing here?' she asked in stunned surprise.

'I've come to see you.' He sat down beside her on

the rug, his manner relaxed and confident, as if they always met like this on a Saturday afternoon in the park. 'Liam told me you were coming here today for a picnic.'

'Did he…?' Gemma could hardly concentrate for thinking how attractive he looked. Marcus was half Italian and he had dark Latin smouldering good looks, olive skin and jet-black hair that gleamed almost blue in the sunlight. Blue chinos and a faded blue shirt sat well on the tall broad-shouldered frame.

Every time Gemma saw him she was struck afresh by how gorgeous he was, and she could remember forcibly what it was that had drawn her so firmly under his spell in the first place. There was something very powerful about Marcus Rossini and it wasn't just that his body was well-toned and muscular. It was everything about him; the set of his jaw, the chiselled, strong profile and the gleam of his velvet dark eyes. As those eyes held hers now, Gemma felt a shiver of apprehension.

'You look well,' he said politely.

'Thanks.'

'Seems ages since I saw you.'

She felt his eyes running in a quick assessment over her long blonde hair and slender figure; felt them as acutely as if he were touching her and it stirred up a renewed feeling of heat inside her. And suddenly she knew why she was so careful to avoid contact with this man. There was something about him that could stir her senses with just a glance.

'So what do you want, Marcus?' Her voice was sharper than she intended but he didn't appear to notice.

'There is something I need to discuss with you,' he said calmly.

Gemma remained silent; she knew what was coming. He was going to tell her he was getting married. She was surprised he had bothered to come and tell her in person. She supposed it was decent of him...supposed it was the civilized way to proceed. After all, they had a duty to their son to handle this in an adult way. Trouble was, she suddenly wasn't feeling at all civilized.

Gemma took a deep breath and tried to prepare herself to react appropriately. She would wish him well and sound as if she meant it.

As their eyes met she felt her heart slam against her chest. Suddenly from nowhere she was remembering the night she had told him she was pregnant, and her feelings when he had proposed. She had felt the same heavy weight of emotion pressing against her chest then. The need to cry, to wail against the unfairness of the fact that this man just didn't love her and would never love her. She had been left with no option but to turn him down. A marriage without love was no marriage at all.

Now he was about to tell her he was marrying someone else. There was a bitter taste at the back of her throat.

She looked away from him over towards Liam. He was swinging higher and higher, a look of intense concentration on his face, and he hadn't even noticed that his dad was here yet.

'I'm leaving London, Gemma,' Marcus said quietly beside her. 'I'm going back to live in Italy and I want to take Liam with me.'

Gemma stared at him blankly, shock waves pounding through her. This wasn't at all what she had expected.

'I know this is a shock, but when you calm down and think about it rationally you'll realize this is a sensible move. This is the best thing for Liam. He is part Italian, he has a heritage and a way of life to learn about. He has the security of a large family waiting for him—cousins, uncles, aunts, not to mention a grandfather who loves him deeply.'

Gemma didn't know why she was allowing Marcus to continue with this conversation. It was quite frankly crazy, but she was so shocked she couldn't find her voice to stop him.

'Liam belongs back home in Italy.'

'Liam's home is here with me.' When she finally managed to speak, her voice was so full of anger that it didn't even sound like her.

'I understand this is going to be a wrench for you Gemma.'

With a fierce stab of panic Gemma noticed that he spoke as if this was already a fait accompli.

'And I know how much you love Liam. That's why I think you and I should get together on this and sort out a compromise that will suit us all.'

'It's not going to be a wrench because it will never happen.' She cut across his calm words with a fierce determination and started to pack away the bottle of lemonade and the cups, needing to get away from this situation as quickly as she could.

He watched her frantic, angry movements with a cool detachment.

'Look, I suggest that we put our own feelings aside and concentrate on what's best for Liam now.'

The sheer arrogance of those words made Gemma look sharply up at him. 'I have always concentrated on what is best for Liam,' she said furiously, her blue eyes blazing with emotion. 'How dare you suggest otherwise?'

'Gemma, all I'm saying—'

'I hear what you're saying and you are talking rubbish. You waltz in at weekends and high days and holidays and think you are God's gift to fatherhood. Well, let me tell you that you're not. You have no idea of the day-to-day reality of being a parent. This idea is just a passing fancy…like everything else in your life.'

She couldn't resist the sarcastic dig. 'And you wouldn't last two minutes if you had Liam full time.'

'Well, that's where I think you are wrong. I would be more than capable of having Liam full time.'

She noticed that his voice had lost the cool, pragmatic tone and there was an edge of annoyance showing now. Good, she thought furiously. How dared he calmly arrive and tell her he intended to take her son away? 'No judge in the land would take a baby away from his mother without extreme good cause,' she added tersely. 'So just go away, Marcus. Go back to your dream world and don't bother me again.'

'He's not a baby, Gemma. He will be starting school in September.'

Gemma ignored the comment and continued to tidy away the chocolate wrappers from the rug.

As she reached to fasten the lid on the basket Marcus stretched out and caught hold of her wrist. The contact of his skin against hers sent a jolt of shock shooting through her as if an electric charge had passed through her body. 'This is something we need to sort out together. If it goes to court you will regret it, Gemma.'

Although the words were softly spoken the meaning was clear. Nobody took on the might of the Rossini family and won. They had money and influence and they always got what they wanted. Gemma tried very hard not to let panic show in her eyes as she looked over at him. 'You are not in Italy now, Marcus,' she reminded him. 'This is my home turf, and a court will never allow you to take Liam away from me.'

'I don't want to fight with you, Gemma,' he said softly. 'But if you insist on it, then I will use any means possible to make sure I win. If you play with fire then you must expect to be burnt.'

'Daddy!' Liam's excited voice cut through the tense atmosphere and Marcus let go of her and turned as the little boy came running across the grass and flung himself into his arms.

Gemma watched the instinctive way Liam curled his arms around his father's neck, cuddling in to him as close as he could get. 'Daddy, will you push me on the swing? Will you? I can go really high, almost up to the sky and…'

'Hey, steady on, partner.' Marcus laughed. 'Give me time to draw breath.'

'Liam, we have to go now,' Gemma cut in anxiously. She just wanted to be away from this situation. Her nerves couldn't stand being around Marcus a moment longer.

'Ah, Mum!' Liam groaned. 'Daddy's only just come! Can't he push me on the swings, can't he, please?'

'You can see him later.' Gemma stood up and pretended to busy herself brushing down the folds of her long dress. 'You're spending tonight over at Daddy's house. You can play on the swing in his garden.'

Marcus watched the way her long hair fell silkily over her shoulders, gleaming a rich honey gold in the sun; noticed the deep V of her sundress revealing a tantalizing glimpse of her curvaceous body.

'Can I stay here with Daddy?'

The words caused a sharp rush of pain inside her.

'No, you can't.' Gemma glanced over and met Marcus's eyes. She imagined there was a gleam of triumph in them, a look that said, See, my son wants to be with me, not you. 'Please stand up from the rug so I can fold it away,' she asked him coldly.

Liam seemed set to argue some more. But, surprisingly, Marcus cut across him. 'Do as Mummy says, Liam,' he said, getting to his feet and lifting Liam with him so that Gemma could pack the rug away.

'Thanks.' Her voice was prickly.

'We need to talk some more,' Marcus said quietly as he watched her place the folded blanket over the top of the basket.

'There is nothing to discuss. I've given you my answer.'

'That's not good enough.'

'Why? Because it isn't the answer you want?' Gemma shrugged. 'Well, tough, Marcus. I know you are used to getting your own way, but not this time.'

Anger glimmered in Marcus's eyes. 'We'll see about that.'

The quiet way he said those words disturbed the cool veneer she had managed to wrap around herself. 'The whole notion is ridiculous, Marcus, so just forget it.'

As her voice rose, Liam looked over at her. 'Are you and Daddy arguing?'

'No, darling, we're just talking.' Gemma held out her hand to him. 'Come on, we have to get home. Uncle Richard said he might call.'

Marcus felt a flash of annoyance at that remark. 'Uncle Richard' was around at the house far too much recently for his liking.

'We'll talk again later in the week,' Marcus said as he put Liam down.

'I told you, there's nothing to talk about.'

'On the contrary, there is a lot to talk about,' Marcus

said coolly. 'How about having dinner with me next Friday night? Will your mother babysit?'

'Dinner?' Gemma looked at him as if he'd gone mad. 'No, she wouldn't.'

'Okay, I'll come over to you, then.'

'Marcus, that isn't convenient.'

'I'll ring you later in the week to confirm.' Marcus's voice was steely.

Gemma was going to tell him flatly not to waste his time but Liam was watching and listening intently. So she just reached to take hold of the child's hand. 'Goodbye, Marcus,' she said with as much cold finality in her voice as she could muster.

Marcus watched as she walked away from him across the grass, her long hair swinging glossily behind her in the softness of the breeze, her back ramrod straight.

Liam was skipping beside her and kept turning to wave at him but Gemma did not look back.

But she would do as he wanted, Marcus told himself grimly. By the time he had finished she would be begging him to compromise and he would have her exactly where he wanted her: back in his life.

CHAPTER TWO

GEMMA groaned and put the letter down on the table, pulling a hand distractedly through her long hair. 'This is all I need!'

'What's the matter?' Her mother walked into the kitchen just at that moment. 'It's not a letter from Marcus's lawyer, is it? This custody battle isn't going to court?'

'No!' Gemma looked over at her mother, horrified by the words. 'There is no custody battle, Mum. Marcus is trying his luck, that's all. He won't dare go to court because he knows he'll lose.'

Her mother didn't look convinced. 'Marcus has never struck me as a man afraid of losing,' she said curtly.

The words were not what Gemma needed to hear. She was desperately trying to convince herself that this problem with Marcus would sort itself out, that he would change his mind before things started to get nasty.

'What's in the letter?' her mother asked now.

'It's from the letting agency, informing me that the landlord is putting this house up for sale. They've invited me to make an offer, as he will give me first refusal, apparently.'

'Would you be able to afford it?'

'They haven't said how much he wants for it, but I doubt it. The houses in this square are going for a fortune these days.'

'I suppose you've done well getting it for such a low rent for all these years. I don't know how you've managed it. Your friend Jane is paying twice as much for her small flat.'

'Yes, I suppose it was too good to last.' Gemma had thought her luck was really in when she had found this place. It was a large Georgian house close to her publishing job in the heart of London and within walking distance of her mother's house. Fully furnished with the most exquisite antiques, there was even a large office where she could work. The rent had been preposterously low but apparently the landlord's main concern was to have a good tenant who would look after the property, as it had once been his mother's home. 'I thought he might bump up the rent one day but somehow I didn't expect him to sell,' Gemma reflected sadly.

She watched as her mother lifted the letter and shook her head in dismay. 'Maybe you could ask Marcus for some help to buy the place,' she suggested tentatively. 'I'm sure he would—'

'No, Mum.' Gemma turned and opened the kitchen door to call up the stairs to Liam. 'Liam, your nana is here to take you to nursery.'

'A house like this would be nothing to a man of Marcus's wealth and he is always offering you financial assistance,' her mother continued determinedly as if Gemma had said nothing. 'I don't know why you keep turning him down. You're so damn stubborn sometimes—'

'Mum, I am not going to ask Marcus for help.' Gemma put on the jacket of her smart black business suit and checked her keys were in her bag. She was running late and she had a stressful day at work ahead of her: she didn't want to think about Marcus, let alone talk about him. 'He's the man who wants to take Liam away from me, remember? The last thing I'll do is go to him cap in hand.'

'It doesn't need to be like that. Marcus is a decent enough man, and I'm sure—'

'You can't be sure of anything where Marcus is concerned. And I don't need his help. I'll manage,' Gemma said positively before going out into the hall to call upstairs again. 'Liam, Mummy will be late for work.'

Joanne Hampton followed her daughter out into the hall. 'How will you manage?' she persisted. 'The cost of living in London is going through the roof, Gemma. You have to be practical. It's hard being a single parent.'

'I've got a good job, Mum,' Gemma reminded her patiently. 'And I'm in line for promotion again. If I get this new job, who knows, maybe I will be able to put in a bid for this house.' As she spoke she swallowed down nervous anticipation. She did have a good job and her career had been going from strength to strength over these last few years. She had worked her way through the various editorial departments of *Modern Times*, a glossy monthly magazine, and had been made deputy editor last year. Now she was up for consideration for editor because Susan Kershaw, the present editor, was leaving.

Everyone said she stood a very good chance of getting the top job. She was talented and she was driven. Even Gemma was quite confident that she could outperform the competition. Circulation of the magazine was up and she had more than proven herself over the last year. In fact, she had been feeling quite relaxed about the whole thing until rumours of a take-over bid for the magazine had started a few weeks ago. And suddenly her rosy picture for the future had developed a few disturbing black clouds.

No one was certain who had made the take-over bid, but if it was successful there might be redundancies. The first to go would be the top jobs, as the new company were likely to want to put their own key people in.

But even if she lost her job she would walk into another one, she told herself confidently. She had a great CV.

All right, maybe she wouldn't earn enough to buy a house as beautiful and in such a good area as this, but she could afford to rent something decent around here. And as long as she maintained her independence and a nice way of life for Liam, that was all that mattered.

Gemma glanced towards the stairs again. 'Liam, I'm going to come up in a minute,' she warned.

'What's he doing up there?' her mother asked.

'Playing with a train set Marcus bought for him last week. The tracks are all the way around his bed.'

Joanne smiled. 'He's a good man. Gemma, why don't you go out for dinner with him tomorrow night. I've been thinking about it and the pair of you should sit down and talk about Liam's future, work this custody matter out. I'll babysit for you.'

'There's nothing to work out,' Gemma insisted. Marcus had rung several times that week and had left messages on her machine, but she hadn't called him back and she wasn't going to. 'Marcus has my answer and that's the end of it.'

'Nevertheless, you need to talk to him about it, soften your attitude.'

'Soften my attitude!' Gemma looked at her mother in consternation. 'If I do that he'll walk away with my son, and that will be that.'

'Marcus is a reasonable man. I'm sure you can come to some compromise.'

'Not over this.' Gemma shook her head firmly. She wished her mother wouldn't always talk so positively about Marcus. She never tried to hide the fact that she thought he was wonderful and at every opportunity she thrust the fact at Gemma. Over the years Gemma had got used to it and accepted it. But given the circumstances, the fact that Marcus wanted to take Liam away, she would have thought her mother might be seeing things a little more from her side at the moment. It was disturbing that she wasn't—hurtful, even.

'Do you think Liam is right and Marcus is getting married?' her mother asked suddenly. 'Maybe he's settling down with that Italian girl. What's she called? Sophia? Maybe that's why he's moving back there.'

'Maybe.' That thought had already tormented Gemma through several long sleepless nights. 'But, whatever the reason, he is not having Liam.'

Gemma was relieved when Liam appeared at the top of the stairs, bringing the conversation to a close.

As he hurried down to stand beside them, Gemma noticed he looked a little flushed. 'Are you okay, darling?' she asked, bending to put one hand on his forehead.

His skin felt clammy under the coolness of her hand. 'Are you feeling ill?'

'I'm okay.' Liam shrugged.

'He's probably been racing around after that train,' his grandmother said with a laugh.

'I've built tunnels under the bed and a big loop by the bathroom door,' Liam said with a grin. 'Come and look, Nana.'

'Maybe later.' Joanne smiled. 'We have to go now. Otherwise, Mummy will be late for work and I'll be late for my bridge club.'

* * *

Thank heavens Liam hadn't been ill this morning, Gemma thought, as she sat at her desk half an hour later and dealt with a mountain of paperwork. If she'd had to have today off it could have been disastrous. The office was chaotic and a lot of the top executives were huddled together in the boardroom, giving a sense of urgency to everything.

'They're calling a meeting later.' Richard Barry, the new features editor of the magazine, paused by her desk on the way to get himself a coffee. 'Looks like the take-over is going through after all.'

Gemma felt slightly ill at those words. If that was the case, it was likely that all her hard work for the job of editor wouldn't pay off.

'Hey, don't look so worried.' Richard perched on the edge of her desk for a moment. 'You are one of the most talented editors I've ever worked with, you'll get your job.'

'Thanks for the vote of confidence, Richard, but I doubt it.' She smiled up at him. Richard was an attractive man and he had become a close personal friend over the last couple of months. She really liked him. Liked him more, perhaps, than any other man she had met in the last few years.

'Shall I get you a coffee from the machine to cheer you up?' he asked now.

Gemma laughed at that. The coffee from the machine was so bad that it had become a standing office joke. It was said that anyone who wanted to end it all only had to overindulge by a few cups to achieve their aim. 'Go on, then. I'll live dangerously, thanks.'

As Richard left her office she watched him through the glass walls of her office. She had one of the few private offices on the floor but her door was always open and the glass walls made her feel part of what was going on out in the main body. Now she noticed there was a stir up by the reception area, and as she glanced over she saw with a shock that Marcus Rossini had just stepped out of the lift.

The nerve of the man, she thought furiously. How dared he come to confront her at work? She watched with a small gleam of satisfaction, knowing that if he didn't have an appointment, Clare, the receptionist, would not let him in without gaining clearance from her first…clearance she had no intention of giving. Marcus could get lost.

She waited for the phone on her desk to ring, but instead, a few minutes later, Gemma watched incredulously as Marcus strode on in through the office in the direction of her desk. What the hell had he said to Clare? she wondered. Probably turned on that fabulous Italian charm of his, or maybe he had merely smiled. She noticed the effect he was having on the other women out in the office as he walked past them: they were all looking at him with ill-disguised appreciation. It was always the same, Gemma thought with annoyance, women just fell at Marcus's feet. But not her, she thought grimly. She was older and wiser now and knew the dangers of that particular pitfall.

She had to admit, though, he did look good. The dark business suit did incredible things for an already very desirable physique. Annoyed with herself for allowing that thought to cross her mind, she glared at him as he strolled nonchalantly into her office.

'What on earth do you want?' she asked sharply. 'Because I'm telling you now, Marcus, I haven't got time for whatever it is.'

'That's hardly a congenial welcome, Gemma,' he chastised softly.

'That's because I'm not feeling particularly congenial where you are concerned.' She felt a tremor of apprehension as he shut the door behind him, closing her into the confined space with him. 'That door always remains open,' she told him, but he ignored her completely and left it closed, taking a seat in the chair at the other side of her desk.

He looked extremely relaxed and yet more formidable than ever, his expression as businesslike and serious as his clothing.

'Clare shouldn't have allowed you in here,' Gemma said heatedly. 'In case you hadn't noticed, I'm trying to work and this isn't a convenient time.'

'Unfortunately, there never seems to be a convenient time, does there, Gemma? As you have not returned any of my calls, you've left me no option but to come in here to sort things out in person.'

She didn't like the sound of that at all. It made a nervous flutter start in the base of her stomach. 'Marcus, I have nothing to say to you, and I want you to leave now.'

As he made no effort to move she continued in a more heated tone. 'Look, I've asked you nicely, but if you continue to refuse you'll leave me no option but to ring through for Security to remove you.'

Far from seeming worried by that, he looked slightly amused. 'I never realized before what a fighter you are, Gemma,' he murmured. 'But I have to warn you that if you take such an action, you might get more than you bargained for. You might find that you are the one who is removed from the office.'

Gemma shook her head contemptuously. 'Your arrogance never ceases to amaze me, Marcus. You may have been able to charm your way around the receptionist, but two burly security guards will be a different matter.'

'Why haven't you returned my phone calls?' he asked, totally ignoring that.

'You know why.'

'You've been working day and night for the last few days?' he said sardonically. 'When I dropped Liam back on Sunday your mother told me you were working. And I've left several messages on your answering machine now, the first on Sunday evening, the last yesterday morning.'

'I've been busy.'

'Too busy to make time to discuss our son's future?'

The nonchalant question fired her blood. 'There is nothing further to discuss.'

He didn't answer that. 'Nice office you've got here,' he remarked instead. 'And I hear you're looking to move even higher within the company.'

'How do you know that?'

'You seem to forget that I'm a player in the publishing world myself. Let's say I've got my ear to the ground.'

If ever there was an understatement, it was that. Marcus didn't just 'play' at publishing: he ran one of the largest companies in Europe. Rossini House was massive; it owned some of the most well respected publishing firms in the business. *Modern Times* was very small fry compared to anything Marcus ran or was remotely interested in.

'Well, I'm flattered that you're taking such an interest in my career,' she replied sardonically. 'Obviously, you have a lot of spare time on your hands. Or is life just incredibly dull for you at the moment?'

'Life's pretty good, Gemma. Thank you for your concern,' he replied smoothly, completely ignoring her sarcasm. 'So what do you think your chances are of getting this promotion?'

'I don't know…I suppose I'm quietly confident.' She frowned, wondering why he was asking her this.

'If I remember rightly, you're not bad at your job,' he reflected.

'Not bad?' Her frown deepened. 'Actually, I'm damn good at my job, as you well know. It's the reason I was offered a job all those years ago at one of your companies.'

He regarded her steadily for a moment as if she were a piece of artwork he was thinking of buying. Her blonde hair was tied back in a schoolgirl ponytail, which showed the perfect proportions of her face, the high cheekbones, the soft, sensual curve of her lips, the large, vivid blue eyes. She wore light make-up but she didn't need any; her skin was flawless and creamy.

Her body was still ripe perfection.

At twenty-nine, Gemma had hardly changed since the day she had first walked into his office five and a half years ago. 'Your work wasn't the only reason you were offered a job,' he said with soft emphasis, then smiled as he saw a bright flush of colour light her skin.

'I'm sure you haven't come here to reminisce about old times, or ask about my work, so perhaps you had better just get to the point,' she said, annoyed with herself for allowing that remark to unsettle her.

'I think you know what the point is,' he said quietly.

'Liam is not going to live with you in Italy, so you may as well just give up on the idea and go away.'

'Giving up isn't an option, Gemma.'

She glanced beyond him towards the main office. People were looking over at them; curiosity was obviously rife out there. 'You are causing a scene, Marcus, and I want you to go.'

'Not until you've agreed to come out for dinner with me tomorrow.'

'I can't—'

'Your mother informed me that she would gladly babysit for us, so what time shall I pick you up?'

'Watch my lips, Marcus. I will not go out with you tomorrow. And where Liam lives is not up for discussion. He is staying with me.'

'I'll book a table at Bellingham's for seven-thirty. How does that suit?'

'You can get a table at Buckingham Palace for all I care. I still won't be there.'

Why was he being so insistent about taking her out for dinner? she wondered furiously. Did he think that was the best place to tell her he was planning to get married? Gemma shivered at the thought…that was a bit too civilized for her taste.

She tried to return her attention to her work, to pretend he wasn't there. And hoped he would just get the message and leave.

'Is it always going to be like this between us?'

The softly spoken question made her look up. 'Like what?' she asked, puzzled.

'Guns drawn at twenty paces.' He gave a small smile.

'That's not fair, Marcus. I have always been very cooperative with you. I've let you see Liam whenever you want. Even at very short notice, I change my plans to fit in with your work schedule. I think I've been more than helpful—'

'What about the fact that I don't agree with the school you are sending him to in September?' Marcus cut across her suddenly.

She frowned, the remark taking her by surprise. 'There's nothing wrong with that school. It's close by—'

'I don't like it.'

'What do you mean, you don't like it? What would you know about it?' she asked impatiently.

'I just think we could send him somewhere better.'

'You mean to a school with colossal fees?' She shook her head angrily. 'Just because a school costs a lot doesn't—'

'That's not what I mean at all, Gemma.'

'So what do you mean?' she asked, and then promptly wished she hadn't when she noticed the smile of satisfaction on Marcus's face.

'You see, we do have things to discuss.'

'Discussing local schools is a very different proposition to discussing taking Liam out of the country completely,' she said quickly.

'Yes, but up to two minutes ago you didn't even want to discuss local schools,' Marcus pointed out coolly.

He was right; she didn't. The simple fact was that she was scared of Marcus taking over completely. It was in the nature of the man: he was arrogant, and he was powerful. If she gave him even an inch he would take the whole nine yards. He thought he could say and have anything he wanted…and maybe he could, maybe that was really what scared her. He had always had the strangest effect on her. Just sitting this close to him across the desk made her heart rate increase, made her whole body turn to red alert. Having sensible, unemotional talks with Marcus was something she was incapable of doing.

'I just want to be more involved in my son's upbringing, Gemma. Is that such a bad thing?'

Gemma stared at him in exasperation. She couldn't honestly say that it was.

'But you don't let me help you in any way—'

'If you're going to start talking about money, you can forget it, Marcus. We have been all through this subject before and I've told you I don't want or need your help. I'm managing perfectly well by myself, and that's how I like it.'

She saw his face tighten, saw the flare of annoyance in his dark eyes, but she held his gaze with determination. She was resolute on this, because she knew if she handed over the financial reins to him he would really have a hold over her.

'And don't worry about the school,' she continued hurriedly. 'It will be good for Liam. My friend's little girl, Annie, goes there as well, so he will feel right at home,' she continued firmly.

'Oh, well, if Annie goes there it must be fine,' Marcus grated sarcastically. 'To hell with academic achievement.'

'He's four years of age, Marcus. He can train to be a brain surgeon a little later on,' she retorted with equal sarcasm. 'My main priority at the moment is that he's happy.'

'If that's the case, then come out for dinner with me tomorrow night.'

'So we can fight between courses. I don't think so. Liam is not going to Italy, he is staying here with me, and he is going to a local school.' She glanced beyond him towards the office again. There was a sense of unreality about being closeted in here with Marcus discussing schools of all things on a stressful Thursday with deadlines looming and chaos reigning in the boardroom. The day had started on a bad note and seemed to be going rapidly downhill. She wondered if it could get any worse.

'You are the most stubborn woman I have ever met, do you know that?' Marcus said quietly.

Gemma noticed Henry Perkins, the company director, coming out of the boardroom to get himself a coffee from the machine. He looked as stressed as she felt, she noted. Although he was a relatively young man at forty-five he seemed to have aged ten years in the last few weeks.

'The fact remains that, no matter what you say to the contrary, Liam is a very happy child.' She returned her attention to Marcus. 'He's well adjusted and secure, and I want to make sure things stay like that. And anyway, maybe if you cared a little more about Liam and a little less about yourself, you wouldn't be thinking of leaving him and going to live in Italy.'

She knew she had scored a bulls-eye with that remark as she saw his face darken angrily. He wasn't the only one who could use emotional blackmail to get what he wanted, she thought with satisfaction.

'Things aren't that black and white,' he said crossly.

'They never are.' She hesitated before asking curiously, 'So what's drawing you back to Italy? Some nubile woman waiting in the wings, I take it. Or are you finally going to make an honest woman of Sophia?'

There was a moment's silence, then Marcus grinned. 'Hell, Gemma, you sound almost jealous.'

'Don't be ridiculous.' She wished she hadn't asked now, wished she had contained both her curiosity and the barbed comment. 'On the contrary, I hope you will be very happy.'

'Thank you.'

Was that all he was going to say? Was he not going

to enlighten her at all? She stared at him in frustration, wanting to ask him more but not daring to in case he thought she really was jealous…which, of course, she wasn't, just consumed with curiosity.

'So, while we are on this new and enlightened "be nice to each other" path, how about agreeing to have dinner with me tomorrow night?'

'The answer is still no, Marcus. Now we've had our conversation, and I want you to go. I'm stressed enough at the moment without you coming in here making trouble.'

'What are you stressed about?' he asked calmly.

For a second she contemplated telling him about the rumoured take-over bid for the magazine, then decided the less he knew about the details of her financial life the better. 'Let's just say that today is not the best of days in this office, and your presence here is making matters worse.' She glanced up, noticed Richard hovering outside the door with her coffee and waved him in, in the hope that Marcus would go once someone else was present.

As the door opened Marcus glanced coolly around. 'Wait outside, will you?' he said to a startled Richard, who had only taken a step inside. 'We are having a private conversation.'

'Oh, right you are.' To Gemma's annoyance, Richard immediately retreated and closed the door again.

'How dare you talk to Richard like that?' she flared angrily. 'He's the features editor, not one of your lackeys.'

'I don't care who he is. Richard can wait,' Marcus ground out tersely.

She glared at him.

'You think you can manage very well on your own,

Gemma, but you are being naïve. It's hard being a single parent—'

'I know it's hard. You're preaching to the converted, Marcus. It's you who has no idea of reality. Now, if you don't mind, I have a living to make and a son to support.'

His eyes narrowed. 'I know you like to think of yourself as very independent, but believe me, without my support you would find things very tough…very tough indeed.'

The quietly spoken words puzzled her. 'I don't need any support from you, Marcus. I never have and I never will.'

'Really?' Marcus rose from his chair, his manner very cool suddenly. 'Such big words…let's hope you're not speaking rashly, Gemma. Because, from what I hear, your life is in a state of flux at the moment.'

'What do you mean?'

'Well, for one thing, I hear that the house you are renting is up for sale,' he said casually.

'How do you know about that?' She stared up at him in confusion and then the mist cleared. Obviously, her mother had contacted him this morning, had gone ahead and asked for his help. Was that why he had rushed around here now, because he thought he could use this to his advantage? Furiously she shook her head. 'Look, Marcus, I don't know what Mum has told you, but…'

'Your mother hasn't told me anything.'

'So how do you know the house is for sale? It hasn't even gone on the market yet.'

He leaned on the back of the chair and stared at her, a wry look on his face as he watched her perplexity. 'Oh, come on, Gemma, you didn't honestly think you could rent a house like that for what you've been paying?'

'You mean you've been paying my rent?' She struggled blindly to comprehend what was going on here.

'I've waived your rent,' he said nonchalantly. 'The house belongs to me. You see, I know you have been determined not to accept my help in any way but I have been doubly determined that you should.'

'Well, you had no right!' All colour drained from her skin and she stood up to face him on legs that were decidedly shaky. 'I told you I didn't want you interfering in my life—'

'I wasn't interfering and I didn't do it for you, I did it for my son,' he said calmly.

'And now, when it suits, you're throwing us out...' Her tone was icily cold. 'And you wonder why I didn't want to accept any help from you in the first place.'

'I'm not throwing you out. You can continue to live there for as long as you like. I'm just giving you a wake-up call. I've tried to tell you nicely, now I'm telling you clearly. I won't allow you to shut me out of Liam's life for a moment longer.'

'Well, here's a wake-up call for you,' Gemma retorted furiously. 'I wouldn't want to live in that house now if it was the last one left standing in London. Liam and I will be moving out at the end of the month.'

'When Liam moves out of that house he will be accompanying me back to Italy,' Marcus replied calmly.

'Not while there is a single ounce of strength left in my body.'

Marcus walked slowly around the desk until he was standing very close to her, then reached out and touched her face. Considering the fact that they were both intensely angry it was a strangely tender caress and it made her shiver deep inside. 'I can think of better ways for that beautiful body of yours to expend energy,' he murmured.

Her eyes locked with his and she felt her breathing quickening, her pulses racing in disarray. She tried to tell herself to move back from him, but it was as if he held her under some kind of spell and she was unable to break free. Her body was a whisper breath from his and she felt the electric magnetism of him invade her very soul.

'I don't want to fight with you, Gemma. We both have Liam's best interests at heart,' he continued softly. 'And I am willing to compromise.'

Somehow she managed to take a step back from him. 'You'll allow me to come to Italy for my holidays, you mean?' she murmured shakily. 'No thank you, Marcus. I'll pass on that.'

'And I wouldn't blame you for passing on that. I don't want to be a part-time parent in the holidays, myself.'

'Then don't leave England.' Her voice held a husky tremor that made it sound more of a plea than an ultimatum.

'I have to.'

'She must be some woman if you are choosing her over your son.'

'I'm not choosing anyone over my son,' he said firmly. 'I'm hoping I can have it all.'

'Nobody can have it all, Marcus,' she said quietly. 'Not even you.'

'When I've made up my mind to something, I usually get what I want.'

The quiet confidence of that last remark made Gemma's heart thud heavily and unevenly in her chest.

'Look, I haven't got time for this,' she murmured. She

glanced beyond him towards the office and noticed that Henry Perkins was looking directly at them. 'I can't afford to slack today. In case it's escaped your notice, things are pretty hectic in here. The managing director is in and there's an important board meeting.'

'Yes, I know.' Marcus glanced at his watch. 'I'm going to have to go.'

'Well, don't let me detain you,' she muttered sardonically.

His dark eyes seemed to sear through her. 'So I'll pick you up tomorrow night, seven-thirty.'

Gemma made no reply. Arguing with Marcus was getting her nowhere. Maybe the best way to deal with this was to allow him to think he'd won and then just phone his secretary tomorrow and cancel.

'Good.' Marcus seemed to take her silence as acquiescence. 'I'll see you later.'

Gemma felt like collapsing in a heap as he turned to leave the room. She felt as wrung out as if she had just been through the spin cycle of her washing machine. But she wasn't going to let him win, she told herself firmly. She would hold her nerve and refuse to meet him tomorrow and hopefully he would realize that if he left the country he would be leaving his son as well.

'By the way.' He turned suddenly and looked at her. 'Now that I've taken over, you can be assured that your application for the position of editor will be treated with fairness and impartiality.'

'Taken over?' She repeated his words in confusion. 'What do you mean, *taken over?*'

But she was alone in the room now and he had closed the door quietly and firmly behind him, leaving her with a slowly dawning sense of horror.

Marcus nearly walked straight into Richard Barry,

who was still hovering outside Gemma's office door, this time minus the coffee, Marcus noticed.

He was younger than Marcus had imagined. In fact, he looked even younger than Gemma...probably about twenty-four or twenty-five. He had an unruly shock of thick blond hair and a worried expression in his grey eyes.

So this was the man who had started trying to play dad to Liam, started to hang around Gemma. Marcus instantly disliked him. He wasn't Gemma's type at all...was he? Despite the dark suit he looked like he'd just escaped from some trendy boy band.

'You're Liam's dad, Marcus Rossini, right?' he said, extending his hand. 'I'm Richard Barry—'

'Features editor, yes. I know who you are.' Marcus shook his hand.

'I've heard about you, too,' Richard said with a grin. 'Liam mentions you quite a bit.'

He had a weak handshake, Marcus noted.

'He's a great little chap, isn't he, I'm very fond of him,' Richard continued brightly when Marcus made no reply.

'Yes, he's quite a character.' Marcus felt like gritting his teeth. 'You can go on into Gemma's office now if you want. We've finished our discussion...for now.'

'Thanks.' The younger man smiled and moved away from him. 'See you around, then.'

'Oh, you can count on it,' Marcus replied with soft emphasis.

CHAPTER THREE

'WHAT on earth is going on?' Richard murmured as he watched Marcus being greeted enthusiastically by the MD, before being steered towards the boardroom.

'I think we have our answer as to who is behind the take-over bid,' Gemma said in a tone that wasn't at all steady. They were both momentarily stunned into silence as the vice president of *Modern Times* arrived in the office and went straight over to shake Marcus's hand.

'And I think we can safely assume it was a successful take-over bid as well,' Richard said, with a low whistle of surprise.

No wonder Henry Perkins looked stressed, Gemma realized bleakly. Once Rossini House had decided to take them over they wouldn't have stood a chance. It was like a plastic toy soldier trying to stand up to an invading army.

'But why would Rossini want *Modern Times*?' Gemma shook her head in disbelief. She could hardly take this in. 'We're hardly in the big league. Why would Marcus Rossini buy us out?' Even as she asked the question she was remembering the look of determination in Marcus's eyes as he told her he usually got what he wanted. And suddenly she had her answer. What he wanted was Liam.

He owned the house she was living in. He owned the company she worked for. It seemed Marcus was taking her over piece by piece, and his ultimate goal was to get Liam.

'Hey, don't look so worried. Marcus seems like a nice enough guy.'

'Looks can be deceiving,' Gemma murmured distractedly.

'I'd say your promotion is in the bag,' Richard said confidently. 'Rossini knows you are over-qualified for the job. In fact, this could really work in your favour. He could offer you something even bigger and better with one of his other imprints. The sky could be the limit—'

'Richard, come back in from dreamland,' Gemma said impatiently. 'I think it's more likely that I can kiss my prospects here goodbye. Marcus won't give me the promotion.'

'How do you know that?'

'Because I know Marcus, and I know what he really wants is Liam, and if I don't hand him over—which I won't—then I'll be out of here.'

'Come on, Gemma. I think you are over-dramatising things. He's not a member of the Mafia, he's a wealthy, upright businessman with a reputation to uphold. He'd hardly take over a company just to get his child. This is big business.'

'This is chicken feed to Marcus Rossini,' Gemma maintained firmly.

'Well, even if you're right and he has bought this place with ulterior motives in mind, it won't get him anywhere. Apart from offering you incentives and pleading with you, there is nothing Marcus Rossini can do to get his son—nothing.'

'You think not?' Gemma looked up at him uncertainly. She really wanted to believe that.

'Honey, he could have all the money in the world but

the judges will still come down on the side of the mother. He must know that.'

Gemma started to feel calmer. 'I suppose you're right…I mean, it's not as if I'm a bad mother, is it?'

Richard smiled and perched on the edge of her desk. 'You are a wonderful mother and Liam adores you.' He reached out and touched her face in a gentle caress. The contact was similar to the way Marcus had traced a finger down and along her skin a few moments ago, but this stirred no feeling of fire inside her, created no chaos, no wild clamour of heartbeats…nothing. Gemma wished it had, and the feeling of emptiness and panic welled up inside her all over again.

'How about I take you out tomorrow night for dinner?' Richard suggested lightly.

'I'm seeing Marcus so we can discuss the future.' She felt the words cause a tremor inside her.

'Okay, well, Saturday night, then. We'll have dinner and take in a movie as well. How's that?'

'Sounds like fun.' Even as she accepted the date, Gemma's thoughts were backtracking towards what she had just said. Without even realizing what she was doing, she had told Richard she was seeing Marcus tomorrow.

Was she really going to go for dinner with Marcus after all her strong and determined words to the contrary?

'Anyway, I'd better get back to my desk, pretend to be busy whilst the new boss is in the building.' Richard smiled.

Gemma smiled back, but she was only half listening.

'And don't worry, Gemma.'

Easy for him to say, Gemma thought darkly as the door closed behind him. Marcus always got what he wanted. Freddie had told her that a long time ago, only he had said it in an admiring way. Freddie had adored his big brother, had hero-worshipped him. Long before Gemma had even met Marcus, she had heard all about him from Freddie.

Even now, when she thought about Francis Rossini—Freddie, as his family and friends affectionately called him—there was still an element of pain.

They had met at Oxford University and an instant friendship had sprung up between them. It was hard not to like Freddie; he was so full of enthusiasm and fun. Wherever Freddie was, there was sure to be a crowd of people gathered around him, laughing and having a good time. He had cut a dashing figure around Oxford in his bright red sports car and women had flocked to him, adoring his dark Latin good looks.

Francis Rossini could have had any woman he wanted but he had wanted Gemma. And that was where the problem had started because, although Gemma had thought Freddie was wonderful, she hadn't been in love with him. From the first moment he had kissed her she had known he wasn't the man for her and she had gently tried to tell him so.

'I love you dearly as a friend,' she had told him firmly. 'But the chemistry between us isn't right.'

'You want thunderbolts and lightning?' Freddie had said, undeterred. 'Then let me take you to bed and I'll give you the best electrical storm you've ever known.'

'No electrical storms, Freddie,' she had said, trying not to smile at the melodramatic tone of his voice. 'Just friends.'

But it had made no difference; Freddie had still pursued her with fervour. He had showered her with flowers and gifts. And in the final year at University, just before they graduated, he had proposed. Gemma had been stunned. She hadn't thought Freddie was that serious! In fact, he had had a bit of a wild reputation where women were concerned and she had assumed that a lot of his displays of affection were just down to his Latin charm. As gently as she could, she had turned him down.

He had taken the refusal well, and they had continued to be friends, but Gemma had been careful to keep him at a distance, never to see him on his own but always to be accompanied by their circle of friends.

After graduation, Gemma had found it difficult to get the kind of job she wanted. She had gone for interview after interview and everywhere the answer had been the same; her qualifications were good but they were looking for someone with more experience.

'How do you get experience if no one will give you a chance!' she exclaimed in disgust on her fourteenth interview of the week. 'I could be the best damn person in the world for this job but you're never going to find out if you don't employ me.'

'We're a national publication group, Ms Hampton,' the editor said patiently. 'We need someone experienced for this position. However, I do have something that might suit. There is a vacancy for a junior on features—'

'I'll take it,' Gemma said instantly.

'Well, I haven't told you yet what it entails.'

'It doesn't matter. I won't be there long, once you discover how good I am.'

The editor smiled at that. 'I like your style, Ms Hampton. Welcome to the *Morning Sentinel*.'

The job was even more menial than she had expected. The pay was lousy, as were the hours, and the main job skills needed seemed to be making tea and being the chief gofer. But she hadn't minded because at least she was in where the action was, and she was content to wait for the chance to prove herself.

That chance came sooner than she had anticipated. The paper wanted to run an article on Marcus Rossini, but the man in control of the Rossini publishing empire guarded his privacy fiercely and never gave interviews. Gemma seized her opportunity and went straight to Freddie to ask for his help.

'If I pull strings and get you an interview, what's it worth?' Freddie asked, a gleam of mischief in his dark eyes.

'I'll treat you to dinner at the Ritz.'

'How about accompanying me to my sister's wedding this summer? I'm short of a date.'

'Freddie, you are never short of a date. You have any number of glamorous woman falling at your feet.'

'But it's not them I want.'

She looked at him in consternation, scared suddenly that he still harboured romantic feelings for her.

Immediately he held up his hands. 'Hey, I'm not getting any ideas. I'm just asking you as a friend. My father's house has enough bedrooms to sleep an entire football team. And everyone would love to meet you. You'll love it…and you'll fall in love with Rome.'

'Rome! The wedding is in Rome!' Gemma's eyes widened. 'I couldn't possibly go with you, Freddie. It's too far away.'

Freddie laughed at that. 'It's a couple of hours on a plane.'

'People will think I'm your girlfriend—'

'Well, you are a girl and you are a friend, aren't you? Anyway, do you want this interview with my big brother or not?'

'That's blackmail, Francis Rossini,' she admonished sternly.

'That's life, Gemma Hampton.' He grinned back.

And so, against her better judgement, she agreed. She was hungry for success and she knew the interview would be a coup, launching her career forward in style. But she hadn't been prepared for it to change her life quite so radically.

Gemma remembered everything about that first meeting with Marcus in vivid detail.

She remembered his office looked more like a penthouse suite than a place of work. Huge chesterfield settees graced one end and picture windows commanded fabulous views out over Green Park.

Marcus was seated behind his desk but he rose to his feet as she walked in. As their eyes met she felt the impact of that glance almost as if he had touched her.

'Good afternoon, Mr Rossini,' she said politely, hoping that she didn't sound as nervous as she felt. There was something awesome about Marcus, something that made her feel suddenly shy and awkward. 'Thank you for agreeing to see me.'

As Gemma's hand was grasped in the firmness of his handshake she felt a jolt of electricity flow through her.

Had her hand lingered too long in his?

Afterwards she wondered a lot about that. The moment had a misty blur of unreality; the only thing she knew was that she was totally captivated. It was as if those thunderbolts that she had joked about had suddenly crashed around her, an electric storm of unimaginable proportions whipping up inside her.

'Pleased to meet you, Ms Hampton,' he said formally.

Gemma noticed that, like his brother, his English was perfect, with hardly a hint of an accent. 'Please call me

Gemma,' she said huskily. And he smiled—a smile that did unimaginable things to her insides.

'Then you must call me Marcus.' He waved her towards the chair opposite his and then sat back down behind the desk again.

'You seem to have made a big impression on my younger brother,' he said easily.

'I wouldn't go that far,' Gemma said with a smile. 'But we are good friends.'

'Just good friends?'

The coolly asked question threw her senses into disarray.

'Yes…just good friends.' She tried to keep her voice light, unsure if he was just making polite conversation or if he was taking a more personal interest. As she looked up into his eyes she found herself hoping sincerely it was the latter.

'Would you mind if I record our interview? It's just so I can check back and make sure I have my facts right.'

'By all means.'

As she took her recorder from her bag Marcus left the office momentarily to say something to his secretary.

'Sorry about that,' he said with a grin as he returned and sat down again. 'Now, fire away with your questions.'

He seemed to be studying her intently and she wished that she had worn something more exciting than her blue suit and that she had put her hair up instead of allowing it to fall freely around her shoulders. She wanted to look as stylish and as beautiful as she was sure the women he dated would look.

She cleared her throat nervously. 'So, Marcus, would

you mind if I asked you about the background of the Rossini publishing house first?'

'By all means.' He settled more comfortably in his chair, almost as if he were about to watch an entertaining film. He seemed very at ease, extremely relaxed, and there was a gleam of amusement in his eyes as if he knew she was nervous.

Honestly, life could be very unfair sometimes, Gemma thought wryly. She had been nervous about the interview to begin with because it was her first really important one. The fact that she found herself overwhelmingly attracted to the man she was interviewing wasn't helping.

He just wasn't at all what she had been expecting.

She had thought he was going to be an older version of Freddie. But, although Freddie was almost as tall as Marcus and their colouring was similar, jet dark hair and eyes that were almost coal black, they were worlds apart in looks. Next to Marcus, Freddie, who was her own age, suddenly seemed terribly young...somehow very immature.

At thirty-three, Marcus Rossini was spectacularly handsome and all male. There was an air of power and sophistication about him and the dark eyes that held hers were cool and serious and seemed to reach into her very soul.

'Your father founded the Rossini publishing business, I believe?' With difficulty she made herself concentrate.

'That's right. I took over the reins six years ago, after my mother died and my father lost interest in the business.'

'Your mother was English, wasn't she?'

'Yes, she was from Surrey. Freddie has obviously been filling you in on the details.'

'Well, he's told me a few things. You were very young for such an awesome responsibility. Did you find the pressure hard at first?' she pressed on, not wanting to be sidetracked from her line of questions.

Marcus grinned at that. 'I thrive on pressure, and I love a challenge.'

The phone rang and he snapped it up and it was several minutes before Gemma could resume her interview. The same thing happened just a little while later and after the third and fourth interruptions Gemma started to get irritated. 'Do you think you could get your secretary to hold your calls for a while?'

He looked unrepentant. 'I'm sorry, Gemma, but as I explained to Freddie, I am a very busy man.'

It was then that Gemma took a calculated risk. 'Well, maybe now isn't a good time. Maybe we could continue our discussion in more congenial surroundings later on. How about dinner tonight?'

He fixed her with that quizzical, deep look that she was beginning to recognise. For a second Gemma thought he was going to turn her down and tell her she either put up with the interruptions or she did without the interview. 'Okay, dinner tonight. It's a date,' he said casually. 'But on one condition.'

'Yes?' She felt suddenly breathless.

'You leave your recorder at home.'

'Okay, but I must warn you my shorthand isn't very good,' she said with a smile.

'Well, I promise I'll take things nice and slow,' he drawled lazily.

Something about the way he said that, the way he looked at her, made her senses leap.

'Come to my place for about seven-thirty. That way we can be assured of no interruptions.'

Had she imagined the look in his eye as he said that, Gemma wondered later, as she frantically went through her meagre wardrobe looking for something suitable to wear.

In the end she borrowed a designer outfit belonging to her flat-mate, Jane; a silky, pale grey creation that managed to look sensual and yet smartly chic at the same time.

She felt more nervous than ever as her taxi turned in through gates leading down to a huge Georgian residence that backed out on to the river Thames. There was a feeling inside her that she was out of her depth. She wanted to focus entirely on the interview so that she could write an article that would get her noticed at work…but disturbing her train of thought was the little fact that she was deeply attracted to Marcus Rossini. There was a part of her that was hoping it wouldn't all be business tonight.

A housekeeper opened the door to Gemma and led her through to a drawing room that was furnished with antiques that were stylishly in keeping with the Georgian era. A log fire blazed a welcome in a large open grate. 'Mr Rossini will be with you in a moment,' the housekeeper said, closing the door behind her.

She probably only waited for Marcus for about five minutes but it felt like an eternity. The ornate clock on the sideboard chimed the half hour and Gemma noticed the framed photographs beside it and went over to have a look. She had just lifted one up when Marcus walked in.

'Good evening, Gemma.'

'Evening.' She put the photo down and swung around to face him, feeling slightly breathless as their eyes connected.

'You look very nice.'

'Thank you.'

As Marcus's eyes swept over her admiringly, she sent up a silent thank you to her friend, Jane.

He walked closer to her and she thought he was going to shake her hand but to her surprise he kissed her on each cheek in true Mediterranean style. For a moment she was so close to him that she could feel the warmth of his body radiating against hers. The scent of his aftershave pervaded her senses, clouding her mind, and she felt a rush of desire sharper than anything she had ever known.

As he stepped back and she looked up into the darkness of his eyes she knew beyond a doubt that she really wanted this man…wanted him with a fierceness and a passion beyond even her wildest dreams.

'I see you've been admiring my gallery,' he said, looking at the photos beside them.

'Yes.' Grateful of the excuse to turn her attention away from him, she picked up the photo she had been looking at before. 'Are these your brothers when they were young?'

'Yes. This is Freddie.' He pointed to a cheeky-looking child who was at the front of the picture. 'And that is Leonardo…and next to him Bruno, Nicholas and then me.'

Gemma looked with interest at the photograph of Marcus as a young teenager. Even then he had been good-looking.

'And are these your sisters?' she asked, picking up the photo next to it and studying the two young women, who were dark haired and very beautiful.

'No, I have only one sister.' Marcus pointed to the

young woman to the left of the picture. 'That's Helene. She's getting married in a few months' time.'

Gemma remembered her promise to attend the wedding. 'And who is the girl next to her?' she asked, trying not to think how Freddie was going to feel when he found out she was attracted to his brother.

'That's Sophia Albani. She is a friend of the family—her father and my father were business partners. They started the publishing house together.'

'Really? I didn't realize that Rossini House had started as a partnership.' She was instantly interested in an angle she could use for her article.

'Yes, Filippo Albani was my father's closest friend. They were in business together for quite a while. They went their separate ways in the late seventies when my father bought Albani out.'

'Was it an amicable split?'

Marcus smiled. 'You have your reporter's hat on now, I hear it in your voice.'

'Well, that is why I'm here,' she said lightly.

'Yes.' He reached out and touched her face in a feather-light caress that sent shivers racing down her spine. 'But I hope that isn't the only reason.'

The door opened at that moment. 'Dinner is served Signor Rossini,' the housekeeper announced, her cheerful tones cutting through the sudden tension and excitement curling between them.

Maybe she had imagined it, she told herself over the delicious meal. Maybe Marcus hadn't been making a pass at her, because his manner throughout the meal was, although charming, impeccably polite and correct, with no hint of the dangerous undercurrent of passion.

Somehow she managed to resume her questions over

the meal. Marcus told her in fascinating detail about the business split between his father and the Albani family.

It was a story Gemma itched to write, a story of friendship and big business. All had ended happily, it seemed, and the two men were still good friends today. Filippo had gone into politics and was now a well-known member of the Italian parliament.

'So is the interview finished?' Marcus asked suddenly as he leaned across to fill up her wine glass.

'Just about.' She grinned at him. 'Apart from the personal details, like are you dating anyone special at the moment…any wedding bells on the near horizon?'

'The only wedding on the near horizon is my sister Helene's. What about you, are you seeing anyone special?'

The sudden way he turned the question back on her took her by surprise. 'No, no one serious.'

'Good.'

The way he said that, and the way he looked at her, made her heart miss several beats.

The housekeeper came in to clear the table.

'Maybe we should retire to the other room and make ourselves more comfortable,' Marcus said, pushing his chair back. 'Then maybe I can turn the tables and shine the spotlight on you. You can tell me all about yourself.'

'There's not that much to tell.' She followed him back to the drawing room and sat on the settee, watching as he put another log on the fire.

'I don't believe that for a moment.' He sat in the chair opposite her. As she glanced over and their eyes met she found herself wondering what it would be like to be kissed by him. And the need to find out was like an ache inside.

'It must have been nice growing up as part of a large

family,' she said, trying desperately to turn her mind away from such dangerous ground. Marcus Rossini was out of her league, she told herself firmly. He was almost ten years older; he was a sophisticated and worldly-wise man who probably ate women like her for breakfast, and then promptly forgot about them as the next willing woman fell at his feet.

He nodded. 'We're quite a close family. All of us work in the same business…except for Freddie, of course.' He smiled. 'Freddie has always been a law unto himself. Considering he is the only one of my brothers currently living in London, I hardly see him.'

'He's probably too busy enjoying himself.'

'I know. I keep telling him he'll have to get a job soon, but he pays no attention.'

Gemma smiled and noted the undercurrent of teasing affection in Marcus's voice. He obviously cared a great deal about his brother.

'So, have you got any brothers or sisters?'

Gemma shook her head. 'No, my father died when I was eight and there was just Mum and I.'

'Was that lonely?'

Gemma thought about that for a moment. 'Not really. Mum did a great job bringing me up on her own. But I think it was difficult for her sometimes because she had no family around her at all, no network of support. I used to find myself worrying about her quite a bit because she worked so hard and always looked so tired… Anyway…' She trailed off in embarrassment, wondering why she had told him all that. 'I don't know why I'm telling you this. *I'm* supposed to be interviewing *you*, not the other way around.'

'I was hoping the interview was over…apart from the

personal stuff.' There was a gleam of humour in his eyes.

'Ah, yes, let's get back to that,' Gemma joked and then some spark of mischief made her repeat something his brother had once told her about him. 'Freddie says you have had numerous beautiful women in your life, and that you break hearts.'

'Francis should watch what he says to members of the press,' Marcus said lightly.

'Don't worry, it's off the record.' Gemma grinned. 'In fact, as I have no tape recorder with me, I might have to come back to check I have my facts straight on any of this.'

'I hope you do.' Marcus held her eyes for a long time and she felt her heart speeding up in her chest. Warning bells rang deep inside her, and she found herself finishing her drink hurriedly and standing up. 'Well, I really ought to be going,' she said brightly. 'Thank you for the interview and for dinner.'

'You're welcome.' He also got to his feet.

'I had better ring for a taxi.'

'I suppose so.' As he walked towards her she felt every nerve in her body tighten in anticipation.

He reached out and lifted her chin so that her eyes were forced to hold with his. Then he lowered his head and without warning he kissed her with an intensity and a passion that sent rivers of fire running through her.

'I've been wanting to do that all night,' he said softly as he moved back.

'So have I,' she admitted huskily.

He moved closer and kissed her again. The only sound in the room was the fire burning greedily in the grate and it seemed to echo the heat inside her. Never had she felt this wild intensity of desire. It was incredible...it was terrifying. Because she didn't want to move back; she wanted so much more.

As his hands started to move over her body she welcomed them.

She felt him touch her breast through the silk of her blouse, his thumb caressing her, feeling how she hardened instinctively. Then he kissed her again, his mouth possessing her totally in the most sexual kiss she had ever experienced.

'Ever since you walked into my office this afternoon, I've wanted to do this.' His hands moved beneath her top and pushed the lace of her bra to one side, cupping the warm curves of her body in his hands. The feeling of his skin against her naked flesh made her gasp with need.

Her body was so close to his she could feel the strength of his arousal and she wanted him even closer. His fingers teased her erect nipples, and she longed to be free of the constraints of her clothes, to feel his body against hers, taking total possession.

'God, you're beautiful.' He kissed her neck and the side of her face before finding her lips again in a kiss that was even harder and more demanding, making her body crave his and press even closer.

Then suddenly he pulled back from her, leaving her shaking and torn with desire.

'Why have you stopped? Don't stop.' Her voice was a husky plea, and he smiled.

'Let's go upstairs.' He took hold of her hand and led her towards the door. She went willingly with him, her heart thundering so hard against her chest with wild anticipation that she was sure he could hear it.

He brought her up into an exquisitely lovely bedroom. A four-poster bed dominated the room, draped with white embroidered cotton. A fire blazed in the Adam fireplace. Outside the window there was a view towards the river, just glimpsed through a tracery of trees. It was snowing, and there was a silent tranquillity about the scene that was totally at odds with the raging heat inside Gemma.

Then she noticed the champagne that was chilling on the bedside table and the two champagne glasses.

'It looks like you were expecting me to stay?' Her eyes moved to his.

'Let's say I was hopeful,' he replied with a lazily attractive smile.

The arrogant confidence of the man threw her senses into confusion. And suddenly she was angry. Was he so used to having any woman he wanted that he just took it for granted that he only had to snap his fingers and a woman would come to him? Or maybe he just thought that she was easy?

That thought really unsettled her. The fact was that she was far from 'easy'. She'd had a lot of boyfriends and all of them had tried to get her into bed—all of them had failed. No one had ever turned her on enough for her to want to go the whole way. In fact, she had started to wonder if there was something wrong with her, if maybe she was just not capable of feeling such intense passion. But a few moments ago that fear had been well and truly shattered. At twenty-three she was still a virgin, but it wasn't because she was frigid—it was because she needed the right man to ignite the fire inside her. That that man now thought she was easy was galling in the extreme.

'Hey, don't look so annoyed.' He reached out and touched her face but she flinched away from him before the touch of his fingers could disturb the clarity of her thinking.

'I think I should go, Marcus. I'm sorry…this is just all happening a little too fast.'

'Yes, I suppose it is.' He grinned teasingly. 'But I only promised to take things slowly with the interview, not with what happened afterwards. And I've got a confession to make.'

'Oh, yes?' She watched warily as he opened the champagne and poured it into two glasses. 'What is it?'

'I asked my secretary to keep interrupting us this afternoon so that I could suggest seeing you tonight.'

'You are incredibly sure of yourself, Marcus Rossini.'

'Maybe I am, but I was just about to ask you to have dinner with me when you asked me first.' He grinned and there was a gleam of such charming mischief in those dark sexy eyes that she felt herself smiling back.

'So I did,' she admitted.

'And I have to confess I'm not the most patient of men. It's taken all my self-control to sit through dinner and answer your questions. You're very distracting, you know…extremely desirable, and that top you're wearing skims over your figure in a very tantalizing way.'

'Does it?' She felt her heart start to speed up again. There was something about the way he was speaking, the way his eyes were moving over her, that was mesmerising.

'If wanting someone is a crime, then I'm definitely guilty.' He put the champagne bottle back on ice. 'All evening I've wondered what it would be like to kiss you. Hold you. How you'd taste…how your body would feel against mine.' He glanced back at her.

There was an electricity rippling through Gemma now that made her writhe inside with longing. She had never experienced anything like it in her life. Where other men had struggled to arouse her with caresses and kisses, this man could switch her on like a light bulb with just a few words and the touch of his eyes.

She stood awkwardly in the middle of the room, telling herself that she should turn and leave, but unable to.

'Come here.' Although he held out his hand to her, the words were a command.

'I'm not going to sleep with you, Marcus Rossini, because you are far too arrogant for my liking,' she said sternly, yet at the same time she was crossing over to stand beside him.

'That's perfectly okay with me...' He reached and pulled her down beside him. 'Because I wasn't planning on doing much sleeping.'

Arrogance like that in any other man would have made Gemma turn tail and leave, yet with Marcus the power he exerted over her held a dangerously intoxicating edge.

'Tell me you want me.' He trailed a finger down over her cheek and the feeling sent butterflies fluttering in her stomach. Then he laced his fingers through her hair and held her so that he could kiss her with an expert passion that made her senses reel. 'Tell me,' he demanded huskily as he pulled away again.

Looking deep into his eyes, Gemma could feel herself trembling with need. 'You know I do,' she whispered unsteadily.

She liked the dominant way he started to undress her. The firm, confident way he took her into his arms, the words he murmured against her ear.

Marcus Rossini knew what he was doing when it came to seduction. He was a master at turning a woman on and he found erogenous zones she never knew she had. He turned her from a cool and controlled person into a wanton hussy totally under his spell. She would have done anything for him…anything.

When finally she lay naked and trembling with desire beneath him, she sobbed for him to take full possession of her, unable to take the sweet ecstasy of need any longer. She cried out as he entered her and there was a sharp moment of pain before pleasure took over again.

But he pulled back from her instantly. 'Are you okay?'

The concern in his voice made her insides melt like wax under a flame.

'Yes.' She reached up, running her fingers through the dark, soft texture of his hair. 'Don't stop.' Her words trembled unsteadily and then she reached to kiss his lips with a sweet and yearning passion, pulling him down towards her again. He tempered his passion with gentleness after that, rocking her and cradling her in his arms until the world seemed to turn to liquid around her in a dizzying hue of astonishing and wild sensations.

Afterwards they lay wet and hot in each other's arms and for some reason they both started to laugh. He kissed her on the tip of her nose and smiled down at her. 'Wow…' he murmured huskily.

'You can say that again.' She wound her arms around his shoulders, holding him tight against her, and she had never felt so complete or so happy.

Now just remembering the wildness of that first time and the intensity of pleasure made her heartbeats increase, made her body tingle with a deep, aching void.

She got up angrily from her desk, furious with herself for thinking about such things. Okay, they had enjoyed a wild and tempestuous affair for a few short months. But that was all it had been…an affair. Marcus had never cared about her in any deep, meaningful way; she had just deluded herself into thinking he had. The reality of the situation was that Marcus had just been using her.

Gemma opened the filing cabinet and raked blindly through the contents of the drawer. She needed to concentrate on her work and put memories of Marcus out of her mind, because they didn't help. She found the file she was looking for and sat back down at her desk just as the phone rang.

'Ms Hampton?' a voice at the other end enquired.

'Yes.' She was busy taking notes from the file while she spoke, her mind only half on the call.

'This is Mrs Robertson from the nursery. I'm afraid I'm going to have to ask you to come and pick Liam up. He really isn't at all well. He has a temperature of one hundred and four.'

Suddenly everything that Gemma had thought was important that day melted away. 'I'll be right there,' she said swiftly.

CHAPTER FOUR

THE board meeting finished at the same time as Gemma emerged from her office. She was vaguely aware of Marcus in the centre of a group of men and there seemed to be a lot of backslapping going on and a lot of frivolity, which was a total change from the sombre mood this morning.

Henry Perkins looked over at her in consternation, noticing the handbag over her shoulder and the purposeful glint in her eye as she headed towards the reception area. 'Gemma, are you going somewhere? This isn't a good time to leave the office because I'm just about to call another meeting.'

'I'm really sorry Henry, but my son is ill and I'm going to have to pick him up from nursery.'

Henry frowned.

'What's wrong with him?' It was Marcus who asked the question.

'I don't know. He's got a very high temperature.' As she was speaking Gemma was walking away. She didn't care how busy it was, or how bad a time it was for her to leave—she was going.

She pushed the button on the lift and then spoke to Clare on Reception. 'I doubt I'll be back this afternoon, Clare. So will you put the transcript of the interview with Rick Simmons on Richard's desk. Oh, and don't forget to send Ali for the photos we need.' It was an effort to concentrate on work; she just wanted to be with Liam. One hundred and four was a very high temperature.

The lift doors opened and she stepped in, but before they could close Marcus stepped in with her. 'I'll come with you,' he said. 'I've finished here, anyway.'

'There's no need,' she assured him quickly. The last thing she wanted was Marcus's company. 'I'll phone you on your mobile to tell you how he is. He probably just has a summer cold.'

'If that's the case then I'll pick him up and you can get back to work. You've got a busy day in the office anyway.'

Gemma glanced over at him sharply. 'So you can accuse me of being a bad mother to some judge at a later date?'

'Now you're being ridiculous.'

'Am I?' She stared over at him. 'I know how you operate, Marcus. I've figured you out.'

'Have you?' His eyes held with hers for what seemed like a long moment. 'Then you'll know I was just trying to be helpful.'

'Just trying to take over, you mean,' she muttered under her breath. 'I know what you're up to, Marcus. I know why you've bought *Modern Times*.'

'Do you? And why's that?' he asked calmly.

'Because it puts you in a position of power over me and you are going to use it to exert pressure to get Liam.' She spoke matter-of-factly now. 'But it won't work.'

'I hate to disillusion you but I've bought this magazine because it was a good investment. I'm a businessman first and foremost.'

'Yes, when it suits you,' she grated sarcastically. 'But I don't trust you one inch, Marcus Rossini, and under the circumstances I'd prefer to go and see to Liam myself.' In an effort to end the conversation she smiled at him over-brightly. 'So just go away and leave me alone.'

Far from looking upset or annoyed, Marcus simply looked amused. 'You know, I'd almost forgotten what a fiery temperament you have,' he drawled huskily. 'I always did enjoy sparring with you. You are a very worthy opponent.'

As their eyes held she was suddenly very aware of the close confines of the lift and earlier memories filtered uncomfortably back into her mind. Memories of how fiery things had once been between them. And how that fire had spilt over into the bedroom in a wild and turbulently wonderful way.

The lift doors opened into the basement car park and it was a relief to step out and away from him. Hurriedly, she fumbled in her bag for her car keys.

'We may as well take my car,' Marcus said easily.

Gemma frowned. 'I thought I made myself clear. I'm going over there on my own, Marcus. It doesn't take two of us.' Nervously, she dropped her keys and, before she could retrieve them, he swooped to pick them up for her.

'Thanks.' She held out her hand, but he was walking on in front of her now.

'Yes, well, I'm finished for the day, anyway,' he said over his shoulder.

'Marcus!'

'I'm parked over the other side.' He was striding between the rows of cars so quickly that she practically had to run to keep up.

'Marcus, will you hand me my keys back?'

He ignored her totally and, as they approached his black sedan, he unlocked it with a flick of a button and climbed in.

Hell, but the man was infuriating, she thought angrily. She wrenched open the passenger door and glared at him. 'Marcus, will you hand me back my car keys, please?'

'Get in or I'll leave you behind.' As if to illustrate his point he started the engine.

'For heaven's sake!'

He revved the engine and, alarmed that he really might just go, she hurriedly jumped into the car. 'This is ridiculous. I don't know what you're playing at.'

'I'm not playing at anything.' He reversed the car out of the space and then casually tossed her keys over on to her knee. 'I'm accompanying you over to the nursery. I don't think that's unreasonable.'

Gemma said nothing to that. *She* thought it was unreasonable...but then she was starting to think everything Marcus did was unreasonable. He was so damn arrogant, he thought he could do or say or *have* anything he wanted. Well, he couldn't, and she was going to prove that to him if it was the last thing she did. He might have taken over the company she worked for, but he wasn't taking her over as well.

The car roared smoothly up the ramp and out into the bright mid-afternoon sunlight. She glanced at the clock on his dashboard. It was almost fifteen minutes now since the nursery had called.

She hoped Liam was okay, and that he wasn't crying or distressed. He had looked flushed this morning. A curl of guilt stirred inside her as she remembered that. Maybe she shouldn't have sent him to school? But she had honestly thought he was hot because he'd been running around playing.

'I thought Liam was a bit off-colour on Sunday,' Marcus remarked nonchalantly into the silence as he turned the car into the heavy flow of traffic.

'Did you?' She frowned. 'You never said anything.'

'That's because I didn't see you when I dropped him back…as per usual,' he added dryly. 'But I did mention it to Joanne. She said he was probably overtired.'

'Well, Mum was possibly right. You let him stay up far too late when he stays over.'

'Do I?' Marcus glanced over at her wryly.

'Yes, you do. He's always exhausted when he comes back from your house. You try to pack far too much into a weekend—he's only four.'

'I don't pack too much in. We have fun together, that's all.' Marcus's voice was derisory. 'But maybe you've forgotten what that word entails.'

'I beg your pardon?' She glared at him furiously. 'What the hell do you mean by that?'

'Well, you are always working, aren't you? The fact is, Gemma, that you are a very ambitious career woman, you always have been.'

'Your point being?' she asked crisply.

'The point being that you have a four-year-old, and I know how tough your job is, how much pressure must be on you, especially now you're working so hard towards the promotion you want. Balancing that and Liam can't be easy on your own. There can't be much time left over for just having fun with him.'

'We have lots of fun and I'm managing very well.' Her voice was stiff with fury. 'And if this is your way of trying to tell me I'd be happier without him, then you can just forget it. My world revolves around Liam. I adore him.'

'I know you do.'

'And, as for having fun, in case you've forgotten, I let you have the relaxing time with him at the weekends. I cope with the routine stuff in the middle—the important things like making sure he eats sensibly and has brushed his teeth. Real life isn't letting him eat sweets at midnight and every meal at hamburger joints.'

'I don't let him eat sweets at midnight.'

'Hah!' Gemma turned away from him to stare sightlessly through the car window. 'That's not what he tells me.'

'I don't care what he tells you.'

'And we do have fun together. I took him for a picnic on Saturday when you let him down—'

'I didn't let him down. I just had some business to deal with which made it impossible to have him on Saturday morning.'

'Well, whatever.' She shrugged airily. 'But it's funny how it's okay for you to have business pressures and not me.'

'I didn't say that.'

'Didn't you? Sounded like it to me. And, for your information, I not only work hard, I play hard, Marcus,' she added icily.

There was a long moment of silence between them as she strove to get her temper back under control.

Marcus glanced over at her. He noted the tense way she was sitting. The way her black skirt had ridden up a little on her long shapely legs.

'In fact, Richard and I are planning to take Liam away on holiday to Spain soon…not that it's any of your business.' She turned to look at him again, her eyes glinting like chips of blue ice.

'Really?'

'Yes, really,' she said coolly. This wasn't entirely true. Richard had mentioned going away together but she hadn't given him an answer yet. She was still unsure about how involved she wanted their relationship to get. However, telling Marcus this half-truth did give her a momentary feeling of pleasure, especially as she noted how his hands tightened slightly on the steering wheel. 'And Liam adores Richard,' she added for good measure.

'Well, I'm pleased for you, Gemma, but I have to admit I'm surprised that you and Richard are hitting it off so well.'

'Why's that?' She was momentarily distracted from her anger by that statement.

'He just doesn't strike me as your type.' He grinned over at her. 'You're spirited, ardently passionate, very tempestuous... Richard strikes me as being a bit dull for you, and a trifle weak—not the type to be able to handle you at all. And certainly not the type to turn you on.'

'That is total rubbish!' His statement horrified Gemma, but the thing that most dismayed her was that he was absolutely right. Richard didn't turn her on. She did find him a little dull. Immediately the thought crossed her mind she was cross with herself. Richard was one of the nicest men she had met in a long time. And anyway maybe safe was better than exciting...look where exciting had got her, she thought as she glanced over at Marcus.

She had once delighted in the dominant hold Marcus had held over her senses. Sexually speaking, she had found his strength of character and his confident manner a complete turn-on. He'd only had to look at her in a certain way and say a few words, and she had been his. Richard didn't have that effect on her at all...in fact, no other man ever had. But there was no way on earth she would ever let Marcus know that. He was bigheaded enough.

'I absolutely adore Richard,' she lied vehemently. 'He

really turns me on *and* he's a gentleman,' she added for good measure.

'Unlike me, you mean,' Marcus grinned.

'Yes, unlike you.'

'Well, I may not have been a gentleman but I definitely turned you on.'

'Go to hell, Marcus.'

He laughed at the outrage in her tone. 'You really don't like being reminded of what we had, do you? Why is that?'

'Because it's something I've forgotten long ago,' she said heatedly.

'You know what, Gemma? I don't believe you,' he said quietly. 'For one thing, you never forget your first time…' He watched her face flare with bright red colour.

'I rest my case,' she said tersely. 'You are no gentleman.'

He pulled into a parking space outside the nursery. 'And, just for the record, I absolutely loathe and detest you,' she added, reaching for the door handle and getting out of the car.

She had hoped that he would wait for her in the car, but he followed her inside the building. They walked side by side, not speaking, and the atmosphere between them was thick with tension.

Good, she thought heatedly. She hoped she had really hurt him, because he was insufferable and impossible.

As they turned the corner of the corridor, she saw Liam sitting beside Fiona Campbell, the young woman who had been his nursery teacher for the last year. Gemma felt a jolt of shock as she looked at her son. His eyes were large and feverish and seemed to dominate his tiny face, and his skin was a strange greenish-white colour. As he saw her he started to cry and she ran towards him to take him in her arms.

'It's okay, darling. It's okay, Mummy is here.' She held him tight against her. 'How long has he been like this?' she asked his teacher quietly as their eyes connected over the child's head.

'He's been worse over the last ten minutes,' she answered softly. 'He's complaining of a severe headache...' She paused before adding gently, 'And I've noticed a rash.'

The word *meningitis* instantly jumped into Gemma's mind, and the thrust of fear that shot through her was unbelievably sharp. She looked over at Marcus, her eyes wide.

He came and crouched down beside the child. 'Liam, let me see you,' he said gently, holding out his hands. The calmness of his voice stilled the child's cries and he obediently turned.

'Now then, what's all this noise?' Marcus held a hand over his son's forehead to check his temperature. His manner was quiet and assertive and it seemed to soothe Liam's distress...and Gemma had to admit it soothed her too. She was suddenly fiercely glad that he was there.

'Okay, let's look at this rash.' He checked Liam's arms and legs and then pulled up the blue T-shirt to check the child's stomach. The rash was only faintly visible, but it was there.

'We'll have to get him to a doctor immediately,' Gemma said, trying to soften the urgency of her tone so as not to alarm Liam.

'Yes, I think you are right.' Marcus reached to pick the child up.

'Thanks for looking after him, Fiona,' Gemma said hurriedly.

The woman nodded and smiled sympathetically. 'Hope he feels better soon.'

'I'll keep you posted.'

'Bye, Liam, hope you feel better soon.' Fiona waved at him but he was clutching hold of Marcus and his cries were getting louder and more distressed.

Gemma practically had to run to keep up with Marcus as they headed for the car, but this time she wasn't complaining. She sat in the back seat with Liam on her knee while Marcus drove. The traffic was horrendously heavy and the short drive to the nearest hospital seemed to take an eternity. Liam was so hot she could feel his body burning against hers. And between cries of pain and distress, he seemed to be slipping in and out of consciousness.

'It's okay, darling, we are nearly there.' She kept stroking his forehead, trying to soothe and reassure him.

'My head hurts,' he whimpered.

'It'll be okay. We'll soon get a nice doctor to make it better,' she whispered, kissing him and holding him tight.

Marcus watched her from time to time in the rear-view mirror, noting the tenderness in her touch and the way Liam clung to her. 'Is he still as hot?' he asked.

'Yes...he seems to be burning up.' Her eyes connected with his in the driving mirror and for a moment there was a unity between them, a shared feeling of anxiety that went deeper than any words.

Marcus pulled the car through the gates to the hospital and then parked directly at the front of the accident and emergency department. He hurried around to help Gemma from the back seat, taking Liam up into his arms. Then together they ran through the front doors.

In one way it was a blessed relief having doctors and

nurses taking over and yet in another the sense of helplessness as she watched the medical staff around him was the worst feeling in the world. She tried to concentrate on the questions the doctors were asking her. What was his name? How old was he? What was his medical history? What had he eaten that morning? And all the while his cries tore into her and she just wanted to go over and pull the nurses away, take him into her arms again and just hold him.

'Mrs Rossini?' The doctor pulled her attention away from Liam again. 'Has he been vomiting?'

She shook her head. At the back of her mind she registered the fact that the doctor was calling her Mrs Rossini. It was an easy mistake, as Liam's surname was Rossini.

'How long has he had the high temperature?'

She faltered a little before answering. 'He was hot this morning but I didn't think he had a temperature. He'd been running around playing…' She trailed off as guilt struck her forcibly. 'I shouldn't have sent him to school, I should have stayed at home with him today…'

'He can't have been that bad this morning.' Marcus reached and took hold of her hand, squeezing it reassuringly. 'His teacher didn't ring until after two o'clock this afternoon, remember.'

She nodded and bit down on her lip. She felt as if she was holding on to control by a whisper. She wanted to cry like Liam, uncontrollably and noisily. She felt the weight of her tears pressing down in her throat like a golf ball wedged solidly there. 'Has he got meningitis?' she asked, her voice a half whisper of fear.

'Too early to tell what it is yet. We're going to run a few tests.' The doctor sounded very matter-of-fact. 'Don't worry, Mrs Rossini, he's in good hands.'

The medical staff allowed them to remain present as they carried out their tests and they both tried to soothe and placate Liam so that he would allow them to proceed. It was one of the most traumatic and difficult afternoons of Gemma's life and she had never felt more helpless or more scared. There was also an overwhelming sense of relief at having Marcus by her side. He was incredibly calm and his strength helped her to stay focused and to hide her fear from Liam. She noticed how wonderful he was with his son, how he could cajole and soothe and even raise a smile under the most stressful of circumstances. No wonder Liam loved him so much, she thought, her heart thumping unsteadily against her chest as she watched them together. It had always been obvious from the way Liam talked about his dad, the way his eyes lit up at the mere mention of Marcus's name, that there was a close bond between father and son. But Gemma had never witnessed the relationship so closely before and it was so special and so touching that it took her completely aback.

They put Liam in a small private room with the blinds pulled firmly across to keep the evening sun out. He was quieter now, drifting in and out of consciousness. Gemma and Marcus sat beside him, taking it in turns to bathe him with cool water to help keep his temperature down.

Liam looked tiny in the big bed, so vulnerable and so ill that Gemma's heart ached.

'He'll be okay,' Marcus said gently as he noted the look of anguish on her face when two of the doctors who had been treating him stopped outside the door to consult their notes.

She nodded. She had to believe that, it was all that was getting her through. 'I wish I could change places with him,' she whispered huskily. 'I wish it was me who was so ill.'

Marcus reached out and took hold of her hand. It was the second time that day that he had done that and she found it strangely comforting. 'Thanks,' she whispered.

'Thanks for what?'

'For being here...for being so good with Liam.'

'He's my son, Gemma. You don't need to thank me for that.' His voice was gruff, but his hand didn't leave hers. She stared down at it and her eyes blurred for a second with tears. She was very glad that the room was in semi-darkness. 'I'm sorry I said some of those things to you today,' she muttered unsteadily.

'Which things in particular?' He sounded amused for a second.

'Well...you know...that I loathe and detest you. You're not really that bad...'

'Hey, don't go too far with the compliments,' Marcus said with a half-smile. 'You'll only regret it once Liam is up and running around again.'

'Probably.' She smiled through the haze of tears and looked up at him. 'You are just so damn irritating and arrogant sometimes.'

'Hey, you're spoiling things now.'

She smiled. 'But you're a very good dad,' she admitted huskily. 'Sometimes the fact that he adores you so much really winds me up. I hear about you a million times a day.'

'Well, I hear about you a trillion times a day,' Marcus said with a small smile. 'Mummy always kisses him better when he falls down... Mummy has a special way of making soldiers for his boiled eggs... In fact, everything you do is wonderful, according to Liam.'

'Really?' Her voice trembled a little.

'Yes, really.' He reached out and wiped a tear away from her face with a gentle finger. 'He loves you to bits.'

'I've been thinking a little about what you were saying to me earlier—how I work so many hours. Maybe you're right. He's going to big school soon and I haven't had as much time as I'd have liked with him as a baby.'

'You're doing fine, Gemma,' he said softly. 'It's not easy being a single parent.'

She shrugged awkwardly. 'But maybe I shouldn't have been so awkward and so proud…maybe I should have accepted more help from you.'

'It's not too late,' Marcus said quietly. 'We can start again.'

Suddenly Gemma wanted to go into his arms. She wanted him to hold her close and reassure her that there was going to be a chance of starting again. 'You think he'll be all right, don't you?' she asked softly.

'Yes, I do. I think he'll be fine.' He said the words firmly, as if he wasn't going to allow Liam to be ill, as if he had it all under control.

But as they looked over at the child who seemed so peaceful now in his hospital bed, they both knew that this was beyond their control.

The door opened and the doctor came in. Gemma knew from the look on his face that he had the test results.

They both stood up and Marcus put a steadying arm around her waist.

'Well, the good news is that your son does not have meningitis,' the doctor said immediately, and Gemma felt herself go weak with relief.

'But he is giving us cause for concern. He appears to have a rare viral infection that is working its way through his immune system.'

CHAPTER FIVE

'I DON'T know, Mum, that's all they've said.' Gemma stood out in the corridor at the pay phone, one hand over her ear so she could hear what her mother was saying amidst the noise around her. 'They can't give him antibiotics because it's a viral infection. We just have to wait now for his fever to break. They say once they've got his temperature down he'll have turned the corner.'

Gemma glanced down the long corridor and saw a nurse going into Liam's room. 'I'll have to go, Mum. I don't want to be away from him for too long...yes, Marcus is here, thank God.' Her voice shook slightly. 'I'll ring you as soon as there is any change.'

She put the phone down and hurried back. It was nine in the evening now and through the window she noticed the sun was still blazing outside. Entering Liam's room felt like entering a bad dream, the blinds were drawn and he lay surrounded by monitors, still deeply unconscious. Marcus and the nurse were talking quietly.

'Any change?' Gemma asked, anxiously looking from one to the other.

'No, no change,' the nurse said gently. 'I was just telling your husband that there is a canteen up on the third floor. Maybe you should take it in turns to go up and have something to eat, Mrs Rossini. It could be a very long night for you and you need to keep your strength up.'

She supposed she should correct the assumption that Marcus was her husband, but it seemed easier just to let it pass. 'Thank you, I'll have something later,' Gemma murmured. The last thing she wanted right now was food. She went over to check on Liam, stroking his hair back from his forehead.

The nurse went out of the room, leaving them alone, and Marcus came to stand at the other side of the bed. 'What did your mum say?'

'She wanted to come down. But I told her there was no point. I tried to play it down a bit so that she wouldn't worry too much.'

Marcus nodded. 'You should sit down.' He indicated the chair behind her. 'You look exhausted.'

'Do I? I feel okay.'

'Well, sit down anyway. I'll get us both a coffee from the machine outside.'

'Aren't you going to go up and have something to eat?'

'Like you, I suspect, I couldn't face anything right now.'

She nodded and pulled the chair behind her closer towards the bed. In the few moments that Marcus was gone there was just the steady bleep of the monitor and she felt her anxiety levels rise even further. 'Please get better, Liam,' she whispered to him. 'Get better and Mummy will give you anything you want.'

He lay so still that he almost looked unreal, with not a flutter of his eyelashes or a hint of any movement.

Marcus returned with the coffees. He handed hers over and then sat down at the opposite side of the bed. She noticed he'd taken his jacket off and his tie, and the top couple of buttons on his white shirt were unfastened. Even in this time of anguish she couldn't help but notice how attractive he was. There was a slight shadow at his jawline and his dark thick hair looked ruffled, as if he had been running his hand distractedly through it. For a second Gemma longed to be closer to him, to be able to lean over and straighten the collar of his shirt, to brush the stray strand of hair on his forehead back soothingly. She wanted to touch him so badly it hurt.

He looked over and caught her eye and immediately she felt foolish.

'I can't remember the last time we sat and had a coffee together,' he said softly.

'No....neither can I.' She looked away from him towards Liam. She noticed how much he looked like his father, same texture of hair, same dark colouring.

The sad thing was, she could remember exactly the last time they had sat and had a coffee together. It had been a few weeks before his sister's wedding, the day she had tried to tell him she was pregnant.

'When Liam is up and about again we'll go out for dinner together.'

'To discuss your move to Italy?' She looked back at him, her heart thumping against her chest.

'To discuss where we go from here.'

'Don't go back to Italy, Marcus. Please.' She hadn't intended to say those words but they came out in a sudden rush. 'Liam needs you.' There was a part of her that wanted to add that she needed him too, but she stopped herself. She was feeling vulnerable because Liam was ill. She didn't need Marcus Rossini, she told herself crossly. She had managed perfectly well without him so far, why should she need him now? 'And don't tell me that you are taking him to Italy with you, because that's just nonsense. He needs us both, Marcus.'

'I agree. But I have to go back,' he said quietly.

'Why?'

'Because the business there needs me.'

'So this has nothing to do with you getting married?'

She watched one dark eyebrow lift in surprise.

'Liam told me,' she said flatly. 'He overheard you on the phone the other night.'

Marcus went very quiet for a moment. 'He must have heard my conversation with my father.'

'So it is true, then?'

'Well, I haven't actually proposed yet,' Marcus said dryly. 'Give me a chance to get around to it before the jungle drums start declaring it to the world.'

'I'm not writing an article on you now, Marcus,' she said softly. 'I'm just asking because of Liam.' She glanced away from him over at her son.

'Well, put it this way. If there is any news on the wedding front you'll be the first to know.'

'Thanks.' She didn't look back at him and she didn't ask if he was finally going to settle down with Sophia. There was no way she would allow him to think she was jealous—his accusation about that this morning still rankled. And anyway he was right; it really was none of her business.

'Do you think Liam's colour is a little better?' she asked, putting a hand on the child's forehead.

'Maybe. Does he feel any cooler?'

She shook her head. Then her eyes moved to the monitor beside her. The steady beep seemed to reflect the beating of her heart.

'I don't know if he can hear us or not, but a few moments ago I promised him anything he wants if he'll just get better.'

'That could cost you very dear,' Marcus said with a half-smile.

'I'd do anything if I could just have him back.'

'Would you come to Italy with me?'

The quietly asked question made her heart miss a beat and she looked across at him in shock.

'Why are you asking me that?' Her voice was so low as to be almost a whisper.

'Why do you think?' His mouth twisted ruefully. 'If this has taught us anything, Gemma, it's taught us that Liam needs us both. I watched how you held him on your knee today in the back seat of my car, how he clung to you, how you kissed and cuddled him and made him feel secure, and the knowledge of how much he needs you hit me like a force ten gale.'

Gemma didn't say anything to that, but she knew exactly where he was coming from because the same feeling had hit her as she had watched him with Liam a little while later.

'If you came to Italy we could be a family together. Think how much that would mean to Liam.'

How could they ever be a family when he was marrying someone else? Maybe he thought they could all be friends together...she had a sudden vision of being invited to the wedding, of wishing him and Sophia all the best for the future. She knew for Liam's sake that would be a good thing but she didn't think she would be strong enough to be able to do it. The very idea made her feel slightly sick inside.

'I don't know, Marcus...my life is in England. Things here are just starting to go in the right direction for me.'

'Richard might be the right direction for you, but is he right for Liam?'

She hadn't been thinking about Richard. She had been thinking about the fact that she liked her job, about her mother and her friends. She was settled in London. Asking her to give that up to live on the sidelines of his life was asking a lot…even if, deep down, she knew it would make her son happy.

'I don't know, Marcus, I can't think about this now.' Distraught, she looked back at Liam.

Please wake up, darling, she thought fiercely. Please.

As she stared at him, willing him to recover, she thought she saw the flicker of his eyelashes. 'Liam?'

Marcus stood up and rang the button for the nurse to come.

'Liam?' Gemma stroked his hair. 'Liam, darling, wake up.'

To her immense relief his eyes suddenly opened and locked with hers. 'Mummy, where am I?' he asked, his voice small and frightened.

'You're in hospital, remember?' Gemma swallowed down a lump in her throat. 'The doctors and nurses are making you better.'

'Can I go home now?' Liam looked over at his dad.

'Not just yet.' Marcus leaned closer and stroked a hand tenderly and protectively down over Liam's face. 'You've given your mum and me a bit of a scare. How are you feeling now?'

'I'm okay.'

The door opened and the nurse came in. She smiled as she saw Liam was awake. 'Looks like our patient is on the mend,' she said brightly.

'I think his temperature is coming down,' Marcus said, moving away from the bedside to allow the nurse to check him over.

'Yes, you're right.' The nurse smiled at Gemma. 'The doctor will be along in a few moments to check him out but it looks like the worst is over.'

The relief that swept through Gemma as she heard those words made her feel weak inside. And as Marcus put an arm around her shoulder she turned and buried her head against his chest, allowing herself to draw strength from his closeness for just a moment.

She was unprepared for the fierce stirring of emotion that the close contact with Marcus had on her senses. The last time she had been held like this in the circle of his arms they had been lovers, and although that had been years ago the familiar feelings that surged through her now made it feel like yesterday. In that instant she remembered everything about their relationship, not just the heat, passion, and fiery intensity, but the tenderness and depth of feeling. She had loved him deeply, wildly…completely. His betrayal had hurt so much that she had thought she would never get over him. And maybe she never had. Maybe there was a part of her that would always love Marcus.

That thought was so horrifying that it made her break contact with him and move swiftly away.

As the nurse left Liam's bedside she went to sit beside him.

'Can we go home now?' Liam asked her tentatively. 'I want to play with my train set.'

'You must be feeling better.' She smiled at him through a haze of tears.

'Why are you crying, Mummy?' He looked at her in consternation.

'Because I'm happy and I'm relieved.'

As soon as the doctor confirmed that Liam was getting better Gemma went out to phone her mother again. When she returned to the room Liam no longer had the monitors attached to him and the nurse was tucking the blankets in around him, telling him he should settle down to sleep.

'Dr Tompkins said they'll be keeping him in for a

couple of days' observation but he thinks that all being well he'll be able to go home on Sunday,' Marcus told her quietly as she stood back giving the nurse room to work.

'Well, that's good news.' Gemma couldn't bring herself to look at Marcus; the memory of the way she had clung to him a few moments ago was too fresh in her mind. She was appalled at herself for such weakness.

'If you want to go home and get some rest I'll stay here with him,' he continued briskly.

She shook her head. 'Thanks, but I really don't want to leave him.'

As soon as the nurse left the room Gemma moved to sit next to the bed again. 'How are you feeling now, darling?' she asked gently as Liam looked over at her.

He smiled. 'Okay…a bit sleepy.'

She brushed his hair back from his forehead with a tender hand. 'So close your eyes and rest,' she said softly.

For a while he seemed to fight against sleep but his eyes were heavy and soon his breathing deepened as he drifted into a peaceful sleep.

Marcus left the room and she wondered if he was heading home, but he returned almost immediately with a blanket and a pillow in his hand.

'You may as well make yourself as comfortable as possible in that chair,' he said gently, handing them over to her.

'Thanks.' Gemma was finding his thoughtfulness and his gentleness over these last few hours very hard to handle. She didn't want him to be nice to her; it made it harder to remember the reasons why she had to keep her distance from him.

'You don't have to stay,' she said quickly as he sat back down in the chair opposite.

'Yes, I do, Gemma,' he said quietly. 'I don't just want to be around Liam because he's my responsibility. I love him too, you know.'

'Yes, I know you do.' For a moment their eyes met and then she looked quickly away from him again and busied herself arranging the pillow behind her head. 'Well, I suppose we should try and get a few hours' sleep,' she said brightly.

But trying to sleep in the chair was almost impossible. Not only was it extremely uncomfortable but her mind was in turmoil. She kept running through the events of the day. They flashed through her mind like a series of picture cards in a wildly jumbled order.

Liam looking so ill, Marcus holding her hand, the tests and the uncertainty. Then Marcus asking her to go to Italy with him. Had he meant that, she wondered, or was it just something he'd said in the heat of the moment?

Then she remembered the feelings that had flooded through her when she had been held in his arms and that made her even more restless. She had to keep in mind that, although Marcus was marvellous with Liam, he was still the man who had hurt her badly. He was not a man to fantasize about, she told herself fiercely.

Her mind flashed back to the moment when they had sat having coffee together. She had lied to him when she had casually agreed that she couldn't remember the last time they had done that. Of course she remembered…it was etched in her mind for all time.

She'd persuaded him to meet her in her lunch hour at a coffee bar around the corner from her office and he had agreed with a hint of reluctance. 'I've got a really hectic day ahead of me, Gemma.'

'So have I,' she had told him swiftly. 'But let's just grab a quick lunch together. I need to talk to you.'

Gemma had arrived at the coffee bar first and had found a table at the back of the shop. She remembered the place had been packed with people from surrounding offices and shops, and the din of voices and the noise of the steam machine they used for espressos and cappuccinos had made her wonder nervously if this was the right place to tell Marcus the momentous news that she was pregnant. But she had tried to tell him when they were alone, and the problem was that as soon as they were behind closed doors Marcus would reach for her and everything else would be forgotten.

Their affair had been going on for over three months, and it had been the most exciting three months of Gemma's life. She had felt as if she were on some wild and wonderful roller-coaster ride. Their time together in the bedroom had been wild, tempestuous and utterly blissful. And even out of the bedroom, just hearing his voice had made her body tingle with exhilaration. But their relationship hadn't been at all conventional; outside the bedroom they had talked mostly about work. Gemma had been keen to get ahead in her career and, to her delight Marcus had taken an interest in her professional development.

The interview with him had got her the promotion she had so greatly craved. But Marcus had read her article and told her she could have done better. The remark had hurt, but when he had gone on to tell her where she had gone wrong she had taken note. He wasn't one of the biggest names in publishing for no reason; Marcus had an instinctive feel for good journalism. Not only had he years of experience but it just seemed to run in his veins. So when he had taken her under his wing she had been only too thrilled to have him as a mentor. It had certainly made for sparkling and animated conversations… sometimes too animated; things could get very heated when they disagreed. But for the most part she had taken his judgements and his advice on board and her work had improved. She'd been offered another promotion, but Marcus had thought she shouldn't take it. Instead, he had set up an interview for her with one of his own publications, a paper with a bigger turnover and a prestigious image.

At the time, when she had sat for the interview, it had seemed like the most nerve-racking and important moment of her life. But just over a week later, as she had sat in a coffee shop waiting for Marcus to arrive, all her priorities had changed. And she had realized how little the job really meant to her.

She had discovered a few days earlier that she was pregnant, and the knowledge had gone round and round in her head, blocking out everything else. And she'd been scared because, despite the fierce passion of their union, she hadn't really known what Marcus felt about her. He had never spoken one word of love to her…not one. Oh, sometimes he had murmured words in Italian to her as he held her close and possessed her fully. But they had been just meaningless compliments: he had called her beautiful, desirable…things he could have said to any woman he took to his bed. They had meant nothing.

Those facts hadn't really worried her too deeply until the moment she sat in that café and tried to prepare the words she needed to say to him. And suddenly she had realized how much she wanted him to tell her he loved her—how deeply and emotionally vulnerable she was where he was concerned. The thought of losing him had made her blood run like ice-water in her body: She was wild about him, she adored him, she wanted his baby and she wanted him so much it had hurt.

He had walked into the café fifteen minutes late, his mobile phone to his ear as he had sauntered through the crowds of people. She'd raised her hand to attract his attention and he had acknowledged her with a nod as he sat down in the seat opposite. Marcus had been speaking in rapid Italian but she had followed most of what he had been saying; she had a quick ear for languages and since meeting Freddie and then Marcus her Italian had become almost fluent. It had been a business call, and basically he had been bawling someone out for failing to do what he had asked. It had quickly become apparent to Gemma that he wasn't in the best of moods and she had felt her nerves clench even tighter.

'Sorry about that,' he said to her almost absently as he hung up. 'I've had a hell of a morning.'

'Have you? Mine hasn't been too marvellous either.'

Marcus heard the nervousness in her tone and he smiled in an arrogantly amused way. 'Well, I know why you're so keen to see me this afternoon.'

'Do you?' She was totally taken aback, wondering if he'd guessed her secret. How could he know she was pregnant? She'd only recently found out herself.

'I suppose the anticipation is driving you wild.' He grinned.

She frowned in confusion. 'Marcus, I don't—'

'It's okay. I suppose my telling you is a bit unorthodox but you'd be hearing through the regular channels soon, anyway. You've got the job. Ben Hardwick loved you.'

'Oh, I see.' The job she'd applied for was the last thing on her mind but she managed a smile.

'So congratulations are in order. They will probably want you to start in about eight weeks' time, so there's no rush giving in your notice at the *Morning Sentinel.* I'd wait a couple of weeks.' Marcus held up his hand to attract the attention of the waiter and she noticed that despite the rush hour crowd he came over to Marcus immediately.

That was the thing about Marcus: he had that air of power, that ability to make everyone rush to do his bidding straight away.

'You didn't pull strings for me to get the job, did you, Marcus?' she asked, momentarily distracted from what she really wanted to talk about.

'Well I pulled enough strings to get you the interview. But you did the rest yourself. You're a damn good journalist, Gemma, and Ben recognised that.'

Marcus never gave praise lightly and the words pleased her.

The waiter arrived with their coffee and Marcus glanced at his watch. 'I'm afraid I'm not going to have time for anything to eat, Gemma. I've got to get back to the office. I've got loads on because I'm having to take some days off soon to go to Rome for Helene's wedding.'

It struck her at that point that Marcus had not asked her to accompany him to his sister's wedding. It seemed an ominous sign. Maybe he knew that Freddie had already invited her? 'I've been meaning to talk to you about that,' she said casually. 'You know, don't you, that Freddie has asked me to accompany him to your sister's wedding?'

Marcus paused with the cup of espresso coffee halfway to his lips. 'No, I didn't know.'

'I thought that was why you hadn't invited me yourself.' She waited for him to offer some excuse for not doing so. But none was forthcoming. He just looked at her, a cool expression in his eyes.

'I haven't seen Freddie for a while. Obviously, you have.'

'Well, I see him occasionally. He asked me to go with him to Helene's wedding ages ago. Before I met you, in fact.' She was suddenly at pains to explain in case he jumped to the wrong conclusion and thought there was something going on between her and his brother. But she needn't have bothered; Marcus wasn't the jealous type and he wasn't the slightest bit interested or concerned. He glanced at his watch. 'I'm really going to have to go, Gemma. I've got an important meeting this afternoon. So, if there is nothing else you want to discuss…?'

She wanted so much to tell him she was pregnant, had built herself up for it all morning, but she couldn't just blurt it out when he was being so cool and businesslike. 'There was one other thing,' she managed to say quietly. 'But I suppose it can wait.'

'Good. I'll phone you and we'll arrange to go out for dinner soon, okay?' He reached to kiss her, but the kiss was absently brisk. '*Ciao*, Gemma.'

She watched him walk away from her with a sick feeling inside. Not only had she not told him she was pregnant, but she had a horrible feeling that huge cracks were appearing in their relationship.

That feeling more than intensified over the next two weeks because he hardly had time to speak to her on the phone, never mind see her.

She sat next to Freddie on the plane to go to Rome. She had never felt more confused or alone in her life. It seemed that Marcus had just dropped her out of his life for no real reason.

Gemma wanted to confide in Freddie but, as she had never discussed her relationship with his brother in the first place, she didn't know where to begin. So she told herself that she'd find a quiet time during the weekend to speak to Marcus, either at his father's house or some time during the wedding and that they'd sort things out. But that chance never presented itself and the first time she saw Marcus was when they got to the church. She glanced across and noticed the very glamorous brunette seated next to him.

'Who is that?' she asked Freddie curiously.

He glanced across too and smiled. 'That's Sophia Albani, the woman Marcus is going to marry.'

The matter-of-fact words hit Gemma like a freight train.

'I didn't know Marcus was engaged,' she said icily.

'Well, it's not official yet, but it has always been understood that they will marry one day. They were childhood sweethearts. They are just waiting until Marcus's spell of running the English side of the business is over before setting the wedding date. Sophia doesn't want to live in London, you see—she absolutely hates the place. Although I think she might be getting ready to compromise and go to England because the separation is killing them both. They miss each other like crazy.' Freddie lowered his voice to a whisper. 'In fact, I had a very embarrassing experience this morning. I went around to Marcus's house to deliver the flowers for the buttonholes and there they were in the front lounge *in flagrante delicto*. Those two can't keep their hands off each other.' He noticed the sudden pallor of Gemma's skin and smiled. 'Hey, don't look so shocked. Some people do have sex before they get married, you know, and my brother is a very red-blooded male. In fact, I don't know how he's managing to survive the distance without Sophia.'

'Maybe he has another woman in London.' Gemma's voice was brittle.

'Probably.' Freddie laughed. 'A bit on the side, as you British like to say, and why not? He's still single, he may as well enjoy himself and have a few flings while he still can.'

The words rang in Gemma's ears like instruments of torture. And suddenly everything became crystal clear. She had her answer as to why Marcus hadn't invited her to his sister's wedding, why he had never uttered any words of love. Why he had backed away from her over the last couple of weeks. He didn't love her; theirs had just been a very steamy and brief affair, nothing more. And he was probably livid that she was at his sister's wedding, worried in case Sophia would find out about them. The knowledge hurt like crazy.

She didn't know how she managed to get through that day. Every time she looked around she saw Marcus and Sophia, and it was an unbearable torture. Sophia looked so happy, so much in love as she looked up at him, and Gemma felt humiliated and used.

When she finally found herself alone with Marcus for a few minutes during the evening celebrations, she didn't know if she wanted to cry or to smack his face.

'You forgot to tell me about your childhood sweetheart when I interviewed you for my article,' she said derisively.

'Well, maybe you should have done further background research, Gemma,' he replied coldly. 'I know I certainly should have done some on you. Maybe that way I wouldn't have been so surprised by the fact that you were attending my sister's wedding with Freddie. And we could both have saved ourselves some discomfiture today.'

'Feeling a little awkward, are you?' His cool audacity took her breath away. Obviously, he was only bothered about Sophia finding out about them, not about how badly he had behaved. He hadn't even tried to make excuses.

'Well, aren't you?'

'Why should I feel awkward? Frankly, I couldn't care less,' she lied coldly, pride coming ferociously to her defence. 'It's not as if we were ever serious about each other, is it? We just had a fling.'

He didn't try to argue with her, just nodded his head grimly. 'Look, Gemma as you seem to be so…' he hesitated before saying dryly, '…*close* to my brother I don't think we should fall out. We had a good time while it lasted,' he said firmly. 'And you've got the job you wanted with Rossini House, so no hard feelings.'

It took a tremendous amount of willpower to remain cool. And she was so glad when Freddie came to her rescue, walking over and placing a proprietorial arm around her waist as he asked her to dance with him.

'I'd love to dance with you, Freddie,' she said, smiling up at him. And she walked away from Marcus without a backward glance. If there was a prize for acting ability that night she would certainly have got one. She danced every dance with Freddie, gazing up into his eyes, ignoring the fact that somewhere across the room Marcus was with Sophia.

She told herself that her heart wasn't breaking, that she didn't care. But inside she felt as if she wanted to die.

Marcus congratulating her on her job with a Rossini publication had been the final insult. Had he seen the fact that he had helped her career as a kind of payment in kind for services rendered? The idea appalled her.

In fact, the first thing she did on her return home was to turn down the job with Rossini House. She didn't want anything that was remotely connected with Marcus.

But she did want her baby. She wanted Liam with all her heart.

Freddie was remarkably supportive to her in the days after they returned from Rome and a new closeness developed between them. But Gemma still didn't tell him of her relationship with Marcus or the fact that she was expecting his baby. Somehow she didn't want to spoil Freddie's glowing image of his brother. He looked up to Marcus so much. It was only when Freddie started to make romantic overtures to her again that she had to tell him the truth.

She could still remember the shock in his eyes when she told him that she was pregnant, that it was Marcus's baby. Even now she felt the weight of guilt. She had shaken Freddie's belief in his beloved brother to the core. And he was incredibly angry. Vowed to go over to Marcus to sort him out.

She tried to calm him down, begged him not to say anything to Marcus because he didn't know about the baby and nor did she want him to. But Freddie wasn't in any mood to listen and he left her apartment in a tearing rage.

Gemma was so worried about him that she rang Marcus for the first time since returning from Rome. He wasn't in and she left a garbled message on his answering machine, telling him his brother was very upset and was on the way over.

But Freddie never arrived. His sports car had spun out of control and left the road somewhere between Gemma's apartment and Marcus's house. Freddie had died instantly.

Even now, five years down the line, thinking about Freddie made Gemma's heart turn over with grief. The police had estimated that he had been driving over a hundred miles an hour and that the accident was entirely his own fault. But, deep down, Gemma didn't agree. She felt responsible because he had been so upset when he left her apartment. Every minute of every day she still regretted telling Freddie about Marcus that night…indirectly, she still felt that the accident had been her fault.

She had said as much to Marcus when he came around to see her a few days later. She had blurted out the truth, that she was pregnant with his child, that Freddie had been furious with him and had been going over to confront him.

Marcus had said nothing. He had looked drawn and ill and had walked away without even acknowledging what she had said in any way. A few days later he had come back and asked her to marry him.

He might as well have put the words, 'It's my duty,' before the proposal itself. There had been no pretence at feelings he didn't possess. Gemma had turned him down just as coldly. 'We don't love each other,' she had said. 'So what's the point? I suggest you go away and marry your childhood sweetheart. At least that way one of us will be happy.'

But Marcus hadn't married Sophia. Gemma guessed that it had taken the other woman all this time to forgive his infidelity. It was one thing forgiving an affair, quite another when a child was involved. Especially as that child always took centre stage in Marcus's life.

But obviously Sophia had come to terms with that now. She arrived from time to time to see Marcus in London and Liam didn't dislike her.

Gemma thumped the pillow on her chair and desperately tried to rid her mind of the past.

Taking Liam to live in Italy wasn't an option, she thought angrily. As much as she wanted her son to be happy, she could never happily accept Marcus and Sophia living as man and wife on her doorstep.

CHAPTER SIX

THERE was a strange noise coming from somewhere. It sounded like the rattling of china being stacked in a dishwasher. Gemma opened her eyes feeling disoriented. For a second she didn't know where she was. Then she saw the hospital bed and it all came flooding back to her. She sat up, wincing in pain from the cramped position she had slept in, and checked on Liam. He was still fast asleep, but his colour was a lot better. He looked back to normal.

'*Bon giorno,*' Marcus said gently.

Gemma glanced across at him. Despite also having spent the night in a chair, he looked remarkably fresh and attractive. The dark stubble of his jawline seemed to add a certain edge to his Latin good looks, gave him a kind of sensual come-back-to-bed look.

'Did you sleep okay?' he asked.

'Well, I think I drifted off for about an hour.' Gemma wrenched her eyes away from his. He looked like a male model and she felt a total mess. Her hair had escaped from its ponytail and her black business suit was creased. She ran a smoothing hand down over her skirt. 'Did you sleep?'

'No, not really.'

The clatter of noise in the corridor intensified and she glanced out and noticed they were bringing down the breakfast trolleys.

'Is your neck bothering you?' he asked and she realized she had been rubbing at it absently.

'Yes, I think I was resting at an awkward angle.'

'You were. The pillow dropped and you looked very uncomfortable. I was going to pick it up and try and slide it under your head again but I was concerned that it would wake you up.'

The knowledge that he had been watching her while she slept made her feel self-conscious.

'You were talking in your sleep as well.'

'Was I?' She glanced over at him, horrified by that. As she had been reflecting a lot about him and about the past last night, she hated to think what she might have been inadvertently revealing. 'What did I say?'

'Not a lot that made sense.' He grinned at her. 'Don't look so worried. Your secrets are safe with me.'

'Well, that's a relief.' She matched his teasing tone. 'I'd hate you to find out what I really think about you.'

'It might go to my head, you mean?'

'Something like that.' She moved closer to the bed to look at Liam as he stirred. 'Hello, darling.' She smiled at him as his eyelashes flickered open. 'How are you feeling now?'

Liam yawned sleepily and turned velvety dark eyes on her. 'Okay. A bit thirsty.'

There was a jug of water by the bed and Marcus moved to pour him a glass. 'They are bringing down the breakfast trolleys. How do you fancy something to eat?' he asked, helping the little boy to sit up.

'I don't know.' Liam shrugged. 'Will they have pancakes like you make at home, Daddy?'

'They might do. We'll ask.'

Gemma looked over at Marcus in surprise. 'I didn't know you could cook.'

Marcus grinned. 'I'm obviously better at keeping secrets than you are.'

'Daddy's good at cooking. He can make boiled eggs too, and snake and chips.'

'Snake and chips?' Gemma smiled at Marcus as she fixed the pillows behind Liam so he could lean back. 'That sounds...interesting.'

'Certainly is. You haven't lived until you've tasted my snake...with chips.'

'You burnt it one time, didn't you, daddy, and there was smoke in the kitchen and the smoke alarm was ringing.'

'Okay, son, a little too much information is coming forth now,' Marcus said with a laugh.

Gemma smiled over at him. 'Do you burn snakes in your kitchen often?'

'Only on Friday nights with a nice bottle of Chianti.' Marcus glanced over at her, a gleam in his eye. 'You'll have to come over one night.'

She smiled but didn't answer.

Marcus watched her as she stroked Liam's hair back with a tender hand, noted the watchful concern in her eye as he closed his eyes for a moment. 'Are you still tired, Liam?'

'Just a little.'

'You're bound to be a bit tired,' Marcus said soothingly. 'You were very ill yesterday. It will take you a little while resting to get over it.'

Liam nodded.

The nurse came in and smiled as she saw Liam sitting up. 'Our patient looks much better today,' she said cheerfully.

'He says he is still a little bit tired,' Gemma told her and she nodded.

'How about some breakfast, Liam?' she asked him.

'That should give you more energy, get you further on the road to recovery.'

'Have you got any pancakes?' Liam asked.

The nurse shook her head regretfully. 'No, but we can order you some for tomorrow morning. I've got some scrambled eggs and toast.'

'That would be great, wouldn't it, Liam?' Marcus said positively and the little boy nodded in agreement.

Gemma was surprised at the ease with which he acquiesced; she usually had a major struggle to get him to eat scrambled eggs.

What was more, he ate most of the small plateful of food without having to be prompted.

As they were clearing away the dishes Gemma's mother arrived. 'Well, you look better than I expected,' she said, reaching to give her grandson a hug. 'You had me very worried.'

'I had to have an injection but I didn't cry, Nana,' Liam said.

'Well that's a brave boy.' She sat down on a chair that Marcus brought forward for her. 'Who would have thought when I brought you to the nursery yesterday, Liam, that you would end up in hospital?' she said with a shake of her head. 'I kept thinking about it all night. You didn't look ill yesterday at all. Maybe a bit hot, but you'd been running around.'

'It was certainly a shock when we arrived at the nursery,' Gemma said quietly.

Joanne nodded and looked over at her daughter. 'You look tired. Why don't you let Marcus take you home for a couple of hours' rest and I'll stay and keep Liam company? No point us all being here.'

'No, I'm fine, Mum. I don't want to leave him yet—'

'Your mother is right, Gemma.' Marcus cut across her

firmly. 'You should take the opportunity while Joanne's here to go home. Not only do you need the break but we should pick up some things for Liam, some pyjamas and his toothbrush.'

Marcus was right. She glanced over at Liam, torn about leaving him, but knowing it made sense to go while her mother was there. 'Will you be okay if Daddy takes me home for a little while?' she asked him and he nodded.

'Will you bring my storybook back?' he asked. 'You know, the one with the dinosaurs in?'

'I will.' She went over to kiss him and give him a hug. 'I'll see you in a little while.'

Marcus gave him a kiss and ruffled his hair. 'Look after Nana,' he said with a teasing grin. 'No wild parties while we're gone.'

Liam giggled.

'Do you think he's okay?' Gemma asked as they left the hospital. 'He does look very tired and yet he slept all night.'

'It's to be expected, Gemma. The best thing for him now is to get as much sleep as possible, allow his body to repair itself.'

They walked out into the fresh morning air. The sky glowed pearly-pink with the promise of a hot day to come and the air was a balmy relief after the stuffiness of the hospital. She breathed in deeply.

'It makes you realize how much we take health for granted, coming out of there, doesn't it?' she murmured to Marcus as he unlocked his car and she got in.

'It certainly makes you get priorities in order,' he agreed with a nod.

They didn't speak for a while as he negotiated the Friday rush-hour traffic going into the city centre.

There was something very calm about Marcus, she thought, watching the way he handled the car. There had been many times over the years when she had been infuriated by that cool and powerful self-assurance of his, yet in a real crisis she had found herself relying on those same qualities, grateful for his strength and his level-headedness. And he was wonderful with Liam…

'I meant it, you know, when I said I wanted both you and Liam to come to Italy with me.' Marcus glanced over at her as he pulled the car to a standstill outside her house.

'I can't think about that now, Marcus,' she said. 'I know you aren't a person who likes to take things slowly. But that is a hell of a big decision and we need to take things one step at a time now.'

'On the contrary. I think we have wasted enough time and we need to get our act together fast.'

'This isn't something we can rush, Marcus. For one thing, neither of us is thinking very clearly at the moment.'

His eyes moved over her face, lingering on the softness of her lips in a way that made her heart stand still. 'On the contrary, my thoughts are crystal clear,' he murmured huskily.

She swallowed hard, wondering nervously if she had imagined the look in his eyes, the sudden flare of sensual tension that had ignited from nowhere.

'Come on, we'll discuss this inside,' he said, reaching for the door-handle.

'I'm really tired, Marcus, and I don't want to argue with you right now.'

'Who said anything about arguing? I think we've done enough of that. We should have a sensible discussion. I'll make the coffee. How's that?'

She smiled. 'What, no pancakes?'

'I'll impress you with my cooking skills at a later date.' His eyes moved to her lips again. 'You have a truly beautiful smile, Gemma, do you know that?' Marcus spoke in Italian, and the sudden compliment and the tone made her blush. It also made her remember the more intimate moments of their time together in the past, times when he had taken her into his arms to murmur private words of seduction against her ear.

'Don't try to charm your way around me, Marcus, because it won't work.' Automatically she answered him in Italian, her heart thumping against her chest so loudly she felt sure he would be able to hear it in the close confines of the car.

'You remember your Italian?' He smiled.

'Of course I remember.' She looked away from him awkwardly, as a sudden vision reared in her mind of them lying naked in each other's arms, him teaching her new risqué phrases and laughing at her blushes.

'That's good.' From the husky satisfaction in his tone she wondered if he had been remembering those moments too.

'Liam speaks Italian when he comes home from your house. That's why I'm still reasonably fluent.' She strove to clarify the point.

Marcus smiled. 'Of course,' he murmured. 'Come on, I'll make that coffee.' He turned away from her and got out of the car.

Part of her wanted to tell him forcefully that she didn't want him coming inside the house with her, yet perversely, as she glanced over at him, there was a stronger part of her that was glad he wasn't rushing off. She was scared of the fact that he could get around her so easily. It smacked of the way he had been able to arouse her emotions so easily in the past. She remembered times when he'd only had to make a phone call to her at work telling her in that arrogant, and yet oh, so sensual tone that he wanted her, and she had felt herself going weak inside with need and desire…

She slotted her key into the front door with a slightly trembling hand. Those days had gone for ever, she told herself fiercely. There was no way that Marcus could turn her on so easily now. She had no need to be afraid of his power over her senses now that she had learnt her lesson.

Gemma led him into the hallway, lifting the post as she walked in. 'I should ring the office and tell them I won't be in today,' she said, forcing her mind to practicalities.

'I'll do it for you,' Marcus said, and then grinned. 'After all, they can't argue with the boss now, can they?'

She didn't know whether to be irritated or amused by that remark. 'You love power, don't you, Marcus,' she said, walking away from him with a shake of her head. 'It's a powerful aphrodisiac where you are concerned.'

'I can think of better aphrodisiacs,' he murmured with a grin as he picked up the phone.

She decided it was better to ignore that remark and went through to the kitchen to flick on the kettle before going upstairs to find some night things for Liam. The sight of his train set curving out from his bedroom into the landing made her heart lurch painfully. She remembered how much he'd been enjoying playing yesterday…and how irritated she had been because he had almost made her late for work. It seemed like weeks ago instead of twenty-four hours.

His bed was still unmade and she went to straighten it. As she picked up his favourite teddy bear from the floor on the way past, she had a sudden terrifying vision of what might have been…if the fever hadn't broken last night… She sat down on his bed, burying her head in her hands for a moment in silent thankfulness.

'Are you okay?' Marcus's voice from the landing made her jump.

'Yes.' She looked up at him and he noticed how blue her eyes were in the pallor of her skin. There were times when Gemma looked incredibly vulnerable. Despite her success in her career and her confident manner, underneath it all he sometimes glimpsed a 'little girl lost' look about her. It was a look that brought out a fiercely protective surge inside him. Made him want to take her into his arms and hold her close.

'He'll be okay you know.'

'I know…it was just such a shock.'

Marcus nodded and looked away from her. Forcing himself not to go over to her, he glanced around the small bedroom, noting the mobiles on the ceiling and the shelves of books. He had to play this very carefully, he told himself. He had made up his mind that he wanted Gemma and Liam back into the centre of his life and he wasn't going to give up, despite the fact that the truce between them was tentative and uncertain. When she had instinctively turned to him last night, allowing him to hold her for a moment in his arms, he had felt they had turned a corner. But she could just as easily turn away from him again and he wasn't going to risk that.

He was going to have to play this with cool determination, using every trick, every strategy at his disposal. Marcus was resolute in his intent. When he left for Italy he would be taking his son and Gemma along with him.

Gemma noticed the way Marcus was looking around

the room with a look of intense seriousness on his face. She realized this was the first time Marcus had been into Liam's bedroom. In fact, he had only ever set foot into the front hallway of this house, and that was on rare occasions when he'd arrived much earlier than expected to pick Liam up.

'Is Liam's bedroom at your place like this?' she asked him curiously.

'Similar.' He grinned at her. 'But it's a bit tidier. I still have Mrs Philips looking after things.'

She remembered his housekeeper well from the times she had spent at his house in the past, and smiled. 'I take it she is as efficient as ever?'

'Oh yes, not a speck of dust would dare to settle around Mrs Philips. I might have to take her with me to Italy as well.'

'Maybe it would just be a lot easier not to go,' Gemma said quietly.

'We've been through this, Gemma. I have to go.' His eyes met hers seriously. 'Nicholas is arriving next week to take over the running of the London office. I fly to Rome the week after.'

Gemma felt a jolt of shock that he was going so soon.

Silence fell between them for a moment as she struggled to come to terms with the news. What the hell was she going to tell Liam? she wondered suddenly. He was going to be devastated.

'It's strange that you gave Liam this bedroom.' Marcus changed the subject. 'It's the one I pictured him in. I used to sleep in here sometimes when I was a child.'

'Really?' She frowned.

He nodded. 'This was my mother's house. We used to stay here when we visited her family in the summer holidays.'

She remembered the letting agent telling her that, only of course she hadn't realized then that he was talking about Marcus. 'I didn't realize,' she murmured. 'And when you told me you owned this house I assumed you'd bought it after we'd moved in.'

'No. I steered you towards viewing it by giving your mother the paper with the advertisement ringed for your attention. I told her I'd already viewed it and it looked like a suitable property. But not to mention that the suggestion came from me. I knew if you found out I was in any way connected to the house you'd stubbornly refuse even to consider it.'

The words fell bluntly between them. She couldn't argue with that because she knew he was right. Her mother had obviously realized he was right as well, because she hadn't mentioned the fact that this house had been Marcus's suggestion.

'In a strange kind of way I've found it reassuring over the years being able to picture Liam's surroundings so clearly, knowing that he was in a good environment.'

'I wouldn't have chosen somewhere that wasn't a good environment for him,' she said quickly.

'I know that. But I'm talking about the atmosphere more than anything—this house has happy memories for me. I've liked the security of knowing Liam is here.'

'And now you want to take him away.'

'To something even better. He'll like my villa. It's in the countryside just outside Rome. There's space for him to play, a large orchard, a stable where he can learn to ride…dogs and cats, and lots of family in the area. In fact, everything to make up a secure and wonderful childhood.'

'You've got it all figured out, haven't you?' She glared up at him, her voice filled with sarcasm. 'And where do I fit into this rosy picture? Are you thinking of shoving me into one of the sheds at the bottom of your orchard where I can conveniently pop out to see Liam when it suits you?'

He grinned at that. 'Not quite.'

Gemma put the teddy bear she was holding down and stood up from the bed. 'I can't come to Italy with you, Marcus. The whole idea is absurd. My life is here.'

'You told me once that Liam is your life.' He watched as she made Liam's bed and then moved towards a chest of drawers to get a pair of his pyjamas out.

'Well, he is…of course.' She hesitated. 'But there are other factors to take into consideration.'

'That promotion at *Modern Times* that you want so badly is mere chicken-feed compared to what I can offer you in Rome.'

Her hand stilled and she looked over at him questioningly.

'There's a position becoming vacant soon for editor in chief at *Élan*.'

Her eyes widened. *Élan* was one of Rossini's flagship publications, a prestigious glossy magazine with a huge European circulation. *Modern Times* was a provincial hick by comparison.

'I thought that would get your attention.' Marcus smiled.

'Meaning?'

'Meaning you always were driven by your career.' His voice was dry. 'It's what brought you to me in the first place, isn't it?'

'I suppose you could say that.' She closed the drawer.

'Oh, come on, Gemma, we both know the main reason you graced my bed for so long was that I was helping to further your career.'

She blanched at those words, too shocked to be able to refute them for a moment.

'I didn't mind that.' He shrugged nonchalantly. 'I didn't want anything serious, anyway.'

'I'm sure you didn't, with sweet little Sophia waiting in the wings for you at home in Italy.' Gemma's voice trembled precariously. 'Don't go all pious on me, Marcus. Because I remember very clearly what happened. And if you remember rightly, I didn't take your job at Rossini back then,' she added sharply. 'And I don't intend to take it now.'

'You didn't take the job back then because you were pregnant and Freddie was going ballistic.'

'It had nothing to do with Freddie.'

The shrill ring of the phone cut the atmosphere between them and she hurried out and over into her bedroom to answer it, scared in case it was the hospital ringing to say there was a change in Liam's condition.

It was Richard and she gave a sigh of relief.

'I just got into the office,' he said. 'And they told me about Liam being in hospital. How is he?'

'He's a lot better than he was yesterday.' Gemma glanced over as Marcus came to stand in the open doorway. 'It's okay, it's only Richard,' she told him, covering the mouthpiece for a moment. 'Why don't you go now? I'm going to take a quick shower and I'll head back to the hospital in a taxi.'

'We haven't finished our conversation.'

'I think we have.' She ignored him and went back to talking to Richard, hoping Marcus would take the hint and leave.

'They said they will be keeping him in for a few more days for observation. Yes, I'm sure he would love you to come and see him. Maybe you should wait until tomorrow, though. Ward C.' Gemma glanced over at the doorway and was relieved to find Marcus had gone. 'Okay, Richard… Yes I'll look forward to seeing you… Bye.' She put the phone down.

The house seemed very quiet, ominously so. She felt her heart beating against her chest as she remembered Marcus's hurtful remarks about her only sleeping with him to further her career! Maybe that was his way of justifying the way he had behaved? She remembered that at his sister's wedding he had made a similar remark to her— 'You've got the job you wanted with Rossini House, so no hard feelings.'

Gemma was fiercely glad that she had turned that job down. She had found life difficult as a single parent working full-time, but at least she had proved that she could stand on her own two feet. She had worked her way up without any help from anyone.

And she wouldn't accept this job offer at *Élan* either, she told herself fiercely. She would do as she had planned and apply for the top job at *Modern Times*. Marcus could go to hell. She had always sworn she wouldn't be under any obligation to him and now she could remember quite clearly why not.

Getting up from the bed, she headed for her en-suite bathroom and quickly stripped off to stand under the forceful jet of the shower. But as her temper faded, the question of how she was going to tell Liam that his father was leaving returned.

Gemma had been a bit older when she had lost her own father; she remembered clearly the devastation she had felt. And she knew how much Liam loved Marcus. He hero-worshipped him.

Stepping out of the shower, she dried herself with brisk angry movements, then wrapped herself in a soft white towel and quickly blow-dried her long hair. It wasn't as if Marcus had died, she tried to reason with herself. Liam would see him during the holidays. That would have to be enough.

Returning to the bedroom to get dressed, she was surprised to see Marcus sitting on the side of the bed waiting for her.

'I thought you'd gone!' She clutched the towel more tightly around her body.

'No. I told you we hadn't finished our conversation.' His eyes swept slowly and deliberately over the long length of her shapely legs. There was something blatantly sensual about the leisurely perusal. It reminded her of the way he used to look at her and disconcertingly she felt her body respond just the way it used to, with a quickening of her pulse-rate and a flare of red-hot excitement.

'I want you to go, Marcus. I need to get dressed.'

'Go ahead,' he said calmly.

Irritated beyond words, she went over to her wardrobe, intending to get her clothes and return to the privacy of the bathroom.

'You asked me where you would live if you came back to Italy,' he said, watching her as she flicked through the rails of clothing.

'It isn't going to happen, Marcus,' she said flatly, clutching hold of the bath-sheet and trying to focus on the clothes in front of her.

'I want you to live with me…as my wife.'

For a second she thought she had misheard him. She turned to look at him, incredulity in her eyes. 'I beg your pardon?'

He smiled. 'You heard me—I want us to get married. It's the only way forward. It's the best thing for Liam… for us.'

The arrogance of that statement made her laugh. 'Now I know you are joking.'

'Here's the deal,' he said, getting up from the bed and walking slowly towards her. 'You marry me and live with me at my villa in Rome and I give you a two-year contract at *Élan*.'

She moistened her lips nervously. 'We don't love each other, Marcus, and there's no way—'

'Think very carefully before you refuse me, Gemma.' The warning in his voice made her heart slam against her chest. 'You assume it's a foregone conclusion you'll get custody of Liam if this goes to court, but nothing is certain in a courtroom. And I'll fight you every inch of the way. Both of us could end up as losers. Do you want to risk that?'

She couldn't answer him. Her breathing felt tight and restricted.

'This way we all end up as winners. Liam has the security of being in a family unit. You get the job of your dreams. I get to keep my son with me.'

When she still didn't answer he continued smoothly, 'I'm a very wealthy man, Gemma. I can offer you a very good lifestyle with everything you want. I suggest we give this our best shot…for Liam's sake. But if you are not happy by the end of your contract with *Élan*, I'll let you go with a handsome divorce settlement. No hard feelings.'

'And in the meantime I live at one end of your villa, like a bird in a gilded cage, and you live at the other? We have a marriage in name only?'

He smiled at that. 'That's definitely not what I'm saying…' He reached up and trailed a hand down over her face in a gentle caress that made her heart race. 'I said we should give the marriage our best shot…'

'You mean sleep together?' Her heart was beating very erratically now.

'Don't sound so appalled. That was the one thing we did very well together in the past…as I recall.'

'Your arrogance never fails to astound me.' She shook her head.

'And the way you are able to lie to yourself never fails to astound me,' he replied silkily. 'Sex was always red-hot between us and you know it.'

'I know nothing of the kind.' She angled her chin up defiantly, her blue eyes blazing into his. 'In fact, I can't even remember what sex was like between us,' she lied vehemently, determined to cut his conceited remarks dead. 'So it can't have been that special. And I wouldn't want you to touch me if you were the last man left on the planet.'

'Really?' His lips twisted coolly.

'Yes, really.'

'Are you angling for a reminder, Gemma…a little taste of how things used to be?' He stepped closer and suddenly alarm bells were ringing loudly inside her body.

'Marcus, I—'

But whatever she had been going to say was cut short by the pressure of his lips against hers. She tried to twist her head away from him, but he held her still with remarkable ease, one hand holding her while his lips carried out a thoroughly gentle yet devastating assault on her senses. For a little while she managed not to respond. Her hands were clenched into tight fists at her side and her lips didn't move beneath his.

His skin was rough and scratchy against hers but for some reason that only served to heighten the sensation of complete arousal inside her. She wanted to respond…she wanted him with a melting weakness that tore into the deepest, darkest recesses of her soul.

His lips knew exactly the way to turn her on. They moved gently at first and then with more heated insistence, dominating her senses until her mind swam hazily with desire and she could do nothing but reach upwards and stand on tip-toe to meet the fierce insistent passion with equal need.

His body pressed closer and his lips moved from hers to trail a heated path to her neck and then upwards to her ear. 'You see, Gemma…you've always been mine for the taking,' he whispered fiercely in Italian.

The arrogant words should have restored her senses, should have made her try to push him away again, but as his hands moved beneath the towel, finding the heat of her naked flesh, her body responded urgently to him.

He caressed the soft curves of her breast, feeling the way her nipples swelled and hardened beneath the gentle encouragement of his fingertips.

'Tell me you want me,' he whispered huskily against her ear.

She was aware that the bath-sheet was slipping down; she could feel the soft material of his suit against her skin, and with it the heat and strength of his arousal.

Little shivers of ecstasy shuddered through her body as his hand slid down over her narrow waist, then lower over the curve of her buttocks before moving to stroke between her legs. She gasped as his hand made contact with the most intimate core of her.

He kissed her neck and the side of her face. 'Say it,' he insisted. 'Admit that I turn you on, that you want me.'

Gemma was almost incoherent with need. The force of her desire was like being held in the grip of a tornado.

She'd never known anything so powerful. She wanted to feel him inside her. She wanted the sweet relief of being as close to him as she could possibly get.

'I want you, Marcus…' The words were almost choked out of her. He moved and kissed her lips again, fiercely this time. His hands left her body to cup her face, holding her still while he ravaged her lips with a sweet searing hunger.

Then, just as she thought she was going to go out of her mind with wanting more, with needing him to possess her body fully, he stepped back.

Dazed, she just managed to catch the bath towel before it slipped to the floor. She held it in front of her with shaking hands, looking up into the darkness of his eyes with perplexity.

'Remember now?' he asked her softly.

She couldn't answer him; she was too dazed…too shocked by the fact that he had actually stopped.

'You see, Gemma. Sexually speaking, I think we'll be fine. Think about it. I'll need your answer by the end of the week.'

Then he calmly turned and left the room, leaving her weak and shaken, wanting him so much it was almost a physical pain.

CHAPTER SEVEN

LIAM made steady progress and by the following day Gemma was told that the doctor would discharge him when he made his rounds of the ward later that afternoon.

'Thank heavens for that!' Gemma's mother was in the room with her daughter and she smiled over at Liam. 'You'll be home by tea-time with a bit of luck.'

'Will I be coming back to your house or Daddy's house?' Liam asked, looking over at his mother.

'You'll be coming back to our house, darling.' Gemma frowned. 'Why are you asking that?'

'Because it's Saturday and I usually stay at Daddy's house on Saturday.'

'Oh! Well, not this Saturday,' Gemma said softly, wondering if this was a disappointment to Liam. Did he prefer staying at his dad's house? she wondered suddenly. The thought was cold in the pit of her stomach.

'Where is Marcus?' Joanne asked, cutting into her thoughts.

'He left in the early hours of the morning. Said he'd be back around eleven.'

Gemma could hardly bear to think about Marcus. The atmosphere between them since the incident in her bedroom yesterday had been so tense it was almost tangible. She was furious with herself for allowing him to touch her and for wanting him so much, furious with him for being so damn arrogant and so sexually adept at turning her on.

When they had met up at Liam's bedside again yesterday, the memory of what had transpired between them had been so disturbing she had hardly been able to look at him. But Marcus had acted as if nothing had happened, chatting about nothing in particular, laughing with Liam and the nurses. The more nonchalant he had seemed, the more the episode took on a feeling almost of unreality. Yet her body had reminded her forcefully that it had been no dream. Her skin had still tingled from the touch of his hands, and she could still feel the imprint of his lips, so dominant, so sensually arousing against the softness of her mouth. Every time she thought about what had happened she felt a fierce thrust of desire that refused to go away, no matter how hard she tried to dismiss it.

'How are you and Marcus getting on?' her mother asked suddenly, and she felt herself blush to the roots of her hair.

'We're getting along okay.' She shrugged and looked away.

'I just wondered how it was going…with you spending so much time together.'

Gemma was very glad when the nurse came into the room, taking the focus of attention away from her. 'You know, I think I had better go and ring Richard,' she said suddenly. 'He said he might come and see Liam this afternoon, and I don't want him to have a wasted trip.'

It was a relief to get out of the room away from her mother's perceptive gaze. But she was only halfway down the corridor towards the phone when Joanne caught up with her. 'So what's really going on?' she asked firmly.

'Mum, nothing is going on.'

'Come on, Gemma, I'm not stupid. There was a

strange atmosphere between you and Marcus yesterday and it wasn't just down to the fact that you were both worried sick about Liam. And today you've been really distracted, and yet Liam's better. The doctors are ready to let him go home.'

'Mum, it's nothing.' She turned, and met the shrewd look in her mother's blue eyes and let her breath out in a sigh. Maybe it would be good to talk about this to someone. Maybe once she had voiced the dilemma, it would help her see things more clearly. 'Okay…but I don't want you to get the wrong idea.' She took hold of her mother's arm and led her over to the side of the corridor by the coffee machine. 'Marcus has asked me to go to Italy with him…as his wife.'

She watched her mother's eyes widen and then a smile of pure pleasure crossed her face.

'I told you not to get the wrong idea!' she said quickly. 'This doesn't mean what you think it means.'

'No?' Her mother shook her head, a smug gleam in her eyes now. 'So what does it mean?'

'It means that Marcus is so desperate to get his son that he's prepared to do anything to get him. He doesn't love me, he just sees me as a necessary part of the equation to get his child—'

'Oh, honestly, Gemma, for an intelligent woman you don't half talk some rot sometimes,' her mother cut across her briskly. 'The reason Marcus has asked you to marry him is that he loves you. It's obvious to anyone with eyes in their head.'

'I might have known you'd start to get all romantic and dreamy about this, Mum.' Gemma shook her head. 'You've always had a blind spot where Marcus is concerned. But the truth is that Marcus views me in a cool clear light. We are compatible…in some ways…' She tried not to blush as she said those words. 'But for the most part he views me as a necessary accessory if he is to have his son in his life. His real love is Sophia Albani.'

'So why isn't he asking her to marry him?'

'I don't know...' Gemma shrugged, at a loss now. 'I really thought he was poised to do just that.' She spoke almost to herself.

'I think if he had wanted to marry her he would have done so years ago. She flies backwards and forwards to see him all the time. He must have had countless opportunities to commit to her. But he's asking you. That must mean something.'

'I think it just means that he puts Liam first in his life.'

'Well, that's good...isn't it?'

'It's good in some ways...' Gemma shrugged and lowered her voice to a husky whisper. 'But I have needs too, Mum.' She remembered the way Marcus had so coolly set out to seduce her yesterday, the way he'd kissed her and the heat and passion of his caresses, then the controlled way he had been able to move back from her when he had proved his point. 'I can't marry someone who doesn't love me.'

'So you've turned him down?'

'I haven't given him an answer yet. But it has to be no. He thinks he can have what he wants, that because he has money and power I'll say yes. He's tried to buy me with a fabulous job, with the fact that I'll be in a lovely home with a great lifestyle.'

'Sounds good to me,' her mother said dryly.

'Well, I won't be bought.' Gemma turned away and searched her pockets for some change for the coffee machine. 'I don't need him. He can go to Italy or go to hell for all I care.' She put the coins into the slot with a shaking hand.

'But you love him,' her mother said quietly beside her. 'You've always loved him.'

'No, I don't,' Gemma said fiercely.

'You can lie to yourself as much as you like, Gemma, but you don't fool me.' Joanne's voice was softly insistent. 'I know you. I've seen the way you look at him, the expression on your face at the mere mention of his name. You've never stopped loving him.'

'That's not true.' Gemma's voice trembled alarmingly and the buttons on the coffee machine suddenly blurred behind a mist of tears.

'If you turn him down, what will you be staying in London for?' Joanne continued persistently. 'Not for Richard, that's for sure. Your feelings for him are lukewarm at best.'

'I like Richard,' Gemma maintained stubbornly.

'If you say no to Marcus you will wake up to regret it. Okay, he hasn't told you he loves you, but he has asked you to marry him—*twice*. Maybe in view of the fact that you still have feelings for him, and the fact that Liam adores him, it's time you threw away that foolish pride of yours and met him halfway.'

The words were tough and uncompromising and they tore into Gemma's consciousness with brutal force.

'And, just for the record, I think Marcus cares about you deeply. There's a certain inflection in his voice when he asks about you sometimes—'

'You're really grasping at straws now, Mum,' Gemma said with a shake of her head.

'Marriage isn't all roses around the door, Gemma. But I think if you and Marcus worked at it, you could have something really special.'

'Hi, Gemma,' Richard's cheerful voice called to her down the corridor and she turned to see him heading in their direction with a huge bouquet of flowers and a big box of chocolates in his arms.

'How's Liam? Everything is okay, isn't it?' He looked at her in alarm as he noticed the pallor of her skin and the bright glitter of her eyes.

'Yes, he's fine. In fact, they've just told me they will be discharging him today. I was on my way to phone you.'

'Gemma, this must all have been a terrible ordeal for you.' He put his arms around her and gathered her close in against him. For a second the scent of lilies and carnations assailed her.

Richard was a good man, she thought, decent and kind...why couldn't she be in love with him? But the fact remained that there was no flutter of excitement at being in his arms, no fierce thrill of pleasure at all. The heart could be very stupid, she thought angrily.

As she pulled back from him she saw Marcus walking down the corridor, noted the dark gleam of derision in his eyes as he witnessed their embrace. She remembered how he had poured scorn on her relationship with Richard the other day. What was it he had said? *'Richard strikes me as a trifle weak...not the type to be able to handle you at all. And certainly not the type to turn you on.'*

The arrogance of that remark seared through her angrily. Obviously Marcus believed he had no real competition. That conceited confidence fired Gemma's blood and made her impulsively reach to kiss Richard on the lips as he handed her the flowers.

'Thanks, Richard,' she whispered huskily.

'Well, you're welcome.' Richard blushed slightly and

looked extraordinarily pleased. And suddenly Gemma wished she hadn't done that.

'The chocolates are for Liam.' Richard shyly passed them over to her as well.

'Thanks—you shouldn't have.' Gemma felt flustered as Marcus reached her side.

'Morning, everyone.' He smiled around at them all, his manner relaxed. Then, much to Gemma's consternation, he reached and put an arm around her waist, drawing her close towards him with an easy familiarity. 'Good news—I've just been speaking to the doctor and he's about to discharge our son.'

The touch of his hand and the scent of his aftershave sent her heart into a frenzied overdrive. She noticed how Richard and her mother took in the closeness of their stance and she wanted to wrench herself crossly away from him but she didn't get the chance because Marcus had already moved to shake Richard's hand. 'Good of you to come down,' he said. 'Sorry you've had a bit of a wasted journey.'

'Doesn't matter,' Richard said pleasantly. 'Gemma was just telling me the good news. I'll stick my head around the door and say hello to him anyway.'

'Liam will be delighted.' Gemma moved to take hold of Richard's arm, steering him firmly away from Marcus. She wished she hadn't caught her mother's eye just at that moment, because it was obvious from the expression on her face that she knew exactly why Gemma was gushing over Richard and she wasn't impressed.

Liam was pleased to see Richard but he was more taken with the fact that his father was back and had brought him a new pair of pyjamas with pictures of an

Italian football team on it. 'Wow, Daddy! Wow, thanks!' he kept saying.

'I thought you'd be in here another night,' Marcus said with a grin. 'But you'll just have to save them for home now.'

'Can Mummy and I come back to your house tonight?' Liam asked suddenly.

'Liam, I've told you that you are not going to Daddy this weekend,' Gemma cut in swiftly, trying to ignore the awkward atmosphere that suddenly seemed to have descended with that question, the watchful eyes of her mother and Richard, and the gleam in Marcus's gaze as he glanced over at her.

'Aw, but Mum!'

'Not today, Liam.' His father cut across him firmly. 'But soon.'

Why did he have to say that? Gemma wondered angrily. He just had to tack the word, 'soon' on, to show her that he was going to win this battle of attrition.

'I suppose our dinner date is out of the question tonight?' Richard asked her quietly.

'Well, I don't want to leave Liam at the moment, Richard.' She paused, wondering if she should ask him around to the house for dinner, but somehow she couldn't face the thought of making polite conversation. She wanted to concentrate on Liam and think seriously about where their future lay...here in London, or in Italy with Marcus. 'Let's make it next week instead.' Conscious of the fact that Marcus was listening she tacked on, 'That way we can really relax and enjoy ourselves.'

'Okay,' Richard agreed with her easily. 'Next week it is.' He turned the conversation towards Liam, asking him what it had been like to be in hospital.

Gemma listened to the conversation. Richard was quite serious with him and Liam answered politely, a solemn expression on his little face. It was quite different when Marcus spoke, making Liam chuckle as if he'd said the funniest things in the world.

Her eyes moved between the two men. Richard was dressed sombrely in a pale grey shirt and black trousers. Marcus was wearing jeans and a blue denim shirt that was open at the neck. He looked confident and relaxed, and extremely sexy. Her eyes lingered on his hands, remembering how they had moved over her so possessively.

'Gemma... Gemma.' Her mother reached over and touched her arm. 'I'm going to go now. I'll ring you later.'

'Oh, right.' Gemma hoped her mother hadn't noticed that she had been staring at Marcus. 'Thanks for everything, Mum.'

'Okay.' She leaned forward to kiss her daughter on the cheek. 'Don't make any rash decisions,' she whispered.

Gemma smiled at her and concluded that was code for 'Don't turn Marcus down'.

'If you're going, I'll give you a lift, Joanne,' Richard said, also getting to his feet. 'I'm going in that direction anyway.'

'That's very kind of you, Richard.' Joanne smiled, then waved over at Marcus and gave Liam a hug. 'Be good for your mum.'

'I'll see you Monday morning,' Richard said as he bent to kiss Gemma goodbye.

'I'm not sure, Richard. I'll have to see how Liam is.'

'But you've got your interview on Monday!' Richard reminded her with a frown and she felt her skin overheat with embarrassment as she realized she had forgotten all about the interview. 'Unless Marcus is going to arrange for it to be rescheduled for you?'

'That's not up to me, Richard,' Marcus said smoothly. 'That call is down to Henry Perkins. I'm leaving the day-to-day running of the magazine to him.'

'Well, you'd better give him a ring if you're not going to make it, Gemma,' Richard said with a worried shake of his head. 'You've worked too long and too hard to throw away the opportunity of your promotion now.'

'Don't worry, Richard. I'll sort it out,' Gemma said quietly.

As the door closed behind her mother and Richard, Gemma glared over at Marcus. She didn't believe for one moment that he was leaving the appointment of the new editor entirely up to Henry Perkins. He was just being deliberately obtuse because he had no intention of allowing her to get the job there.

'Don't look at me like that, Gemma. The job interviews are nothing to do with me.'

'Of course they are something to do with you. You own the magazine!'

'So what are you saying? That you want me to pull strings for you?' he asked calmly.

'You know that's not what I mean. I'm saying that I don't want you to interfere in any way.'

'That's fine then, because I don't intend to.'

Gemma didn't believe him, but there was no time to say anything further because Liam's doctor arrived at that moment to check him over.

'He's much better.' The doctor smiled over at them both as he finished making some notes on his clipboard. 'Your son is quite a fighter—his immune system kicked in and fought off the infection much faster than I had expected. But you need to keep a close eye on him now for the next few months. Just to make sure we don't have any recurrence.'

'You mean the virus could come back?' Gemma was horrified.

'I don't think it's likely but he is still a little under par. Nothing to worry about unduly.' The doctor ruffled Liam's hair playfully. 'With a bit of TLC from mum and dad, a bit of fresh air and good food, you should be right as rain in no time, Liam.' He smiled over at Gemma. 'Just keep an eye on him and bring him along to his GP in six weeks for a check-up. I'm sure he'll give you the all clear.'

'We will do that, Doctor. Thank you,' Marcus said with a nod.

'Can I go home now?' Liam asked hopefully.

'Yes, darling, you can come home,' Gemma said thankfully.

Marcus helped pack up Liam's belongings while Gemma changed him out of his pyjamas.

'Have you got your car here?' Marcus asked her as he lifted Liam up into his arms.

She shook her head. 'I got a taxi.'

'Right, we'll go back in mine,' he said, picking up Liam's holdall with his spare hand. 'Come on, let's get out of here.'

Gemma didn't argue with him. She wasn't up to getting taxis, she just wanted to get Liam home as soon as possible.

She sat silently as Marcus drove them back, only half listening to Liam's cheerful chatter in the back. Her mind was focusing on the doctor's words. The fact that the virus could return was frightening.

'Are you okay?' Marcus glanced over at her.

'Yes, I'm just thinking about the doctor's advice. I think I'll take next week off work to keep an eye on Liam.'

'I'll come over and stay with him on Monday if you want to attend your interview.'

The casual offer took her by surprise. 'You'd really do that?'

'I said so, didn't I?'

'It's just...well, I didn't think you wanted me to have that job.'

'I don't.' He glanced sideways at her and his dark eyes seemed to slice straight into her very soul. 'You know what I want. I made that clear yesterday. But it's your decision. If you want to go for that interview on Monday, then go. I'll be there for Liam.'

'Thanks, that's a kind offer—'

He frowned at that. 'He's my responsibility too, Gemma. It's only right that I help out...at least for as long as I can.'

She knew that was a veiled reference to the fact that he would be leaving soon. And the awareness of just how deeply that was going to affect them all was deeply disturbing.

'If you had let me finish, I was going to say that it was a kind offer, but I won't be taking you up on it, because I've decided not to apply for the job after all.'

Marcus looked over at her with a raised eyebrow. 'Does that mean you are going to accept my offer?'

The quietly asked question seemed to reverberate in the silence of the car.

'It means that I've been thinking about what the doctor said and I suddenly realize just how unimportant work is compared to my son's health.' Gemma looked away from him down at her hands, clasped tightly in her lap. 'And I've decided that I don't want promotion—in fact, if anything, I think I should be downsizing my job, so I can spend more time with Liam.'

'That's a mighty big decision.'

'I know…' She smiled shakily. 'But being in that hospital has made me take a long hard look at my priorities, and listening to that doctor just now scared me. Liam is the most precious thing in my life…the job means nothing beside that.'

Marcus pulled the car to a standstill in front of her house. 'Does that mean you are going to come to Italy with me?' he asked softly.

When she didn't answer him immediately, he reached and took hold of her hand. The touch of his skin against hers sent shivers of feeling running through her.

'The job at *Élan* doesn't become vacant until mid-September. So you could take the summer to relax at the villa with Liam, decide what you want to do about work at your leisure.'

Gemma felt confusion strike and suddenly she didn't know what to think any more. The offer sounded remarkably tempting—and did he mean that she could take the summer to consider whether or not she would marry him?

'Are you going to Italy, Daddy?' Liam's little voice in the back of the car brought them both up with a start. He'd been sitting so quietly that they had forgotten he might be listening.

'I'm just talking about it now, Liam,' Marcus said gently.

'Is it business?' Liam asked. He was used to his father making short business trips to the continent.

'We'll talk about it later, Liam,' his father said firmly.

Gemma liked the way he didn't try to lie to him. In

fact, she liked everything about the way he acted around his son.

Marcus turned his attention back to her.

'Why don't you invite me to stay for dinner and we can discuss this further?'

A cheer of enthusiasm from the back seat met the matter-of-fact question. 'Yeah, Daddy can stay for dinner and I can show him how I've put up my train set.'

Marcus looked at her with a gleam of amusement in his eyes now. 'So what do you say?'

Gemma only hesitated fractionally and then shrugged. 'Well, it looks like I've been outvoted. So you'd better come in.'

It seemed strange being downstairs in the kitchen knowing Marcus was upstairs with Liam. She could hear the distant rattle of the toy train and Liam's laughter, and it made her smile with pleasure. It was good having him home, and hearing him so happy was music to her ears. She was never going to take things like that for granted again, she thought.

The fact that Liam was in extra high spirits because his father was here couldn't be ignored either. If she let Marcus walk away from them her son was going to be devastated. So what should she do?

Gemma turned on the stove and then busied herself making a salad. Thinking too deeply about Marcus brought confusion, but it was something that she had to face. Should she go to Italy?

Marriage without love wasn't an option, she told herself sternly. And she didn't love him…yesterday had been a moment of weakness. It had been about sex…nothing else.

Marcus left Liam playing and went downstairs to see

Gemma. He noticed that she had put the flowers from Richard in a crystal bowl in the hall. Their scent was overpowering, almost as overpowering as the fury that had assailed him when he had watched Richard taking her into his arms. She was his, he thought angrily now, and he was damned if he was going to lose her to the likes of Richard Barry.

He paused in the open doorway to the kitchen. Gemma was standing at the kitchen counter, busy chopping peppers on a wooden board and then sliding them into a sizzling pan on the stove. She seemed immersed in the task, completely lost in thought and obviously not aware of his presence at all. What was she thinking about? he wondered.

He noticed the way the evening rays of sunshine were slanting through the kitchen window behind her, capturing the gold lights in her blonde hair, making it shimmer as she turned her head. Noticed the perfection of her skin, the dark sweep of her lashes, the soft curve of her lips. Then his eyes moved lower to the way her blue dress clung to the curves of her body and he remembered the heat and passion that had flared between them yesterday. It had taken all his willpower to be able to draw back from her. He had wanted to follow through and take her completely…he wanted that now, the need for her so strong it was burning him away inside.

Surely she couldn't have responded to him like that if she were in love with Richard? The thought crept into his mind that she had responded to him passionately once before when she had been in love with someone else. His own brother, no less.

He remembered Freddie's hurt expression when he had told him he'd been seeing her. Remembered the pain in his words. *'How could you do this to me, Marcus?*

She's mine, God damn it...she's the woman I'm going to marry...'

He hadn't seen that one coming, Marcus reminded himself brutally. When he had gone to his brother to ask him why he was taking Gemma to Helene's wedding, he had half-expected Freddie to admit he fancied her—or was hoping for a relationship stronger than friendship. That there was already a relationship going on had stunned him.

'Of course, you know why she's seeing you. It's to further her career, nothing more. She loves me... She's saving herself for me and the only reason we haven't slept together yet is because we want our wedding night to be special.'

At least he knew Gemma wasn't looking to further her career with him this time, Marcus reminded himself, trying to cut the painful memories of the terrible argument with Freddie. He had loved his brother and the knowledge of what he had done to him still tore him apart with grief and guilt. Sometimes in his nightmares he could still see his brother's face, his eyes glimmering with rage, with unshed tears of emotion.

For a long time after Freddie's death the conversation had haunted him, and he had hardly been able to bear to look at Gemma, he had been so burdened with guilt. And yet he had never stopped wanting her...desiring her...dreaming of her naked in his arms. When he had seen her out with Richard a few weeks ago it had focused his mind sharply. She hadn't seen him. They had been leaving a restaurant together, Richard's arm firmly around her waist. But the sight of them together had been a shock. And suddenly he had known with a searing clarity that he couldn't afford to have regrets about the past. He had to look to the future, and he saw that future with Gemma and Liam.

He moved and she looked up in surprise. 'How long have you been standing there?'

'Not long.' He walked further into the room and came to stand behind her, watching her as she worked. 'Do you need a hand with anything?'

'No, everything is under control, thanks.' She wished that were true. The food might be under control but her body temperature and her emotions definitely weren't. He was too close to her and she was acutely conscious of his body just a whisper away from hers. All she would have to do was turn around and she would be in his arms.

'What are you making?'

'Nothing exciting, I'm afraid, as I haven't had a chance to go shopping. Just pasta and a side salad.' It was difficult keeping her voice steady and light.

'Sounds good to me.' His breath tickled on the side of her face as he reached across and stole a piece of raw pepper. He didn't touch her but her body was so acutely tuned to the heat of his that it made every nerve ending tingle. In that instant the need to turn around and melt into him was so powerful it was almost overwhelming.

Her mother's words taunted her loudly in her mind. *'You love him. You've always loved him… It's time you threw away that foolish pride of yours and met him half-way.'*

'So what were you thinking about as you chopped away so industriously?' he asked, still not moving back from her.

'Not a lot.' She wondered how he would feel if she were to tell him she'd been thinking about her body's clamouring need to be held by him? He'd probably be arrogantly pleased, knowing Marcus, she reminded herself sharply.

'Did you mean it when you said you didn't want the promotion with *Modern Times*?'

The serious turn to his questions made her heart miss a beat. 'Yes, I did.'

'So will you come away with me, Gemma?' He put his hands at either side of her on the counter. 'You'll love living in Italy, I promise you.'

Gemma squeezed her eyes tightly closed.

'And Liam will love it. He's already almost fluent in the language, he'll be completely at home…and he'll thrive there.'

Still she didn't answer.

'So what do you think…will you say yes to my proposal?' The words were silkily smooth.

She had given up all pretence of work now and her hands clenched into tight impotent fists at her side.

He turned the stove off. 'Gemma? It will be the perfect arrangement.' He whispered the words close to her ear; his breath tickled and tantalized the skin on her neck.

He touched her then, one hand lightly on her shoulder as he turned her around to face him. Then he put a hand under her chin, tipping her head up so that she was forced to meet the darkness of his eyes. His thumb moved to stroke silkily across the soft fullness of her lower lip. The butterfly caress teased the sensory nerve endings, making her tremble inside. She longed for him to kiss her, longed for it so badly that it was like a deep ache inside.

'I think we are mature enough to make a marriage work. We both know what we want…' His hand moved to stroke a stray strand of hair away from her face, tucking it behind one ear. She wanted to tell him not to touch her; the sensation of his skin against hers was exquisite torture.

She loved him. The realisation suddenly screamed through her. *She adored him.*

She could lie to herself as much as she wanted but the truth was that she had been lost as soon as he had touched her again, as soon as she had been held fleetingly in his arms that day by Liam's bedside. All the memories that she had tried so desperately to close out had started to flood in again. And she realized now that her mother was right, she had never really lost her love of Marcus, she had just succeeded in masking it.

Yesterday, as soon as his hands had touched her body, she had been right back to where she had started with him five and a half years ago, totally and utterly under his spell. After all these years of telling herself that she was over him, it was a devastating admission to have to make and it made her incredibly angry with herself for being so weak where he was concerned.

'I never envisioned myself marrying for any other reason than love,' she murmured unsteadily.

'Do you love Richard?' His voice became sharper.

She shrugged and then deliberately lied. 'Maybe…'

'That's a very half-hearted declaration of love,' he grated derisively.

'Yes, well, Liam doesn't have a strong bond with Richard. And I'm a parent first, Marcus, that tends to change the way you view relationships.'

Marcus nodded. 'Yes, I realize that.'

The dry words sidetracked her somewhat. 'Is that the reason you haven't got married before now?'

'It has a bearing on it, yes.' His eyes moved towards

her lips and a flare of desire shimmered through her with sudden intensity.

'If I did agree to marry you, it would only be for Liam's sake…nothing else.' Her voice trembled precariously.

'Of course.' He smiled. 'Does that mean your answer is yes?'

She didn't reply to that. 'I don't want Liam to be without his father, you see…I can't bear the knowledge that if I turn you down I'll hurt him badly.' Her heart was thundering against her chest. She was aware she was desperately making excuses both to herself and him. She hated the weakness inside that desperately wanted to say yes, when she knew the answer should be no.

'Gemma, get to the bottom line.' His voice was abrupt; his eyes seemed locked on her lips. 'Will you marry me?'

'Yes…' The word was a mere whisper in the silence between them. She saw the flare of triumph in his eyes and hated herself for caving in so easily, but she couldn't help it. She wanted him with all her heart. She loved him.

He cupped her face in both his hands. 'You won't regret it. This is the right thing for Liam…for all of us.'

The feel of his hands against her skin was like a brand of possession.

Her breathing felt tight and constricted as he lowered his head towards hers and she realized he was going to kiss her.

His lips, soft and persuasive against hers, created the most intensely erotic sensation. It was as if he were laying claim to her, possessing her hungrily, and her body clamoured for so much more. Her breasts longed to feel his hands; her skin tingled with the need to be closer.

But then abruptly he stepped back. 'We'll leave for Italy next week and get married over there. If I apply for a special licence now that should mean we can have the ceremony within about ten days or so.'

'Ten days?' Her eyes widened. 'That's too soon!'

'No, it's not.' He stroked the side of her face and the soft touch distracted her. 'We've wasted enough time.'

'We should wait and get married here in London…' She was half panicking now, scared of what she was doing, but the other part of her was breathless with excitement. It was one thing agreeing in theory to a marriage without love—was she really going to go through with it?

'I know you'll want your mother and friends to attend and that's no problem. I'll get the air tickets. But we'll be married in Italy, Gemma.'

His voice was firmly decisive. Her senses were in complete disarray from the kiss, from the speed that he was taking things…from the fact that she wanted him to make love to her and talk about wedding dates later.

'I don't know, it seems a bit fast.'

His gaze took in the swollen softness of her lips, the huge blue eyes. 'And as I said, we've wasted enough time. I want you now…'

'Mummy, I bumped my elbow on the staircase.'

The little voice in the doorway took them both by surprise.

'Did you, darling?' She moved past Marcus to go and pick the child up. 'Where does it hurt?' she asked him gently.

'Just here.' He pointed to his arm and watched as she pushed up his sleeve to inspect the damage. 'No harm done. Just a little bump, I think,' she said softly and kissed him. 'There…does that feel better?'

He nodded.

'You look sleepy, darling.' She pushed a tender hand through his hair. 'It's been a long day, hasn't it?'

Liam nodded again and looked over at his dad. 'You're still staying for tea though, aren't you, Daddy?' he asked him anxiously.

Marcus nodded and came closer. 'In fact, you're going to be seeing a lot more of me from now on, Liam.'

Gemma felt her heart starting to bounce unsteadily again in her chest as she met his eyes, saw the question there. 'Shall I tell him?' he asked her softly.

She hesitated. As soon as they told Liam there would be no going back on her decision, she knew that.

'Gemma?' He looked at her with an intensity that tore at her heart. And she nodded.

'Yes, let's tell him.' She cuddled Liam closer to her, taking comfort in the warm little arms that stole around her neck, and in the fact that this was going to make her son very happy.

CHAPTER EIGHT

WHEN Gemma woke up that morning her first thought was that this was her last morning as a single woman.

Outside she could hear the distant rumble of traffic heading towards the centre of Rome. She glanced around the unfamiliar bedroom with its floral wallpaper and heavy wooden furniture and saw her wedding dress hanging on the back of the wardrobe, a delicious pale cream silk that was stylishly understated. Next to it, on the floor, her suitcase sat neatly packed, ready to be taken up to Marcus's villa.

Thinking about the momentous step that lay before her, Gemma felt a tingle of nerves which seemed to work its way up from her toes through her entire body. The alarm clock rang shrilly in the silence of the room. She reached out and switched it off.

Was she doing the right thing? The question had tormented her through the last two weeks. But everything had moved so quickly that there hadn't been a lot of time to think. She remembered the reaction in the office when she had told them she was leaving. Everyone had been shocked, but no one more so than Richard. Just thinking about the look on his face made her sad all over again.

Hurting Richard had not been easy. He had been such a good friend to her, especially over the last couple of months, but at least their relationship, if you could really call it that, had only just started. He had been disappointed and upset, had told her he thought she was making a big mistake rushing into marriage. But they had parted as friends and she had promised to keep in touch.

Gemma got out of bed and pulled back the curtains. The morning sunlight caught the engagement ring on her finger and it splintered into a myriad of dazzling colours. Marcus had presented her with the square-cut diamond solitaire just before they left London last week, but she still wasn't used to wearing it, was still overwhelmed by its beauty.

Her eyes moved to admire the view from her bedroom window; the city of Rome was bathed in the soft golden light of morning. This was the room that she had stayed in when she came to attend Helene's wedding. It was strange being back in Marcus's father's house. The last time she had stood at this window she had felt like her heart was breaking. Who would have thought that she would return, and that she would stand here and admire this view on the day she would marry Marcus?

She put on her dressing-gown and padded quietly across the hall to peep into Liam's room. He was still fast asleep, which wasn't surprising as it had been almost ten-thirty last night before she had been able to settle him down. Excitement had been bubbling inside him and he had talked incessantly, about the wedding, about living in Italy. And the fact that his father had arrived just as she had got him into bed hadn't helped.

'Isn't it bad luck to see the bride on the night before the wedding?' Gemma had asked when she had gone downstairs and bumped into him coming through the front door.

'I'm not the superstitious type.' He had grinned.

'Well, I am,' she had said firmly. 'I never walk under ladders, or put shoes on a table.'

'Well, they are just common sense precautions.'

'So is not letting the groom over the threshold the night before the wedding.'

She didn't know why she had pretended not to be glad to see him, when in reality all she had wanted was for him to take her into his arms and kiss her senseless. But it was a game she had played since accepting his proposal. She had too much pride to let him know that her heart went into overdrive at the mere sight of him.

Marcus had just smiled and stepped past her. 'Well, I won't keep you long. I just thought I'd call and say goodnight to Liam—is he still up?'

'He is now,' Gemma had said as she heard his footsteps on the landing and then the excited squeals of 'Daddy, Daddy, Daddy!'

Anyone would have thought Liam hadn't seen his dad in a fortnight instead of that afternoon. Which, she supposed, went to prove how much she was doing the right thing where her child was concerned. But as far as *she* was concerned, Gemma still wasn't at all sure.

There hadn't been a chance for them to be alone together since the moment when she had accepted his proposal. In one way it was a good thing because emotionally it helped her to keep her guard up. Marcus was so coolly confident about everything and she couldn't let him know that deep down she was scared to death…that she loved him so much it hurt. She had her pride. In fact, it was probably the only thing she had left. Marcus was taking everything else over, forcefully and absolutely.

He'd taken charge of closing up the house, arranging shipping and storage for certain items. He'd arranged for her to leave work without having to serve out the necessary notice. Everything had swept ahead with the force of a tidal wave.

She had said as much to him last night before he had left.

'Having last-minute doubts?' he had asked quietly, turning to look at her.

'Yes, I am, millions of them,' she had said honestly. 'What about you?'

He had smiled. And something about the way his eyes had raked over her face, lingering on her lips, had sent prickles of awareness racing through her.

'Not one. I know absolutely that this is the right thing.'

Those confident words echoed in her mind now as she wandered back to her bedroom and the en-suite bathroom to have her shower. Of course Marcus would feel like that. He was getting Liam…the one thing that made his life complete.

All Marcus's family were thrilled about the wedding, and they doted on Liam. His grandfather Giorgio Rossini in particular was crazy about him. He had been the one who had insisted they stay here before the ceremony. 'I want to get to know my grandson better,' he had said firmly. 'There has been too much distance between us for too long.'

Liam had been a little shy at first and had clung to her. He didn't really know his grandfather very well, having only seen him on a few occasions when Giorgio had visited London. But after the first day it was as if Liam had always known this house and these people. He was running around playing with his cousins and laughing with his grandfather quite happily.

Gemma raised her head to the pummelling pressure of hot water. The house was filled with joy and excitement and it was hard not to get carried away by it all, to believe that this marriage was real and that Marcus really did love her. But deep down she knew that wasn't true. The fact was that her emotions were a lot like the house she had left behind in London, shrouded under dustsheets. She was frightened of looking too deeply under the covers. Scared to examine this forthcoming marriage too closely in case she might not be able to deal with what she found. For instance, she hadn't dared to question Marcus about Sophia, in case she didn't like his answer.

She kept telling herself that the woman would be out of Marcus's life for good now that he was marrying her. But was that the case? Maybe Marcus envisaged some kind of open marriage, where he kept a mistress? Then he'd have the best of all worlds…his family and his lover.

Gemma snapped off the shower and swiftly pushed the idea away. Sophia would surely never tolerate that, not when she'd had hopes of marrying him herself one day. And anyway, Marcus had said he wanted to give their marriage a real chance of working; he'd hardly say that and keep a mistress. She had to put thoughts like that out of her head because they didn't help.

At one-thirty today she would officially become Mrs Marcus Rossini and then everything would start to come right in her world. She would be with the one man she had always loved. And okay, maybe he didn't love her, but she had enough love for the two of them and she would make this marriage work.

As she stepped back into her bedroom there was a knock at the door and Marcus's sister Helene came in with a cup of tea for her. 'How are you feeling?' she asked with a smile.

'Nervous,' Gemma admitted wryly.

Helene laughed. She was a very beautiful woman with

long dark hair and smiling dark eyes. 'Well, if it makes you feel better, I think Marcus is nervous as well. I rang the villa a few moments ago to see how he was going on and his housekeeper told me he'd gone out.'

'Out? At eight in the morning?' Gemma wondered suddenly if Marcus was having doubts about this marriage as well. Maybe that cool confident manner of his was just an act. Maybe deep down he was just as apprehensive and uncertain as she was.

'Oh, he'll be down at the stables having an early morning ride.' Helene grinned. 'He always does that when something important is on the horizon. The day he took over the business from Papà he was up at dawn and out riding for a couple of hours. He says it helps him focus on the day ahead.'

Gemma frowned. It suddenly struck her how little she really knew about Marcus. Even though they had a child together, it was a bit like marrying a stranger. She knew he was a good father, an excellent businessman, and she knew she liked his family. But the man himself was still an enigma to her.

'Oh, by the way.' Helene reached into the pocket of her dress and brought out a small flat box. 'Marcus asked me to give you that this morning.' With a smile Helene put the gift down on the dressing table and headed for the door. 'I'd better go. I said I'd accompany Papà to the airport to pick up your guests, give them a proper Italian welcome.'

Gemma smiled. 'Thanks, Helene.' She had only invited her mother, her best friend, Jane, and her partner, Steve, to the wedding because she had wanted to keep the occasion low key. It was a forlorn hope, because the Rossini family alone would probably pack the church.

As the door closed behind her future sister-in-law,

Gemma reached to open the box. Inside there was the most stunning square-cut diamond on a white gold chain and a note that said simply,

Thought this might look good on you, Marcus.

Not *love* Marcus…just 'Marcus'.

Gemma fastened the diamond around her neck. It looked fabulous. But she would have traded all the diamonds in the world if he had just written that one extra little word on the card.

The festivities for the wedding seemed to be underway even before Gemma had put on her wedding dress. The large double doors leading out to the secluded back garden were open and huge tables groaning with food had been laid out on the patio. People seemed to be arriving in droves and presents and cards were mounting up on the trestle tables in the hallway.

'The Italians certainly know how to party.' Her mother laughed as she came upstairs to help Gemma with the last-minute attention to details. 'I don't know how anyone will be able to eat at the reception after all that food downstairs—' She stopped abruptly as she saw her daughter in her wedding dress. 'You look gorgeous.' She sighed. 'An absolute picture.'

The dress did do incredible things for Gemma's figure. It hugged her tiny waist and skimmed over her curves in a most flattering way. The soft cream silk made her skin look luminous. Her hair was softly caught up with cream roses and around her neck was the necklace from Marcus.

'The car is here,' Helene called excitedly up the stairs and Gemma felt another flutter of nerves.

'Where is Liam?' she asked her mother.

'He left for the chapel with his uncles and cousins five minutes ago.'

Gemma nodded. 'Then I suppose it's time I followed him.'

As the limousine slowly rounded the corner towards the church the first person she saw was Liam, standing at the bottom of the steps. He looked adorable in his dark morning suit, his hair neatly brushed back from his face, and he waved with excitement as he saw the car.

The limousine pulled up beside them and the driver jumped out to open the door for her. As she stepped out on to the pavement her eyes connected with Marcus. Why was he standing outside the church? she wondered anxiously. Was something wrong?

He looked awesome in his morning suit. The penetrating dark eyes that held hers sent shivers of excitement and desire rushing through her.

'What are you doing out here?' she whispered. 'Shouldn't you be inside the church?'

'I wanted to see you arrive. You look beautiful, Gemma,' he said softly, his eyes raking over her body in a possessive way.

She smiled at him and suddenly her doubts were forgotten.

'Daddy said I was to give you this,' Liam said and brought out a single red rose from behind his back.

'Thank you, darling.' Gemma crouched down beside him to take it and then gave him a kiss.

'Hey, that's my kiss you're stealing, Liam,' Marcus said, putting a hand on his son's shoulder, and Liam giggled happily. Gemma straightened and looked up into Marcus's eyes. 'But I'll claim my kiss later,' he said huskily.

And suddenly the thought of the night ahead, of being

in his arms and having him make love to her, burnt through her consciousness.

He held out his hand towards her. 'Are you ready for this?' he asked.

She hesitated for just one second before placing her hand in his. 'As ready as I'll ever be,' she said, trying to feign a lightness of tone, trying to pretend that the touch of his hand against hers wasn't sending darts of electricity dancing through her.

'Hey, Marcus, you should be waiting for us inside!' His father stepped forward with an impatient shake of his head. 'I'm the one who is walking into the chapel with Gemma, you should be waiting with nervous anticipation by the altar.'

'Just going…' Marcus smiled at Gemma. 'See you in a moment.'

'Honestly, my son always has to do things his way,' Georgio said teasingly.

'Yes, I've noticed.' Gemma smiled.

The small church was packed with members of the Rossini family. But Gemma only had eyes for Marcus as she walked towards him down the aisle.

Suddenly this felt so right…

As she reached Marcus's side he took hold of her hand and she felt as if she had arrived somewhere that she should have been a long time ago.

She looked up at him and smiled and he squeezed her hand. 'I'll look after you, Gemma…I promise,' he whispered huskily.

Afterwards, when she looked back, those words were like part of the ceremony. The solemn look in his eyes, the pressure of his skin against hers.

Then the priest was welcoming them and the service began. Gemma's voice was hushed and not altogether steady as she repeated her vows. Marcus, on the other hand, was firm and decisive.

He slid the gold wedding band on to her finger resolutely.

'I now pronounce you man and wife.' The priest said the words in Italian and then repeated them in English. 'You may kiss the bride.'

It was hard to believe that such a short period of time could change someone's life so radically. Gemma looked up into Marcus's eyes with a feeling almost of unreality. Maybe this wasn't really happening to her, she thought dazedly. Maybe this was all a dream. Then Marcus leaned closer and his lips covered hers, not in a gentle way but in a fiercely possessive kiss that claimed her totally as his. And as she felt the answering surge of blazing heat inside her she knew with certainty that this was no dream.

Outside in the full glare of the sunshine they were showered with confetti, and then they paused for photographs before climbing back into a stretch limousine.

'Well, we did it,' Marcus said with a wry grin as he looked over at her.

'Yes, we did.' Gemma waved at Liam who was going to follow behind them in the car with Marcus's father and her mother.

She settled back into her seat and looked over at Marcus.

'You make a very lovely bride, Mrs Rossini.' He smiled.

'Thank you.' Her heart missed several beats. 'And thank you for the necklace. It's lovely.' She touched the diamond around her neck. 'I feel quite embarrassed because I didn't buy you anything.'

He smiled at that. 'You can give me your present tonight,' he said in a low teasing tone and smiled as he saw the flare of colour in her cheeks.

As she looked away from him he reached out and tipped her chin upwards so that she was forced to look at him. 'And I'm looking forward to unwrapping it very slowly,' he added softly. 'Savouring every moment… In fact, maybe I won't be able to contain myself until tonight. I think I've waited long enough…' He leaned closer. She could smell the scent of his cologne, mixed with the scent of the roses in her bouquet. Then his mouth covered hers, plundering the softness of her lips with delicious intent. Her stomach dipped as if she were experiencing the thrill of a fairground ride.

She felt his hands moving up over the bodice of her dress and she longed to feel them more intimately.

'We shouldn't, Marcus…' she whispered unsteadily. 'There's the driver and…people will see us….'

'To hell with people seeing. If I want to kiss my wife, I will.' Marcus grinned, his fingers stroking over the firmness of her body, noting the instinctive rise of her breast beneath his touch.

Then she was kissing him back with heated passion.

The loud blare of horns made her pull away from him.

Marcus laughed as she looked out into the crowded streets to see if there had been an accident. 'Relax. It's just people wishing us well. We'll probably be driving all the way out towards the restaurant accompanied by that noise.'

He was right; the uproarious din of horns continued as they left the city and headed out into the hills. And suddenly Gemma was reminded of Helene's wedding day. The Italian countryside bathed in sunshine, just like this, the fields of corn ripening to pale green gold, scarlet poppies lining the roadsides and cutting swathes through the lush meadows. Only then she had been sitting next to Freddie, painfully aware that the car ahead of them in the convoy held Marcus and Sophia.

'So, where were we…?' Marcus murmured, reaching to touch her again.

'We really shouldn't, Marcus.' She pulled away from him. 'That should wait until later…' She tried to force herself to be sensible but all her emotions were crying out for him to continue.

Marcus smiled. 'I suppose you are right.' Despite the words his hand moved teasingly to stroke the side of her face. 'But it's a pity because you look so ravishing in that dress that right at this moment…I really…want an aperitif…'

He leaned closer and his lips crushed against hers again and she found herself kissing him back hungrily. Her bouquet fell to the floor as the touch of his hand became more heated, his kisses more intrusive.

Then abruptly he pulled away from her and looked out of the window. 'But you are right, there is no time for this now. We'll be at the restaurant soon.'

The words made her hastily try to straighten her dress, smoothing down the ruffles in the silk with a shaking hand.

Marcus watched her with a gleam of amusement in his eye.

'It's not funny,' she said unsteadily, fastening up the top button on her bodice. 'I've got visions of the car pulling up surrounded by all your family.'

He laughed softly. 'Relax, they can't see in here anyway. It's tinted glass.'

Marcus picked up her bouquet and handed it to her. 'How's my hair?' she asked him nervously.

He smiled. 'You look gorgeous…tasted gorgeous as well.'

'Very funny. You've probably smudged all my make-up.'

'You don't need it anyway.'

She glanced over at him reproachfully and then smiled. 'You haven't changed much,' she whispered. 'You're still incredibly…audacious.'

'And you're still incredibly hot. Do you remember that evening when we first started seeing each other? We were supposed to be going out to dinner and then the opera…but we didn't even make it through the main course.'

Gemma held the darkness of his eyes for a long moment. She remembered that evening well. The hurried speed with which Marcus had paid the bill, the way they had started to undress each other as soon as they had stepped through the front door of his house. She had often wondered if that was the night Liam had been conceived.

'Yes, I remember…' She whispered the words huskily and wanted to tell him that no one had ever held such compelling power over her senses, either before or since.

'They were good times,' Marcus said quietly.

The lightness of that remark brought her firmly to her right mind.

'Yes…' She looked away from him sharply. Of course she couldn't tell him how deeply he had touched her. It was far too revealing. Letting Marcus know that she was completely besotted by him would serve little purpose other than to feed his ego. And in the process it would leave her open and vulnerable.

But guarding her heart from her husband was not how Gemma had ever envisioned her wedding day.

She looked down at the gold wedding band on her finger. 'Can I ask you something?'

'Fire away.'

'When Liam was in hospital and you asked me to marry you...'

'Yes?'

'Was it a spur of the moment thing? You know... Were you so worried about Liam and about having to leave that the question just popped out?'

'No, it wasn't a spur of the moment thing.' He said the words firmly, then reached to touch her face so that she would look at him. 'I'd been giving the idea careful thought from the moment I realized I was leaving London. In fact, Liam must have heard me talking about it on the phone just before he was taken ill.'

'I thought you were planning to marry...someone else.' She couldn't even bring herself to say Sophia's name—not on her wedding day.

Marcus shook his head. 'Only you,' he said softly.

The words made her heart bounce crazily against her chest.

'I wanted to take you out to dinner to ask you properly, but you kept refusing to see me...then events were taken out of my hands when Liam became ill.'

'Out of the hands of both of us,' Gemma murmured.

Marcus nodded. His eyes were so cool and serious on her face that she felt them as if they were touching her. 'You've given up a lot to come here...your job, your friends...'

Some small spark of devilment made her say softly, 'Richard was devastated...'

'To hell with Richard.' Marcus's eyes narrowed on her face, and for a fraction of one joyous moment

Gemma wondered if he was jealous. If maybe, deep down, he really did love her…

'You belong to me now, Gemma.' He leaned forward and his lips touched hers with sizzling heat and passion.

It took a moment before either of them realized that the car had come to a standstill. They broke apart and, looking out, saw that they were outside a pretty country inn and that other cars were pulling up around them.

'I guess it's time to get the wedding show back on the road.' Marcus grinned over at her. 'But let's leave as soon as possible…hmm?' His eyes drifted down over her body. 'Because it's time I had you all to myself. Claimed what is rightfully mine.'

The words made her burn inside with desire and need.

CHAPTER NINE

THE setting for their wedding banquet was idyllic. The quaint whitewashed old inn backed out on to the most charming garden where long white-clothed trestle tables were laid up under the leafy shade of a vine-covered pergola.

A bar had been set up at the end of the lawn and for a while the guests mingled, chatting happily as they sipped *aperitivo* wine and ate small salted biscuits. A warm breeze stirred the cypress trees, lifting the intensity of the afternoon heat.

Gemma glanced across the lawn to where Liam was playing happily in the shade with his cousins. In the few days since they had arrived he had caught the sun and his skin was a golden brown. He looked the picture of health and it was hard to believe he was the same little boy who had been so pale and ill in the hospital.

Her gaze moved towards Marcus who was deep in conversation with his father and two of his brothers. The Rossini men were all handsome, but it was Marcus who drew her attention. She couldn't keep her eyes off him. As if sensing her gaze, he turned and looked over at her and smiled. She smiled back.

'And you tried to tell me you weren't in love with him,' her mother said in a teasingly low voice next to her and she felt herself blushing guiltily. 'He's very good-looking, isn't he?'

'Yes,' Gemma agreed. 'Too good-looking for any woman's peace of mind.'

'And I can see where he gets his looks from as well. Giorgio is a very attractive man.'

Gemma smiled and looked questioningly up at her mother. 'Oh, yes?'

Joanne shrugged and then to Gemma's surprise blushed a little. 'He's asked me to accompany him to the opera tomorrow night.'

Gemma remembered that similar invitation from Marcus and her eyes widened a little. 'Well, tread carefully, Mum. The Rossini men can be very charming.'

Joanne laughed. 'This is your old mum you are talking to! It's just dinner and the opera.'

'Less of the "old", you look fantastic,' Gemma said honestly. Her mother did look beautiful in a pale blue suit with a matching wide-brimmed hat.

Some other relatives of Marcus came over to speak to them and the conversation was forgotten. Then, a little while later, everyone took their places at the table.

Gemma sat next to Marcus at the head of the table and then Giorgio opposite to her mother with Liam beside her. In all there were about sixty people at the long table, and, with the exception of Jane and Steve they were all Marcus's family.

There was lots of laughter and the wine flowed with the many courses. The waiters brought out vast silver platters with canapés of smoked salmon and stuffed olives, tiger prawns, lobster. They circulated many times, first with the hot antipasto then the cold. After that they brought different types of pasta, Gemma's favourite being the restaurant's own delicious tagliatelle, and then the main course of aromatic lamb.

All through the meal guests were proposing toasts to the bride and groom. There was much teasing and laughing. Marcus watched how Gemma blushed when someone said that he hoped their union would be blessed with many, *many* children. Then someone else jumped up and said he hoped that their table would always groan under the weight of good food.

That made Gemma laugh. 'I can see I'm going to have to take up lessons in Italian cooking while I'm here,' she said jokingly to Marcus.

'What do you mean, *while* you are here?' He looked at her with a quizzical lift of one eyebrow. 'You're here to stay, Gemma, remember?'

Her heart missed a beat at those words. Then he leaned closer and whispered playfully against her ear. 'And don't worry, I'm a very modern man—I won't keep you barefoot and pregnant in the kitchen…just naked and ready for me in the bedroom.'

She knew he was only joking but there was something so riskily sexual about the vision he conjured up that she felt the heat of pure lust lick deep inside her. He laughed with delight as he saw the echo of that heat in the deep blue of her eyes.

A chant went around the table as suddenly everyone insisted that the groom should kiss his bride.

Marco grinned and leaned closer to oblige. The heat of his lips was seductively mesmerising against hers and as she kissed him back she wished fervently that they were on their own.

There were no stilted formal speeches but as the wedding cake was carried in to loud applause, Giorgio got to his feet to propose another toast. 'I just want to say how glad I am that you two have got together,' he said with deep sincerity in his eyes, 'and to propose a toast to members of the family who are not here. My late wife…Gemma's father…and of course Freddie, who introduced you two in the first place.' He smiled. 'It was a wonderful day when he brought you into our lives, Gemma.'

She smiled at her father-in-law, deeply touched by the words.

The light was starting to fade in the garden as the cake was cut and champagne was served. Fairy lights were turned on and they sparkled amongst the trees and along the trellis. The tables were swiftly cleared so that candles could be placed along the centre and a small band set up next to the bar area and played romantic Italian melodies.

As people got up to dance and mill about near the bar, more guests arrived and came over to congratulate them.

For a little while she was separated from Marcus and it was Helene who introduced her to the late arrivals, most of whom were friends and neighbours of the family.

'And of course you met Sophia Albani at my wedding,' Helene said casually. Gemma turned and with a deep jolt found herself face to face with the woman who had haunted her thoughts for so long.

Sophia hadn't changed a bit. She was still arrestingly beautiful. A turquoise dress fitted tightly over the sensual curves of her body, dipping provocatively at the neckline and skimming her small waist and narrow hips. She had high cheekbones, almond shaped brown eyes and long glossy dark hair.

Although the woman smiled at her, her eyes were cold. 'I believe congratulations are in order.'

'Thank you.' Gemma had never felt more awkward in all her life. She didn't know what to say and she was astounded that the woman was even here. If their situations had been reversed, there was no way Gemma would have attended her marriage with Marcus. But maybe Sophia had moved on…maybe she was in love with someone else by now and didn't care?

'Sorry I didn't make it to the church today but I had another important engagement and I couldn't get out of it.' Sophia took a glass of champagne from the tray of a passing waiter.

'It was a beautiful service,' Helene said. 'Not a dry eye in the place.'

'Yes… I'm sure.' As Sophia lifted the glass to her lips Gemma noticed the sparkle of a wedding ring on her finger and the feeling of relief that swept through her was immense.

'I see you've got married since we last met?' Gemma said, wondering when this event had taken place.

'Yes, two months ago. Alberto is around here somewhere,' she said nonchalantly, her eyes searching the crowds. 'He's probably at the bar with the men.'

Helene turned away from them to talk to someone else and they were left momentarily alone.

'Well, Marcus and I decided it was for the best…' Sophia continued. 'We both had to get on with our lives.'

'Sorry?' Gemma was lost now.

Sophia smiled and there was something rather pitying in her expression. 'You do know that Marcus and I have always…had an understanding? We're soul mates. Have been together from the junior school.'

Gemma wasn't sure how she should be handling this at all—or where it was leading. 'Well, Freddie told me that you used to…date Marcus, if that's what you mean.'

'It was a little more than that.' Sophia's eyes were hard now, like chips of granite. 'Until he went to England and got—how shall I put it…encumbered. Yes, encumbered with a child.'

'I don't think Marcus would put it like that. He adores Liam.' Gemma's voice was equally cold now and her heart was beating angrily in her chest.

'Yes, he does. You were very clever. Produced a son, then played to Marcus's sense of duty. It would have killed him to let go of Liam, so he had to propose, and you got him in the end.' Sophia lifted her glass in a mocking salute. 'I have to hand it to you, it was a very clever strategy. Shame he doesn't love you, though. How do you live with that? It must be awful knowing you've got him by default, and that I'm the woman he really wanted...'

'That is absolute rubbish.' Gemma's voice was very low now and very icy. 'Marcus adores me.' Even as she uttered the lie, Gemma wondered if a bolt of lightning would strike her.

'Does he?' Sophia smiled. 'So how come he spent his last night of freedom in my arms, telling me he wished things were different?'

With a small smile of satisfaction Sophia walked away from her.

'What's the matter?' Helene asked in consternation as she turned back towards Gemma and saw the sudden pallor of her skin.

'Nothing...it was just something Sophia said.'

'What did she say?' Helene asked sharply.

'Nothing.' Gemma shrugged, too embarrassed to tell the other woman the exact conversation. 'Just something about how her and Marcus were childhood sweethearts.'

'Oh, is that all?' Helene laughed. 'Marcus is a grown man now, Gemma. He put away his childhood toys a long time ago. He loves you—he married you. Pay no attention to Sophia. It is a case of...what's the English phrase...sour wine?'

'Sour wine?' Gemma was momentarily distracted. 'Oh, I think you mean sour grapes.'

'That's it!' Helene laughed.

And Gemma had to smile.

Helene put an arm around her shoulder. 'That's Sophia's husband over there.' She indicated a tall man with an ugly profile and balding head. 'Her papà helped her pick him out when it was decided Marcus was no longer...'available'. He's practically a millionaire and very well connected to help Sophia's father, business-wise. Plus he keeps Sophia in very good style, and as she has hardly ever worked a day in her life that suits her fine. But look at him! It's no wonder Sophia is a little bitter.'

Gemma shook her head. 'Maybe he is a lovely person, Helene,' she rebuked lightly.

'Well, maybe he is, and maybe they love each other deeply, but I doubt it somehow. I think their marriage is a business arrangement more than anything.'

Gemma couldn't say anything to that, because deep down she knew her marriage to Marcus was little more than a sham itself. He didn't love her, he was doing this for Liam, and all these people who had flocked to wish them well were just being taken in by an illusion... Everyone except for Sophia, of course.

The buoyant feeling of happiness that had been with her since walking into the chapel today suddenly disappeared completely. She had almost been taken in by the illusion herself. Marcus could play the adoring bridegroom to perfection.

She saw him making his way towards her through the crowds and her heart started to race nervously. Tonight he would want to take the illusion one step further and sleep with her. How was she going to deal with that, knowing for certain that he still loved Sophia?

He reached her side and smiled at her. 'Liam has found himself a girlfriend.'

Gemma glanced over to where her son was dancing hand in hand with Helene's four-year-old daughter, Andrea who looked very appealing in her long white frilly dress.

'Obviously he has inherited the Rossini charm,' she managed to reply with a smile.

'Obviously.' Marcus's gaze moved over her face. 'Shall we have a dance before we sneak away from the party?'

The question made apprehension rise even further inside her. 'Yes…' She nodded. 'Good idea, then we really should take Liam home. He must be exhausted.' Maybe she could delay the inevitable by staying with Liam in his room for a while, she thought desperately. Maybe she could even say that Liam didn't want her to leave him alone tonight…? She just wanted to buy some time to think about this situation.

'Liam is coming back to Papà's house with us, Gemma,' Helene said, glancing at her watch. 'We'll be rounding up all the children in a few minutes.'

This was the first Gemma had heard of such a plan. 'That's very kind of you, Helene,' she said quickly. 'But I wouldn't hear of it. You've got enough children staying at the house, plus you've got my guests.'

'There's plenty of room and there are plenty of adults around to help with the children. Liam is coming with us,' Helene said with equal firmness. 'This is your wedding night, Gemma. You and Marcus relax and enjoy yourselves. We will take care of Liam.'

Gemma wanted to argue further but Marcus took hold

of her hand. 'Come on, let's have that dance,' he said with a grin.

Marcus led her on to the small wooden dance floor and suddenly everyone started to applaud. Gemma was conscious of a sea of faces around them, watching as he pulled her closer into his arms.

'Relax.' He whispered the word against her ear as she held herself stiffly against him.

'Why?' She angled her head up to look at him and couldn't quite conceal the shimmering resentment in her voice. 'Because everyone is watching?'

'Because otherwise I might step on your toes.' He grinned. 'You are fighting against me…relax and go with the flow, let me lead.'

'And that's something you are very good at, isn't it Marcus?' she murmured dryly.

'Yes, it is.' He put a hand under her chin as she made to look away from him. 'What's the matter?'

'Nothing.' She jerked away from him and then, conscious that they were being watched, forced herself to smile at him. 'Nothing…' she said again in a softer tone. She didn't want to start a deep and angry conversation with him now. And anyway, what was the point?

Really, she had no right to be angry with him. She'd gone into this marriage with her eyes wide open. Marcus hadn't lied to her; he'd never said he loved her.

People had joined them on the dance floor now and she was forced to stay close to him in the tightly confined space.

He put an arm around her and held her close. She was conscious of the hard pressure of his body against hers, the delicious tang of his aftershave, the familiar warmth of his arms. She closed her eyes and leaned against his chest, giving herself up to the pleasure of just being held.

'That's better,' Marcus whispered. His voice tickled against her ear. 'Are you tired, my darling?'

The husky endearment made her squeeze her eyes tight against sudden tears. 'A little.'

'It's been a long day.'

'Yes.' She breathed in the scent of him, the delicious tenderness in his manner. She wanted so much to forget that their marriage was based purely on practicalities; she wanted to drown in his arms, accept the passion of his kisses and the heat of his body. The thought of the night ahead tempted her senses beyond endurance. She wanted desperately to shut out every negative and painful thought that was in her mind and just give in to the delights of being with him.

'Shall we go?'

The whispered question was accompanied by the touch of his lips against her neck. The sweet rush of pleasure was almost more than she could bear.

'Yes…' Her heart pounded heavily against her chest. 'I just want to say goodnight to Liam, make sure everything is all right with him.'

'Fine. I'll sneak out and get the car started. Meet you outside the front of the inn in, say, ten minutes?'

She nodded.

It sounded like a secret assignation—exciting, wonderfully clandestine. As she hurried away she pulled herself up. The only clandestine meeting that Marcus would look forward to was a meeting with Sophia.

Was she so pathetically in love that she would take any crumb of endearment? Where was her dignity, her pride now?

She spotted Liam sitting at the table with her mother and four of his cousins.

'Are you okay, darling?' She crouched down beside

him and he nodded happily. 'Do you want to come home with me now?' She knew everyone would be cross with her for taking him, but she didn't want to leave him.

Liam frowned. 'No, I'm going home with Nana and Auntie Helene and Andrea...oh, and Bruno is coming as well. We're going to have a midnight feast.'

'It's almost midnight now. Why don't you come home with Daddy and me?'

Liam shook his head. 'I don't want to. Grandad is going to take us to the zoo tomorrow and Bruno and Peter are coming too.' He indicated the two cousins that were nearest to him in age. 'And Nana is coming...' Liam added excitedly. 'I want to stay with them.'

Gemma's mother put a hand on her arm. 'Leave him, Gemma. You go with your husband now. I'll take care of Liam, I promise.'

Gemma nodded. 'Okay. Thanks, Mum. I'll see you tomorrow.'

Her mother smiled. 'Or the day after...' she added mischievously.

'I'll ring you in the morning,' Gemma said and gave Liam a kiss. 'Be good.'

Gemma headed away from the crowds of people and around the side of the inn. The gnarled shapes of olive and lemon trees were outlined against the bright starry sky. There was a smell of citrus blossom in the night air.

As the voices and the music faded away, all Gemma was left with was the sound of her heart beating heavily against her chest and the tropical sound of the cicadas.

She saw Marcus waiting for her, leaning against the bonnet of a car. He straightened as she walked over.

'Was Liam okay?'

She nodded.

'He'll enjoy being at Dad's house with all the other children.'

'I still think he should have come back with us.' Her voice was brusque. 'We are supposed to be keeping a close eye on him, remember?'

'Of course I remember.' Marcus opened the passenger door for her. 'It's the reason you married me, isn't it?'

There it was—the truth, awkward and painful but inescapable. 'Yes. It is.' She walked towards him to get into the car. 'And for that reason we should have brought him home with us tonight. We're a family, not a couple. We may have to pretend for everyone else's sake that we are madly in love, but at least we can be honest with each other.'

'I thought we were being honest.' Marcus's voice was hard and cutting.

She paused next to him and looked up into his eyes. She wished she could see the expression on his face but it was in shadow. She took a deep breath and launched in before she could change her mind. 'So I really think the decent thing would be for us to sleep in separate rooms.'

There was a moment's silence.

'You don't mean that?'

The arrogance of that remark made her angle her head up defiantly. 'Yes, I do.'

'We have an arrangement, Gemma. You are my wife and tonight we *will* consummate the marriage.'

She opened her mouth to say something further and then closed it again. The ominous dark tones of his voice were not to be argued with. And she supposed he was right, she had made an agreement with him.

'Get in the car.' His voice was softer now. 'We'll talk about this when we get home.'

She did as he asked. Her heart was pumping so heavily in her chest it felt like it might explode.

CHAPTER TEN

IT WAS a short drive along narrow twisting roads towards Marcus's villa. Neither of them spoke along the way and Gemma tried not to think too deeply about the rights and wrongs of what lay ahead.

The truth was she wanted to sleep with Marcus so badly it hurt. And she wished now that she hadn't said anything to him. It was pride that had made her sound off...stupid and misplaced pride. She had already married him. There was no going back. They could only go forward. And the thought of lying in a separate room from him tonight was not agreeable. Where could their marriage go from there? And she wanted this marriage to work...wanted it with all her heart.

The road ahead glinted gold in the lights of the powerful headlights and the landscape around them was bathed in a strange silver light from the full moon. But Gemma hardly noticed anything. All she could think about was the situation she found herself in.

Maybe Marcus wouldn't see Sophia again; she said the words to herself fiercely. Maybe last night had been their final farewell? The notion wasn't even slightly reassuring. In fact, it just smacked of hopelessness.

Marcus turned the car through high gateposts and down a gravel drive lined with sentinel pine trees. A few minutes later she could see the outline of his house silhouetted against the night sky: a huge rambling farmhouse, flanked at each side by majestic black cypresses.

'Home, sweet home.' Marcus's voice was dry.

She didn't answer him.

He brought the car to a standstill by the front door and then climbed out without a word.

Gemma followed him, lifting her long dress to walk up the steps towards the front door.

The silence of the countryside added to Gemma's feeling of unease. She was used to the rumble of traffic night and day in the city. The sounds here were of insects and the rustle of creatures in the hedgerows.

As Marcus put his key in the latch, Gemma looked out over the meadows beside them and noticed pinpoints of flickering, pulsating light. 'What's that?' she asked, putting a hand on his shoulder.

Marcus followed her gaze out across the fields. 'Fireflies.' He looked back at her, momentary amusement in his eyes. 'They won't bite. The only thing that bites around here is me.'

'Very funny.'

The door swung open but before she could precede him into the darkened hallway, Marcus put his arm around her waist and swung her easily up off her feet and into his arms.

'Put me down!' The action took her by surprise and her arms went instinctively up around his neck.

He ignored the request. 'No, I won't put you down, Mrs Rossini.' He smiled, his eyes lingering on her lips. 'I'm observing custom and carrying you over the threshold.'

She wondered if he was going to kiss her. She wanted him to. In fact, she would have liked him to carry her in and straight up the stairs to the marital bed. She was ashamed of herself for such weakness but she couldn't help it.

However, Marcus didn't kiss her and as soon as they

were inside the house he did put her down and then flicked on the hall lights.

She busied herself smoothing down the soft silk of her long skirt. Now that they were under the glare of bright lights she didn't want him to look at her too closely in case she gave herself away…in case he read the desire in her eyes.

'Shall we have a drink?' He moved away from her towards the lounge.

She followed him, glancing curiously around the impressive hallway, with its wide staircase and galleried landing. Marcus had invited her up to the villa a couple of days ago, but she had snatched the excuse of a shopping trip with Helene in Rome instead. She supposed she had been putting off the inevitable, even then.

What exactly was she scared of? she wondered as she watched him pouring whisky into a crystal tumbler.

He glanced over and the darkness of his eyes seemed to slice through her. 'Do you want to join me or are you going to go upstairs to make yourself more comfortable?'

The question brought a blaze of heat to her skin.

'I'll have a drink, thanks.' She moved further into the lounge from the doorway.

Gemma didn't drink whisky, but it was preferable to going upstairs to make herself more 'comfortable'. What did he expect her to do? Go up to the bedroom and take all her clothes off and wait for him?

She accepted the glass from him with a slightly shaking hand and their skin touched accidentally. The sharp feeling of yearning that ran through her at the contact was shocking in its intensity. And suddenly she knew exactly what she was afraid of. *Losing control.* Allowing him to find out just how much she still wanted him…throwing away all the carefully constructed barriers of pride that she had built up around herself over the years.

Once he touched her she was lost and she knew it. *He probably knew it as well.* Hadn't he demonstrated it to her the last time they were alone in her bedroom in London?

Marcus touched his glass against hers in a salute. 'Alone at last,' he murmured sardonically.

Something about the toast reminded her of Sophia's mocking salute earlier. 'Well, you don't have to be alone with me,' she said flippantly. 'The ink is still wet on the marriage certificate—we could probably get it annulled.'

'For non-consummation?'

'Why not?' She shrugged lightly. 'Maybe this marriage was a crazy idea to begin with.'

'Maybe it was.' Marcus regarded her through a narrowed glittering dark gaze. 'But we've already been through the marriage ceremony, so as far as I'm concerned, it's a bit late for cold feet. We made an agreement, Gemma…' As he spoke he was unfastening the silk cravat at his neck.

There was something very purposeful about the move.

Gemma took a sip of her whisky; it burnt the back of her throat and made her cough. She turned away from him nervously, pretended to be looking around the room.

A huge fireplace dominated one wall; it was raised off the floor on a flagstone platform and the stone chimney breast soared to the high ceiling. The furniture was in keeping with the rustic charm of the place; comfortable chairs and a settee in a pale buttermilk colour.

'Well, if I'm going to stay, then I suppose you should show me around the house,' she murmured, trying to turn the subject away from the sleeping arrangements.

There were some photographs sitting on a side table and she picked one of them up absently, noticing that it was the same photograph that she had looked at long ago at Marcus's London house—Marcus as a young teenager with his younger brothers. Her eyes lingered on it for a moment, remembering that night when she had gone to interview Marcus. Remembering how much she had wanted him from that first moment.

Marcus came across and took the photograph away from her to put it face down on the polished surface. 'What's all this really about, Gemma?' he grated harshly. 'You were quite happy to go along with our arrangement this morning...what's changed?'

Gemma didn't answer him immediately. She supposed nothing had changed. She had known when she walked down the aisle that morning that Marcus didn't love her. She had just foolishly tried to convince herself for a few hours that he did. And if Sophia hadn't broken the illusion so brutally she would probably be still fooling herself now...but that was her fault, not Marcus's.

Suddenly she remembered Freddie telling her how he'd come over here on the morning before Helene's wedding to deliver some flowers and had found Marcus and Sophia *in flagrante*.

What was it Freddie had said... *'Those two can't keep their hands off each other.'*

She looked up at him with shimmering blue eyes. 'Nothing has changed,' she whispered unsteadily. 'I suppose you are right and I've just got cold feet...plus I'm a bit tired.'

Marcus frowned. Then he reached out and took the crystal glass from her hand. 'Come on, I'll show you upstairs,' he said softly.

As she followed him out towards the hallway her heart

started to beat with an uneven and nervous tattoo against her chest again.

'The kitchen is over there.' Marcus waved towards a doorway at the other side of the hall. 'And there is a study and a smaller morning room at the back of the house.'

She tried to concentrate on the practical tone of his voice and not on the fact that she was now following him upstairs.

'There are seven bedrooms.' Marcus reached and opened one of the doors. 'This one is for Liam.'

She stepped inside the doorway and looked around. The room was beautifully decorated in pale blue. All Liam's toys were waiting for him, lined up along the shelves. Marcus had obviously given the room a lot of time and thought. His thoughtfulness and his love for his child never failed to move Gemma.

'It's lovely,' she whispered.

He turned away and opened the door next to it. 'And this is our room.'

She stepped into the large bedroom and glanced around at the tasteful décor, the pale cream carpets, the fitted wardrobes, before her eyes lingered on the enormous double bed.

'It's all right, don't look so worried. I've never forced a woman to sleep with me in my life and I don't intend to start now.'

He waved a hand towards another door at the end of the room. 'There's a bathroom through there. And you'll find your clothes in the far wardrobes. My housekeeper should have unpacked most of your stuff.'

'Where are you going?' she asked shakily as she watched him gather up a few of his belongings.

'I'll be next door. If you change your mind and want

to share my bed then just come on through.' He closed the door firmly behind him on the way out.

She sat down on the edge of the bed and glared at the door. Who the hell did he think he was? she thought angrily. *'If you change your mind just come through,'* indeed! If he was the last man left in the universe she wouldn't follow him through there now, not after that arrogant exit.

Gemma caught sight of her reflection in the dressing table mirror opposite. She was extremely pale; her eyes seemed to dominate her small face and her wedding dress looked ghostly and unreal.

Was she going to let Sophia sabotage her marriage before it had even started?

The question ricocheted through her mind. If she let Marcus sleep in another room wasn't it tantamount to handing him to the other woman on a plate?

She stood up from the bed. She didn't give a toss, she told herself fiercely. Sophia was welcome to him.

With trembling fingers she undid the top seed pearl buttons on her dress. Then she realized that she couldn't reach the other buttons down the back of the dress.

She stretched and stretched, but to no avail. Sitting back down on the bed she tried to think what she should do. It was either sleep in her wedding dress or go next door and ask Marcus to take her out of it and she knew very well what he would make of that.

She kicked off her shoes and lay back against the pillows. To hell with it, she'd sleep like this.

But sleep refused to come. Her mind seemed to be racing in a million different directions. Gemma glared up at the ceiling. Then, in an agony of anger and frustration, she jumped up and went out into the hallway to march into the bedroom next door.

Marcus was coming out of the en-suite bathroom with just a towel around his waist. His hair was wet and his bronzed skin still glistened with water. He grinned at her and didn't seem to be the slightest bit surprised to see her.

'It's not what you think,' she said quickly. 'I just want you to get me out of this dress.'

'Really?' One dark eyebrow rose mockingly. 'I've had some invitations from women in my time, but never one quite so blunt.'

'I don't mean I want you to sleep with me.' She tried to make her eyes stay on his face but they kept drifting down to his body. He had an incredible physique—powerful shoulders and chest tapering down to a flat stomach and narrow hips. 'Just unbutton my dress, please.'

'Come here, then.'

The quiet command made her senses jump with nervous anticipation. She walked over towards him and then turned around so that he could see the buttons.

The touch of his hands against her made her heart thump loudly. Deftly he unfastened them down to her waist. Then, before she could move away, he slipped his hand in against her bare skin and pulled her back against him. She could feel the hairs on his chest, damp against her skin. 'I think that deserves a kiss, don't you?' he whispered playfully against her ear.

He kissed the side of her neck and as he did so he slowly pulled the dress down.

Gemma couldn't move, she just stood there transfixed by the sensation of pleasure as his lips trailed heatedly over her shoulders. As his fingers brushed over the curves of her breast she felt weak with longing for him.

She was wearing a lacy strapless bra beneath the dress, and it held the contours of her curves in a very provocative way. One more pull of the dress and the silk slid to the floor, revealing the lacy panties and the hold-up stockings that shimmered glossily on long shapely legs.

'There, that's better.' Marcus turned her to face him then and regarded her with a cool appraisal. Then he reached out and stroked one finger slowly and deliberately over the lace bra. Her nipples were so erect that he could feel them pushing against his hand. There was a gleam of triumph in his eyes as they moved upwards to hold with hers.

'You see, Gemma? Sexually, you want me very much…'

She shook her head, defiance shimmering in her blue eyes, and he thought he had never seen any woman so beautiful in all his life.

'You're a really bad liar, Gemma.' As he spoke he was lowering his head towards hers. Then his lips captured hers in a fiercely provocative and invasive kiss that sent all her senses reeling. After a few seconds she kissed him back with equal fervour—she couldn't stop herself. Her mind was saying one thing but her body was saying another in much more persuasive terms.

'You see? We've always been sexually compatible.' His tone was arrogantly assertive, but she didn't care. He pulled her closer and she wound her arms up and around his neck, standing on tiptoe to kiss him back heatedly.

She wanted him so much it was like an all-consuming fire inside her. And she was melting fast.

Then abruptly he stepped back and placed one hand under her chin, forcing her to keep eye contact. 'Say "please, Marcus make love to me".'

She stared at him mutinously and he smiled. 'I've

never met anyone as stubborn in all my life as you…Gemma Rossini.'

'Why are you playing these games?' Her voice sounded very distorted, not at all like her.

'I'm not the one playing games, Gemma, you are,' he said calmly. 'You pretend all the time. You pretended with Freddie…and probably with Richard too. And with me.'

'What are you talking about?' She was mystified.

'I'm talking about the way you like to tease men. I've seen you in action, Gemma, you are really very good.' He reached out and touched her, smoothed a stray strand of her hair back from her face. 'But it stops here…' he murmured softly. 'Because you belong to me now and there will be no more games…no more pretending…' He reached behind her and unfastened her bra.

'Now repeat after me…"please, Marcus, make love to me".' As he spoke he was caressing the fullness of her breasts with both his hands, his thumbs running over her erect nipples with practised skill, making her catch her breath with a gasp of need.

Then his hands moved to the panties, pulling them down roughly and then stroking between her legs.

She was so aroused now that she was past thinking about anything other than the need to have him possess her completely.

'Please Marcus…' She moved into his arms willingly. 'Please make love to me.'

He pushed her down on to the softness of the bed and then, taking the towel from around his waist, he joined her.

Pinning her to the mattress with his body he slowly kissed her all over—her neck, her shoulders, then lower towards her breasts, taking his time pleasuring her so much that she felt impatient with longing. She just wanted to feel him inside her.

She had forgotten how wonderful his body felt against hers, how he knew exactly where to touch her, what to do to heighten her pleasure completely. As they clung wildly to each other, kissing and touching, Gemma was lost in a spiralling frenzy of pure desire.

When at last she felt his body inside hers she gasped with pure pleasure.

She writhed against him, her hands raking over his back.

'That's so good,' she cried out as he thrust even deeper within her.

'You belong to me, Gemma Rossini.' He ground the words fiercely as he penetrated her deeper and deeper, holding her head with his hands and then plundering her mouth with his tongue. 'Never…ever…forget that…'

Each word was punctuated by an extra push, and she felt the world suddenly spinning off its axis into a blur of complete and utter ecstasy.

Gemma stretched languidly in the bed. She felt unusually stiff and achy. She opened her eyes and looked around the unfamiliar room. Sunlight was filtering through the curtains, playing over the pretty lilac wallpaper and the bowl of roses on the dresser. There was a sound of a bird singing outside the window, but nothing else, no hint of human movement, no roar of traffic.

For a moment she was so disoriented that she couldn't remember where she was. Then as she sat up, she saw the crumpled heap of her wedding dress on the floor and the events of the night before came rushing back like the roar of the incoming tide.

Quickly she glanced over to the other side of the bed.

But it was empty. Memories from the night before trickled hotly through her mind. It was no wonder she was tired. The night had been filled with the heated passion of their lovemaking. Three, maybe four times, Marcus had possessed her. Then in the early hours of the morning he had woken her to take her again. It had been wild and tempestuous…and it was no wonder that her body felt tenderly dazed. She lay back against the pillows, drinking in the memories for a while. Lovemaking with Marcus was fabulous. She remembered now why no other man had ever come close to arousing her like he did. Just thinking about it made her body throb with need again.

Impatiently she pushed back the covers and walked towards the bathroom to have a shower. Standing under the heavy jet of water, she wondered where Marcus was. Wherever he was, she wanted him to come back so that they could continue where they had left off.

She smiled to herself, snapped the water off and reached blindly for a towel. To her surprise, one was placed in her hand. She looked up and saw Marcus standing outside the shower, fully dressed in jeans and a white shirt.

'Morning.' He smiled at her and his eyes raked boldly down over the naked curves of her body.

'Morning.' She grabbed the towel and wrapped it around her. It was ridiculous but suddenly she felt very shy. 'What time is it?'

'Seven-thirty.' He stepped back to allow her out of the shower. 'I thought we might go for an early morning ride.'

'Sounds fun.' She smiled. 'But I'm not very good at riding. You'll have to find me a reliable mount.'

'Oh, I think I can do that all right.' His eyes gleamed with teasing good humour and she felt herself blush.

He reached and pulled her towards him and then kissed her fully on the lips in a sensually provocative way.

The towel slipped to the floor as she reached to wind her arms around his neck.

She felt his hands moving over her possessively, holding her and touching her with arrogant ease. 'See you outside in a little while, okay?' He pulled back from her.

'Okay…' She watched him walk away from her, aware that she was a little disappointed because she had wanted him all over again.

She picked up the towel and hurriedly dried herself, then walked back to the bedroom to find something to put on, before remembering her clothes were in the bedroom next door.

It was half an hour before Gemma went downstairs, dressed in fawn cropped trousers and matching T-shirt. Her hair swung silkily around her shoulders and she had a bounce in her step. She was married to Marcus… The words sang happily in her mind. Maybe he hadn't told her he loved her but he sure as hell had *made love* to her. And suddenly that was enough for now.

She stepped into the kitchen, a high square room with a red tiled floor and beamed ceiling. There was a state-of-the-art cooker and light oak cupboards and also another massive fireplace like the one in the lounge. The house really had a lot of charm, Gemma thought as she opened the fridge and poured herself a glass of fresh orange juice. Moving to open up the back door, she breathed in the scent of the early morning air. It was tinged with camomile and the peppery scent of rosemary from a small herb garden that ran down from the enclosed courtyard towards the orchard below.

Liam was going to love it here, she thought looking at all the open space for him to run and play. Marcus was right; this was a lovely place to bring up a child.

The phone rang and, afraid it might be her mother ringing because Liam was missing her, she went through to the hall to pick it up.

'Rossini residence,' she said with a smile.

'Hi, Gemma, it's Sophia. Will you put Marcus on the phone? I need to speak to him.'

'He isn't here,' Gemma said tersely. She had no intention of fetching Marcus to the phone for her.

'Left you already, has he?' The smirk in Sophia's tone dripped venom.

'Actually, he's waiting to take me out for an early morning ride. In case it has escaped your notice, we are on our honeymoon, and we are very much in love, so please go away and don't ring here again.' With a feeling of satisfaction she slammed the phone down. 'Put that in your pipe and smoke it,' she said, dusting her hands against her hips.

'Who were you talking to?' Marcus stepped out from the kitchen making her jump.

'Nobody.' She whirled around, frightened in case he had heard what she had just said.

He frowned. 'It's a bit early to be ringing anyone.'

'Well, that's okay, because they were ringing me.'

The phone rang again loudly in the silence of the house and Gemma's nerves jangled alarmingly. As Marcus reached to pick it up she put a detaining hand on his arm. 'Leave it,' she said gently. She didn't want him talking to Sophia...and she certainly didn't want

Sophia repeating what she had just said. 'It will be a wrong number again.'

She saw the look of disbelief in his eyes.

'Okay, it'll be Richard again.' She pulled at his arm. 'Let's get out into the sunshine and ignore it.'

To her relief the phone stopped ringing.

'Richard?' Marcus looked at her dryly. 'What the hell did he want at this hour?'

'He'd forgotten there was a time difference...' Gemma turned away from him towards the kitchen. 'He just wanted to tell me who got the job as editor...you know, at *Modern Times*.'

'If you wanted to know who got the job at *Modern Times* why didn't you just ask me?' Marcus glared at her.

'I didn't want to know, that's just what I told Richard.' Gemma whirled around to look at him, one hand on her hip. She hated lying, she was dreadful at it and she could feel her temperature rising phenomenally. Why hadn't she just been truthful and told him it was Sophia? Why was she tying herself in knots? 'Now, are we going for that ride or not?'

Marcus looked at her with dark cynical eyes. 'Yes, let's go.'

CHAPTER ELEVEN

THE Italian countryside was spectacularly beautiful, Gemma thought as they rode silently side by side. The only sound was the soft thud of the horses' hooves on the grass and the occasional snort from Marcus's black stallion, Rufus, who was straining at the reins impatiently, wanting his head. He was a magnificent animal, Gemma thought, noting how his coat gleamed blue-black in the sunshine and his black tail swished from side to side.

Obviously, Marcus was an accomplished rider to be able to handle such a beast. And he looked pretty magnificent himself, she thought wryly flicking a glance up at him.

'You okay?' Marcus met her eyes and she nodded.

'Do want to walk for a bit?'

'Will Rufus allow that?' Gemma asked with a smile. 'He looks like he wants to gallop off.'

'He'll have to be patient,' Marcus said with a grin, stroking the animal's neck.

'Okay, we'll walk for a bit,' Gemma said, quite glad to be able to get down from her horse.

The gentle roan that Marcus had picked out for her was perfect but she was still feeling a little stiff from the activities of the night before. Just thinking about last night set up another ache inside her, but this time it was the dull ache of longing.

Marcus dismounted and then reached to help her. She slid down and for a second was held in his arms.

Instantly her body responded to the intimacy, her senses flaring with heat. Shyly she stepped away from him. It was embarrassing the way she responded to him. She wondered if he found it amusing, or if it merely fed his ego?

She slanted a glance up at him to see if he had noticed, but he seemed deep in thought.

Gemma glanced out over the fields. It was almost high summer and the corn was nearly ripe—it glinted gold in the sun, interspersed with the scarlet of poppies and blue of cornflowers. The sky had the same incandescent blue of the cornflowers and the hills in the distance looked hazily purple. There was not a house or a person in sight.

'London seems like a long, long way away,' Gemma murmured, breathing in the warmth of the air.

'Missing it already?' Marcus asked wryly.

'No, of course not.'

'So why were you ringing Richard this morning?'

'I didn't.' Gemma's face flared red. 'I told you, he phoned me.'

'Just to tell you who got the job at your old office?'

'Yes…'

'So who did he say had got it?'

'Well…he didn't.' She wondered if her face was scarlet now. 'I told you, I said I didn't want to know.'

'Really.' Marcus's tone was dry. 'Was that because you are so upset at not having it yourself?'

'No, it's not.' She shook her head. 'I don't have any regrets at giving up that job, Marcus.' She looked over at him, her eyes clear and candid now. 'Liam has to come first for a while.'

'But I take it Richard doesn't understand that?'

She frowned. 'Yes, Richard understands… And while we are on the subject, what were you talking about last night when you accused me of leading Richard on?' She remembered the conversation suddenly. 'You said something about my leading Freddie on as well. That's absolute rubbish.'

'Is it?' Marcus looked over at her with frank disbelief in his eyes.

'Yes, it is.' Gemma stopped walking and turned to face him.

'Gemma, you should remember that I'm not as easy to dupe as Freddie.'

The sardonic tone made her frown. 'What the hell do you mean by that?'

'You know what I'm talking about.' Marcus shook his head. 'Freddie really believed you loved him, you know...thought you were saving yourself for marriage with him.'

Gemma's eyes widened. 'No, he didn't!'

'Drop the innocent act, Gemma, it won't wash with me,' Marcus said grimly. 'You strung Freddie along, promising him you'd sleep with him eventually. He told me all about it just before Helene's wedding.'

Gemma felt her face flare with furious colour. 'I didn't lead Freddie on in any way,' she said, her voice rising sharply. 'Why the hell would I have done that?'

'Because it was your way of getting what you wanted. By refusing to sleep with Freddie you got a proposal of marriage...by sleeping with me you got the job you were after. That was the way you operated.'

Gemma's mouth fell open in horror. 'You really think I'm that conniving?'

'I think you were once, yes, but not now. Having Liam seems to have changed you. You're warm and caring and you're a wonderfully good mother and—'

'Don't you dare patronize me,' Gemma snapped

fiercely and the horses beside her fidgeted nervously. 'I never once led Freddie on. He always knew exactly where he stood with me.'

'So why did you agree to go to Helene's wedding with him?'

'Because he said he'd get me the interview with you if I agreed to accompany him to Italy.' She waved aside his words as he started to speak. 'And I made it very clear that there were no strings attached and that I was just a friend. In fact I made it clear to the whole house when I arrived. Told your father in no uncertain terms when he made a remark linking us together…you should ask him.' Gemma glared at Marcus furiously, her eyes snapping like jewels in the pallor of her face. She took a deep breath. 'And, as for not sleeping with Freddie because I wanted him to propose, that is utterly preposterous. For a start, Freddie had already proposed to me six months earlier, and I turned him down.'

Marcus frowned. 'So why was he so shocked when I told him I was seeing you?'

'You told Freddie…?' For a second Gemma was sidetracked. 'When did you tell him?'

'I went straight to see him after you told me you were attending my sister's wedding with him. I wanted to know what was going on.'

'There was nothing going on!' Gemma glared at him.

'Yes, well, at that point I needed to hear that from him.' Marcus raked a hand through the darkness of his hair. 'You can imagine my horror when Freddie practically broke down. He was inconsolable…told me you were the woman he was planning to marry. That you were both deeply in love…'

Gemma was so shocked by this that she could hardly

speak. 'That's just not true! Freddie and I were never anything but friends. Why did he say that?'

There was a long moment of silence.

'I can understand him being shocked when you told him you were seeing me,' she continued, trying to go over the past carefully in her mind. 'You see, I could never bring myself to tell him about us. I should have done, right from the beginning. But...' She frowned. 'I guess I was frightened of hurting him. He had tried to get me into bed in the past and I'd always turned him down...how could I tell him that at the first meeting with his brother I fell...into bed.'

Her voice trembled a little, as she nearly said, *fell in love*. 'I remember when I came home after spending that first night with you, there was a message on my answering machine from Freddie asking me how I'd got on with the interview. I rang him back intending to tell him honestly, and then backed away from the subject. I thought if I left it a while, told him things had developed more slowly between us, that it might soften the blow.'

'So you never told Freddie you loved him?'

'No!' Gemma's voice was emphatic. She raked a hand through her hair in confusion. 'What I don't understand is, why did Freddie pretend he knew nothing about our affair when quite clearly he did. Are you sure you told him *before* Helene's wedding?'

'Of course I am. The conversation is etched in my mind for all time.'

'Yet he never said one word to me in Italy about knowing. And when I finally did tell him, after we returned to London, he acted so shocked...'

'Was that the night you told him you were pregnant with my child?'

Gemma nodded.

'Well, that's why he was shocked.' Marcus's voice grated derisively.

'Don't look at me like that, Marcus. I never led Freddie on in any way.'

'You were dancing pretty close to him at Helene's wedding.'

'He was comforting me because you were with Sophia. It was a bit of a shock finding out you were going to marry someone else, Marcus. Freddie told me all about it—how you two couldn't keep your hands off each other, how he'd gone around to the house to deliver flowers that very morning and caught you making love with her in the lounge—'

'He did what?' Marcus looked furious now.

'Look, there is no point being angry with Freddie for telling me that. I needed to know.'

'No, you didn't, because what he told you was a pack of lies.'

Gemma frowned sceptically. 'So there was never any question of you marrying Sophia?'

'There was an understanding once between our two families that Sophia and I would get married. But we were very young then, and it never worked out between us. Freddie knew that.'

'Yeah, right, and that was why you were making love to her in the lounge before Helene's wedding...'

'Freddie was lying, Gemma. There were no flowers that morning at my house, and no Sophia. The only thing that happened that morning was a last and terrible argument between my brother and I about you.'

Gemma stared at him for a few moments, her breath rising and falling heavily in her chest, and then she turned away from him. 'I don't believe you.'

'Think about it, Gemma,' Marcus called after her as

she walked away. 'If Freddie lied to me about how serious his relationship was with you...couldn't he also have lied to you?'

Gemma stopped walking.

'It seems to me that he was playing us off against each other, hoping you'd turn to him for comfort. It might have worked, as well, except for the fact that you were pregnant with my child.'

Gemma let go of the horse's reins and turned back towards him.

'And what about Sophia? Was she lying too?' Her voice was very unsteady now. 'Did she lie when she told me how much you loved her?'

'When the hell did she say that?' Marcus also let go of his horse to walk towards her. 'Things were over romantically between Sophia and I long before I left Italy.'

Gemma shook her head. 'I don't believe you. Because, according to Sophia you've always been in love with her. She used to visit you in London all the time.'

'That's not true, Gemma.' He grasped hold of her, bringing her tightly in against him. 'Yes, she called to see me a few times in London. But she didn't stay with me; she was over visiting other friends. She used to call around with gifts for Liam, she's very fond of him.'

Gemma looked at him sceptically.

'Sophia is like a part of my family, Gemma. She's always been around, but I swear there is nothing between us. There's been no one else in my life since the day I met you.'

Gemma swallowed hard, wanting so much to believe that.

'So where were you the night before our wedding, Marcus?' she asked him suddenly. 'How did you spend your last night of freedom?'

Marcus frowned. 'You know what I did. I came down to see you and Liam.'

'That was just for an hour. What did you do after that?'

'I went home.'

'According to Sophia, you were with her. Telling her how much you wished it was her and not me that you were marrying—' The look of astonishment on Marcus's face made her stop abruptly.

'That's not true, Gemma.' He caught her face in his hands earnestly. 'You've got to believe me. Sophia and I finished years ago…and I don't know why she is saying these things, but we will find out.' His voice shook with such fierce anger that suddenly Gemma could do nothing else but believe him.

'I love you.' He said the words with such emphatic fierceness that she felt her body shake with the force of his emotion. 'I'm crazy about you…always have been and always will be.'

'But…?' Gemma was looking up at him in wonder. 'You kept away from me for so long…even after Liam was born…'

'Because I was a fool.' He shook his head. 'I believed my brother…and every time I looked at you I was filled with remorse and guilt for what I'd done. I broke my brother's heart, Gemma. He died because of me, because of us…'

'No!' Gemma's eyes filled with tears of horror. 'That's not true, Marcus. It wasn't anybody's fault. He was driving too fast—you know what he was like, how careless he could be…' She reached up and stroked the side of his face with tender concern. 'It wasn't your fault…or mine.'

Marcus took a deep breath. 'I realize that now…

but…God, I miss him Gemma, he was my kid brother.'

'I know.' She reached up and suddenly they were in each other's arms, holding each other tight.

Then suddenly their embrace changed, turned from empathy and fierce emotion to a different kind of intensity. Gemma turned her head and found his lips and they kissed, a passionately sweet and searing kiss.

'Oh Marcus…' She raised herself up to hug him closer. 'I want you so much.'

She felt his hands on her body and suddenly it was as if they couldn't get enough of each other. He took hold of her hand and pulled her into the field of corn beside them, laying her down and kissing her again, his other hand pulling at her T-shirt.

Then they were naked in each other's arms, kissing each other, holding each other. Above her, Gemma could see the blue of the sky and the gold of the corn and she felt as if her life had never been so perfectly complete.

'I love you so much, Marcus,' she whispered the words huskily against his skin as she pulled him closer.

'What did you say?'

He pulled back and looked down at her.

'I love you…'

He smiled and leaned down to kiss her. 'God, you don't know how much I've longed to hear you say those words.' The relief in his voice was so deep it was palpable. 'I was frightened that you were starting to have feelings for Richard.'

Gemma shook her head. 'No. I'm fond of him, but…that was as deep as it went.'

'Really?' He held her head between his hands and looked deep into her eyes.

'Yes, really.'

'When I saw you together…' He paused. 'Hell, Gemma I was so jealous. It was as if a mist had lifted, leaving a clear vision of life without you, and I suddenly realized that it didn't matter about the past, all that mattered was the future, and I couldn't bear to lose you. I knew then that I had to get you back.'

Gemma stroked her hands along the sides of his face, tracing the contours of his features lightly. 'Richard is a nice guy but—'

'I don't care how nice he is.' He interrupted her firmly. 'No more phone calls from him first thing in the morning, okay?'

She winced. 'I've got a confession to make. That wasn't Richard this morning, it was Sophia.'

'What the hell did she want?'

'You, I suppose.'

'So why did you lie?' He stroked her hair back from her face. 'You should have told me. I don't know what her problem is, but I'd have dealt with her.'

'I didn't tell you because I didn't want you to know what I said to her.'

'What did you say?'

'That we loved each other and she should go away and leave us alone.'

Marcus laughed at that and pulled her closer, rolling over so that she was lying on top of him. 'I couldn't have put it better myself,' he said softly, then threaded his fingers through the gold of her hair and pulled her down to meet the passion of his lips.

When I saw [illegible]
[illegible]
[illegible]
[illegible]
[illegible]
[illegible]

Gemma [illegible] tracing the contours of his features lightly. 'Richard is a nice guy but—'

'I don't care how nice he is.' He interrupted her firmly. 'No more [illegible] calls [illegible] thing in the morning, okay?'

[illegible]

[illegible] Richard [illegible]

'What the [illegible]'

'You [illegible]'

[illegible]

[illegible]

[illegible] myself,' he said [illegible]

[illegible]

1206/51

THE FORBIDDEN AFFAIR by Peggy Moreland

Years ago Wade Parker had swept Stephanie Calloway off her feet...and then broken her heart. Now he is determined to win her back!

TEMPT ME by Caroline Cross

John Taggart Steele, ex-Army Ranger, is the hunter. Sparky Genevieve Bowen is his prey. And he is out to catch her—at any cost...

THE ELLIOTTS

BILLIONAIRE'S PROPOSITION by Leanne Banks

Gannon Elliott wants to control a dynasty and win a boardroom battle. Erika Layven just wants his baby. Who will outmanoeuvre whom?

TAKING CARE OF BUSINESS by Brenda Jackson

He was a wealthy, successful Elliott, so Renee Walker never expected Tag to be attracted to a quiet social worker like her. But Tag was determined to prove his passion for her!

CRAVING BEAUTY by Nalini Singh

Marc Bordeaux believed beautiful Hira shared the deep soul-connection with him that he felt when he asked her to be his wife. But was he wrong? How could he reach her?

HIS WEDDING-NIGHT WAGER by Katherine Garbera

Shelby Paxton had been paid to leave Hayden MacKenzie at the altar. And now that she's back, he is hell-bent on exacting his revenge...and getting his long overdue wedding night!

On sale from 15th December 2006

Visit our website at www.silhouette.co.uk